Kate Hardy has always loved books, and could read before she went to school. She discovered Mills & Boon books when she was twelve and decided this was what she wanted to do. When she isn't writing Kate enjoys reading, cinema, ballroom dancing and the gym. You can contact her via her website: www.katehardy.com.

Melissa Senate has written many novels for Mills & Boon and other publishers, including her debut, *See Jane Date*, which was made into a TV movie. She also wrote seven books under the pen name Meg Maxwell. Her novels have been published in over twenty-five countries. Melissa lives on the coast of Maine with her teenaged son, their sweet rescue Shepherd mix, Flash, and a lap cat named Cleo. For more information, please visit her website, www.melissasenate.com.

Also by Kate Hardy

Books by Melissa Senate

Discover more at millsandboon.co.uk

REUNITED
AT THE ALTAR

KATE HARDY

DETECTIVE
BARELLI'S
LEGENDARY
TRIPLETS

MELISSA SENATE

MIX

FSC

FSC° C007454

This book is produced from independently certified FSC™
paper to ensure responsible forest management

For more information visit: www.harpercollins.co.uk/green

Printed and bound in Spain
by CPI, Barcelona

MILLS & BOON

First Published in Great Britain 2018
by Mills & Boon, an imprint of HarperCollinsPublishers,
1 London Bridge Street, London, SE1 9GF

Reunited at the Altar © 2018 Pamela Brooks
Detective Barelli's Legendary Triplets © 2018 Melissa Senate

ISBN: 978-0-263-26509-5

38-0718

REUNITED
AT THE ALTAR

KATE HARDY

To Archie, my beloved spaniel,
aka the newest member of my research team,
who always keeps me company when I write.

CHAPTER ONE

'ARE YOU SURE you're all right about this, Abby?' Ruby asked.

'Absolutely,' Abigail fibbed. 'I'm so pleased he agreed.'

That bit, at least, wasn't a lie. Abigail was more than pleased that Bradley Powell had not only agreed to come to his twin sister's wedding, he'd also promised to walk her down the aisle in their late father's stead— especially as he hadn't set foot in Great Crowmell, the Norfolk seaside town where they'd grown up, in the years since their father's funeral. Ruby had been panicking that Brad would make an excuse not to come to her wedding because he still couldn't face coming home.

As for actually seeing her ex-husband again for the first time since their divorce: that wasn't something Abigail relished. But she was five years older now. Infinitely wiser. She could do this. And she *would* do this with a smile, for Ruby's sake. No way was she going to rain on her best friend's parade.

'You know you can bring a date to the wedding,' Ruby said. 'Just give me a name for when it comes to sorting out the place cards. Or you don't even have to do that—bring whoever you like and I'll get someone to write his name on the place card that morning.'

'Thanks, but I don't need a date. I'm going to be way too busy on the day for that,' Abigail said with a smile. 'I've got chief bridesmaid duties to think about, and I want everything to go perfectly for your wedding.' The fact she'd barely dated since her divorce was irrelevant.

Or—a nasty thought hit her—was Ruby trying to tell her something? That she should bring a date, because Brad was bringing his new love to meet everyone and it would be awkward if Abigail turned up alone?

'Is Brad bringing a date?' Abigail asked, trying her best to sound casual and hoping that her suddenly thumping heart didn't show in her voice.

'Of course he's not. He's married to his j…' Ruby winced and clapped a hand to her mouth. 'Um.'

Abigail smiled and finished the phrase. 'Married to his job.' *Whereas he'd once been married to me.* And she knew that was exactly what Ruby was thinking, too.

'Sorry, Abby. I didn't mean to—'

Abigail hugged her best friend. 'It's fine. That water's so far under the bridge, it's already been recycled twice. Brad and I can be civil to each other.' She hoped. She'd been through all the stages of grief at the end of their marriage. Denial that it was over, anger that he was being so stubborn, bargaining with him to see sense, depression when she realised that she just wasn't enough for him, and finally acceptance that it was all over. All laced together with guilt, because she'd been the one to instigate the end.

She'd been so sure that if she walked out on him and went home to her parents, it would shock him into his senses: that he'd miss her and realise that shutting her out wasn't the answer.

And how wrong she'd been. Because, instead of asking her to come back to him, Brad had simply said that her defection was proof that everyone had been right about them. They'd been way too young to get married, they weren't going to make it, and he'd give her a divorce so she could have the chance to make a real life for herself.

Divorce had been the last thing she'd wanted.

But Brad had built a wall of ice around himself after his father's death. He'd shut Abigail out, and she just hadn't been able to reach him. Despite being married for nearly four years, they hadn't been strong enough to weather the storm. She hadn't supported him enough in his grief or been able to hold her marriage together.

So maybe everyone had been right about their relationship, after all. They'd been naive and reckless and immature, eloping to Gretna Green the week before their exam results. Everyone else had thought they were simply doing the coast-to-coast walk from St Bees in the Lake District to Robin Hood's Bay in Yorkshire, raising money for the local lifeboat rescue team—which they had. They'd just happened to go to St Bees via Gretna Green, having quietly sorted out all the marriage paperwork the day after their last exams.

At the time, they'd both thought that eloping would be romantic. That each other was The One. That their love would last for ever.

Yeah. Naive, reckless and immature just about summed it up.

And she wasn't any of those any more.

'Is Brad OK with me being your bridesmaid?' Abigail

asked. 'If he's not, you know I'll step down and keep out of the way on the actual day—but obviously I'll still help you with all the organisation and do anything you need.'

Ruby rolled her eyes. 'For goodness' sake. Who else was I going to ask to be my chief bridesmaid, other than the person who's been my best friend since the day we met at toddler group?'

And who also happened to be her twin's ex-wife.

'Have you actually told him?' Abigail asked.

'Yes. And he—well, he said the same that you did. That you could be perfectly civil to each other at the wedding.'

Civil. All that passion and love and hope reduced to cool, dismissive politeness. It made Abigail want to weep. What a waste.

Not that she was going to let Ruby have the slightest idea about that. Abigail wanted her best friend's wedding day to be the happiest day of her life and she'd do her best to make it happen. 'There you go, then. All's fine.' Abigail smiled. 'Now, we have lists to make. If you will insist on having a whirlwind wedding…'

Ruby snorted. 'Says the woman who eloped.'

'There's a lot to be said for keeping it simple,' Abigail said lightly. 'No worries about seating plans, menus or dresses.'

Ruby looked at her. 'Do you regret it, Abby?'

'Marrying your brother? Or eloping?' Abigail asked.

'You know what I'm asking.'

Abigail sighed. 'I don't regret marrying Brad. I loved him. We just brought the wedding forward to before he went away to study rather than waiting until after he'd finished his degree, that was all.' It had been Brad's idea to elope and, although part of Abby had thought it wasn't really practical to get married when he was about to go away and be a student, she'd been madly in love with him and thought he felt the same about her. So she'd said yes, squashing her misgivings.

'But you regret eloping?'

'Yes and no. Yes, it was romantic and fun to elope.' Just the two of them. And they'd made love so tenderly in their cheap hotel room that night. Eighteen years old, with the whole world ahead of them. 'But, in hindsight,' Abigail said, 'I regret not sharing the day with everyone else. It meant Dad didn't get to walk me down the aisle, our mums didn't get the chance to dress up and make a fuss, you weren't my bridesmaid, and your dad wasn't the best man. Looking back, I realise we were selfish. We should've shared that day.' And maybe if they'd been mature enough to share their wedding, they would've been mature enough to make their marriage last.

'Anyway, there's no point in dwelling on it because you can't change the past.' Abigail opened up her laptop. 'Right. Our list of things to do starts here…'

Six weeks later

Great Crowmell.

Even the signpost made Brad's stomach turn to knots.

The town where he'd grown up.

The town where he'd met the love of his life.

The town where he'd lost her.

He was dreading this. He'd avoided coming here at all since his father's funeral—not for birthdays, not for Christmases, not for an off-the-cuff visit. The longer he left it, the harder it was to face. He'd seen his family—of *course* he had—but not here. He'd met them in London, organised posh afternoon teas and trips to the theatre with hard-to-get tickets, to make up for not coming here.

Every nerve in his body told him to turn the car round again and drive back to London. Back to where he could bury himself in work and forget everything.

But he couldn't be that selfish. His sister was getting married and he had no intention of letting her down. This was the one thing that would make him come back: Ruby had asked him to walk her down the aisle on her wedding day and he'd promised her he'd do it. Even though the last time he'd set foot in that church and walked down that aisle, he'd been one of the pallbearers carrying their father's coffin, he'd suck up his feelings for her sake.

Though Brad hadn't quite been able to face going back to stay in their childhood home, filled with his memories of their father—and with a hefty loading of guilt. Instead, he'd rented a holiday cottage for a few days. One of the ancient two-up, two-down fishermen's cottages in the flint-built terraces just behind the harbour. A place with no memories, so he had a bolthole when the town and everything that went with it got too much for him: all the kindness and concern edged with speculation and gossip. He knew that Ruby understood and he hoped she'd talk their mother round. He wasn't avoiding Rosie; he was avoiding the house. Just as he'd done for the last five years. He knew it was selfish, and it made the guilt worse.

And then there was Abigail.

How was he going to face her?

More layers of guilt weighed down on him. He'd been the one to sweep her off her feet and ask her to elope with him; and when life threw its first hurdle in their way he'd let her down. He'd let her go.

Even before Ruby had diffidently asked if he'd mind that Abigail would be her chief bridesmaid, Brad had known who she'd choose—the woman who'd been her best friend right from toddler group through to high school and beyond. He'd prepared himself for it so when it came, he was able to tell Ruby without batting an eyelid that everything was absolutely fine, and he and Abigail could be perfectly civil to each other on the day. But stupidly he hadn't thought to ask Ruby if Abigail was taking anyone to the wedding. The idea of seeing his ex-wife dancing with her new man, laughing and smiling and kissing him in the moonlight, the way she'd once done with him, made him feel sick.

He dragged in a breath. Maybe he should've asked one of his colleagues to be his plus one, just in case. There was still time; the wedding wasn't until Saturday. Though who could he ask, without either giving out the wrong signals—and he really didn't want the complication of someone at work thinking he was interested in a relationship—or having to explain the situation and becoming an object of pity throughout the lab and the office?

Maybe he should've made an excuse not to come to the wedding in the first place. Maybe he should've said he was speaking at a conference and, because Ruby had only given him a few weeks' notice, there simply wasn't enough time to find someone to take his place.

But then he'd hate himself for letting her down.

He needed to brace himself and deal with it. Be the cool, calm, analytical scientist he'd spent the last five years turning himself into. The one who kept his feelings completely locked away and could deal with almost anything without betraying a flicker of emotion. There was no place in his professional life for guilt, for nervousness and wondering how people were going to react to him, so he shouldn't let any of that have a place in his personal life, either.

He could do this. The taste of bile in his mouth, the way his hands felt cold and tingling with adrenaline—that was all psychosomatic and he was going to ignore it. And he'd grab some paracetamol to deal with the tension headache that had started more than an hour ago, as soon as he'd crossed the county border to Norfolk.

He pulled into the car park in the middle of the town, fed coins into the meter to get a pay-and-display car park ticket to tide him over to the next morning, and stuck the ticket on the inside of his windscreen.

The letting agent had warned him that parking was tricky outside the rented cottage so he left the car and made his way to the address. He pulled up the four-digit key code for the safe box where the house keys were stored from the last email from the letting agent on his phone, retrieved the keys and dumped his luggage next to the stairs in the living room. When he headed into the kitchen at the back, there was a tray on the small kitchen table containing a plate, a mug, a spoon, a box of tea-bags and a tin of good instant coffee. There was also a white paper bag, and a note propped on top of it.

Welcome to 2 Quay Cottages. There's milk and butter in the fridge, bread in the cupboard, and a little something in the paper bag to keep you going until dinner. Any problems, please call in at number 1.

Clearly the neighbour was happy to act as a kind of caretaker. That was reassuring, given that the letting agent was in London. OK, Brad thought, and opened the paper bag.

A blueberry muffin.

Home-made? he wondered. From the neighbour? Though surely the neighbour would've put his or her name on the note. Or maybe they'd been interrupted while they were writing the note and simply forgot to sign it. Whatever, the gesture was appreciated.

Brad realised then that he was hungry. He'd worked through his lunch break so he could leave early and miss the worst of the rush-hour traffic for his three-hour drive from London to north Norfolk, but then he'd been too keyed up to eat when he'd stopped for a rest break. He hadn't bothered to stop at the large supermarket on the edge of town—one that hadn't been there on his last visit—and he hadn't even thought about dinner. He'd just been focused on driving to Great Crowmell and facing all the memories.

He took a bite of the muffin. And it was fabulous.

For a second, he was transported back to the early days of his marriage. When Abby had made blueberry muffins for breakfast on Sunday mornings, and he'd woken to the smell of good coffee and cake. They'd always eaten the muffins in bed and lazed around until lunchtime…

He shook himself. Long, long gone.

Coffee. That would sort out his head. And it would help the paracetamol to tackle his headache, too.

He took the kettle to the sink and turned on the tap.

Nothing.

The neighbour hadn't left a note about there being any problems with the water.

Frowning, he went upstairs to the bathroom and tried the taps on the sink and the bath. Nothing there, either. When he flushed the toilet, the cistern didn't fill up. Clearly someone had turned off the stopcock, for some reason, and forgotten to turn it back on. It would be easy enough to fix.

But he couldn't actually find the stopcock. The obvious place for it to be located was under the sink in the kitchen, but it wasn't there—or in any of the other cupboards. It wasn't in the bathroom, either.

Great.

It looked as if he was going to have to disturb the occupant of number one, after all, to see if he or she knew what the water problem was and where the stopcock was located.

Leaving the little cottage, he walked to the neighbouring house and knocked on the white-painted front door. And he stared in utter shock when it opened, putting him face to face with Abigail Scott for the first time in nearly five years.

CHAPTER TWO

'BRAD?' ABIGAIL LOOKED as shocked as he felt, the colour
draining from her face as she stared at him. 'What are
you doing here?' she asked—at exactly the same time
as he asked, 'What are you doing here?'

'I was looking for the owner of number one Quay
Cottages,' he said.

'That would be me.' She frowned. 'So that means
you're hiring number two this week?'

'Didn't the letting agency tell you?'

'They don't always give me a name. They just said it
was a single person who'd booked a Monday-to-Monday
let.'

Which was clearly why she'd left him the fresh muffin today as a welcome gift. 'I didn't realise you lived
here.'

'No.' She raised an eyebrow, as if to point out that it
was really none of his business, since he was no longer
married to her. 'I assume there's a problem next door?'

'Yes. There's no water,' he said.

'Ah.' She grimaced. 'Number three had a leaking
pipe and the plumber borrowed the spare keys from
me to turn off your water this morning, just in case it
caused a problem in your house. Obviously he forgot

to turn the water back on before he returned the keys,
and I didn't check because I assumed he would've already done that.'

'And the stopcock isn't in an obvious place.'

'When these cottages were done up, let's just say the
building contractors made some unusual choices,' she
said. 'I'll come and show you where it is.'

'Thanks.'

Abigail looked hardly any different from the way
she'd looked five years ago, when Brad had last seen
her. She was still the most beautiful woman he'd ever
met, with eyes that he remembered being sea-green
when she was happy and grey when she was sad, a
heart-shaped face and a perfect cupid's bow mouth.
The striking difference was the way she wore her dark
hair; he remembered it falling halfway down her back,
and now it was cropped in a short pixie cut that made
her grey-green eyes look huge.

'Audrey Hepburn,' he said.

She frowned. 'What?'

'Your hair. *Breakfast at Tiffany's*.'

She inclined her head. 'Thank you, but actually she
had long hair for that film. This is more like her hair
was in *Sabrina*.'

Of course Abigail would know. She and Ruby loved
Hepburn's films and had binge-watched them as teens
in the summer holidays. And it was a stupid thing to
say. 'Sorry.'

'It's not important.' She ushered him out of the house,
and waited for him to let her into the cottage next door.
'OK. The stopcock's here in the lean-to at the back.'

He found the right key, unlocked the door and dealt
with the stopcock.

'I'll wait to make sure the water's working,' she said. 'And I'd better ask the agency to put a note about the stopcock's position in the file they leave for clients.'

'Good idea,' he said. Abigail always had been practical and organised. She'd made him feel grounded and back in the real world after a hard day at the lab—and he'd missed that.

Not that he had a right to miss it.

He'd been the one to insist on a divorce. Even though he'd been sure he was doing the right thing for her, he knew it had hurt her.

There was nothing he could do to change the past; but he wanted things to be at least on an even keel between them, for the sake of Ruby's wedding.

'Thank you for helping,' he said, turning on the taps and noting that thankfully the water ran clear.

'No problem.'

Abigail knew this was her cue to leave, and to make herself a little bit scarce over the next few days.

Except Brad looked like hell, with dark smudges under his eyes. And she knew why: because he was back in Great Crowmell for the first time since his father's death. Home, where he felt he'd failed. Even though Jim's death most definitely hadn't been his fault, Brad had blamed himself, and that was when their life together had started to unravel.

They were divorced, she reminded herself. This was none of her business.

But Bradley Powell had been her first love. Her one and only love, if she was honest with herself. Right now, she could see he was suffering. She couldn't just leave him like this. OK, so she knew he didn't love her any

more and she'd learned to accept that; but, for the sake
of what he'd once been to her, she wanted to help him.

'Are you OK?' she asked, her voice gentle.

'Yes.'

He was lying. Putting a wall between them, the same
way he'd done five years ago. She could walk away, like
she had last time; or, this time, she could challenge him.
Push him the way she maybe should've pushed him
back then, except at the age of twenty-two she hadn't
quite had the confidence to do that.

Now, things were different. She knew who she was
and she was comfortable in her own skin. And she was
no longer afraid to challenge him. 'That's the biggest
load of rubbish I've heard in a while.'

He looked at her as if not quite believing what he'd
heard. 'What?'

'You're not OK, Brad,' she said. 'You're lying about
it—which is crazy, because I'm the last person you
should need to keep a stiff upper lip in front of—and
I'm calling you on it.'

He lifted his chin, as if to argue. 'I…' Then the fight
went out of him and he sighed. 'No. You're right. I'm
not OK.'

'Because you're dreading this week?' she asked.
'That's why you booked into the cottage, isn't it? So
you wouldn't have to go home and see the ghosts.'

He raked a hand through his hair. 'You always could
see through me, Abby. Except back then…'

'Back then, I would've let you get away with it.' How
young and naive she'd been. In the last five years she'd
grown much wiser. Stronger, more able to deal with
tricky situations. She'd changed. But had Brad? 'You've
just had a three-hour drive from London, in rush-hour

traffic. I'm guessing you didn't have time for lunch and you were thinking about your current project while you were driving, so you didn't bother to get any shopping on the way here either. Apart from what I left you, your fridge and cupboards are all empty. But there's an easy solution. Come and sit in my kitchen while I make you something to eat.'

He shook his head. 'I can't ask you to do that.'

She folded her arms and looked at him. 'You're not asking me. I'm telling you.'

'Bossy.' But there was the hint of a smile in the tiny crinkles at the corners of his eyes. A smile she wished she hadn't noticed, because it still had the power to make her knees weak.

We're divorced, she reminded herself. I'm just doing this for Ruby, to make sure Brad doesn't get over-whelmed by the past and bail out on her before the wedding. Bradley Powell doesn't make my knees go weak any more. He *doesn't*.

'Just shut up and come next door,' she said, more to cover her own confusion than anything else.

'Is there anything I can do to help?' Brad asked when he'd followed her into her kitchen.

Abigail shook her head and gestured to the small bistro table in the nook that served as a dining area. 'Sit down and make yourself comfortable.'

'Thank you.' He paused. 'So how long have you been living here?'

'Two years. Didn't Ruby tell you?'

'She doesn't really talk to me about you.' He looked at her. 'Does she talk to you about me?'

'No,' she said. 'Though obviously your mum told me

you'd got your doctorate. She showed me the graduation photos.'

He'd nearly not bothered with the graduation ceremony—until his sister had pointed out that she and their mother would quite like to be there, so it would be a bit selfish of him not to go. Brad had felt he didn't deserve the fuss, but he'd given in for his mother's sake.

'Uh-huh.' He didn't want to talk to Abigail about his graduation and how much he'd missed his father. How it had been a physical ache. How he'd longed to say to Jim, 'See, I told you I'd make something of myself doing the subject I love.'

He grabbed at the nearest excuse to change the subject. 'Nice house.' It looked as if it was the same layout as the cottage he'd hired for the week: the white-painted front door opened straight into the living room, and stairs led between the living room and kitchen to the upper floor. But whereas next door was all furnished in neutral shades, as far as he'd seen, Abigail had gone for bright colour. Her living room was painted a warm primrose yellow, with deep red curtains and a matching deep red sofa opposite the cast-iron original fireplace with a huge mirror above it, a wall full of books and a massive stylised painting of a peacock on another wall, which looked very much like his sister's handiwork. And the kitchen walls here were painted a light, bright teal; the cupboards were cream and the worktop was grey. It was stylish and homely at the same time.

The perfect size for two.

He didn't let himself think about who might have sat at this table opposite her. It was none of his business who she dated. She wasn't his wife any more.

'Are there any dietary things I need to know about?' she asked.

'Such as?'

She shrugged. 'I know you don't have any food allergies, but you might have given up eating meat or fish since we last ate together.'

Had she? He really had no idea. As for himself, he barely noticed what he ate, since she'd left. Since he'd pushed her into leaving, he amended mentally. 'No. Nothing's changed. But I don't want to put you to any trouble. I can walk up the road and get some fish and chips—assuming the chip shop's still there on the harbour, that is?'

'You're not putting me to any trouble,' she said. 'I haven't eaten yet this evening. It's as quick to cook for two as it is for one.'

'Then, if you're sure you don't mind, whatever you want to cook is absolutely fine with me,' he said. 'Thank you.'

'You told Ruby we could be civil. So did I. We might as well start here and now.'

'A truce. OK.' He could do that. And maybe, if he could get things on an even keel with her, it would take some of the weight of guilt from him.

'Coffee?'

'Thanks. I'd love one.' He paused. 'That muffin you left next door—did you make that yourself?'

'Yes. This morning.'

'I appreciated it. And it was very good.'

'Thank you.'

She'd gone slightly pink. Was she remembering when she'd made muffins in his student days and they'd eaten them in bed together? Not that he could ask her. That was way, way too intimate.

She made coffee just the way he liked it, strong and sugarless with a just dash of milk. He remembered how she took her coffee, too. And the fact that she never drank tea. Funny how all the memories flooded back, as if their years apart had never happened.

Wishful thinking. It was way too late to do anything about it now.

She chopped onions, chilli and garlic, then heated oil in a pan and started to sauté them. The kitchen smelled amazing. She added diced chicken, and he realised just how hungry he was. Abigail always had been good in the kitchen; rather than going away to study for a degree, she'd planned to join her family's café business when she left school. She was going to work her way up while he studied, and they were going to get married after he graduated.

Until Brad, after a huge row with his dad, had rebelled; he'd asked Abby to elope with him before they got their exam results. All wide-eyed and trusting, young and full of hope, she'd agreed. And she'd put her plans aside, moving with him when he left for university, getting a job in a café in Cambridge and ending up managing the place within a year.

Ruby had been economical with the details but Brad guessed that, after Abigail had moved back to Great Crowmell, she'd gone with her original Plan A and joined the family business. Given that her parents were in their late fifties and would be looking at retiring, he'd guess that she was taking more responsibility every year. Maybe she was even running the place now.

'So how's the café?' he asked.

'Fine. How's the lab?'

'Fine.'

Stonewalling each other with single-word answers wasn't going to do anything to help the situation. Brad decided to make the effort and try some polite conversation. Offer some information, which might make her offer information in return. 'My team's working on developing a new antibiotic.'

'Sounds good—we definitely need that.' She paused. 'So are you happy in London?'

He hadn't been happy in the last five years. But he did like his job. And she was asking about his job, right? 'Yes. How about you? You're happy here at the café?' If he focused on work rather than the personal stuff, then she wouldn't tell him about her new love.

'Yes, I'm happy at the café. Like you, I'm developing something, except mine's rather more frivolous.' She paused, then said brightly, 'Ice cream for dogs.'

'Ice cream for dogs?' The idea was so incongruous that it made him smile.

'Don't knock it,' she said, smiling back. 'Think how many people bring their dogs to the beach, then come and sit with them outside the café.'

He knew that Scott's Café, on the edge of the beach, had tables outside as well as inside, plus water bowls for dogs; it had always been dog-friendly, even before it became trendy to welcome dogs.

'Half of the customers buy an ice cream for their dogs to help cool them down, too, but obviously the sugar's not good for the dogs' teeth and the fat's not brilliant for their diet, either,' Abby said. 'So we've produced something a bit more canine-friendly.'

He raised an eyebrow. 'So you're telling me you're making chicken-flavoured ice cream?'

She laughed. 'Not quite. It's more like frozen yoghurt. We do a carrot and cinnamon one, and a cheese one.'

He stared at her. 'Cheese ice cream?'

'They serve Parmesan ice cream at the posh restaurant round the bay in Little Crowmell,' she said. 'That's what gave me the idea. Especially as Waffle—' her parents' dachshund '—will do anything for cheese. He loved being one of my beta testers. So did your mum's dog.'

He wondered who'd taken her to Little Crowmell and had to damp down an unexpected flicker of jealousy. He had no right to be jealous. She was a free agent. It was up to her who she dated, he reminded himself yet again.

'Dinner smells nice,' he said, reverting to a safer subject.

'It's not that fancy. Just chicken arrabbiata.'

He'd always loved her cooking. 'It's still better than I could've made.' Not that he really cooked, any more. Cooking for one didn't seem worth the effort, when he was tired after a long day in the lab. It was so much easier to buy something from the chiller cabinet in the supermarket and shove it in the microwave for a couple of minutes. Something he didn't have to think about or even taste.

Abigail's chicken arrabbiata tasted even better than it smelled.

And how weird it was to be eating with her again, in this intimate little galley kitchen, at this tiny little table. Close enough so that, when he moved his feet, he ended up touching hers.

'Sorry,' he said, moving his feet swiftly away again and banging his ankle on the chair leg.

She gave him a half-shrug. 'Not a problem.'

She might be immune to him nowadays, he thought, but he was far from immune to her. There was a time when they would've sat at a tiny table like this together, their bare feet entwined. When they would've shared glances. When dinner would've been left half-eaten because he would've scooped her up and carried her up the stairs to their bed.

And he really wasn't going to let himself wonder if she slept in a double bed.

It was none of his business.

This was supposed to be civil politeness. A truce. Getting rid of the awkwardness between them, so Ruby's wedding would go smoothly at the weekend. So why did he feel so completely off balance?

He forced himself to finish the pasta—she was right, he did need to eat—and then cleared the table for her while she rummaged in the freezer.

She was close enough to touch.

And that way danger lay. Physical contact between them would be a very, very bad idea. Because seeing her again had brought back way too many memories—along with a huge sense of loneliness and loss.

He retreated to the bistro table, and she brought over two bowls, spoons and a plastic tub.

'Are you selling tubs for people to take home, nowadays?' he asked, suddenly curious.

'Yes, but they're half-litre paper cartons rather than like this. Ruby designed them for me—pink and white Regency stripes, with "Scott's" written across it in black script,' Abigail said.

'So you're expanding the business?'

She inclined her head. 'Certain local restaurants stock our ice cream, and we have pop-up ice cream stalls for events. Regency-style carts. Ruby's having one at her wedding.'

And how different his sister's wedding would be from his own. A big affair, with the church filled with family and friends. The complete opposite from his and Abby's: no frills, no fuss, just the two of them, and two witnesses that the wedding planner at Gretna Green had provided. Abby had worn an ordinary but pretty summer dress and carried a posy of cream roses, and he'd worn the suit his mother had bought him for his interview at Cambridge. It had got a bit creased in his rucksack, but he hadn't cared. He'd just wanted to get married to Abby and be with her for ever and ever, and prove to his dad that he was wrong, that they weren't too young and he wouldn't find someone else in the first week away at university—that their marriage would last.

The summer when they were eighteen.

How young and foolish they'd both been.

All that was left from that day now was a handful of photographs.

He shook himself. They were meant to be talking about her business, not their past. 'Sounds good,' he said lightly. 'So what's this?'

'A new flavour. I'm still tweaking it, so it's not in production yet. Let me know what you think.'

She actually wanted his opinion? Something shifted inside him.

She put a scoop into the bowl. 'If you hate it, don't be polite and eat it—just tell me what you don't like about it because that'll be much more useful. I also have salted caramel in the freezer.'

His favourite. And he knew that she remembered. Just as he remembered that she loathed chocolate ice cream.

He looked at the bowl she'd just given him. The ice cream was a dusky pink, studded with pieces of deep red fruit. He took a spoonful. 'No more tweaks needed,' he said. 'Cherry and almond.'

'Cherry and amaretto, actually—but that's close enough.' She looked pleased. 'So the amaretto isn't overpowering?'

He tried another spoonful. 'No. You've got a good balance. It's not too sour from the cherries, but it's also not oversweet.'

'Analysed like a true scientist.'

There was amusement in her voice, but there was also respect. And maybe, he thought, a note of affection? But he'd managed to kill her love for him, five years ago. He'd shut her out, hadn't let her help him deal with the shock of his father's death. He didn't deserve her affection. 'It saves time,' he said.

'Thanks. I thought I might have got it right with this batch, though I was thinking about adding pieces of crushed amaretti biscuits.'

He shook his head. 'It'll change the texture too much. This is rich and soft and—well, *nice*.'

'Good. Help yourself to more. Or there's salted caramel,' she said.

He realised then that he'd finished the bowl. 'I'm fine,' he said. 'But thank you.'

He insisted on doing the washing up. And, even

though he knew he really ought to go, how could he refuse when she offered him another coffee?

Her living room was just as cosy as the kitchen.

'Is that one of Ruby's?' he asked, gesturing towards the peacock.

'Yes. It was a special commission,' she said with a smile. Then she grew serious. 'It's going to be hard for you, this week.'

There was no point in lying. He knew she'd see through it. 'Yes.'

'I imagine you came back early so you could face things before the wedding on Saturday, instead of being hit by the whole lot on the day.'

How well she knew him. 'It seemed the most sensible approach.' Doing the lot in one day tomorrow would be easiest in the long run; and if he did it now he'd cope better at the wedding.

'I'm working tomorrow,' she said, 'but I'm pretty much off duty from Wednesday so I can help Ruby with any last-minute details.' She paused. 'If you want someone to go with you to…' She paused, and he knew what she wasn't saying. To the church. To his father's grave. To all the places in the town that held so many memories, they threatened to choke him. 'Well, you know where I am,' she finished.

It was a really generous offer, especially considering how he'd pushed her away before.

But he also knew he had to face this on his own. 'Thanks, but I'm fine.'

Brad wasn't fine. Abigail could see it in his dark, dark eyes.

But he was as stubborn as his father had been. Which

wasn't always a good thing. He was making himself miserable, and that made his family miserable. Why couldn't he see that?

'Brad. It's been five years.' And everyone else had moved on, except Brad himself. 'I hope by now you've worked out that you weren't to blame.'

He said nothing.

'Your dad was a stubborn old coot. I loved Jim dearly, but he didn't help himself and he didn't listen to anyone.' Maybe now wasn't the right time to say it—but then again, when would be the right time? 'I think you're going the same way.'

'What?'

There was a simmering, dangerous tone to his voice. But Abigail wasn't backing down now. It was a boil that had needed lancing years ago. The poison needed to come out so Brad could move on instead of being stuck in the misery of the past. 'Jim was the one to blame for his death, not you. If he'd listened to his doctor and taken his angina medication out with him on the boat—or, better still, waited until the following weekend when you could've gone out on the boat with him and he wouldn't have been on his own—he wouldn't have had the heart attack in the first place; or at least if he'd had his GTN spray with him he would've been able to buy himself enough time for the emergency services to get to him and treat him in time.'

He clenched his jaw. 'My dad's *dead*.'

'And you're still alive, Brad.' Though he wasn't living. Just existing. 'Stop wearing that hair shirt and thinking you have to atone for something that really wasn't your fault.'

His face shuttered. 'I don't want to have this conversation.'

'No,' she said, not sure whether she was more angry or sad. 'You wouldn't face it then and you won't face it now. Brad, for pity's sake—you might want to keep punishing yourself, and that's your choice, but please make sure you don't punish your mum and Ruby at the same time.'

'I think,' he said, 'I'd better go. Before we say something we'd both regret.'

He was shutting her out again and refusing to discuss anything. So he hadn't changed. How stupid she was to think that five years might have made a difference. 'You do that,' she said. 'But if you're not smiling all day until your face hurts on Saturday, then you'll answer to me.'

His eyes widened as if he was shocked that she could even think that he'd do anything less than be delighted for his twin. 'Ruby's my sister.'

'And you've been there for her?' It was a rhetorical question, because they both knew the answer. He hadn't. He'd shut himself away in his lab, suffering in silence and not letting anyone comfort him—and that had also meant he wasn't able to comfort anyone else.

A muscle worked in his jaw. 'That's none of your business.'

'That's the attitude you took when it *was* still my business,' she said. 'Stubborn, refusing to see any other point of view except your own.' The anger she hadn't realised she was suppressing flared up, and the words came out before she could stop them. 'That's what killed your dad. Don't let it kill you, too.'

He stood up, his dark eyes full of answering anger, and walked out without a word.

He didn't even slam the door behind him. Just left it open.

Abigail stared after him, the flash of anger suddenly gone and leaving her full of guilt.

Oh, God. What had she done?

She was supposed to be civil to the man and start pouring oil at the first sign of any troubled waters. But instead she'd stirred up the storm. Big time.

OK.

Tomorrow, she'd apologise. And hope that she could repair the damage in time for Ruby's wedding.

CHAPTER THREE

EVEN THOUGH BRAD was tired after the three-hour drive, he couldn't sleep. He just stared into the darkness, replaying Abby's words over and over again in his head.

'You might want to keep punishing yourself, and that's your choice, but please make sure you don't punish your mum and Ruby.'

Was he punishing his mother and his twin?

'Stubborn, refusing to see any other point of view except your own. That's what killed your dad.'

No, what had killed his dad was Brad's selfishness.

He should've come home for the weekend and gone out on the boat with his dad, instead of going off with Abby for a romantic weekend away. OK, so she'd won the trip in a competition, but she could've taken Ruby with her instead and made it a girly weekend: and then Brad would've been there for Jim. He would've made sure that his dad had his angina medication with him on the boat. He could've administered it, bought time until the emergency services could get to them.

Though he was horribly aware that Abby had said pretty much the same thing. If only Jim had listened to his doctor and taken his medication with him. If only Jim had waited.

But everyone knew that James Powell was a Type A personality and the word 'wait' simply wasn't in his vocabulary. Jim was a larger-than-life character, a sharp barrister who'd lived for his job and been bored stiff being stuck at home. Of course he wouldn't have waited to go out on the boat until someone else could be with him. He would've argued that he was perfectly capable of crewing the boat alone. He'd hated the whole idea of having to retire early on the grounds of poor health. Being diagnosed with a heart condition that could kill him if it wasn't kept under control had been the worst thing that could've happened to him. He'd needed something to fill his time, and the boat was the one thing that had stopped him going crazy.

If Brad had only come home, that weekend...

But he hadn't.

And Jim had taken the boat out on his own. He'd had an angina attack and collapsed. The chest pain had been so bad, he hadn't even been able to call the emergency services; he'd only been capable of hitting the last number redial on his phone.

Brad's number.

'Chest. Hurts. On boat. Call coastguard,' he'd gasped.

'I'll do it now. Where's your medication, Dad?' Brad asked.

'Home.'

Meaning that there had been nothing to help with the pain.

Abby had been in the spa, having a facial, but thankfully she'd left her mobile phone in their room. With shaking hands, Brad had put his dad on speaker on his own phone and called the emergency services from Abby's.

'I'm getting someone to you now, Dad.'

'Should've waited.' Jim had squeezed the pain-filled words out.

'That doesn't matter now, Dad. Stay with me. Stay with me. It's going to be OK. I've got help coming. I know it hurts to talk, so I just want one word from you every couple of minutes so I know you're still with me. OK?'

'Yes.'

'Stay with me, Dad. I love you. It's going to be all right.'

But Jim had been in trouble way before the helicopter and the lifeboat had reached him. Miles and miles away from the coast, knowing it would take him hours to drive to Great Crowmell even if he left the hotel that very second, Brad had been unable to do anything to help. He'd heard the clatter of the phone onto the deck and guessed that his dad had dropped it.

'Dad! Dad! Stay with me. Pick up the phone. Please pick up the phone,' he'd pleaded.

But Jim hadn't answered. All Brad had been able to hear was the hum of the engine and the screaming of the seagulls, until finally the phone had been picked up by one of the lifeboat crew.

'This is the lifeboat. We've winched down the paramedic from the helicopter. You're his son, who called us out, right?'

'Yes.'

'OK. We're going to fly your dad back to hospital. Can you give us some information?'

'Anything you need,' Brad had said, and had gone through his father's medical history.

But it had been too late.

Jim had had a massive heart attack in the helicopter and the crew hadn't been able to resuscitate him. He'd died on the way to hospital.

Stop wearing that hair shirt and thinking you have to atone for something that really wasn't your fault.

Now that was where Abby was wrong. Brad didn't blame himself for his father's death. Even if he'd been there, if he'd given his father the medication, there was a very high chance that Jim would still have had that heart attack and died on the way to hospital.

That wasn't what crucified him every single day.

It was the fact that he'd been the last person to speak to Jim while he was still alive—while his father was still conscious—and he'd known that he couldn't do a thing to save his dad. That the lifeboat and the air ambulance wouldn't get to him in time. And then, in the days after the funeral, he'd realised that he would never get the chance to prove to his dad that he'd made the right career choice, following his heart to become a scientist rather than following in Jim's footsteps and becoming a barrister.

Brad just hadn't been able to cope with it all. To keep himself functioning, he'd had to build a wall round his heart. And that hadn't been fair to Abby: so he'd done the right thing by the love of his life. He'd set her free to find happiness with someone else.

And she thought he was being self-indulgent and wearing a hair shirt?

He stared into the darkness.

If only things had been different.

If only.

Eventually, he slept. His dreams were vivid, to the

point where he actually reached out for her, the next morning, thinking she was curled up in bed beside him.

Of course not. How stupid of him. Those days were long gone. She wasn't next to him, she was next door. There was only a single brick wall between them, but they might as well be on different planets.

Brad dragged himself out of bed and had a hot shower, but he didn't manage to scrub away the guilt and remorse. Or the sick feeling that today he was going to have to face everything he'd spent years avoiding.

Toast and coffee—thanks to the supplies Abigail had left him—made him feel more human.

OK.

He'd do the hardest bit first.

He headed into the centre of the town to renew the ticket for his parking space, then went to buy flowers. It meant he had to walk past the quay, and he could see another boat moored in the place where his father's used to be. Well, of course there would be. His mother had never really been into boats, so there was no reason for Rosie to keep the boat or the mooring after Jim's death.

But it still felt as if a little piece of his dad had been wiped away.

He bought a bunch of flowers from the shop in the middle of the high street, then walked to the church on the edge of town. It was a big old barn of a place, built of flint, with a massive tower, a lead roof and tall arched windows.

What he liked best was the inside of the church, and not just because it was full of light from those enormous windows. He turned the massive iron handle and pushed the heavy door open. He could remember coming here with his father, who'd showed him the ancient graffiti of the old-fashioned sailing ships scratched into the stone pillars, explaining they were probably prayers of thanksgiving for safe returns from long voyages.

If only James Powell had made a safe return from his last voyage.

But you couldn't change the past.

Brad shook himself and wandered through the church. There was the hexagonal stone font with its carved wooden cover and the smiling stone lions at the base—the font where he and Ruby had been christened as babies. And the ancient wooden pews with their poppyheads and carved bench ends, parts of the carvings polished smooth over the centuries where children's hands had rubbed against them. He'd always especially loved the carvings of a cat carrying one of her kittens and the mermaid.

This was the church where, if they'd waited until after his graduation, he would've married Abigail. Just as Colin would wait for Ruby on Saturday, Brad would've waited at the altar for Abby. But, because he'd been young and impetuous and desperately in love with her, he'd wanted to marry her before he went away to university. He realised now how much they'd deprived their families of a celebration. How stupid and selfish he'd been.

There were tea-light candles on a wrought-iron stand near the font, a couple of which were already lit. He lit one for his father using the wax taper provided, and stood watching the flame flicker for a while before putting some money into the slot in the wall safe.

Outside, several more graves had been dug in the churchyard since he'd last been here. And it was the first time he'd actually seen his father's headstone.

His mum had made a good choice. Together with the dates, she'd kept the words simple: *James Powell, beloved husband, father and son.* And on the back there was a carving of a boat, his father's favourite thing.

The stone vase-holder in front of the headstone was already full of flowers. Of course it would be; either Rosie or Ruby would've made sure of that. He should've thought to buy one of those pots on a spike that you could push into the earth, or bring some kind of jam jar to put his flowers in. Too late, now. He placed the wrapped bunch of flowers on the grass next to the vase, and sat cross-legged in front of the stone.

'Well. I guess it's about time I showed my face here,' he said.

Understatement of the century.

He could almost see his father's rolled eyes and hear the sarcastic comment.

'I'm sorry, Dad,' he said quietly. 'I'm sorry I couldn't save you. I'm sorry I was too far away to help.' He dragged in a breath. 'I'm sorry I've made such a mess of my life—though at least my career is doing OK. I know you were disappointed I didn't follow in your footsteps, but I would've made a lousy lawyer. I'm a good scientist. I love my job. And I think you'd approve of me being one of the youngest managers ever in the pharmaceutical company, in charge of a really big project.'

No answer. Not that he expected one. But a sudden gust of wind or an unexpected ray of sunlight would've been nice. A sign that his father had heard him.

'I'm sorry I haven't been there for Mum and Ruby,' he said. 'I wasn't trying to neglect them. It was the whole idea of coming back here. Where I'd failed you. I know, I know, I should've manned up and driven here instead of always expecting them to come and see me in London. But, the longer I stayed away, the harder it was to come home. I couldn't face walking into the house, expecting to see you and then seeing the space where you weren't there—it'd be like losing you all over again and I just couldn't bear it.'

And how he missed his father. They'd had a difficult relationship at times, but Brad had respected his father and what he'd achieved, even though they'd disagreed about Brad's career choice. James Powell was a big bear of a man, always laughing and joking, full of outrageous stories about his days in court. Brad had sneaked into the public gallery at court one day, to watch his father at work, and he'd seen how brilliant James was—persuasive, knowledgeable, putting his client's case in a way that the jury understood but without patronising them. He'd been spellbinding. A father to be proud of.

And he'd died way, way too soon.

Brad sighed. 'You were right about me and Abby. We were too young to get married. Of course it didn't last.' And how selfish he'd been to drag Abby into his teenage rebellion. If he'd waited, maybe they would still be married now. But they weren't. Another failure. Something else he hadn't wanted to face, here in Great Crowmell. The place where he'd fallen in love with Abigail Scott.

The break-up had been entirely his fault. He'd been the one to push her away.

Though seeing her again had made him realise that his old feelings for her were still there. They'd never really gone away. He'd ignored them, buried them even; but now he was home and close to her, it was harder to block them out.

He couldn't possibly act on those feelings. He didn't trust himself not to mess it all up again, and he wanted to give Abby the chance to be happy—even if it was with someone else. But maybe they could be on better terms than they'd left it last night. When she'd told him things he hadn't wanted to face and, instead of talking it over with her, he'd walked out and refused to discuss it.

'Did you ever regret things, Dad?' he asked. 'Did you ever wish you hadn't said things, or that you'd done something differently?'

Of course there was no answer.

Though his father had always been so confident, so sure that he was right.

Abby's words slid back into his head. *Your dad was a stubborn old coot. I loved Jim dearly, but he didn't help himself and he didn't listen to anyone.*

She was right; and that was probably why James had been so confident. He didn't listen to anyone who didn't say exactly what he wanted to hear. And Brad couldn't ever remember his father apologising; though Jim had come close to it in that last phone call, when he'd admitted he should've waited instead of going out on the boat on his own.

Brad sighed. 'Abby loved you. Even though you were stubborn and didn't listen to anyone except maybe your clients, she loved you.'

She'd loved Brad, too. And he'd been so sure he was right, not listening to her. Just like his father. Funny, he hadn't thought that he could be as difficult as James, but maybe he was. Being stubborn and refusing to give up had stood him in good stead professionally; the flip side meant that being stubborn and refusing to talk about things had ruined his marriage.

'I owe her an apology,' he said. 'For a lot of things. I need to go and talk to her. But I'll be back. I'll come and see you on Saturday. And we're going to smile all day until our faces hurt, for Ruby's sake.'

When he walked back into the florist, the assistant raised her eyebrows. 'Back again?'

He nodded. 'Can you wrap up six roses for me, please?' And there was only one colour he could choose. 'Cream ones.'

'Going to see your mum now, are you?'

That was the thing about growing up in a small town; everyone knew you, and they knew your business, too. 'No. Actually, I'd like a different bouquet for her, please—something with lots of pinks and purples.' Her favourite colours. 'Can I pick it up in an hour? Oh, and if you have one of those vases on a spike you can use in the churchyard, I'd like to buy one of those, too, please.'

'Sure.'

He paid for everything, taking just the roses and the vase with him, then bought a bottle of water in the newsagent next door.

Then he noticed the shop next to the newsagent. Scott's Ice Cream Parlour. That was new. He'd been so focused on visiting the churchyard that he hadn't noticed it when he'd walked here before. So where would Abigail be today? Here, or at the café by the beach?

Inside, there was a young girl serving; he didn't recognise her.

'Can I help you?' she asked with a smile.

'Um, I was wondering if I could have a quick word with Abigail, please?'

'She's not here, I'm afraid. Can I take a message?'

'No, it's fine.' It looked as if he'd have to catch her at home.

'Do I hear someone asking for our Abby?' An older woman came out of the back of the shop and stared at him in surprise. 'Oh. Brad. You're back.'

'Hello, Gill.' He remembered her from the beach café, years back. 'Yes, I'm back for Ruby's wedding.'

She eyed him warily. 'I can get a message to Abby, if you like.'

It was kind of nice that Abby's staff were protective about her, he thought, not actually telling him where she was until they'd checked with her first. Though it didn't help him.

'I'm not going to fight with her,' he said softly. 'I just wanted a quick word with her about wedding stuff.' That last bit wasn't strictly true, or anywhere even vaguely near the truth, but the first bit was heartfelt.

Gill frowned, and he thought she was going to stonewall him. But then she nodded. 'OK. It's Tuesday, so she'll be at the beach café.'

'Thank you, Gill.'

'You're welcome.' Her gaze dropped to the flowers and the vase he was carrying, and this time there was more sympathy in her expression. 'Going to see your dad?'

'Yes.' She didn't need to know it was for the second time—or that these flowers were for Abby.

'He was one of a kind, your dad. He's still missed around here.'

The words put a lump in his throat. 'Thank you.'

At the church, he sorted out the flowers he'd left at the grave earlier, pushing the spike into the earth and then filling the vase with water; then he headed for the beach café. He'd forgotten what a long walk it was from the harbour to the beach. It had always felt like seconds when he was a teenager, walking there hand in hand with Abby. Now, it seemed never-ending. And he couldn't remember the seagulls being quite so irritating and screamy, either.

Or maybe he was just out of sorts because of what he'd been doing that morning.

As he neared the café, he saw that all the tables outside were full. Dogs were sitting next to their owners or lying half under the tables; it looked idyllic. The perfect English beachside scene.

He was pretty sure that Gill would have called the café as soon as he left, so Abby would be expecting him. Hopefully she hadn't decided to leave and avoid him, or he'd have to come up with a plan B. He took a deep breath and walked inside.

She was nowhere to be seen in the café.

'Excuse me, please,' he said to the young man at the counter—someone else he didn't recognise. 'Would it be possible to have a word with Ms Scott, please?'

The young man eyed the flowers curiously.

And then it occurred to Brad that he might be causing problems for Abby if she had a new partner. A stranger bearing a bunch of roses wouldn't go down well. Even if she explained that the stranger was her ex-husband, and he was simply trying to apologise for a fight they'd had and keep things on an even keel between them for the sake of his sister's wedding.

'I'll go and get her,' the assistant said.

Abby came out from the back and he could see the second that she spotted him, because the welcome in her face turned to wariness. He sighed inwardly. It was his own fault. He'd done that with his behaviour last night.

'I know you're at work, and I don't intend to hold you up or get in the way,' he said, 'but please can I talk to you for three minutes?' And hopefully she'd realise he meant not in front of other people. He didn't want any gossip. Gossip was the thing he'd hated most about growing up in a small town.

She nodded. 'Come into the office.'

He followed her behind the counter, ignoring the curious looks from the people round them.

She closed the door of her office behind them and gestured to a chair. 'Have a seat.'

'Thank you.' He handed her the roses. 'For you.'

She frowned. 'Why?'

'A mixture of things,' he said. 'One, to say thank you for stocking my fridge.'

She lifted one shoulder in a half-shrug. 'Barely. It's what I do for all the guests next door.'

He ignored her protest. 'Two, to say thank you for sorting out the water problem. Three, to say thank you for dinner last night.' And here was the big one. 'Four, to apologise for walking out on you last night when you tried to talk to me.' He knew he owed her more than that. 'Five, to ask if you'd let me take you to dinner to-night to apologise properly—that is, if it won't cause a problem with your partner?' Because he had to face it. A woman as warm and lovely as Abigail Scott wouldn't be alone for long.

'Will it cause a problem with your partner?' she asked.

Which didn't tell him anything. Though he could

hardly call her on answering a question with a question. 'I don't have a partner,' he said.

After a long, long pause, she said, 'Ditto.'

And why did that make the day feel as if the sun had suddenly come out? Crazy. He wanted Abigail to be happy. Rekindling their relationship wasn't on the cards, because he couldn't risk hurting her again. He ought to want her to have a partner instead of being alone. But a more selfish part of him was glad that she wasn't involved with anyone else.

'And six,' he said, changing the subject, 'just because five roses is an odd number. Literally and figuratively.'

That last bit made her smile, to his relief. 'Thank you. They're lovely.'

'I *am* sorry, Abby,' he said. 'I was tired and out of sorts last night, and I shouldn't have taken it out on you. I was rude, ungracious, and stubborn.'

'So only part of a chip off the old block, then,' she said.

Meaning that, unlike his father, he actually apologised? 'Maybe.' He looked her straight in the eyes. Today, they were sea green. 'Abby, I meant what I said. I'd like to take you to dinner tonight. To say thank you for looking out for me, to apologise, and to kind of cement a proper truce between us so Ruby's wedding day is perfect.'

She was silent for so long that he thought she was going to say no, but then finally she nodded. 'All right. I won't finish here until seven, though.'

'Fair enough. I'll book somewhere local for, what, eight? Will that give you enough time to be ready?' Not that Abby had ever been the high-maintenance sort who took hours and hours to get ready. Though he had no idea how much she'd changed since their divorce. Maybe she was different, now.

'That's fine,' she said.

'And I'll call for you at quarter to eight.'

She nodded. 'That'd be nice.'

'I can see you're busy,' he said, 'so I won't hold you up.'

'Thank you.'

'I'll see you tonight.'

He was at the door when she said softly, 'Brad.'

He turned round to face her. 'Yes?'

'Did you go to the church?'

He inclined his head. 'And I'm going to see Mum now.'

'That's an awful lot to face in one day.'

The quayside. The church and the churchyard. His childhood home. 'I might as well deal with most of the ghosts at once. I'll live.' It was time he stopped avoiding his past; and maybe being stubborn about it would help, for once. Doing it today would give him a couple of days' breathing space before the wedding, so he could get his mask perfect again. 'I'll see you at quarter to eight.'

Brad walked up the driveway to his parents' house—his mother's house, he corrected himself—just as he'd done so many times before. The house hadn't changed; although the paint was fresh the colour was the same and the flowers growing in the front garden were the same.

He paused with his hand on the doorbell. How many times he'd stood on this step as a teen, hoping that his dad wasn't working from home, ready with a lecture about how many more opportunities Brad would have with a law degree than with a chemistry degree. Or the row over the Cambridge college he'd applied to—not the one where James had studied. Brad had never been able to get through to his father that he loved him dearly but didn't want to follow in his footsteps; he wanted to make his own way, not trade on his father's reputation.

And now he never would.

He took a deep breath, nerving himself to ring the doorbell, when the front door opened abruptly; his mother swept him into a hug, and Ollie the Collie bounced around, barking madly.

'Brad, it's so good to have you home,' Rosie said.

Home.

'And you know you don't have to ring the doorbell. You're not a guest. This is always your home, any time you need it.'

A home with an empty space where his father should be.

Brad hugged his mother a little bit tighter, then made a fuss of the dog. 'I know, Mum.'

Her eyes were full of tears, but she blinked them away. 'It's so good to see you.'

'And you.'

She squeezed his hand. 'Last time you were here…'

She didn't need to say it. They both knew. The day of James's funeral.

'I know this is hard for you, Brad.'

It was. And her understanding made him feel worse. The lump in his throat was so huge, he could barely get the words out. 'I'm sorry, Mum. I should have come back before.'

'You video-call me twice a week and you spoil me in London. That's an awful lot more than some mothers get,' Rosie pointed out.

'I guess.' He took a deep breath. 'It's weird, being

back. And it must be so hard for you—imagining Dad's going to walk in any second now.'

'I've had time to get used to it. Which isn't a criticism,' Rosie said. 'And I know your dad used to give you a hard time.'

'I let him down by not following in his footsteps.'

'You would have let me down if you'd done that,' Rosie said. 'You needed to live your own life, not relive your dad's for him. And actually he was really proud of you. I know he probably never told you, but I used to hear him talking about you to his friends. "My son, the scientist. He's going to change the world."'

'Seriously?' Brad couldn't quite square this with his memories. All the criticisms, all the witticisms, all the little digs.

'Seriously. But telling you himself would have meant admitting he was wrong, and your dad didn't do that.' Rosie raised an eyebrow. 'I thought you were heading the same way, but I'm glad you're not. I hear you've seen Abby.'

The grapevine hadn't taken long to get the news to her, he thought. 'And had a fight with her—and bought her flowers to apologise,' he said ruefully.

'But you're going to have a truce for Ruby's wedding?'

'Absolutely,' he said. 'Nothing and nobody is going to spoil my twin's special day.'

'I'm glad to hear it,' Ruby said, walking into the hall from the kitchen. 'Welcome home. It's good to see you here instead of having to trudge all the way to London.'

'You mean the place where you get free accommodation and dinner, and plenty of time to spend at exhibitions,' Brad retorted. 'Not to mention theatre tickets.'

'Yeah, yeah.' But her smile was slightly wobbly.

'I was never going to let you down,' Brad said. 'And I've been to the church. I've been to see Dad. I put flowers on his grave.'

'That's a lot of ghosts to face in one day,' Rosie said softly. 'I think you need some lunch.'

'The bread's home-made,' Ruby said. 'Though I guess we should have got you a fatted calf.'

'Except you would have made friends with it, called it "Fluffy" even if it was a fully-grown bad-tempered bull, and it would have had a regular supply of best bovine treats,' Brad said with a grin.

Ruby punched his arm. 'Not only do you look like Dad, you *sound* like him. He would've been so pleased.'

'I'm not sure whether that's a compliment or not,' Brad said. 'And I wasn't the one who kept trying to tempt you away from being a vegetarian by cooking bacon sandwiches every single day.'

'Just as well, or we would've had to call the fire brigade,' Ruby said.

And this time, when he smiled, it didn't feel forced.

'So you and Abby—you're OK?' Ruby asked.

'We're OK. Really.'

'Only I heard—'

'They're fine,' Rosie said, and hugged her daughter. 'Come on, lunch. It's good to have both my babies home.' At the look on their faces, she laughed. 'You might be twenty-seven, but I can assure you that you're still my babies. You always will be.'

'It's good to be home,' Brad said. And this time he really meant it.

CHAPTER FOUR

CREAM ROSES.

Brad had bought her cream roses.

Had he remembered that had been her wedding bouquet, Abigail wondered, a posy of half a dozen cream roses they'd bought last-minute at the local florist? Or had he just decided that roses were the best flowers to make an apology and those were the first ones he'd seen?

She raked a shaking hand through her hair. It might not have been the best idea to agree to have dinner with Brad tonight.

Then again, he'd said he wanted a truce for Ruby's sake, and they needed to talk.

But seeing him again had stirred up all kinds of emotions she'd thought she'd buried a long time ago. She'd told herself that she was over her ex and could move on. The problem was, Bradley Powell was still the most attractive man she'd ever met—those dark, dark eyes; the dark hair that she knew curled outrageously when it was wet; that sense of brooding about him. She'd never felt that same spark with anyone else she'd dated. She knew she hadn't been fair to the few men who'd asked her out;

she really shouldn't have compared them to her first love, because how could they ever match up to him?

She could still remember the moment she'd fallen in love with Brad. She and Ruby had been revising for their English exams together in the garden, and Brad had come out to join them, wanting a break from his physics revision. Somehow he'd ended up reading Benedick's speeches while she'd read Beatrice's.

"'I do love nothing in the world so well as you: is that not strange?'"

She'd glanced up from her text and met his gaze, and a surge of heat had spun through her. He had been looking at her as if it were the first time he'd ever seen her. As if she were the only living thing in the world apart from himself. As if the rest of the world had just melted away…

It had felt crazy.

Abigail had known she shouldn't let herself fall for her best friend's brother. Apart from anything else, they had been way too young. Sixteen. There had been no chance their relationship would last, and she certainly hadn't wanted to put any strain on her friendship with Ruby. Brad had been the last boy she should have dated.

So she'd damped down the feelings.

But then Ruby had set him up as Abigail's date for their school's end of year prom, the week after their exams, on the grounds that neither of them had had a date and she had, and Ruby hadn't wanted either of them to feel left out.

It had been strange. The boy she'd known since she was a toddler, run around on the sand with and thrown snowballs at, had suddenly been a man, in a formal suit. And the look in his eyes when he'd seen her dressed up in a proper long, off-the-shoulder dress—it had been the same for him, too. Instant recognition. Shock at the changes in each other. A realisation that they weren't kids any more: they were grown up.

They'd danced together, and it had felt as if she were floating. They'd danced to music she hadn't even liked—and she really hadn't cared, because she had been in Brad's arms. She had barely been aware of anyone else being in the room.

At the end of the night, he'd taken her out into the grounds of the ancient hotel where the prom was being held and he'd kissed her among the roses. Moonlight, the scent of roses, the sound of a song thrush warbling into the night air—she would always associate those with the night Brad had first kissed her.

And from then on they'd been inseparable.

Ruby had gone to art college in September, while Brad and Abby had stayed on at their school's sixth form. And Abby had been happier than she could ever remember, spending as much time as possible with Brad. Of course she'd said yes when he'd asked her to marry him on the night of her eighteenth birthday. They'd kept their engagement secret, even from Ruby.

The original plan had been to wait until after Brad had graduated, but late one night he'd climbed up the drainpipe outside her bedroom window and said he didn't want to wait another three years to marry her. He'd suggested eloping to Gretna Green.

They'd got married in secret the week before their exam results had come out; and she'd moved to Cambridge with him when he'd started university in October.

Life had been perfect. Brad had studied while she'd

worked in one of the local cafés, and they'd spent every evening and every night together. First love, true love, for ever and ever and ever. She'd been blissfully happy, and she'd thought it had been the same for Brad.

Until the weekend when she'd won a competition for a spa break.

And then everything had fallen apart.

Brad had never got over his father's death. He wouldn't talk about it, but she was pretty sure that he'd never stopped blaming himself for not being there to save his dad. And he'd built a wall of ice round himself that Abby just hadn't been able to breach. Even leaving him hadn't been enough to shock him into breaking that wall; the idea, born from sheer desperation, had blown up in her face. Brad had been supposed to realise how much he missed her and come after her and talk; instead, he'd ended their marriage completely.

Five years.

For five years she'd tried to move on.

And right now it felt as if she was back where she'd been at the start. Raw, aching, wanting a man who clearly didn't want her any more. Wanting a man who'd shattered her belief in love.

How stupid was this?

Somehow Abigail got through the rest of the day. Though those roses haunted her every time she looked up and they caught her gaze. And they haunted her even more when she went home to put them in water on her kitchen windowsill.

She had enough time to shower, change into a little black dress and reapply her make-up by the time Brad rang the doorbell.

'You look very nice,' he said.

'Thank you. So do you.' He was wearing a formal shirt and dark trousers, with perfectly polished shoes; she knew that was from his father's influence. 'So where are we going?'

'The Old Boat House,' he said.

She blinked. The restaurant in Little Crowmell, the next village round the bay, took its name from the building it had been converted from. The food was amazing—unsurprisingly, as the chef had a Michelin star—and you had to wait weeks for reservations. 'How did you manage to get a table?'

He shrugged. 'It's a Tuesday night, so I guess it's less busy than at weekends.'

It was somewhere they'd never been together—on a student budget it simply wasn't affordable—but since she'd moved back to Great Crowmell Abigail had been there with Ruby for her birthday, and a couple of times with her parents as a major treat.

She needed to remind herself that this wasn't a *date* date. It was simply sorting things out between them and setting the terms for a truce, for Ruby's sake.

'Ready to go?' he asked.

No. She was panicking inwardly, worried that she was going to make a fool of herself over him. 'Sure,' she fibbed, trying to brazen it out.

She locked the door behind her and followed him out to his car. He didn't say much on the way to the restaurant, but put the radio on to a classical station. It suited her not to have to talk, too, and to pretend to listen to the music while her thoughts were whirring round.

Just where did they go from here? she wondered. Had he bought those roses because he too remembered their wedding day and missed the love they'd shared? Did he miss her as much as she'd missed him? Was this the first step towards repairing the bitterness of the past, maybe even trying to rekindle their lost love?

They were both older now, wiser, maybe more able to cope with life. But, if they did try again, there was no guarantee that their life together would be perfectly smooth. Unexpected things happened; the odds were that they'd hit a sticky patch. So what would happen at the next bump in their relationship? Would Brad shut her out again, just as he had when his father had died? She couldn't bear that, to make a fresh start but then go on to make exactly the same mistakes again.

Maybe it would be better to keep things between them just as friends.

And she'd tell him that tonight.

Abigail was as beautiful now as the day when he'd first fallen in love with her at their school prom, Brad thought. He'd gone as Abby's date simply as a favour to his twin, who didn't want her best friend to feel like a wallflower because Ruby was going to prom with her boyfriend. But there was something subtly different about Abby, that night. She wasn't just the girl who spent almost as much time at their house as his sister did and who felt like part of the furniture. She'd haunted him a bit since he'd read the lines from that Shakespeare play out loud and seen the wonder in her eyes, but he'd told himself that he couldn't possibly get involved with his sister's best friend. They were only sixteen, and the inevitable breakup would have too much fallout.

But at the prom he'd danced with her all night, and for him there had been nobody else in the room. Just Abby.

And then he'd taken her out into the grounds and

kissed her in the middle of the rose garden. He knew at that moment that he'd met his one and only. The woman he wanted to marry. The woman he *did* marry. The woman he'd been so happy with—until he'd ruined everything.

He really didn't know where they could go from here. Maybe he could ask her to give him another chance, after Ruby's wedding. But, then again, how could he trust himself not to ruin things a second time? He was the one who'd wrecked their marriage. OK, while life was smooth, things would be absolutely fine between them; but what would happen when they hit a rocky patch? Life wasn't always perfect. Would they be strong enough as a couple to weather whatever Fate threw at them, this time round? Or would he end up letting her down again?

He didn't have the answer.

So maybe it would be better to keep things between them just as friends.

And he kind of wished he hadn't asked her out tonight. He knew they needed to talk properly and cement their truce, but all the feelings he'd once had for her had come flooding back. It was so unexpected—and it was seriously messing with his head. He really didn't know what to do. Being here with her made him feel like an awkward teenager all over again.

The same awkward teenager in a creased suit who'd married her over the anvil in Gretna Green, promising to love and cherish her for eternity...

He opened the car door for her, and she acknowledged his courtesy with a smile. His hand accidentally brushed against hers as they walked to the restaurant, and he felt a tingle through his whole body; he didn't dare look at her in case it showed in his eyes and she noticed.

What was she thinking? What was she feeling? He didn't have a clue. And asking her would break open too many things he needed to keep buried.

The *maître d'* seated them at their table with an amazing view of the sea.

'I know we won't see the actual sunset from here,' Abby said, 'but we'll still get to see the sky looking pretty, reflected in the sea.'

Not as pretty as her.

And not that Brad would be gauche enough to actually say that out loud. 'Uh-huh,' he said instead.

The waiter brought their menus over.

'Would you like wine?' Brad asked.

Abby shook her head. 'Even though I'm not officially on duty at the café again until next week, I have things to do with Ruby tomorrow, including the final dress fitting, so I'd rather keep a clear head. Still water's fine for me, please.'

He smiled at the waiter. 'Still water for both of us, please.'

He looked at the menu. 'It's been a while since I've eaten somewhere this fancy.'

She glanced at him over the top of her own menu. 'You picked it.'

'I wanted to take you somewhere nice.' And she'd mentioned it inspiring her new range of ice cream, so he'd thought she might like it here.

'It *is* nice. Thank you. I love eating here.'

When the waiter came to take their order, Brad discovered they'd both chosen the same. He should've guessed. They'd always had similar taste in food;

though he'd seen food more as fuel than anything else, since she'd left.

'So how was it?' she asked.

'Which bit?'

She spread her hands. 'All of it.'

Of course she wasn't going to let him get away with fudging the issue. This was Abby. The woman who knew him as well as he knew himself—if not better. He sighed. 'OK. Confession time. I realise now I should've come back before. I wasn't fair to Mum or to Ruby.' Or to Abby, for that matter. 'I left them to deal with it and didn't support them enough.' He'd abandoned Abby, too.

'Well, you're here now,' she pointed out. 'You're not still running away.'

Though part of him wanted to. He'd never actually told her about his clashes with Jim and how much he regretted them. He knew she was close to her own parents and he wasn't entirely sure she'd believe him, because it was so far outside her own experience. But talking about it now wouldn't change things, so he didn't tell her. Instead, he said, 'It's when you're expecting someone to walk into a room and they don't. That's the hard bit.'

She reached over the table and squeezed his hand briefly. 'I know what you mean. Every time I sit at your mum's kitchen table, I half expect your dad to walk in and ask if there's any more coffee and where are the doughnuts. It must be so much harder for you.'

'Mum says you get used to it.' He blew out a breath. 'Though I'm glad I'm staying at the cottage so I don't have to face it all day, every day.'

'That's understandable,' she said, and he was grateful that she didn't point out his mother had to face it all day, every day. 'How was the church?'

'Seeing Dad's grave was tough,' he said. 'So was walking past the quay and seeing someone else's boat in the spot where his used to be. Though of course I didn't expect Mum to keep Dad's boat. It's much better for it to have gone to someone who'll use it and enjoy it.'

'I'm glad you see it that way,' she said.

'There's no other sensible way of seeing it, and I'm not that selfish.' He hoped. Though he knew he'd already been selfish enough in the past and he needed to make amends. He needed to sort that out in his head before he talked about it, though, so he switched the subject. 'I noticed you had a new shop on the quayside.'

'The ice cream parlour. I opened it last year. It's for people who don't want to walk all the way down to the beach to get one of our ice creams,' she said, 'or maybe they just want to pick up a half-litre tub to eat at home that evening.'

'Your idea?'

'Another new direction for Scott's,' she said. 'Yes. Mum and Dad want to take it easier and—' She stopped and winced. 'Sorry. That wasn't tactful.'

'Spend time together in semi-retirement? It's what married couples of that age do,' he said. 'What my parents would've done, if Dad had been more sensible with his medication and looked after himself better instead of leaving it all to Mum.'

She said nothing, simply looked at him.

'You were right,' he said softly. 'Everything you said about Dad, last night. He was stubborn, he didn't listen to anyone—and I really ought to learn from his mistakes.'

'Does that include looking after yourself better, rather than spending twice as many hours as you ought to in the lab and living off sandwiches and microwave meals?' she asked.

It was how he got by.

But he was saved from answering by the arrival of their first course: heritage tomato salad with pesto and burrata, all soft and wobbly and creamy.

'This is fabulous,' he said.

He managed to keep the conversation going about food during the second course, too: monkfish wrapped in Parma ham, served on a bed of lentils with samphire, plus a cauliflower and saffron purée.

'I'm a bit disappointed not to see your Parmesan ice cream on the menu today,' he said to Abigail after the waiter brought the dessert menu.

'If you really want to try it, I can always make you some,' she said. 'It was very popular in the eighteenth century. Though one glass of ice cream cost about the same as the average daily wage, so really it was only for the super-rich.'

'Have you thought about making historic recipes?' he asked. He remembered she'd always loved history. It had been her favourite A level subject.

'I do sometimes. I have an ancient brown bread ice cream recipe. But I'm experimenting with a few "free-from" options at the moment. Mum's been diagnosed as having coeliac disease, so that led me to source gluten-free wafers. And I've been making non-dairy ice cream with oat milk or almond milk for people who have dairy allergies. Or vegans—you know Ruby's thinking about taking the next step from being a vegetarian.'

He didn't. And he felt another twinge of guilt that he really hadn't paid enough attention to his sister.

'She's my main beta tester.' Abigail smiled. 'I get

people to fill in comment cards in the shop and the café, too—if they do, they go in a monthly draw to win a voucher for Scott's. Plus then I have their details for our mailing list when we release a new product.'

He wasn't surprised that Abigail had moved the business forward. Or that she'd turned out to be a savvy, thoughtful businesswoman. That had been so obvious in their Cambridge years; she'd been bubbling over with ideas and it was easy to see that she had what it took to grow Scott's. Only now he was seeing that potential actually realised, and it was a bit of a jolt to see that the naive, shy teenager he'd married was now well on the way to becoming a tycoon.

'And everything I sell is made from local ingredients, as much as possible,' she said. 'The local dairy supplies my dairy products; the farm shop supplies my fruit and veg; I have an arrangement with the local fishmonger and butcher; my flour's stone-ground from a local watermill—actually, they supply my bread as well—and even my coffee's roasted locally.'

'That's impressive,' he said.

'I want to make a difference,' she said. 'Yes, it's a little bit more expensive than using the cash and carry supermarket, and my prices reflect that—but my customers know that when they buy from me they're supporting local businesses and reducing their carbon footprint. And that's important to them as well as to me.'

He could just see Abigail being named local businessperson of the year. And he was proud of the woman she'd become: bright, confident and with a huge heart. The woman he'd always known she'd become. The woman he missed so very much…

Not that he could tell her that. He didn't have the right. Not any more.

'It sounds as if you're really settled. Though I'm guessing the hours you work are ridiculous.'

She shrugged. 'I don't mind. I love it here. I love the café, I love my staff, and I love Great Crowmell.'

Which was a timely warning for him. He didn't love it here. He didn't love the town, he didn't want to come back here, and his job was in London. There was no room for compromise, not when they lived three hours apart. That would be way too much of a commute for either of them.

So keeping things polite and a little bit distant would be the best the two of them could do. As for that weird yearning: he'd just have to try and bury it until he was back in London.

He managed to make polite conversation until the end of the meal, and then drove her back to Great Crowmell. Even if he hadn't hired the cottage next door to hers, he would've walked her home—his father had impressed the importance of good manners on him.

'Goodnight,' he said outside her front door, and leaned forward to kiss her on the cheek. Just to prove to both of them that they could do this—that they would be fine around each other at the wedding.

Except somehow his lips didn't meet her cheek.

Instead, they brushed against her lips. Very gently. Very lightly.

It felt as if he'd been burned.

But, instead of backing away sensibly, he found himself kissing her again. Then he drew back far enough to look her straight in the eye.

Sea green.

Not grey.

And her lips were parted very, very slightly. Inviting him. Telling him that it was the same for her—that right at this second she wanted them to kiss, too.

Memories collided in his head. The first time he'd kissed her, in the moonlight among the roses. The first time he'd kissed her before making love. Kissing her over the anvil in Gretna Green, their first kiss as a married couple.

How he'd missed her.

How he wanted her.

And he couldn't help leaning forward again. This time, she let him deepen the kiss, sliding her hands round the back of his neck and twining her fingers in his hair. And he wrapped his arms round her, holding her close, feeling the thud of her heartbeat—just as she must be feeling the thud of his.

Her mouth was so soft. So sweet. And it felt as if every nerve end in his body had just burst into life after five years of being dormant.

Shaking, he broke the kiss, and they stared at each other.

That really, really wasn't supposed to happen, Abigail thought. Right now Brad was more off limits than he'd ever been. It was Ruby's wedding in four days' time and they were supposed to be keeping a truce, not trying to rekindle the past. She was supposed to be telling him that they could be friends and nothing else.

But the way he'd just kissed her had blown her mind.

His hands were still splayed on her back and her hands were still loosely round his neck. Right now, they were like the teenagers they'd once been, kissing in a doorway.

And she felt just as she had the first time he'd ever kissed her, in that rose garden. Light-headed, needing to hold on to him to stop herself falling over.

This was a really bad idea.

They needed to stop.

Now.

She slid her hands back from his neck and took one step backwards, not quite trusting herself to stand upright, but thankfully that one step meant she could lean against her front door. And he clearly felt the same way that she did—spooked by the strong sensual reaction between them and not knowing what to do—because he stopped holding her, but he didn't move from where he was.

What now?

It would be oh, so easy to step forward again, kiss him and lead him upstairs to her bedroom. But she knew it would be a hideous mistake and they'd both regret it in the morning. They couldn't go back. Shouldn't go back.

'I...' Her voice sounded cracked to her own ears.

'We shouldn't,' he said, his own voice sounding just as hoarse.

'We have a truce. For Ruby's sake.' She forced the words out. 'And we'll be polite and civil to each other.'

'Agreed.'

'I'm going to bed now,' she said. When she realised that it sounded like an invitation, she added, 'Alone.' And her voice *would* have to squeak on that word, wouldn't it?

'Me, too,' he said. Though his expression said otherwise. The heat in his eyes told her he wanted to repeat their wedding night, to carry her over the threshold of their bedroom and then make slow, sweet love to her until they were both dizzy.

But they couldn't go back.

They *couldn't*.

'Goodnight,' she said, and turned away. While she still had the strength to do it.

Brad couldn't sleep. When the early-morning light poured in through the thin cotton curtains, he gave up trying, pulled on some clothes and a pair of running shoes, and went for a run to clear his head. It was early enough that the streets were mostly deserted—too early for anyone to go into the town to pick up a newspaper or a pint of milk before rushing to work. He'd forgotten how steep and narrow some of the back streets were, sloping up away from the harbour, and he'd worked up a decent sweat by the time he got back to the cottage. Which would have to be at exactly the same time that Abigail, also dressed in running gear, got back to the front door of her own cottage.

He could make this awkward.

Or he could keep it light and pretend that the kiss last night never happened.

It might be cowardly; but it might also be kinder to both of them.

'Fancy seeing you here,' he said.

'Anyone would think we lived near each other,' she said wryly. 'Temporarily.'

'Do you go running every morning?' he asked, suddenly curious. She'd never really been one for sport when they'd been together, preferring to curl up with a book or listen to music. That was another area where she'd changed.

'Yes. It clears my head and sets me up for work. Well, not that I'm at work today, but it's a good habit.' She looked at him. 'You?'

'Same.'

This was his cue to smile, say good morning, and walk inside.

But his mouth clearly wasn't with the programme. 'Maybe we could have lunch.'

'Sorry. I've got a final dress fitting with Ruby and Izzy.'

'Izzy?' It wasn't a name he knew. The dressmaker, perhaps?

'Isabella. Colin's niece—the other bridesmaid. She's seven years old and very sweet.'

Ruby had probably already told him and he hadn't been paying attention. Guilt twisted through him again.

And that was her cue to say good morning and walk away. Except her mouth clearly wasn't with the programme, either, because she said, 'Maybe we could grab some fish and chips tonight.'

'And eat them on the harbour wall.' Like tourists, or like the teenagers they'd once been. He liked that idea. 'What time?'

'How about seven o'clock?'

'That's fine. I'll knock for you.' He smiled. 'Have a good day.'

'You, too.'

At seven precisely, Brad knocked on Abigail's front door.

'Hi.' She was wearing faded jeans and a T-shirt, and no make-up.

'How was the dress fitting?'

'Fine,' she said. 'How was your day?'

'Fine. I spent most of it with Mum.'

'But you sneaked in some work?' she asked.

He smiled. 'As if you didn't.'

'I ticked a few things off my to-do list,' she admitted with a grin. 'My staff are great, but I don't want to take unfair advantage of them and dump my responsibilities on them.'

'Same here,' he said. 'I never used to understand what you meant about getting to know your team and developing them, when we were in Cambridge. I do now.'

'So you like managing a team?'

'As part of a project, yes. Watching their confidence grow and knowing I've helped that—it's a good feeling.' Something else they had in common, now.

They walked to the fish and chip shop and bought cod and chips, then ate them out of the cardboard box with a wooden fork while sitting on the harbour wall.

'Remember doing this, years ago?' he asked.

She nodded. 'And sitting on the dunes on the beach, watching the stars come out.'

'Star light, star bright…' And he thought, that the wish he'd make now wasn't achievable because the past couldn't be changed. 'We could do that now.'

She blinked. 'What?'

'Go and sit on the dunes and watch the stars,' he said.

She was silent for long enough that he thought she was going to refuse, but then she nodded. 'OK.'

When they'd finished their meal, they walked all the way from the harbour to the dunes. They didn't talk on the way there but it was an easy silence, not an awkward one. Especially as their hands had brushed against each other and their fingers had ended up entwined; he didn't want to say anything to break the spell, and he guessed it was the same for her.

And he couldn't get that kiss from last night out of his head. Had it been a mistake? Or had it been one step closer towards changing things between them? Towards making things better?

They sat on the dunes, still holding hands, just listening to the swish of the sea and watching the sky change colour; the band of deep purple at the horizon shaded up to pink, apricot and finally to blue.

'Look, it's the first star.' She pointed up to it with her free hand. 'Though I know it's a planet, not a star, because it doesn't twinkle. I remember you telling me that.'

He remembered that evening, too. 'It's Jupiter.'

She smiled. 'Trust you to know that.'

He gave a half-shrug. 'I don't see the stars much in London.' And that was one thing he missed about Great Crowmell. Out here, they were far enough away from the town for the sky not to be so affected by the light pollution. 'Every so often, I see news reports about sightings of the Northern Lights out here.'

'And every time I see those reports, Ruby and I gnash our teeth,' she said. 'We always manage to miss them, even though I get email alerts from the university about when a sighting's possible.'

He knew that was top of her bucket list, seeing the aurora borealis. He'd always intended to take her to the Arctic Circle, the winter after he'd finished his doctorate, so she could see them. Except life had changed unimaginably before then. The winter after he'd finished his doctorate, they'd already been divorced for a long, long time.

Trying to keep things light, he pointed out some of the constellations to her.

Even though it was summer, the night was still cool; he loosened his fingers from hers and slid his arm round her. 'Because it's cold,' he said. 'And, scientifically speaking, sharing body heat is the most efficient way of keeping warm.'

It was true, on a superficial level; but he knew it wasn't the real reason why he'd put his arm round her. He'd wanted to be close to her. And she hadn't moved away…

Then he looked at her. Her eyes were huge and her mouth was slightly parted.

What else could he do but kiss her, here under the stars, with the sea swishing gently in the background?

When he broke the kiss, he whispered, 'I'm sorry. For so very much.'

'It wasn't all you,' she said.

He didn't deserve this kindness, and his heart broke a little more. 'We were young. I handled everything badly. And I'm truly sorry I hurt you so much.'

'Apology accepted.'

He noticed that she didn't say it was all right. Because it wasn't all right. The past couldn't be changed.

But the fact she'd accepted his apology meant that perhaps they could both move on instead of being stuck.

'You have wedding stuff to do with Ruby tomorrow,' he said. 'We'd better head back.'

He resisted the urge to kiss her again. Though, when he offered her his hand to help her to her feet, he didn't let her hand go until they were outside the row of cottages.

It would be oh, so easy to ask her to come in. To stay with him tonight.

But that wouldn't be fair. He couldn't offer her a future. And he'd let her down before.

Instead, he brushed his mouth against hers. Lightly. Not demanding. 'Goodnight, Abby. Sleep well.'

And he unlocked his door and went inside before he did anything stupid—like picking her up and carrying her over the threshold.

Abby let herself indoors and curled up on the sofa.

That kiss yesterday had blown all her defences wide apart.

And tonight, eating fish and chips with him on the harbour wall and then going to the dunes to watch the stars come out—it was like reliving the best bits of their teenage courtship.

The worst thing was, she realised she was more than halfway to falling in love with Brad all over again. If she'd ever actually fallen out of love with him. Which she was really beginning to doubt.

She needed to get herself under control. He wasn't going to stay here, and this was where she belonged. They couldn't have a future together. Their lives had gone off at tangents from each other, and there was no way they could compromise.

At least she'd be busy for the next couple of days with Ruby, too busy to spend any time with Brad. She'd keep herself under rigid control at the wedding, making sure she was polite but keeping a distance between them. And then, after the wedding, he'd leave again— and she would have time to bring herself properly back to her senses.

CHAPTER FIVE

SATURDAY DAWNED BRIGHT and sunny: perfect weather for a wedding.

As the stand-in for the father of the bride, officially Brad didn't have anything much to do before the wedding apart from getting dressed and then accompanying Ruby to the church. But he knew exactly what James Powell would've done. He would've shooed his wife out of the kitchen and told Rosie to get ready with the girls, and he would've been the one dispensing cups of tea and terrible jokes and lots of hearty laughter.

Well, Brad could do that. Maybe not the hearty laughter and terrible jokes, because he wasn't a showman like his father had been; but he could do tea and calmness.

Colin was staying overnight with his brother Richard, mindful of all the old wives' tales about not seeing the bride on the morning of the wedding until she walked down the aisle. Brad and Abigail had got dressed together; maybe that had been one of the first in a long line of mistakes. Along with not having something old, something new, something borrowed and something blue, he thought.

He shook himself. Today wasn't about himself and

Abby—or the fact that she'd managed to avoid him ever since the night they'd sat and watched the stars come out and kissed each other. They'd be polite and civil to each other today, and maybe they could talk tomorrow.

He made mugs of tea for his mother, sister, Abby and Isabella's mother Sadie, and added a glass of milk for Isabella, then took the tray upstairs and knocked on Ruby's door. 'I'm leaving a tray of tea outside,' he said. 'By the way, the wedding flowers are here and they all look perfect. And there was an extra delivery for you, Ruby.'

A single deep red rose, with a message from Colin—no doubt telling her how much he loved her and how he was looking forward to marrying her later that day. Yeah. Brad remembered that feeling. How excited he'd been, hardly able to wait for the rest of his life to start—his new life as Abby's husband.

Older, wiser, he reminded himself. And divorced.

He dispensed bacon rolls—a hummus and falafel wrap, in his sister's case—mid-morning; and dispensed more tea when the hairdresser and make-up artist arrived.

And then finally it was time to head for the church.

Ruby emerged in a gorgeous strapless lacy gown, her hair in an updo and a tiara securing her veil. Brad had a lump in his throat as he looked at her. 'You look amazing. Dad would've been so proud of you.' He hugged her, careful not to crease her dress or spoil her make-up. 'You look fabulous, too, Mum.'

'Thank you,' Ruby and Rosie chorused.

'And you, Isabella. You look very pretty.'

But the one who really made his jaw drop was Abby. She looked stunning in a deep red dress with a V-neck and tiny shoulder straps; it was fitted at the waist and fell to the floor. And he knew every curve under that dress, knew every inch of skin. The memory practically poleaxed him.

What did he say to her?

His throat dried.

Polite and civil. That was what they'd agreed. He didn't dare meet her eye, and he drew on every reserve he had to make sure he didn't give a keynote speech worthy of a conference. 'You look very nice, too, Abigail.'

'Thank you,' she said, her tone equally polite and civil.

Had she guessed at how much his thoughts were churning? He hoped not. 'The cars are here,' he said.

He made sure that his mother, Abigail, Isabella and Sadie were all comfortably seated, then helped Ruby into their own car.

'Thank you,' Ruby said when he'd closed the door. 'You and Abby—I have to admit, I did worry a bit. Especially as she's been very quiet about you.'

So obviously Abby hadn't said a word to his twin about the kisses they'd exchanged. Or maybe they'd put her in as much of a spin as they'd done to him, and that was why she'd used the excuse of chief bridesmaid's duties to avoid him for the last couple of days. Not wanting to make today difficult, he'd backed off. 'It's fine,' he said. 'We're fine.' Even though they weren't, they *would* be for today. He'd make sure of that. Ruby's wedding wasn't going to be collateral damage from any problems between himself and Abby.

'I wish Dad was here,' Ruby said, a slight crack in her voice.

'Me, too.' He took her hand. 'But I'm pretty sure he's here in spirit. And he'd really love the woman you've become.' He looked at her. 'Don't cry. Mum and Abby will kill me if your make-up's even the slightest bit smudged.'

Ruby blinked hard. 'I won't cry.'

'Be happy, Rubes,' he said. And he wanted her to be as happy as he and Abby had been at the start of their own married life. Except he wanted that happiness to last for his sister for ever. 'Colin's a good man and I like him very much. But I know what Dad would be saying to you right now, and because he can't say it then it's my job to say it for him. I love you, and if you've got even the slightest, tiniest doubt about marrying Colin then you don't have to walk down that aisle today. I'll sort everything out for you so you won't have to worry. Nothing matters except that you're happy.'

'I don't have any doubts. I want to get married to Colin.' Ruby looked straight at him. 'Did you have any doubts when you married Abby?'

The question felt like a sucker-punch to his gut. He'd never told anyone why he'd rushed Abby off to Gretna Green—not even Abby herself. 'No. But don't repeat my mistakes, OK?'

His sister regarded him narrowly. 'Are you sure you're going to be OK with all this?'

'It's your wedding day. Of course I'm sure,' he said. 'You're going to have a lovely wedding and a lovely life with a man who adores you.'

She squeezed his hand. 'Love you, Brad. And I wish…'

'Yeah. Me, too.' He wished a lot of things. That his dad were still there. That he hadn't shut Abby out. That he could find some compromise to suit them both.

He couldn't change the past. But could he change their future?

At the church, he helped Ruby out of the car. Abigail straightened Ruby's veil and made sure she was ready for the first batch of photographs.

And then it was time to walk down the aisle.

This service would be a much happier occasion than the last one he'd attended here.

To the sound of Pachelbel's *Canon*—one of their father's favourite pieces of music, and he knew that was why Ruby had chosen it—he walked his twin down the aisle and gave her away to Colin in the middle of the ceremony. But when he took his place in the pew for the rest of the service, he wasn't looking at the bride and groom; he only had eyes for the chief bridesmaid. She looked wistful. Was it just the way women always looked at weddings—or was she thinking of their own wedding, right now, the way that he was? Remembering all the tiny details, all the little things that had made that day so special?

After Ruby and Colin signed the register and walked back down the aisle, there was a blur of photographs.

Brad chose that moment to sneak away to visit Jim's grave. 'I hope I did you proud today, Dad,' he said softly. 'Ruby looks so happy. I wish you were here with us, but I'll raise a glass to you later.'

Once the photographer was happy she'd got the shots she wanted, everyone headed to the big gorgeous hotel on the edge of town, which had once been the local mansion. The reception was being held in the former ballroom; the places were all immaculately set with silver and fine china and crystal glasses, and there were fresh flowers on every table.

Ruby's table arrangements were a little unconventional, though Brad was relieved he wasn't sitting near Abby—or anywhere near where he could see her and be distracted. Right now, he was focusing on making his sister's day as perfect as it could be, and he knew that Abby was doing the same. Having to face each other would complicate things.

His was the first speech after the meal, in the place of the bride's father. 'I'd like to thank everyone for coming and to welcome you to Ruby and Colin's wedding,' he said. 'And I'd also like to make a toast to our dad, who I'm sure is with us in spirit. I have to admit, I'm finding his shoes pretty hard to fill and I'm not going to do the kind of witty speech that he would've done—I'm going to keep it short and simple. But what I do know is that Dad would've been so proud of the wonderful woman my sister has become, just as I am. I'd like to welcome Colin to our family and it's good to have a new brother. In fact, it's rather nice to have another Y chromosome around to even things up a little in our family.'

Everyone duly laughed, and he relaxed. 'I give you the bride and groom, Ruby and Colin.'

'Ruby and Colin,' everyone echoed.

Colin made a speech about how much he loved his new wife that had a lump in everyone's throat; and then Richard, his brother, lightened things up again by telling the traditional best man's funny stories about the groom.

Then Ruby stood up. 'I'd like to say a big thank you to everyone for coming,' she said. 'And to my twin, Brad, for standing in for Dad today—and Dad would've been just as proud of our brilliant scientist, too. To Colin, for making me happier than I've ever known. To Mum, for being the best support ever. To Izzy, for being the greatest flower girl. And especially to Abby, because I could never have organised this without my best friend. We've known each other since we were toddlers and I love her like a sister. Please raise your glasses to my chief bridesmaid and ice cream maker extraordinaire, the woman behind the ice creams you'll all be eating in the garden this afternoon, Abigail Scott.'

Guilt flickered through Brad. Abby *had* been Ruby's sister—well, sister-in-law—until he'd messed everything up. But he was glad their friendship hadn't become collateral damage in the divorce.

Somehow he and Abby were both too busy with wedding details to speak to each other for the rest of the afternoon; she was supporting her staff at the old-fashioned ice cream cart and checking if there was anything they needed, and he was making sure that everyone had a drink.

Finally, it was time for the evening reception and the DJ announced the first dance; Ruby and Colin walked onto the dance floor together to George Michael's cover of 'The First Time Ever I Saw Your Face' and began a slow, sweet waltz.

The words of the song were so perfect; and they made Brad think of Abby. Unable to help himself, he glanced over the other side of the ballroom at her—to see that she was looking right back at him.

Was she thinking the same that he was?

Polite and civil, he reminded himself. That was the order of the day. Polite and civil. He could absolutely not be a troglodyte and scoop up the chief bridesmaid, haul her over his shoulder and carry her off to his lair. Particularly as his cottage was a couple of miles down the road. And particularly as lots of their family and friends were there to witness everything and he was very aware of the speculative glances.

Plus it was time for the traditional father-daughter dance. He couldn't help smiling as the music Ruby had chosen came on: ABBA's 'Dancing Queen'. It was the song she and Abby claimed would get anyone up on a wedding dance floor. Colin was dancing with his mother, Frances. Then they swapped round and Colin danced with his new mother-in-law, Rosie, while Ruby danced with Jeremy, Colin's dad; and Richard, Colin's brother, was dancing with Abby.

'Don't you dare try to sneak off this dance floor,' Ruby warned Brad as she passed him.

'As if I would,' Brad fibbed. But he was dreading the moment when he knew he was supposed to dance with Abby. How could he keep things polite and civil, when his emotions were raging inside him? That sense of loss and regret, knowing it was all his own fault and wishing things were different, wishing he had the right to hold her close and remember their own wedding day and kiss her under the stars...

The rest of the guests joined in and the DJ kept things upbeat for a while, getting all the generations doing their particular versions of dances to wedding classics.

'I guess the chief bridesmaid and the bride's brother ought to dance,' Abby said, coming to stand next to him. 'Before the bride starts fretting that they're having a fight.'

Polite and civil, he reminded himself. They could do this. 'Sure,' he said lightly.

He was expecting another upbeat song, one he could cope with—but, to his shock, the DJ chose that precise moment to dim the lights and slow things down with an old, old slow song.

They could hardly back out of it now, not without making a scene and making everyone feel awkward.

But dancing close to her like this...

Especially to this song. Art Garfunkel's 'I Only Have Eyes for You'—it was horribly appropriate. Because right now, there was nobody else in the room for him. Was it the same for her?

Maybe it was because, when the song ended and he forced himself to break the dance hold and take a step backwards from her, she looked as dazed as he felt.

Thankfully Stuart, her father, stepped in to dance with her; and Rosie came to dance with Brad.

'That was a lovely speech you made, darling,' she said.

'It's a lovely wedding, Mum,' he said, smiling at her.

'It is.' Rosie looked slightly anxious. 'Do you mind about George being at the wedding?'

'George?'

She looked pained. 'I told you about George earlier in the week.'

Of course. Her new partner. The one Brad hadn't met because George's elderly and frail mother had been taken ill last weekend, and George had gone to be with her. He'd come back today for the wedding, and Brad had shaken hands with him this afternoon and made polite and anodyne conversation.

How could he have forgotten? The emotion of the wedding—and of dancing with Abby—must've pushed it all out of his head.

But he really appreciated the fact George hadn't tried to take Jim's place on the day. He'd been diffident and decent and kept in the background, near enough to support Rosie but without pushing himself forward. He was a good man. And, most importantly, Brad liked the way that George looked at his mother.

'Mum, I want you to be happy,' Brad said.

'I know how badly you took your dad's death. I wasn't sure how you'd react to the idea of me seeing someone else. I've wanted to tell you about George for the last year,' Rosie said. 'I should've told you before this week.'

Except he'd made himself unavailable. Been utterly selfish. Maybe Abby was right about that hair shirt. 'I wish you had told me about him before,' he said. 'It would've been nice to meet him sooner and get to know him properly.' And he meant it.

'So you really don't mind that I'm dating someone?'

'Mum, you're not exactly wizened and ancient. You can't be on your own for the rest of your life,' he said. 'Dad wouldn't have wanted that for you either. He loved you enough to want you to be happy, not being a—a—' He struggled to find the right words. 'A Miss Havisham.'

'Wrong character, darling. Miss Havisham was a jilted bride, not a widow,' Rosie pointed out with a smile.

'I'm a scientist, not an English Lit graduate,' he reminded her, smiling back. 'You know what I mean, Mum. Isolating yourself and being miserable and living in the past. That's not what any of us wants for you, and Dad wouldn't have wanted that either. George seems a nice guy, Ruby likes him, and if he treats you the way you deserve then that's good enough for me.'

She hugged him. 'Thank you.'

'It's Ruby's special day,' he said. 'I want her to be happy—and I want you to be happy, too.'

'I am, but I worry about you. So does Ruby.' Rosie looked at him. 'I saw you dancing with Abby earlier.'

'We're both adults. We can be civil to each other,' he said mildly. Even though 'civil' didn't even begin to cover the complexity of his feelings towards her.

'She's still part of our family,' Rosie said.

'She's Ruby's best friend. Of course she's part of the family.' Even though she wasn't still married to him.

'She's not just Ruby's best friend. I still think of Abby as a daughter and I love her dearly. I just wish...' Rosie broke off and sighed.

'I know, Mum.' He hugged her. 'But you can't change the past. Now, go and dance with George, and let me get you both a glass of champagne first.'

Abby was dancing with someone he didn't know, someone who was clearly attracted to her by the way he was holding her. Jealousy flickered through him. And how bad was it that, when she didn't accept a second dance, he was pleased about it?

He ought to let her move on. Find someone else. Hadn't that been the whole reason he'd walked away from their marriage, to give her a chance to find happiness?

The problem was, his twin's wedding had brought back so many memories of his own.

Of dancing with Abby in their room on their wedding night, with music playing on his phone.

Of making love with her...

He managed to keep his distance for a full hour and a half.

But then another slow song came on. 'Moon River.' The song he'd always associated with Abby's favourite Audrey Hepburn movie and it made him itch to hold her. Before he knew what he was doing, he was right by her side.

'Might I have this dance, Ms Scott?'

'Sure.' She gave him a polite, civil smile.

But the dance wasn't polite and civil at all. They moved closer and closer together until their feet were barely moving and they were just swaying together; her heels were high enough that all he had to do was dip his head slightly and he could press his cheek to hers.

And how good it felt to be cheek to cheek with her. Holding her close. Feeling the warmth of her skin against his, the regular thud of her heartbeat.

But this time he was all too aware of the people around him. Right now, he wanted to be alone with her. Find out what was going on in her head.

'Do you want to go and get some fresh air?' he whispered in her ear.

'Good idea,' she whispered back.

He broke the dance hold and just about stopped himself taking her hand, but they walked out together into the garden. There were fairy lights strung all round the garden through the trees and shrubs, creating a soft warm glow in the twilight. The romance of the garden was intensified even more by the roses, where all the blooms were out and it felt as if they were breathing nothing but the sweet scent of them.

They'd been here before. A different function and a different garden, but it felt the same. The same as the night they'd first got together at their school prom.

He could hear the music from the ballroom, another slow song.

'Dance with me here?' he asked.

And it was just as if the years had melted away, as they held each other in the light of the moon and the fairy lights. Dancing cheek to cheek.

Except this time he moved so he could kiss the corner of her mouth.

And she responded by twisting slightly to brush her lips properly against his.

And then they were really kissing, holding onto each other as if to save each other from drowning in the sudden sea of emotion that threatened to swamp them both.

When he broke the kiss, he was shaking and her pupils were enormous.

He stroked her cheek. 'This reminds me of prom. The day when I really noticed you for the first time.'

'So before then I was just your sister's annoying friend?'

He smiled. 'No. I always liked you. But that time in the garden when I helped you and Ruby revise your Shakespeare—I felt something different, then. I knew I shouldn't get involved with you because you were my sister's best friend, and that made you off limits.'

'But you let her fix us up on a date for prom, a few weeks later,' she pointed out.

'I did it as a favour to Ruby. She was worried that you'd be a wallflower.'

'She told me she was worried that you wouldn't have a date because you were the biggest nerd in the world,' she countered.

'She was right. I was. I probably still am,' he said. He laughed, and stole a kiss. 'Abby. Today. We're supposed to be polite and civil to each other.'

'So why are we alone in the garden together? Why did you kiss me?'

'And why did you kiss me back?' he asked.

'I...' She shook her head, as if unable to find the words.

'Maybe it's just the emotion of the wedding.' He

knew that he was lying. He was here because he wanted to be here. He'd kissed Abby because he'd wanted to kiss her. Because he couldn't help himself.

'It's a good wedding.'

He nodded. 'And it's made me realise how selfish we were, eloping the way we did.'

'We were so young,' she said. 'Just eighteen.'

'And we didn't think of anything or anyone else,' he said. 'Just Gretna Green.'

She wrinkled her nose. 'We deprived everyone of a good party.'

'But I never, ever regretted marrying you,' he said.

She looked straight at him. 'So why did you divorce me?'

The big question. And he owed her honesty. 'Because I thought I was doing the right thing.'

She rolled her eyes. 'Are you trying to tell me there was a shiny suit of armour on top of that hair shirt of yours, and you were riding a white horse at the time?'

'Abby, I was a mess. I felt I was dragging you down.'

'That's the point of wedding vows, for better or worse. We should've stuck it out,' she said.

She could say that now? 'You were the one who left me,' he pointed out.

'I wasn't deserting you when you needed me.'

'It felt like it, though.'

'I simply wanted to shock you into realising what you were doing and stop you pushing me away all the time.' Her eyes filmed with tears. 'But it backfired. You divorced me. It wasn't supposed to be like that.'

He hadn't wanted the divorce, either. He'd wanted Abby—but he'd tried so hard to be unselfish, to un-shackle her from the mess he knew he'd become so she would have a chance to be happy. 'It's nearly five years.' He rested his palm against her cheek.

She turned into it, kissing his palm, and it felt as if he'd been galvanised. 'And neither of us has really moved on, have we?'

No. They hadn't. That was a problem they needed to solve, because they couldn't go on like this.

Though there was a solution. An insane one. She might say no if he suggested it, and he'd accept that. Then again, she might say yes. And how he wanted her to say yes. His heart thumping, he said, 'Maybe we need closure. To get things out of our system at last.'

'Closure. Getting things out of our system. Maybe you're right.' Her eyes were sea green. 'The bride and groom have slipped off to their honeymoon suite. We don't have to be here any more.'

So she was thinking along the same lines that he was? 'We could get a taxi. Go…' No. It wasn't home. Nowhere had felt like home since she left him. Not the flat they'd shared, not the college rooms he'd moved into after the divorce, not the flat he'd bought when he'd accepted the job in London. 'Back to the cottage,' he finished.

She was silent for so long that he thought she'd changed her mind. But then she nodded. 'I'll text my mum and say I'm fine but I have a bit of a headache and I'm going home for an early night, so nobody worries about me.'

He stole a kiss. 'Good thinking. I'll do the same.'

And from there it was easy.

A taxi was there in five minutes.

They didn't say a word to each other all the way back to the centre of town. They didn't need to. He paid the taxi driver, unlocked the door and ushered her inside.

'Coffee?' he asked.

'That'd be nice.'

While the kettle was boiling, he switched on some music then held out his hand to her. 'Dance with me?'

She took his hand and let him draw her into his arms. They swayed together, and when his mouth found hers the rest of the world felt a million miles away.

Coffee forgotten, he carried her up the stairs to his bed. Unzipped her dress and hung it neatly over the back of a chair, then let her strip off his tailcoat and waistcoat.

'Nice,' she said when she'd undone his tie and shirt, then ruffled his hair and grinned. 'You always did look sexy when you came home from the lab, all dishevelled because you'd stuck your hands through your hair like an absent-minded professor while you were thinking about a problem and it never occurred to you to look in a mirror or comb your hair before you came home.'

She remembered? Warmth spread through him.

'And you've always been the sexiest woman I've ever known,' he said, his voice husky with longing.

'Yeah?'

'Yeah. The day we got married. Me in that crumpled suit and you in that pretty summer dress.'

'You and me, always. That's what we said. And it didn't happen.' Her eyes filled with sadness.

He kissed her. 'Let's remember the good stuff, not the bad.' The beginning of their marriage, all those years ago.

And maybe tonight would be closure.

Closure on all the hurt and pain between them.

A chance to move on.

And maybe tomorrow the future would look bright instead of bleak.

CHAPTER SIX

ABIGAIL HALF OPENED her eyes as the light filtered through the curtains.

Then she was instantly awake.

Her own curtains had blackout linings. These ones didn't—because they weren't her curtains. This wasn't her bed. And the man spooned against her, with one arm wrapped round her waist holding her close to him, hadn't slept in the same bed as her for nearly five years.

Oh, help.

Had this just been the worst mistake of her life?

Maybe it was the wedding that had got to her; it had brought back memories of her own wedding day and how happy she and Brad had been. And it had been, oh, so easy to fall into his arms yesterday. To kiss him in the garden. To let him carry her to his bed when they'd caught a taxi back to his cottage.

She had absolutely no idea what would happen today. They'd both said they needed closure, but had this been the wrong way to do it? There hadn't been any kind of closure when they'd got divorced. The whole process had all been cold and distant, done through their respective solicitors, and it had left her with so many unanswered questions. Had she not been enough for Brad in the first place, that he'd let her go so easily? Or should she have tried harder to fight for her marriage?

Maybe she ought to leave. But right now she was warm and comfortable, with his arms wrapped round her, and she didn't want to go anywhere.

How stupid was she, trying to cling on to the past?

They couldn't go back. She knew that.

But making love with Brad again hadn't got him out of her system. At all. If anything, it had made her realise just how much she missed him. She filled her life with work—and she loved her business, her staff and her life here—but she knew perfectly well that she kept herself busy to stave off the loneliness. And, although she'd dated a few men during those years, nobody had ever managed to make her feel even the tiniest bit the way Bradley Powell had. So the fairest thing to do had been to keep all her relationships platonic and just not bother dating.

But what now?

How would Brad feel, when he woke?

Would he think last night was a huge mistake? Or...

She didn't dare let herself hope.

Either she'd fidgeted so much that she'd woken Brad, or he was awake already and was waiting to hear the change in her breathing to tell him that she was awake, because he said softly, 'Good morning.'

'Um, good morning,' she said awkwardly, wriggling round to face him.

He stroked her face. 'Sunday morning. I do actually have food in the house, so I could make pancakes, if you like.'

It was the best thing he could've said to make her relax again, because she had a flashback to the only time he'd ever tried to make her pancakes, one Sunday morning back in their Cambridge days. She laughed. 'What, and set the smoke detector off?' He'd burned the pancakes so badly that the alarm had shrieked madly, and he hadn't been able to stop it. Although she'd finally managed to make it stop by flapping a damp tea towel beneath the smoke detector, the noise had woken everyone in their block of flats and she'd had to bake a massive batch of cookies to mollify their disgruntled neighbours.

He laughed back. 'Or maybe we could go out for breakfast. Though not in Great Crowmell—maybe somewhere a bit further down the coast.'

'Breakfast.' Where was he going with this? Was this some kind of date, or did he have something more serious in mind?

'We need to talk,' he said.

'You have a point.' At least if they were out somewhere, she could always leave and get a taxi home if things got too much for her. If they had breakfast next door, or even here, it could be awkward. Better to be somewhere that had an escape route. 'I'll meet you next door in twenty minutes.' Which would give her enough time to shower, wash her hair and change.

'Twenty minutes,' he said.

And the way he brushed his mouth against hers was so sweet it almost made her cry.

Fortunately nobody spotted her going from his cottage to hers. It wasn't exactly a walk of shame, but as she was still wearing her bridesmaid's dress it would be obvious that she hadn't slept in her own bed, and she'd hate someone to see her and gossip about her. Especially as she didn't have a clue right now where this thing between her and Brad was going. Was that kiss just now a goodbye or a hello? Was he going to say a final goodbye to her over breakfast? Was that what he'd meant by closure? Or did she dare hope that last night had meant something to him, just like it had meant something to her, and he'd ask her if they could maybe try again?

Could they make it work, this time?

Then again, today was the last full day on his lease of the cottage. Brad was due to go back to London tomorrow, and for all she knew he might have decided to return today. He'd been away from the lab for a week, and she knew he'd be itching to get back to his work.

She'd better not hope for too much. It would be naive, foolish—and, worse, it would be setting herself up to have her heart broken all over again.

Brad knocked on her door twenty minutes later. Like her, he was dressed casually in jeans and a T-shirt. 'Ready?'

No. Part of her was terrified. 'Sure,' she fibbed, and walked over to his car with him. He drove to a larger town a few miles down the coast, and they found a café that was part of a chain. As they sat down, Abigail felt almost too sick to eat.

As if he'd guessed, Brad said gently, 'You need to eat and so do I.'

She ordered coffee and an almond croissant; she could do with the sugar rush. Brad, as she could've predicted, chose a full English breakfast.

She crumbled half the pastry on her plate and forced herself to eat the other half.

And then she looked at him. 'So. Closure. I assume you're leaving either today, or tomorrow morning before eleven because that's when the cleaners come in to get the place ready for the next holidaymakers.'

He tipped his head on one side, an old gesture that made butterflies swoop in her stomach. 'I was planning to go back tomorrow. But it doesn't have to be that way.'

She frowned, not understanding. 'How do you mean?'

'You and me. We can't go back.'

So this *was* goodbye, then. 'Uh-huh.' She couldn't trust herself with actual words.

'We're different people now. Older. Wiser. And maybe if we'd met for the first time yesterday at the wedding, we might have…'

He actually blushed.

'Well, I wouldn't have been quite such a troglodyte with you,' he said. 'It's not my style. But I would have asked to see you again.'

He was still attracted to her. Just as she was still attracted to him.

'And if we'd met for the first time yesterday, I wouldn't have gone from the wedding reception straight to your bed,' she said.

'That's not your style, either,' he agreed.

'But if you'd asked me out…' Was that what he was trying to do now?

That meant this all hinged on her.

She could say no. Leave the past in the past.

But saying yes didn't mean that she was trying to recreate the past, either. She knew what he meant. If they'd just met for the first time, they'd maybe start dating. Take things slowly. See where things took them.

But that was the problem. They couldn't do that. Not when they lived more than a hundred miles apart.

It wasn't a commutable distance, and she didn't want a weekend-only relationship. Particularly as she worked at least part of every weekend. 'Your life's in London,' she said.

'And yours is here. I know.' His dark, dark eyes were as irresistible as a puppy's. 'But let's ignore that for the moment. When you opened your new ice cream parlour, you didn't do the whole lot in a day, did you? Just as I don't expect a whole project to be sorted out in a day. Things take time. You need to do a critical path analysis before you start—work out what the steps are and in which order they have to be taken.'

She couldn't help widening her eyes at him. 'You're seeing us as a *project*?'

'No. I know it sounds as if I'm being a nerdy scientist, but I'm not.' He raked his hand through his hair. 'What I'm trying to say is that the obstacles you think are going to be a problem at the start of something don't always turn out to be obstacles. And, if the end result is important enough to you, then you can find ways to work around the obstacles.'

'Right.'

'So we could agree to put the issue of where we live to one side for now,' he said, 'and see where things take us. Starting with whether we actually like the person each of us has become.'

She coughed. 'I woke up in your bed this morning, Brad. I'd say that means we still like each other—at least physically.'

He smiled. 'The Abby I knew would've been too shy to say that.'

'I'm not shy any more. I'm comfortable in my own skin.'

'I'd noticed.'

Was that a criticism?

The question must've shown in her face, because he said, 'That was a compliment, Abby. Confidence is sexy.'

'Oh.' This time it was her turn to blush.

'So we've established that we're still attracted to each other,' he said. 'I have a lot of annual leave accrued. I could shock everyone in the lab and actually take some of it—and maybe we can spend some time together. See what else there is between us.'

Her frown deepened. 'You want to have a holiday here? With me? But I can't just take time off from work at short notice, Brad. That's not fair to my team.'

'I know, and you don't need to. I know the summer's your busiest time. It would just be nice to spend time with you—say, when you're free in the evenings or on your days off.'

'What I don't understand is, why now?' Why had he waited five years, if he'd still wanted her? Why had he even divorced her? She wasn't buying his knight on a white charger line.

'Because I had a few conversations at the wedding that made me think,' he said.

'Conversations?'

'With people who took a second chance at happiness,' he explained.

She couldn't remember anyone on the guest list who'd broken up and got back together. Her confusion must've been obvious, because he said, 'My mum, for starters.'

'You mean your mum and George?' She blinked. 'I saw him at the wedding yesterday. So your mum told you about him?'

'Yes. I don't expect her to spend the rest of her life alone,' he said. 'She's still relatively young. She should be enjoying life instead of being miserable and lonely and mourning Dad.'

Abigail really hadn't expected him to take the news so well. 'I'm glad you recognise that,' she said carefully.

He narrowed his eyes at her, as if to say that of course he did—that he'd grown up in the years since Jim's death.

'I assume you met him yesterday, then, and talked to him?'

Brad nodded. 'He seems like a nice guy, though I'd like the chance to get to know him better, to talk to him properly away from the hustle and bustle of the wedding.' He sighed and pushed his plate away. 'I want Mum to be happy. And Ruby.' He paused. 'And maybe you and me… Are you working today?'

'No. Lucy, my second in command, is in charge until tomorrow.'

'Then spend today with me, Abby.'

How could she resist those dark, dark eyes? 'What did you have in mind?'

'You. Me. A trip out.' He gave her a sudden grin, reminding her of the teenage boy she'd married, and her heart felt as if it had done a funny little flip. 'But we need to get you some travel-sickness tablets first.'

She suddenly realised what he was planning. 'You want me to go out on a boat?'

'Not piloted by me, but yes.'

'The Broads?' The medieval peat diggings that had turned into a waterway system over the centuries would hopefully be calm, like a millpond. As someone who'd grown up at the seaside, Abby knew she should've developed a decent pair of sea legs, but within five minutes of being on a boat she usually turned green. The swell of the ocean, even at its mildest, always made her queasy.

'I was thinking the North Sea,' he said. 'It's been a while.'

Five years. Unless he'd gone out on a boat some time this week, which she doubted—she rather thought he might have told her about it—she was pretty sure Brad hadn't been anywhere near a boat since Jim's death. So was this his idea of closure?

Then again, he'd just been talking about coming back for a few days. Spending more time with her.

It left her more confused than ever.

'What do you want, Brad?'

'Right now—a boat trip to see the seals at Blakeney Point,' he said.

She knew he'd avoided her real question, but she wasn't sure she was ready to hear the answer; she wasn't sure she could answer the question herself. Plus she liked the idea of the trip; it would be fun to go out and see the summer colony of common seals basking in the sunshine on the spit of sand, with their huge eyes and pretty faces. It had been years since she'd done it. 'OK, if we can get tickets.' It was a popular trip and weekends were usually heavily booked.

'I'll get tickets.'

He was so sure. And it was easier to go along with him, to buy bottled water and seasickness tablets and take the medicine to give it time to work.

He took her hand as they walked back to the car, and it felt weirdly like their early dates, when just the touch of his hand against hers made her feel as if fireworks were going off in the sky.

This was dangerous. Totally stupid, in fact. OK, so they'd spent last night together and she had no regrets about it whatsoever—but, even though Brad had told her to ignore the obstacles, she couldn't get away from the fact that his life was in London and hers was here. She wouldn't expect him to give his up for her, just as she wasn't prepared to give hers up for him.

Wouldn't it be better just to part now, as friends?

By the time she'd gathered her thoughts, he'd already driven them to Blakeney, they'd picked up their tickets and were walking across the marshes towards the harbour.

'Just for today,' he said, 'I think we should forget the past. We're not going to pretend it didn't happen—but we have to accept that we can't change it. All we can do is learn from it and move on. I know I hurt you and I'm sorry. I was too young to deal with what happened. Which honestly isn't an excuse, by the way, it's an explanation.'

She nodded. 'I understand. I was too young to deal with it, too.' And she needed to be fair about this. He wasn't the only one to blame. 'We both made mistakes. I hurt you, too.' She'd left him when he was vulnerable and in pain and totally unable to deal with his feelings, when she should've tried harder to support him. 'I'm sorry.'

'Apology accepted.' He stopped and spun her round to face him, then kissed her.

His mouth was soft and so very sweet, and it sent a shiver of pure desire through her.

'Enough of the past. Today's all about you and me discovering a bit more about who each other is now,' he said. 'Let's have some fun.'

He climbed easily into the boat and helped her in beside him, then slid his arm protectively round her when they sat down. The captain took the boat out to the narrow strip of land at Blakeney Point, where everyone could see the seals basking on the sand. Some were lumbering along in an ungainly fashion; others were just sunning themselves. There were a few groups of a cow, a bull and a pup; Abigail knew that the pups on the land with their mothers were less than three weeks old, still needing to be fed.

Around the boat, seals were gliding through the water, looking far more elegant than they did on land and totally at ease; others were frolicking in the shallows, splashing their flippers in the water. It was utterly charming and Abigail lost herself in the moment, enjoying the sight.

'Smile for the camera,' Brad said, and took a snap of her on his phone with the seals in the background. She smiled at him and took a shot of him on her phone, too. Today was a good day. One to make memories.

'Would you like me to take your photograph together?' a middle-aged woman sitting near them asked.

'Thanks, that'd be lovely,' Brad said, and handed over his phone.

'Are you on honeymoon?' she asked as she took the photograph. 'You look like newlyweds.'

Abigail had no idea how to answer. The truth was much too complicated.

Brad simply smiled and said, 'Something like that. It's a lovely part of the world,' as if neither of them had ever been here before.

'Well, I wish you both every happiness,' the woman said, and handed his phone back.

'Thank you,' Brad said.

'Yes—thank you,' Abigail added with a smile.

Once they were back at the harbour, they climbed out of the boat and walked hand in hand back to his car.

'OK?' he asked.

'Yes. It was lovely. I'd forgotten how gorgeous the seal pups are,' she said. 'And those big eyes.' Dark and expressive and utterly captivating.

Though she could've been talking about Brad.

'Sea legs holding up?'

'They're pretty much propped up by the sickness tablets,' she admitted. 'But I'm OK. You?'

His hand tightened round hers. 'Good company and the perfect view. I'd forgotten how lovely the seals are, too.' He paused. 'Shall we go for a drive and find a pub somewhere for lunch?'

'Sounds good.'

Though Abigail couldn't shake what the woman had said about them looking like honeymooners.

This felt almost like a honeymoon. Not that theirs had been a conventional one: after Gretna Green, they'd done the coast-to-coast walk to raise money for the local lifeboat service and stayed in little guest houses along the way. They hadn't been able to afford an expensive holiday abroad when Brad was a student, though they'd pooled their birthday and Christmas money and managed a couple of nights in Paris. His dream of trekking through the Australian outback and hers of seeing the Northern Lights had been completely out of range of their budget. But they'd enjoyed snatched days out, visiting museums and booking train tickets well in advance to keep costs to a minimum.

There had been good times. Plenty of good times. It hadn't mattered that they didn't have much money. The only thing that had mattered was being together.

Just like they were now; they didn't have to fill every moment with chattering. That hadn't changed over the years, and she was glad that they could still find an easy silence between them.

And it was easy for lunch out to stretch into pottering around antique shops in one of the Georgian market towns, and then afternoon tea, and then strolling along the beach and watching the stars come out.

Outside her front door, he said, 'I can't quite bear to let you go yet. Come and sit with me for a bit?'

But curling up together on the sofa led to kissing. Which led to him taking her back upstairs to the king-sized bed and making love with her; and then she was too comfortable to move.

'Stay with me tonight,' he said, wrapping his arms round her.

Common sense meant she ought to go. 'I have work tomorrow. And you've got to pack and be out of the cottage by eleven,' she pointed out.

'It won't take me long to pack,' he said. 'And I'll be leaving early. I have things to do in the lab.'

Back to the real world. Where no doubt Brad would think about this weekend and realise that this was all a pretty fantasy, but it couldn't work in real life. The logistics were impossible.

'But I'll be back. Give me a few days to sort things out,' he said. 'I need to make sure the project's still on track, and then I can call in a few favours and take a few days off.'

Maybe he would. Maybe he wouldn't. He'd been away for a week already; what if there had been some real developments on his project while he was away that meant he had to stay in London? What if he couldn't use his leave because some of his team had already booked holiday and that would mean the lab was short-staffed?

Her worries must've shown on her face because he kissed her gently. 'Stop overthinking things, Abby.'

'Habit,' she said.

'Tonight, let tomorrow take care of itself,' he said. 'Go to sleep.'

She didn't think she'd sleep, but eventually the warmth of his arms around her did the trick and she drifted off.

The next morning, he woke her with a tray of coffee and toast.

'Breakfast in bed?'

'Time to wake up. It's an hour and a half after sunrise,' he said with a grin.

'At this time of year, that means it's still really early,' she reminded him.

'Early enough for you to have time for your run before work.' He kissed her and climbed back into bed beside her. 'So. I'll leave by seven, which means I'll be back in London at around ten. I'll let you know as soon as I've sorted out some time off. I'll book a room in a hotel.'

'So you're not staying with your mum?'

'No. Though, this time, it isn't because I can't face the memories. Now I've been back to the house—and, thanks to you making me talk—I know I can. This time, it's about you and me,' he said, 'and we're keeping it simple. Staying at my mum's would mean that she'd ask too many questions.'

Abigail sipped her coffee. 'I guess the simplest thing would be to ask you to stay at my place.'

He shook his head. 'I wasn't fishing. And, actually, staying with you would complicate things.'

'How?'

'I think we both need our own space while we work out what's happening between us and what we want to do about it,' he said. 'I'm going to stay at Little Crowmell rather than here, if I can.'

Where the staff would be less likely to know him and less likely to be curious. 'OK. Well, let me know.'

'I will.'

When they'd finished breakfast, he kissed her goodbye. 'Thank you for giving me a second chance,' he said. 'I don't intend to let you down again.'

But there was a wide, wide gap between good intentions and what actually happened, she thought. They could start again. But what if they hit a rocky patch? Could she be sure that he wouldn't close himself off again?

'Uh-huh,' she said, not wanting to start a fight.

'I'll call you,' he said. 'Enjoy your run and have a nice day.'

'Safe travels,' she said. 'And I hope you don't get stuck in a traffic jam.'

'Thanks.'

When Abigail came back from her morning run, she saw that his car had gone.

And how ridiculous was it that she felt so flat?

She needed to prepare herself for the fact that Brad might get back to real life in London and change his mind. That in a few days she'd have a cool, apologetic text from him saying sorry, he'd realised that it wasn't going to work and it was best to keep things formal and polite between them.

But in the meantime she had work to do. A business to run. So she'd concentrate on that.

CHAPTER SEVEN

ABIGAIL THREW HERSELF into work to keep herself occupied and stop herself checking her phone constantly during the day. Brad didn't text to let her know he'd got back to London safely; then again, she thought, he was probably doing pretty much the same thing as she was. Plus he'd been away from the lab for longer than she'd been away from the café, even if he had been in touch with his team by phone. He'd be too busy to think about anything else but his job.

She finally picked up a text from him that evening, just as she finished locking the café behind her.

Hope you've had a good day. Can I video-call you later?

So was this it? Had he had time to think about it and change his mind? If so, at least he was going to tell her sort of face to face.

Sure. What time?

She didn't get an answer until she was back at her cottage.

Let me know when's a good time.

So the ball was in her court. I'm home now.

To her surprise, a few seconds later, her phone buzzed with a video call.

'Hey.'

She narrowed her eyes as she noticed the background. Unless Brad had turned his home into a lab... 'Are you still at work?'

'Um, yes,' he admitted.

'Brad, it's gone eight o'clock.'

'I know, I know. But I started late.' He smiled at her. 'How was your day?'

'Busy but good. Yours?'

'The same. I'm calling in a few favours, and I'm taking ten days off from next Monday evening.'

So he really meant it. He was actually coming back to Great Crowmell, to spend time with her and see whether they still had something between them. And she was shocked to realise how relieved that made her feel. 'OK,' she said, hoping that both her voice and expression were light and cheerful and didn't betray her feelings too much.

'I'd better let you get on,' he said.

Which was Brad-speak for *I'm busy but I don't want to be rude to you*, she remembered. 'Don't spend all night in the lab.'

To Abigail's surprise, Brad contacted her every day during the week; sometimes it was just a brief text, sometimes it was a phone call, and sometimes it was a video call. But every day she knew he was thinking about her, and that made her feel good.

On Thursday morning, a parcel arrived for her at

the café. She opened it to discover a paperweight in the shape of an ice cream, together with a message in Brad's neat handwriting.

Just wanted you to know I'm thinking of you.

She knew he'd be busy in the lab, so she didn't want to disturb him with a phone call; instead she texted him a picture of the paperweight on her desk, so he could pick up the message at a time to suit him.

Thank you. It's brilliant. And very useful.

And what was sauce for the goose…

She wasn't set up to do mail order cakes, but she knew a good local supplier. And they'd just released a new flavour of sponge cake: sticky toffee pudding. Brad's all-time favourite dessert, unless that had changed—and somehow she didn't think it had. It took only a couple of minutes to order one to be delivered to him the next morning, together with a message.

Don't stay too late in the lab tonight.

Much later in the day, her phone pinged with a text in reply to her photograph.

My pleasure. Flowers would've been more conventional but would also have meant gossip, so I thought you'd prefer the paperweight.

He had a point.

And he actually called her in the middle of the day

on Friday. 'I just got your delivery. Thank you. Is this the next step in your empire?'

Abigail laughed. 'No. But it's a local firm and Ruby's office uses them,' she said, 'so I've tried four different varieties. I nearly sent the apple crumble one—it's gorgeous with lots of cinnamon—but then I saw the sticky toffee pudding and I was pretty sure you'd like it.'

'It's fabulous. My team says to thank you, too.'

'My pleasure. Don't work too late.'

'Yeah, yeah.' But she could hear the laughter in his voice. 'Speak to you soon.'

And did she actually hear him mutter 'love you', just before he disconnected the call, or was that just what she'd wanted to hear so her ears were playing tricks on her?

She didn't have the courage to ask him. But there was definitely an easy affection between them again. A warmth that hadn't been there for a long time—a warmth she'd missed. She liked the man he'd become, and she rather hoped he liked who she'd become, too.

Abigail was run off her feet over the weekend, and was pretty sure that Brad was just as busy in his lab; but then on Monday evening, when she left the café, she picked up a text from him.

Leaving now.

The message was timed an hour ago, so he was already on the way.

Staying at the Bay Tree Hotel in Little Crowmell.

The hotel was attached to a golf course and had a spa; her stomach tightened for a second as she remembered the last time she and Brad had stayed in a hotel with a spa. The weekend away she'd won in a competition. The weekend when everything had gone wrong, and their life together had unravelled faster than she'd ever believed could happen.

She shook herself. Five years. Older and wiser, she reminded herself. They were different people now, and these were different circumstances.

Meet me in the bar for a drink at about nine?

Just the two of them. The start of something that might or might not work out.

But that was the whole point of this time together. To see what they might still have—and whether it was worth the possible upheaval. Because, if they were to have a future together, they'd have to find some kind of compromise about where they lived.

See you at nine, she texted back. She knew he wouldn't get the message while he was driving, but he'd maybe pick it up if he stopped for a break, or when he got to the hotel.

She changed into a pretty top and smart black trousers, and called a taxi to take her to the hotel for nine; it meant she could have a glass of wine with Brad without worrying about being over the limit for driving home. And how strange that she felt like a teenager about to go on her first date with a boy she'd secretly liked for months. Second time round, shouldn't it all be calm and collected and adult? But she could hardly wait to see him. Just like the years when they really had been teenagers, sneaking time together between their studies.

There was a group of businessmen in the bar, all

wearing lanyards; clearly they'd been at some sort of conference in the hotel and were letting off some steam after a hard day's work, judging by the amount of hearty laughter and empty glasses at their table. There was no sign of Brad. Maybe he was still in his room.

Abigail went over to the reception desk. 'Excuse me, please. I'm meant to be meeting Bradley Powell here. I wondered if you could call his room for me, please?'

The receptionist checked her computer. 'Sorry, he hasn't checked in yet.'

He'd probably been held up in traffic, Abigail thought. 'When he does check in, could you let him know that Abigail Scott is waiting for him in the bar, please?'

'Of course,' the receptionist said with a smile.

Feeling slightly awkward, Abigail ordered an orange juice at the bar, and tried to find herself a quiet corner. She was playing a word game on her phone to keep herself busy while she waited, when one of the businessmen came over to her, holding an almost empty pint glass.

'On your own, sweetheart?' he asked.

'No, I'm waiting for someone,' she said.

'Well, you can have a drink with me while you're waiting.'

He sounded slightly drunk, slurring his words, and Abigail sighed inwardly. She was used to dealing with difficult customers over the years, so she knew how to keep the situation from escalating. She kept her voice calm and anodyne. 'It's very kind of you to offer, but no, thank you.'

'But a girl as pretty as you *needs* company.'

She forbore from correcting him that she was a

woman, not a girl, and suppressed her irritation. It looked as if she was going to have to take the cracked record approach. 'It's very kind of you to offer, but no, thank you,' she repeated firmly.

'Go on, sweetheart. What's the harm in it?' He swayed towards her.

'No, thank you,' she said yet again.

'It's only a little drink, sweetheart. Come and join me and the boys. We could do wi—'

'I said no, thank you,' she cut in. 'Now, would you please leave me alone?'

'You don't mean that, sweetheart.' He looked her up and down. 'Or maybe just you and me, then, not the boys.'

Abigail had had enough. She stood up and was at the point of walking over to the bartender and asking him to deal with the man when Brad walked over to her.

'Sorry I'm late, darling. Reception told me you were waiting in here for me.' He greeted her with a kiss. 'Traffic was horrible and my phone decided not to work, so I couldn't call you and warn you how late I'd be, and...' He looked at the man who'd been trying to chat her up, and suddenly seemed to be six inches taller and broader. 'I'm sorry, I don't believe we've met,' he said politely, though his voice contained a hint of steel. 'Are you a friend of my wife's, or maybe one of her business associates?'

'I... Sorry.' The man raised his free hand in surrender and backed away as if he'd been scalded. 'No offence, darlin'. I didn't know. I didn't mean anything.' And, to Abigail's relief, he stumbled off back to his colleagues.

'Wife?' Abigail asked quietly, raising her eyebrows.

Brad smiled. 'I forgot to add two letters and a hyphen.' Then his expression became more serious. 'It looked as if the guy was pestering you.'

'He was. I was about to go and talk to the bartender and ask for help,' she admitted.

'It might still be worth having a word with the reception desk, so they're aware of the situation and can make sure he doesn't behave like that to anyone else,' he said. 'Though obviously that's your call.'

She liked the fact that Brad wasn't bossing her around. 'I will. Have you checked in?'

'Just about. And, actually, I did text you to say I was stuck in traffic and I'd be late.'

'I didn't get your message.'

'I'm sorry.' He paused. 'Have you eaten tonight?'

She nodded. 'Have you?'

'I grabbed a burger from the place on the corner, on my way out of the lab. It's fine. Can I get you another…?' He looked at her glass. 'That looks like orange juice, so I'm assuming you drove here.'

'Actually, I got a taxi so I could have a glass of wine or something with you.'

He smiled. 'That's good. Let me order a bottle of wine, and maybe we can go and drink it on the terrace.' He looked at her. 'Or I believe my room has a balcony, if you want to go somewhere quieter. And, just so you know, that offer doesn't come with any strings attached.'

The bar was becoming noisy and she really wanted to get away from the group of businessmen. Their over-hearty laughter was starting to irritate her. 'Actually, your balcony would be nice.'

'OK. What would you like me to order?'

'Dry white, please. Or red, if you'd prefer,' she added

swiftly, not sure what he drank nowadays. 'I really don't mind.'

'Dry white's fine with me.'

Part of Abigail felt sad that they still had to be polite to each other. There was a time when Brad would've known what she'd like without having to ask, just as she would've known what he wanted.

'I'll talk to the hotel reception about that guy while you sort out the wine,' she said.

The receptionist was horrified and apologetic. 'I'll ask the duty manager to have a quiet word with him and make sure the bar staff don't serve him any more alcohol this evening,' she said.

'Thank you,' Abigail said. 'I'm fine, but anyone younger or less able to deal with the situation might have struggled, and I'd hate someone vulnerable to be in that position.'

She'd just finished talking to the receptionist when Brad came to join her, carrying a bottle of Sauvignon Blanc and two glasses. 'All OK?' he asked.

'Everything's fine,' she confirmed.

They went up to his room, and she noticed that he hadn't even unpacked; clearly he'd just dumped his suitcase on his bed and come immediately to find her.

He opened the French doors to the balcony, which overlooked the golf course on the top of the cliffs, and the sea glittered in the distance. There were two wrought-iron chairs, a small wrought-iron table just big enough for a couple of drinks, and one of the hotel's trademark bay trees in a terracotta pot.

'Very nice,' she said.

'Indeed.' He gestured to her to sit down, and poured

them both a glass of wine. 'I'm sorry I was late. There was a traffic jam.'

'It isn't your fault that the text didn't come through.'

'But I'm still sorry. If I'd been on time, you wouldn't have been bothered by that guy.'

She reached over to squeeze his hand. 'I'm not blaming you. And it's fine. No harm done.' She smiled at him. 'So you've got ten days, you said?'

'I did,' he confirmed. 'Sunetra—my assistant manager—is keeping all the projects ticking over. I can review things through my laptop here during the day, and she'll call me if there's anything she needs.'

Abigail would be busy herself during the day, so his work wouldn't intrude on their time together. 'That's good.' She looked at him. 'So does your family know you're here?'

'Ruby's on honeymoon. She doesn't need to know. But, yes, I told Mum,' he admitted. 'She's promised not to interfere. What about you—did you tell your mum and dad?'

'They kind of noticed that we left Ruby's wedding at the same time,' she said. 'So, yes, they asked me about you.' And her mum was worried about it; she'd seen how long it had taken Abigail to pick herself back off the floor and dust herself down after the divorce.

'They don't approve, do they?' Brad asked wryly.

'They have some reservations,' she said. 'But they won't interfere. This is between you and me. Our chance to work out if we like who each other is now and if we want to do something about it.' She paused. 'So what's the plan?'

'Plan?'

'You were the one who talked about running a project. About critical path analysis.'

He smiled. 'I'd hardly call you a project, Abby. But the plan, as you put it, is to spend time with you. If we were dating under normal circumstances, we'd see each other, what, once or twice a week?'

'About that,' she agreed.

'Then think of this as a kind of speed-dating. If we see each other every day for the next ten days, it's the equivalent of nearly two months of dating at once or twice a week. And then we'll have a better grasp of the situation.'

'We'll know whether we want to take this thing further or not.' And, if they did, then they'd have to decide which of them would be the one to uproot their life.

'We could make a list,' he said. 'Things we want to do, places we want to go. Make it as off-the-wall or as touristy as you like.'

She looked at him with a smile. 'Spoken like a true scientist.'

'Isn't that what you do in business?' he asked. 'Make lists and plan things?'

'I have a list of new flavours I'm planning to try, and promotional activity, yes,' she admitted.

'So let's start here. I don't mind being scribe—I'll copy the file and send it to you when we're done, and then we can whittle it down.' He took his phone out of his pocket and flicked into what was obviously a note-taking app.

'Let's do the obvious ones,' she suggested. 'A walk on the beach, a visit to the gardens of a stately home, a walk in the woods.'

He typed them in. 'A trip on one of the steam trains—

I'm fairly sure there was a nineteen-forties weekend listed in the local newspaper. That could be fun.'

'OK. Visit a ruined castle, go somewhere quirky for afternoon tea.'

'Agreed. And we need stuff for rainy days. I know it's summer and this is the driest part of the country, but this is England and that means rain. Museums, art exhibition, ten-pin bowling.' He typed them in swiftly.

'The cinema,' she said. 'Maybe going to see a local band.'

'And the lighthouse,' he said. 'I haven't been there for years. We need to make that on a day when it's open to the public and we can climb up to the lamp.' He smiled. 'There are so many things on that list I've never done before. I guess you always take where you live for granted.'

Not just where you live, she thought. It was too easy to take people for granted, too. Maybe that had been part of the problem between them, the first time round. She'd been so sure she knew how he'd react in any situation—and how very wrong she'd been.

'Well. To us and our list,' she said, lifting her glass. 'And may it give us our answers.'

'I'll drink to that,' he said, lifting his own glass. 'So when are your days off? Then we can plan to do the further away things on those days.' He narrowed his eyes at her. 'You're smiling.'

'You really are making this into a project, aren't you?'

'It just makes sense to do it this way and make the most of our time.'

'Like you did when we went to Paris.'

'You remember Paris?' His voice was suddenly husky.

She nodded. 'You had a list of all the places we wanted to visit, the opening days and times, whether they were covered by our museum card, and you even marked everything on a map.'

'But we got to see everything,' he pointed out. 'The Mona Lisa, Notre Dame, the Eiffel Tower, Montmartre, and all the Monets.'

'True. Though it would've been nice just to go for a wander in the city and see what we could find.'

'But we only had three days. If we'd been wandering around aimlessly, we would've missed all the other stuff we actually wanted to see,' he reminded her.

How different their approaches were: Brad with his strict itineraries, and her own preference for just seeing what they came across. Maybe they were too different now for things to work between them. Nowadays, she would've insisted on one of those three days in Paris being spontaneous. On closing their eyes and putting a finger at random on a map, and using that as their starting point for exploring. But was that too far out of Brad's comfort zone?

'Do you remember, we bought all those postcards at the art galleries and museum and stuck them on our living room wall, because we couldn't afford a proper print in a frame?' he asked.

'I remember. And that guy did a charcoal drawing of us at Montmartre,' she said, 'when we were both sitting on that wall outside the church.'

'What happened to that?'

She spread her hands. 'No idea.' The drawing had been another casualty of their broken marriage.

As if Brad realised they were heading into dangerous territory, he backtracked. 'So, when are your days off?'

She made a show of checking her diary, even though she knew her schedule without having to look it up. 'This week, I have a full day off on Thursday, and a half-day on Sunday. Next week, I have a day off on Monday; I need to go in on Wednesday first thing, but I'll be done by ten.'

And then on the Thursday he'd go back to London.

When it would be decision time.

Would they make it together as a couple—or would they agree to part for good and ignore the pull of the past?

Right at that moment she had no idea.

Brad made a note. 'I'll work through our list and make—'

'—an itinerary,' she finished.

'You say that as if it's a bad thing.'

'No. Just sometimes it's good to be spontaneous.'

'I can do spontaneous.' And he proved it by putting his phone down, coming over to her side of the table, scooping her out of her chair and then sitting in her place and settling her on his lap.

And of course she had to put her arms round his neck for balance.

She could hardly complain, given that she'd been the one to make a fuss about him being so buttoned-up and such a planner.

'I thought you said your balcony didn't come with strings?' she asked.

He stole a kiss. 'It doesn't. I'm not expecting you to sleep with me, and I'm not asking you to stay the night with me. Even though we're sort of speed-dating for the next few days, I'm not going to rush you.' He stole another kiss. 'But it's good to hold you again, Abby.'

She stroked his face. 'It feels good to have you hold me, too.'

'I'm glad that's settled.'

And then there was no need to talk. They just sat there together, warm and comfortable and snuggled up, watching the afterglow of the sunset and the stars shining more brightly in the sky as the night darkened.

Finally, he kissed her again. 'You've got work tomorrow. And I meant what I said about no strings and not expecting you to stay the night.'

'It'd just confuse things. We're meant to be seeing how it goes, what we still have left between us,' she agreed. 'I'll call a taxi.'

'But if you want to come for breakfast tomorrow, just show up,' he said.

'Maybe.' She slid off his lap and called the taxi. 'They'll be ten minutes.'

'OK. And thank you for giving me a second chance.'

'I think we're giving each other a second chance,' she corrected.

But had they both learned enough from the past? Would they make the same mistakes all over again? Was this going to be the best idea they'd ever had or a complete disaster?

CHAPTER EIGHT

ON TUESDAY, ABIGAIL took her usual early-morning run to see the sun rise over the harbour, and thought about whether to turn up at the Bay Tree for breakfast with Brad.

Then again, today was supposed to be their second date. And she had a pile of work to do. In the end, she sent Brad a brief text.

Up to eyes this morning. See you tonight. A x

He responded with an email she picked up at her desk.

See you tonight. Let me know what time. Itinerary attached. B x

She opened the file, read it and smiled. The whole way he'd organised it was so very Brad. A table, with the date in the left-hand column, and suggestions for what they did, split between fine weather and wet weather, and with notes of opening times for the places they'd wanted to visit.

Tonight's itinerary was a walk on the beach after

work—unless it was raining, in which case they'd go to the cinema or ten-pin bowling. He'd even noted which films were showing during the week, so she could choose what she liked.

He'd already crossed out the gory ones—so he obviously remembered that horror films gave her nightmares, even if they were award-winning and brilliantly written. But there was a comedy and a sci-fi film listed that she thought they might both enjoy, so she marked them as possibles.

She texted him.

Thanks for itinerary. See you at seven.

Then, on impulse, she added, Can't wait.

Can't wait to see you either, came the reply.

It warmed her all day and, although Abigail had intended to experiment with a new flavour of ice cream that morning, she ended up messing up the recipe twice because she was thinking of Brad and couldn't concentrate. And she found herself clock-watching when she was doing admin during the first half of the afternoon—until she noticed that it was raining. The kind of deceptively fine rain that would soak you to the skin and make any beach walk completely miserable; and she knew that the café would start to get really busy with holidaymakers who were fed up with the rain and wanted a hot drink to warm them up. Now wasn't the time to daydream about her beach walk with Brad, which she was pretty sure would have to be postponed. She wasn't a ditzy teenager any more. She had a business to run and staff to support.

She went into the café and helped out behind the

counter until the rush had died down; and, when even
the diehard dog-walkers had left and the café was practically empty fifteen minutes before they were due to
close, she sent everyone home early.

'But don't you want us to clear up before we go?'
Joe asked.

'It's fine, sweetie. I'll sort it out. We're practically
empty now and you were all rushed off your feet earlier.' She patted his shoulder. 'Off you go.'

Once the last customers had finished their drinks and
left and she'd cleared up, locked the door, and stacked
the chairs, she was just about to wipe down the tables
and mop the floor when there was a knock on the door.

Frowning, she went over to explain that sorry, the
café was closed now until tomorrow—only to see Brad
standing there. Much earlier than they'd agreed.

She let him in. 'Hey. I wasn't expecting to see you,
yet.'

'I thought maybe you could do with a hand.'

She hadn't expected that, either. 'Are you just bored
waiting for me?'

He laughed. 'A tiny bit. But my plan was, if I help
you clear up, you'll be finished more quickly and then
you can come and play with me.'

'Spoken like a true scientist. Do you want to do the
floor or the tables?'

'Whichever you don't want to do.'

She handed him the mop and bucket.

'So do you clear up on your own every night?' he
asked.

'No, but after the rain caught out some customers,
it drove the rest away so I sent everyone home early.'

He looked at her. 'Now I get why your staff are so protective of you. You're good with them.'

'They stay late without being asked if we've got a rush on,' she said, 'so it's only fair to let them go earlier if we're not busy.'

'And the fact that you're prepared to do every single job in the café, including mopping floors and cleaning toilets.'

'Are you telling me you don't help your team scrub the glassware if you've been really busy in the lab?' she asked.

'Of course I do. We're a team.'

'Exactly my point,' she said. 'I might have got the job originally because I'm the boss's daughter, but I worked my way up from the ground floor. And I don't expect my staff to do anything I haven't either done myself or am prepared to do.'

'You didn't get the job because you're the boss's daughter,' he said. 'You worked your way up in Cambridge. You already knew how to run a team and how to organise your stock. You got the job because you earned it.'

She *had* earned it. She'd thrown herself into work, put in crazy hours, to stop herself thinking of Brad after they'd split up.

And now they were dating again. Ten days of speed-dating to see if there was still something between them and if they could make a go of things second time round.

Did she need her head examined? Was this going to be a huge mistake? Had they both changed enough for this to work, or had they changed so much that they'd be even further apart?

Suddenly flustered, she said, 'Well, this café isn't

going to clean itself,' and busied herself cleaning tables. Between them they finished cleaning the café so it was ready for the morning; and while they were working the rain grew heavier.

'I think our beach walk might've been rained off,' he said ruefully as rain lashed against the plate-glass windows.

'Just a tad,' she said with a smile. 'Thanks for helping.'

'No problem.' He tipped his head on one side, and her heart felt as if it had done a little flip. 'Cinema or ten-pin bowling?'

'Toss a coin?' she suggested.

'Heads, cinema; tails, bowling. That OK with you?' At her nod, he took a coin from his pocket and tossed it. 'Ten-pin bowling it is. Where are you parked?'

'Outside my house,' she said. 'I walk in when the weather's good—which it was, this morning.'

'That makes things easier. I'm parked right outside,' he said.

She locked up, and they walked hand in hand to his car.

'So I guess this is our first official date?' she asked, once they were sitting in his car.

'It is. Which means I have to be gentlemanly and let you win at bowling.'

She loved the way his eyes crinkled at the corners and scoffed. 'Bring it on.'

'So you're telling me you don't need the bumper bars up at the sides any more when you play?' he teased.

'I'll have you know zig-zagging the ball is a perfectly valid form of bowling,' she said.

He laughed. 'In your dreams.'

He drove them to the out-of-town complex which housed the bowling alley, cinema and half a dozen restaurants. 'Actually, I haven't done this for quite a while,' he said.

'Getting your excuses in early for when you lose?' she teased.

'Just saying.' He smiled. 'Have you already eaten, or shall we grab something to eat first?'

'Dinner sounds good,' she said. 'So I'll buy dinner and you can pay for the bowling.'

'Strictly speaking,' he said, 'the dating was my idea so it all ought to be my bill.'

'Strictly speaking,' she countered, 'we made that list together, so we're going halves. No arguments. So I'm buying dinner and you're paying for the bowling, and I might let you buy me a beer at the bowling alley if you're good.'

Brad really liked the woman Abby had become. Funny, smart and confident. In the old days, she would've simply gone along with his suggestions. Now, she had the confidence to say what she wanted. 'OK. Halves, it is.'

They went to one of the fast-food places and ordered a sharing platter of grilled chicken, sweet potato wedges, garlic bread and avocado salad. And every time his fingers accidentally touched hers as they reached for garlic bread or sweet potato wedges at the same time, every nerve-end in his body tingled. Anyone would think he was seventeen again, not twenty-seven. Though at least nowadays he was more articulate than he'd been as a nerdy teen.

'Thank you for dinner,' he said when she insisted on picking up the bill.

'My pleasure.'

And funny how her smile made his heart feel as if it had done a somersault. It was anatomically impossible; but she was the only woman who'd ever made him feel that way.

He enjoyed the bowling, too. He was so aware of Abigail and the graceful way she moved, even though she was still absolutely terrible at ten-pin bowling.

After the first game he ended up putting up the bumper bars for her. 'At least this way we can both have some fun. There's nothing duller than seeing your ball go in the ditch every single time,' he said.

'You just want to admire my zig-zag skills,' she said, brazening it out.

He laughed and stole a kiss. 'You bet.'

They'd had so much fun as teens. And as a young married couple, even though money was tight, with him as a student and her with a low-paid job. They'd just revelled in being together.

Tonight had reminded him very much of how much he'd appreciated her company. Why had he ever been so stupid as to let her go?

The more time he spent with her, the more he wanted to be with her. This week was his opportunity to convince her to give him a second chance. He needed to work harder at this than at anything else he'd ever done in his life.

At the end of the evening, he drove her home and parked in the nearest space he could find to her front door.

Crunch time.

Had he done enough for her to let him see her again tomorrow? There was only one way to find out. And he was shocked by how nervous he felt. This was worse than sitting his driving test, his finals, and his viva for his doctorate all rolled into one. And the outcome also felt more important.

'Was tonight's date OK enough for you to meet me tomorrow?' he asked, trying to keep his tone light.

'Ten dates. That's what we agreed,' she said.

Whether she'd enjoyed tonight as much as he had or not, she was at least going to be fair about it. Give him a chance to prove himself. 'OK. So tomorrow evening's a walk on the beach,' he said. 'Or, if it's raining, this time we can maybe do the cinema.'

'That sounds good.' She leaned over and kissed him, and it sent a shiver of pure desire through him. 'Thank you. I had fun, tonight.'

'Me, too.' And, because he didn't want to push her too far, too fast, and ruin any progress he might have made, he didn't ask if he could come in for coffee. He simply brushed his mouth against hers really lightly, not deepening the kiss the way he really wanted to. He knew they were still compatible in bed, but that wasn't what this was about. It went much, much deeper than that. 'Goodnight, Abby. See you tomorrow.'

He waited until he'd seen her close the front door behind her, then drove back to the hotel.

On Wednesday evening, it was dry, and the café was still incredibly busy when Brad got there.

He could offer to help clear up again; but that would leave her open to gossip. He was pretty sure a couple of her staff recognised him, and the last thing he wanted was for them to start asking awkward questions. He'd left his car in the town, so he couldn't sit there and wait until she was ready. In the end, he bought a cold drink and sat at a quiet corner table until one of her staff—one who didn't know him—said, 'I'm ever so sorry, sir, but we're closed now.'

'And you need to put the tables and chairs inside. Of course.' Brad stood up.

'Thank you.' The young man smiled at him. 'Have a nice evening.'

'Thanks.' Brad smiled back, and went to sit on the dunes. Abby clearly wasn't going to finish dead on seven tonight, so he texted her to make sure she didn't feel pressured.

Sitting on dunes right now. Didn't want to get in the way of your staff. Come and find me when you're ready.

It was another twenty minutes before Abigail emerged. 'Hey. Sorry I'm late.'

'Not a problem.' He stood up, and, as he'd hoped, she kissed him hello.

'Had a good day?' she asked.

'Yes. Sunetra sent me a file to review, so that took a while. And I had lunch with Mum.'

'Who was dying to know the latest?'

'Yes, but I'm giving her credit—she didn't ask.'

'She's waiting until you're ready to tell her.' Abigail smiled. 'That's one of the things I like about your mum. You know she's concerned and she's there, but she's not pushy.'

'No she's not.' He took her hand. 'How was your day?'

'It's always busy when it's sunny. Which is how I like it.' She slipped her hand into his. 'Where did you park?'

'In town. I assumed you walked here this morning, as it was dry, and I thought I could walk you home from here.'

'That's nice.'

And it *was* nice, walking hand in hand on the beach. The tide was starting to come in, but not massively fast, so he knew they still had time to wander along the shoreline for a bit.

Out of sheer habit, he glanced down at the sand. As usual, there was a scattering of razor shells, cockle shells and limpets; but in between he spotted a pretty banded shell and stooped to pick it up. 'For you,' he said, and handed it to Abigail.

She inspected it. 'That's a nice one. It'll go well in the dish of shells on my bathroom windowsill. Thank you.'

'Do you remember, we always used to look for stones that look like letters?' he asked. 'After you saw that picture of a stone alphabet on the Internet.'

'We found an S, once and what could almost have been a Y,' she said. 'But we never did manage to find an A, a B and an X, did we?'

'Though we did find a heart-shaped stone.' He still had it, tucked away in a drawer somewhere, a memory of much happier times. 'Do you still look for letter-shaped stones?'

She shook her head. 'Not since you.'

'Shall we?'

She looked at him, and there was the ghost of sadness in her eyes. But then she nodded, and they continued walking hand in hand along the beach. It didn't matter that they weren't chattering; the silence was companionable rather than awkward. Eventually, she tugged at his hand, then bent down to pick something up from the sand.

'Not a heart-shape or a letter,' she said, 'but still interesting.'

The stone had a perfect hole bored right through the centre.

'A hag stone,' she said. 'Legend has it that you can see through the hole into fairyland and it can protect you against bad luck. It's meant to be lucky to hang it from a ribbon.'

'Superstition,' he said. 'It's actually a composite stone where the softer part's been worn through by water.'

'Sometimes it's more fun to forget the science and enjoy the old stories,' she said.

'You don't have to forget the science,' he said. 'You can see a sun dog in the sky and know it's caused by the refraction of sunlight off tiny ice crystals—but knowing how it works doesn't mean you can't still appreciate the beauty of the phenomenon.'

'Brad?' she asked.

'Yes?'

'Shut up.' And, just to hammer her point home, she kissed him.

His head was spinning by the time she broke the kiss. She clearly knew it, because she grinned. 'I'm glad that still works.'

He couldn't help laughing. 'OK. I was being pompous.'

'Just a little bit. But at least you know it.' She handed him the stone. 'Thread it on a ribbon,' she said.

'I will.' And he meant it. 'Let's head back into town. Have you eaten since lunch?'

'No,' she admitted. 'I've been too busy.'

'Fish and chips or pizza?'

'Pizza,' she said. 'We could eat at my place.'

'I'd like that,' he said.

They picked up a takeaway pizza from the pizzeria in town, then headed back to Abigail's cottage.

'So how is it, being back again?' she asked.

'As a tourist? Fine.'

'Why did you stay away for so long?' she asked. 'I mean, I can understand it'd be hard for the first year, with the first birthday, Father's Day and Christmas to get through.' And the mess of their divorce. So many memories to stop him in his tracks. 'But why did you never come home after that, even for Christmas or your mum's birthday?

'I always see Mum for her birthday and Christmas,' he protested. 'And I see Ruby. I video-call Mum at least twice a week.'

'Which isn't the same thing as coming home.'

He blew out a breath. 'I know. Since you ask, I just couldn't face it. There were too many memories, too much unfinished business that will never get closure now.'

'Unfinished business?' She didn't understand. Like her, Brad and Ruby had had an idyllic childhood, growing up with parents who adored them. They'd all been popular at school and done well academically; Brad had won every single science prize. She couldn't think of anything that would count as unfinished business. Unless... 'Do you mean *us*?'

He shook his head. 'Not that. It doesn't matter.'

She thought it did, but he had that closed-off expression in his eyes that she knew only too well. Time to back off. Maybe if she gave him time to think about it, he might open up and help her understand what was in his head—and she could help him deal with it.

'But yes, before you ask, I feel guilty about not coming back. I know I was selfish. But I can't change the past, Abby.'

'No.' But you could learn from it. 'Was it as bad as you thought it would be?'

'No,' he admitted. 'I think, the longer I left it, the more it built up in my head and the worse I felt. It was easier to use work as an excuse to avoid coming here. But I'll make more effort in the future.'

She hoped so—for his mum's sake. 'OK. I think you're talked out for now. Are you up for something different for pudding?'

He looked relieved that she wasn't pushing him any further. 'Bring it on.'

'Correct answer,' she said, and took a tub from the freezer.

'New recipe?'

'Very, very old one, more like,' she said. She served him a scoop, then sat with her elbows propped on the table and her chin resting on her hands, watching him.

'Aren't you having any?'

'Maybe later. I want to see your reaction,' she said.

'Are you turning into a scientist, now?' he asked.

She laughed, liking his sense of humour. 'No. I just want to see your face when you try it.'

'I'm not even going to ask,' he said, and tasted a spoonful.

She saw the exact moment he realised what he was eating. And that it wasn't actually sweet.

'That,' he said, 'is really not what I was expecting.'

'Is that you being polite and you don't like it?'

'No. Now I've adjusted my mindset, it's quite nice.'

'Normally I'd serve this with slices of fresh apple or pear,' she said. 'Or really good crackers. But I wanted you to try this on its own, first.'

'For the shock value.'

She laughed. 'Busted.'

He took another spoonful. 'So is this what sparked off your idea for dog ice cream?'

'Yes—after I tried it at the Old Boat House, I looked up some old recipes and gave it a go. Mum brought Waffle over and I dropped some on the floor—and you know what dachshunds are like. He scoffed the lot. And that was my lightbulb moment.' She smiled. 'But I use cheddar for the dogs rather than Parmesan.'

'I still can't quite believe I'm eating cheese ice cream.' He took another spoonful. 'It's good.'

'Thank you. I haven't actually got any crackers in at the moment, but I can slice you an apple if you like.'

'It's fine just as it is,' he said with a smile. 'When you were talking about my reaction, I did wonder if you were going to give me the dog ice cream.'

'I could,' she said. 'I only use human-food-grade ingredients—partly because the owners don't believe it at first and want to taste it themselves. But I have an official panel of canine testers, including Waffle, Ollie the Collie—' his mum's dog '—and the dogs of all my staff.'

'So you have regular doggy tasting evenings?'

'Give me a sec.' She flicked into the photo albums on her phone, found the picture she was looking for, and handed him her phone. 'Here we go.'

He chuckled. 'I love it. Doggy testers all in a row, with their owners holding the tubs for them to lick. And is that a chocolate flake?'

'No, it's a mini dog biscuit,' she said.

'You ought to send this to the local press,' he said.

'I got there before you. It's their photograph,' she said. 'My suggestion, and they loved it.'

'You're amazing. I always knew you were creative, but this is something else,' he said. 'Your mum and dad must be so proud of you.'

'I like to think I'm taking the family business forward. In a couple of slightly different directions, admittedly—but it's all customer-driven.' But it really warmed Abigail that Brad thought her parents should be proud of her. That he recognised the hard work she'd put in to Scott's in the years since they'd split up. That she'd changed and grown.

'You're amazing,' he said again.

He insisted on washing up; but he accepted her offer to stay for a while. And it was nice, just being curled up on the sofa together with his arms wrapped round her and soft music playing in the background.

Maybe she should ask him to stay.

But the whole idea of these two weeks was speed-dating—ignoring their past and looking towards their future. In terms of that, they were two dates in: the equivalent of a week in a relationship. So asking him to stay the night would be too soon.

As if he was thinking the same thing, he shifted so that he was sitting properly on the sofa again. 'I ought to go.' He leaned over and kissed her lightly. 'So I'll see you tomorrow at ten.'

'And we'll climb the lighthouse.'

'It won't matter if it's raining because we'll still have amazing views. And I thought we could have a picnic somewhere afterwards, maybe go inland and find a nice shady forest if it's really hot. Or sit in the car if it tips down.'

Typical Brad: he planned all outcomes. 'Sounds good. What would you like me to bring?' she asked.

'Nothing—the picnic's all mine. And yes, I know I probably ought to buy it from Scott's, but...' He wrinkled his nose. 'Then it wouldn't be a surprise.'

She laughed. 'I'm not that territorial.'

'Good.' He stole a kiss. 'Is there anything you'd rather I didn't get?'

'I'm fine with whatever you'd like to pick,' she said with a smile. 'Surprise me.'

'I think you win on the surprise front with the Parmesan ice cream,' he said wryly, and kissed her goodnight. 'Sleep well.'

On Thursday, Brad knocked on Abigail's front door at ten; as he'd expected, she was ready. She never had been the sort who took hours to get ready.

They headed further down the coast until the red and white striped lighthouse came into view.

'Can you imagine what it'd be like, living in a lighthouse?' she asked. 'This one's actually on the mainland so it wouldn't have been so bad. But it must've been so tough, years ago, if you were the keeper of an offshore lighthouse. No telephone, no mail, no visitors— just you and the lighthouse and the other keepers for months, and no fresh food because there wouldn't be space to grow any.'

'You'd have a boat coming to bring your mail and

supplies once a week, and you could go fishing when you weren't on duty in the lighthouse,' he pointed out.

'Yes, but you'd have hardly any fresh vegetables and fruit, except on the couple of days after the supply ship came, and think of the sheer isolation.' She shuddered.

'But think of the views—all the stars you'd see.' He looked at her, remembering one of her big bucket list items. 'Maybe even the Northern Lights.'

'If you were in one of the lighthouses in Northumbria or Scotland, perhaps,' she said.

'And the birds you'd see. It would be great if you were an artist—Ruby would love it.'

Abigail laughed. 'Your twin likes being smack in the middle of modern life. She'd enjoy the sketching for maybe a week, and then the isolation would drive her crackers. And imagine her with no phone coverage.'

'True,' he admitted.

'I think it'd be too isolated for me,' she said. 'Though I guess for you it'd be like being in your lab.'

He smiled. 'I'm not that isolated in my lab. Apart from the fact that I work as a team, I have to go to way too many meetings during the week.'

He parked the car and they walked down the track to the lighthouse; it turned out they were among the first to queue for the tour and were let up with the first batch of holidaymakers.

'It's barer than I expected,' Abigail whispered when they were inside. 'Obviously this bit must've been for storage because the lighthouse keeper had a cottage next door.'

There were colourful displays around the walls, with old photographs of the lighthouse and former lighthouse keepers, but when Brad looked up there was nothing between them and the very top floor of the lighthouse.

Their group followed the guide up the narrow stone steps that clung to the walls in a spiral, first of all up to a room full of maps, which showed all the shipping hazards in the area and the locations of other lighthouses nearby.

'When the lighthouse was first built here, it took three keepers to run. And they had to be really good friends because they worked together and lived together for months at a time. It wasn't so bad here on the mainland, but in somewhere like the Needles Rock on the Isle of Wight it meant living in a tiny room, with no running water or heating.'

Brad looked at Abigail, who grimaced at the thought of it.

Then they climbed up the steep ladder to the lamp itself; from the top, there were amazing views over the cornfields and the sea.

Brad was fascinated by the fact that the light was only five hundred watts but was visible eighteen miles out to sea, thanks to the angles of the glass slats around the lamp. But, as the guide talked, he thought about how much his dad would've loved this, and a wave of sheer misery and loss hit him. It felt like a wall slamming into him and he was barely able to pay attention to what the guide was telling them about how the lamps worked in the early days and what the keepers had to do, from lighting and checking the lights to keeping records of the weather and any shipwrecks.

Abigail frowned. Brad had gone very quiet and it was as if all the sunlight had been sucked from his face.

Something was definitely wrong. Was this something to do with his 'unfinished business'?

Would he talk to her about it? Or would he block her off again?

She had to concentrate on going backwards down the steep ladder from the top, and going down the spiral steps was definitely more scary than going up them, but as they walked to the car she took his hand and squeezed it. 'Are you OK?'

'Sure.'

But his tone was flat. Years ago, she would've left it. Now, she called him on it. 'You don't look OK or sound OK.'

He sighed. 'I was thinking about Dad. He would've loved this, all the stuff about boats in olden times. I could've brought him here and taken him out for a pub lunch or something afterwards.'

'I know. It's a shame you never got to do it.' She turned to face him and splayed her hand over his heart. 'But your memories of him are still right here and you'll never lose them—and you can still share this with him in your head.' She added quietly, 'And today you've shared it with me.'

'I know. Sorry. I'm not good company right now.' He grimaced. 'Do you want me to take you home?'

At least he was talking to her. 'No, let's go for a walk somewhere. It will clear your head.'

He was quiet all the way as they drove inland to a patch of woodland. He was quiet, too, when they walked hand in hand through the trees, and she didn't push him to talk.

Eventually, he sighed. 'I'm sorry. I don't want to

bring you down with my mood, but I don't want to shut you out either.'

Relief flooded through her. He wasn't going to close himself off again. 'It's fine,' she said lightly. 'Everyone has good and bad days.'

'Do you get bad days?'

She had when they'd first split up; she'd managed to pull herself out of it, but it had taken her a while. And she'd really needed the support of her parents and her best friend—support she guessed Brad either hadn't had or, more likely, had refused. Support she should have given him instead of letting him down. 'Yes. Obviously both my parents are still here, so it's not the same thing that you went through, but I'm only human. I get days where just about everything seems to be wrong.'

'So what do you do? How do you deal with it?'

'Hit my kitchen,' she said. 'Baking always works for me. I think it's the scent of vanilla that does it. Actually, I read an article saying it's not just childhood associations with the scent that cheers people up—there's something in the fragrance that's calming and reduces stress, the same way as lavender works to help you sleep and lemon's good for if you're feeling sick or need to be mentally sharp. And that's proper peer-reviewed science, not the woo-woo stuff,' she added with a grin.

He smiled. 'You sound a bit like me.'

'It's where I got it from,' she said with a smile. 'I kind of picked up from you what to look out for and what to ignore. But, seriously, do you want to skip the picnic and go back to my place for a baking session and see if it works for you?'

He raised an eyebrow. 'Have you forgotten the time

I made you pancakes and we couldn't shut the smoke alarm off?'

She laughed. 'No, but I'll be supervising, and I promise it's the easiest recipe ever. It's also the best management tool ever.'

'Management tool?' He looked mystified.

She grinned. 'I make them for my staff—they love me and will say yes to almost anything once they've scoffed the brownies.'

'Got you.' He nodded. 'OK. I'll give it a go. But it'd be a shame to waste the picnic.'

'Let's eat first, then.'

They headed back to the car, where he retrieved the cool bag containing their lunch, before finding an empty table at the picnic area.

Brad had chosen a wonderful selection of food: sourdough bread, Brie, tomatoes, ham carved off the bone, local crab and chilli pâté, local raspberries and smoothies from the local deli.

'This is fantastic. Excellent choices,' she said.

'Glad you like it,' he said.

On the way back to the car, they saw magpies. Three of them.

'One for sorrow, two for joy, three for a girl,' Brad said, recalling the old rhyme.

'Maybe Ruby will have a honeymoon baby,' Abigail said lightly.

She and Brad hadn't discussed children when they'd got married; their tacit agreement was that they wouldn't even discuss it until he'd finished his studies. By then, they'd been divorced, so it wasn't an issue. Now, it might be. She'd barely dated since Brad, let alone met someone she'd think about settling down with and having a family with, and she was pretty sure it was the same for him.

But now they were on the verge of trying again...

They looked at each other, and she knew both of them were thinking the same thing, wondering if the other wanted children.

It was a conversation they might need to have—but not yet. Not until they'd decided what was happening between them.

'Let's go make some killer brownies,' she said.

She could see in his face that he knew she'd chickened out of the conversation—but that he was relieved she hadn't made an issue of it.

Back at her house, she took the ingredients from her cupboard.

'Do you always have ingredients for brownies?' Brad asked.

'These ones, I do.'

And it was so simple: weighing the dry ingredients into a bowl, measuring the wet ones into a jug, and stirring the lot together with a whisk.

'See? It's not so very different from lab work,' she said.

'Oh, but it is,' he said with a smile.

But as the scent of the brownies spilled from the oven, she could see his mood change. He relaxed enough to make them both a mug of coffee—and funny how nice it felt to have him pottering around her tiny kitchen.

He kissed her when she'd taken the brownies out of the oven. 'Thank you. You're right. The scent of vanilla and chocolate *has* made me feel better.'

'Of course I'm right. I have two X chromosomes.' She gave him a cheeky grin.

He didn't correct her; he just smiled and kissed her again.

'Now go and take these to your mum, then take her out to dinner. You can return the pan later,' she said.

'Are you sure?'

'I have stuff to do,' she said, 'and I think you need some time with your family right now.'

'Yeah.' He held her close. 'You're wonderful, do you know that?'

'I'm just me.'

But it warmed her all the way through when, an hour later, her doorbell went and the local florist handed her the most beautiful arrangement of flowers.

The card was in Brad's handwriting and said simply, *Because you make my world a better place.*

Abigail had to blink back the tears. Today had been a little bit of a hurdle, but they'd overcome it. So maybe, just maybe, there was hope for the future.

CHAPTER NINE

BRAD CALLED FOR Abigail at seven on Friday evening and she greeted him with a kiss. 'Thank you for the flowers. I know I texted you, but it's good to say thank you in person, too. They're gorgeous.'

'You're welcome.' He looked slightly awkward. 'Sorry I was a bit difficult yesterday.'

'It's fine. You talked to me.' And that was the big difference between now and five years ago, she thought. The thing that gave her hope for the future. There was still stuff he was keeping inside, but she'd give him space and let him talk when he was ready.

'Mum says thanks for the brownies.' He handed her the now clean cake tin.

Abigail smiled. 'She's already texted me to say thanks.'

His eyes widened. 'Did she ask…?'

'Of course she did. She's your mum and she worries about you. But I told her,' Abigail said softly, 'that we're talking, that right now we're not in a place to make any decisions, but she'll be among the first to know when we do.' She stroked his face. 'And she's not going to rush us. When we make the decision, it has to be right. For both of us.'

'Agreed.' He kissed her. 'Come on. Let's go and play.'

He'd got tickets for them to see a singer-songwriter in a tiny venue in Norwich, where the bar was lit by fairy lights and the stage was just about big enough for three people, two guitars and a piano. It reminded her of their years in Cambridge when they'd go to see a band in some tiny room and stand at the front, with his arms wrapped round her, swaying along to the music and enjoying the closeness as well as the atmosphere.

They couldn't go back to the past.

But maybe they could move forward and bring the best bits of the past with them.

On Saturday night, they went to the cinema, and Brad even put up with a rom-com and held her hand all the way through it. He got his steam train trip on Sunday afternoon, and their seats were in an old-fashioned carriage with seats opposite each other and a corridor, with a uniformed inspector coming to clip their tickets. And Abigail had to admit it was fun, with the sulphurous smell of coal in the air and the sight of the steam wafting past the windows as they went round a bend in the track.

Monday felt like a honeymoon: a day to themselves in Norwich, where they went to an art exhibition in the castle and wandered through narrow streets full of quirky, independent shops. They had afternoon tea in a café where all the china was clearly vintage and none of the tables and chairs matched, but she loved the ambience: ancient pine dressers where jars of local honey and home-made jam were stacked for sale, the paintings on the walls were all by local artists and were for sale, and they had a kitsch cuckoo clock which gave the café its name. The scones were light and fluffy, the sandwiches were perfect and the red velvet cake was the best she'd ever tasted.

On Tuesday, Brad picked her up after work and they had a fabulous dinner on the terrace at his hotel before sitting on his balcony with a bottle of champagne, watching the sun set.

Two more days, she thought, and their speed-dating thing would be over. It would be time to make their decision about the future.

Dating him over the last few days had shown her that yes, she was still physically attracted to him and still enjoyed his company. Spending time together was fun.

And if she was honest with herself, she knew she was still in love with him. In love with the man he'd become rather than the memory of the teenager she'd married. Brad was thoughtful, kind, and he made her laugh. If he asked her to stay with him, she knew she would.

But how did he feel about her?

He'd sent her those flowers. He'd opened up to her— at least, he'd tried to. He'd said that she made his world a better place; that was how she felt about him, too.

So if he did feel the same way that she did… What then? How was it going to work, given that her life was here and his was in London? It wasn't a commutable distance. How were they going to compromise?

'You're quiet,' he said, his arms wrapped round her and his mouth against her hair.

'Wool-gathering,' she said, not wanting to push the point.

'I was thinking,' he said. 'I know you have to be up early tomorrow, but right now I don't want you to go home.'

Her stomach suddenly felt as if it were filled with butterflies. 'You're asking me to stay the night?'

'Yes.' He twisted slightly so he was facing her, and snatched a kiss. 'I know we said we weren't going to complicate things, but I want to wake up with you in my arms.'

She wanted that, too.

'And I'll drive you back to your place tomorrow morning at whatever time you like.'

'It'll be really early. Well before breakfast,' she warned.

'I don't care, as long as you stay,' he said.

In speed-dating terms, they were practically two months in to their new relationship. And although she knew they'd both held off sleeping together again because they hadn't wanted sex to get in the way, she was already clear about what she wanted. The fact that he wanted it, too—and he'd talked about waking with her, not about sex—gave her hope.

And how could she resist those beautiful dark eyes? She took a deep breath. 'Yes.'

'Good.' He kissed her, scooped her up at the same time as he got out of the chair they'd been sitting in together, and carried her to his bed.

Abigail was awake early the next morning. Brad was still asleep and the light was just starting to filter through the curtains. He really was beautiful, she thought as she watched him lying beside her. But more than that, she loved the man he'd become.

They'd find their compromise somehow. Even if it meant that she was the one who had to uproot her life and move to London. Maybe she could open a branch of Scott's there, while putting a manager in to run the Norfolk side of the business.

She'd miss her parents, Ruby, her friends and her colleagues. She'd miss seeing the sea every day. She'd miss the tiny flint cottage she'd grown to love. Leaving here would be a massive wrench.

But it meant she would be with Brad.

No more loneliness, no more wishing that she'd done something different and managed to save her marriage.

Tomorrow, they'd talk about it and make their decision.

And please let him want the same thing that she did.

She woke him with a kiss. 'Hey, sleepyhead.'

He was almost instantly awake. 'I need to drive you home.'

'I can get a taxi.'

'I promised you last night I'd take you home, no matter how ridiculously early it is.' He kissed her. 'Good morning. I can try sweet-talking the kitchen staff into letting us having some very early breakfast.'

She smiled. 'It's fine. I'll grab something after I've had my shower and changed.'

In the end, he drove her home and made her coffee while she showered and dressed, and instead of her usual morning run she made toast and had breakfast with him.

And how nice it was to do something as simple and everyday as having breakfast together. She'd missed that. Missed him making her coffee, missed doing the crossword together on Sunday mornings, missed waking up in his arms.

'I'm afraid I have to go now, but I'll be done at the café by ten,' she said.

'Sure. I'll do the washing up while you're gone.'

'It's fine. Leave it. A couple of crumb-filled plates and jammy knives really don't matter,' she said, flapping a dismissive hand. 'But thanks for the offer.'

She let him drop her at the café on his way back to the Bay Tree.

'I'll pick you up at the café at ten?' he asked.

'See you then,' she said, kissing him goodbye.

She could hardly wait to see him again. And she loved the gardens of the house he'd discovered that only opened to the public four times a year; it was full of specimen trees, and early summer was the perfect time to show it off. They wandered through the gardens hand in hand, and Abigail gasped when they went down to the lake and saw the hundreds of azaleas there reflected in the water.

'I've never seen anything like this in my life. Our mums would both love it here.' She took a photograph.

'And with that bridge over the lake—it's stunning.' He squeezed her hand. 'I always meant to take you to Giverny to see Monet's gardens. I know you love that picture of the bridge and the lily pond.'

'And all the tulips in his spring garden,' she said. 'I'd love to see that.'

'I had so many plans for us,' he said. 'I wanted to make all your dreams come true.'

'All I wanted was to be with you.' And maybe it was time she took a risk and told him how she really felt about what had happened. 'I loved you, Brad. I thought you loved me. I had a few doubts when you asked me to elope, but I was so sure you loved me as much as I loved you. And then, when I realised you didn't, it was too late.'

'I loved you,' he said. 'But I admit I asked you to elope for the wrong reasons.'

It felt as if he'd slapped her, and her recoil was involuntary. As were the tears she had to blink away fast.

Clearly he'd noticed, because he said, 'That came out wrong. I meant every word of my wedding vows. I just…' He blew out a breath. 'I've never really talked about this to anyone, but Dad and I had a bit of a strained relationship.'

'What? But your dad adored you.'

'He wanted me to follow in his footsteps,' Brad said. 'Our fights weren't in public. But it was all the little comments he made. He never once criticised Ruby about her choice of career—I guess he could see that she lived for her art and that she was really good at it—but he didn't think much of my choice. "You'll never make a proper living. Lab technicians are ten a penny." He said that to me so many times.'

'You're not a technician. You're a researcher,' she said. 'Actually, I think you would have made a good lawyer, because you pay attention to detail and you pride yourself on doing a job properly—but your heart wouldn't have been in it. You did the right thing, choosing the subject you love.'

He looked at her. 'That's not how Dad saw it.'

And then she realised why Brad had really stayed away. Why he'd reacted so very badly to his father's death. *This* was the unfinished business. 'And you never got your chance to show him that you'd made the right choice because he died while you were still a student.'

Brad said nothing, but she saw the muscle clench in his cheek.

'Your dad,' she said, 'loved you very much. And if he'd wanted you to read law—well, yes, of course he'd be disappointed that you didn't. But, as I've said to you before, your dad was stubborn and wouldn't listen to anyone. It would have choked him to say, "Brad, you did the right thing." Even if you won the Nobel prize for chemistry, and you made the biggest scientific discovery of the century, he would probably still say that he was proud of you but you should have been a lawyer.'

Brad looked at her as if the whole weight of the world were on his shoulders.

'And then at his chambers he would have been telling everyone within earshot—and that would include the set of chambers three buildings away—how his clever son was a brilliant chemist and he was going to change the world.'

'You really think so?'

'I've got no reason to lie to you, Brad. He loved you and he was proud of you. Telling you to your face would have meant admitting he was wrong about your career choice, and that isn't what your dad did. But ask your mum. Ask Ruby. I bet they'll tell you the same thing.'

He sighed. 'I just wish I'd had the chance to show him I did the right thing for me.'

She hugged him. 'I reckon he knows. He's watching you right now, huffing about how his boy's gone soft in the head and of course he loves you. But then he'd add there was still time for you to do another degree and maybe specialise in science law.'

Brad was shaking.

Oh, dear God. She'd just sent him into another meltdown. 'Brad, it's OK,' she said, desperately wanting to reassure him.

But when he pulled back, she could see that he was laughing.

'What?' she asked, puzzled.

'What you just said… That's exactly what he would have said.'

'So I'm right about the rest of it, too.'

'I guess.'

'I loved your dad. I thought he might be a bit of a nightmare to live with—so full-on hearty, the whole time, it must have been a bit wearing—but I never realised he gave you such a hard time about your studies. I wish you'd told me. I could've…' She sighed. 'Maybe not.'

'Made it better? I think I needed to grow up and see it for myself,' he said. 'Which, thanks to you, I have, and I'm sorry I didn't trust you enough to tell you years ago.'

'Is that why you asked me to elope? So you'd be living with me instead of having to come back here and be nagged about your degree?'

He shook his head. 'It was a fit of rebellion. We had a big fight, that night. And it wasn't just the usual stuff about my career; he started on about you. He said we were too young even to be engaged. And I wanted to prove him wrong.'

She bit her lip. 'So you didn't actually want to marry me.'

'I always wanted to marry you,' he said. 'Dad was wrong about some of it—I never met anyone who even began to match up to how I felt about you—but he was right about us being too young to get married. I still had a lot of growing up to do. The fact I pushed you into eloping instead of having a wedding like Ruby's was proof of that.'

'I really thought you loved me. And when your solicitor sent me that letter…' Her throat felt as if it had closed up.

'More proof that I needed to grow up,' he said. 'I

really loved you, Abby. But I was a mess and I really thought setting you free to find happiness with someone else was the right thing to do.'

'I never wanted anyone else.' She swallowed hard. 'I think you broke me for a while. I cried so much I couldn't see, my eyes were so swollen. And you wouldn't even speak to me.'

He held her close. 'I'm so sorry I hurt you. I'm not going to ask you to forgive me, because I can't ask for that. But I've learnt a lot about myself over the last few weeks and I know I'd react differently in the future.'

The future. The thing they were meant to be discussing tomorrow.

Did they *have* a future?

'I felt as if I wasn't enough for you,' she said. 'And it made me wary of dating again. In case whoever I started seeing felt like that about me—that I wasn't enough.'

'Any man who had you in his life would count himself the luckiest man in the world.'

'You didn't,' she pointed out.

'Because I was young, I was hurting, and I was very, *very* stupid.' He stroked her hair. 'I can't change the past, Abby. I wish I could. And, if I could, I would never...'

'...have married me?' she finished.

'Have let you go,' he corrected.

'So are you saying you want to try again?'

'I'm saying,' he said carefully, 'we might both need a bit more time to think. We've told each other things we maybe weren't expecting to hear.'

She certainly hadn't had a clue about what he'd told her.

'We need to make the right decision for both of us,' he said, 'for the right reasons. And at this precise moment I feel as if someone's just put me on one of those loop-the-loop rollercoasters at triple speed.'

'So you want to go back to the Bay Tree on your own?'

'No. I want to walk through this garden with you, hand in hand,' he said.

Now she got it. 'And not talk.'

'Not talk for a little while,' he agreed. 'But I want to be with you.'

Walking in the sheer beauty of the gardens helped to clear her head. Maybe his, too, because finally he tightened his fingers round hers. 'I'm sorry.' He grimaced. 'I seem to be saying that a lot, today.'

'Maybe we need to put it all behind us,' she said. 'We can't change the past,' she said. 'But know that not all of it was bad.'

'Agreed.' He looked at her. 'Right now, I really want to kiss you. But it kind of feels—I don't know. Insensitive. And I'm trying to be sensitive.'

'You might be thinking too much,' she said.

'How?'

'This,' she said, and reached up to kiss him. 'That's better.'

He wrapped his arms around her and kissed her back. 'You're right. Much better. So here's the plan. I take you somewhere nice for dinner, we watch the stars come out over the sea—and then, if I'm not being too pushy, I want to fall asleep with you in my arms.'

'That,' she said, 'sounds like an excellent plan.'

CHAPTER TEN

BRAD STAYED WITH Abigail at the cottage that night, and it was good to wake in his arms. To wake and make love—except, when she got out of the shower, she realised that she was going to be late for work.

'I know I'm the boss, so technically speaking I can walk in any time I choose, but I need to set an example,' she said. 'I don't want anyone to think I'm slacking off.'

'Nobody thinks you're slacking off. I'll drive you in,' he said.

In the end, she was only ten minutes late, though it was enough to fill her with guilt.

He kissed her lightly. 'Go. I need to get back to the hotel, pack and check out. I'll see you at seven and I'll book a table somewhere tonight for dinner.'

'See you at seven,' she echoed.

But when Abigail walked into the café and smelled the bacon grilling, the scent made her feel queasy.

Maybe it was something she'd eaten at dinner last night. Something that hadn't agreed with her.

When her usual mid-morning mug of coffee made her stomach turn as well, to the point where she couldn't even take a mouthful of the stuff, she started to wonder. Was she being paranoid, or was she…?

She did a quick mental calculation and realised that her period was late. It should have started a week ago.

Panic skittered through her. Had they even used a condom, that first night—the night of Ruby's wedding? They'd definitely used protection since then, but that first time... Her mind was horrifyingly blank on the subject. She'd been so swept away by Brad that she couldn't think straight. She simply couldn't remember.

Could she really be pregnant? The dates would tie in. Friends who'd had a baby had talked about a super-enhanced sense of smell in the very early days of pregnancy and feeling sick, being tired, going off coffee, and their breasts feeling tender. And every one of those symptoms applied to her right now. She'd felt sick at the smell of cooking bacon, she didn't want coffee, and her bra felt too tight...

She pushed the thought away. How utterly ridiculous. The nausea could be anything, and not fancying coffee could be down to that too; she was tired because she was still putting in all the hours at work and seeing Brad every night; the tightness of her bra was purely psychosomatic because now she was half convinced that she was pregnant; and the date of her period was probably a bit off kilter because her emotions had been turned upside down over the last couple of weeks. The dates had nothing to do with it. Of course she wasn't pregnant.

But the thought kept nagging at her, along with the fact they'd seen those magpies in the woods the other day. *Three for a girl, four for a boy...* For pity's sake, it was just an old superstition. She wasn't pregnant.

By mid-morning, Abigail had had enough. There was only one way to find out the truth.

It was her admin day in the office at the café, so if

she went out for a bit it wouldn't cause any problems with the staff at the counter. She made an excuse that she needed to go and see a supplier, and walked back to her cottage to pick up the car. She could've gone to the pharmacy in town or even the supermarket, but everyone knew her in Great Crowmell and she didn't want even the faintest bit of gossip to start. Instead, she drove to a supermarket in one of the bigger market towns where nobody knew her and bought a pregnancy test kit. A digital one, so there would be no margin of error.

She didn't want to wait and do the test at her cottage, so she went into the nearest café and ordered a cheese scone and a mug of hot chocolate.

She was probably being ridiculous. Of course she wasn't pregnant by her ex. She couldn't be. Though the test felt as if it were burning a hole in her bag.

How pathetic was that? She was twenty-seven, not seventeen.

But what if she was pregnant? What if? What if? The question ran round and round in her head.

She gritted her teeth, forced herself to eat the scone and drink the hot chocolate, then headed for the bathroom.

Thankfully it was empty and there were three cubicles, so she didn't feel guilty about causing any kind of queue. She did the test and stared at the little white stick.

One blue line, to show it was working…

And there it was. In stark black text, so she couldn't pretend she'd make a mistake and misread the result.

Pregnant.

She swallowed hard.

What was she going to do now?

Last time she and Brad had done something reckless—eloping to Gretna Green—they'd kept their castle in the air going for a few years… And then it had all come crashing down and she'd realised how naive and foolish they'd been.

Nearly ten years later, they hadn't learned a thing, had they? They'd been reckless and stupid, and had a crazy affair. Something that both of them had known deep down could never last. Abigail didn't expect Brad to give up his job for her—and, even though the other day she'd thought that maybe she could follow him to London, now it came down to it she wasn't so sure that she could. Her life was here. Her family was here. In London, she'd be isolated.

Or would Brad offer to give up the job she knew he loved and come back to Great Crowmell? Would he consider taking a job that maybe he didn't love so much? Would he want to make a life here with her?

And then the doubts came slamming in. What if he didn't? What if Brad did expect her to give up everything for him and move to London? What if she put a manager into the café and ran the business from a distance, so she wasn't letting her parents down—would things really work out between them? Because, the last time they'd been together and life had thrown up a major change, their marriage had disintegrated. Brad hadn't coped with the shock of his father's death and he'd frozen her out.

What if he did the same if things went wrong this time round?

OK, so she'd had the confidence to push him when he'd gone quiet on her at the lighthouse, and he'd opened up to her. But that was over something relatively small. What about something bigger? What if—God forbid— something happened to his mum, or to Ruby? What if he was made redundant and it was difficult to find another job? Would he talk to her and let her help him through it, or would he shut himself off again?

And a baby would be a huge, huge change to both their lives. They hadn't discussed having children; she had no idea how he felt. Was it too soon for him? Or didn't he want children at all?

Plus she knew that a baby was never the answer to a sticky patch in a relationship. Those early days, with all the broken nights and worry and stress, would put extra strain on them and would widen any rifts between them, to the point where those rifts couldn't be bridged any more. What if the baby made him feel trapped? What if he froze her out again? Because this time it wouldn't just be her, it would be the baby as well.

But could she do this on her own? Could she have a baby and keep running her family's business as a single mum?

There was another option, but she pushed it away. She'd made a choice that had led to a pregnancy, and getting rid of a baby just because it wasn't convenient felt wrong. Not that she'd ever judge anyone else for making that decision, but for her that wasn't the right option.

OK. She knew her parents would stand by her. So would Ruby, and Brad's mum. They'd all be supportive. But Brad himself...

She had absolutely no idea how he was going to react. Or how she was going to tell him. The only thing she knew was that they had to talk about it. Tonight. And only then could they decide if they wanted to move on together—or apart.

And until then she just had to keep going. Pretend that everything was just fine and she'd had a business meeting.

She splashed water on her face, then drove back to the café and buried herself in all the admin tasks she hadn't done that morning. And please, please, let her find the right words to tell Brad.

The Abby Brad had dropped off at the café that morning had been laughing and bubbly, a little flustered and cross with herself, but happy.

The Abby he met at seven was quiet. Too quiet.

'Is everything all right?' he asked.

'Of course. Why wouldn't it be?'

But he'd seen a flicker of panic in her eyes. Which were grey, not green, another tell-tale sign that she was upset.

'Abby. Talk to me. Tell me what's wrong.'

'There's nothing wrong.' Her tone was light, but he could tell it was deliberately so; and it increased his conviction that something had happened.

He waited until they were seated at the quiet table he'd booked in a pub and had ordered their meal before tackling her again. Maybe something had happened to the business. 'Something's wrong,' he said gently. 'I'm guessing it's work. What's happened? Someone's gone bust, owing you a lot of money and you need a temporary loan to keep on track?'

When she said nothing, he pushed on. 'Because I've got savings, Abby, and they're yours if you need them. I've seen how you've grown your parents' business and you're a good manager, so I know you'll get through this. I'm more than happy to invest in Scott's if you need me to.'

'It's not that.'

To his horror, a tear slid down her cheek, followed by another. And then the tears were unstoppable.

He knew she'd hate it if the waiter came over and saw her crying like this. And he also knew something was really, really wrong. She needed him, and she needed them both to get out of here. Now.

'Go out to the car. I'll deal with everything here and then I'll be with you,' he said, handing her his car keys.

He went to see the waiter. 'I'm really sorry, but something's cropped up and we can't wait for the meal we've ordered. Can I pay the bill? And if I could have a bottle of water to take away, that'd be great.'

The waiter was nice about it, but it felt as if it was taking for ever to sort everything out; and Brad was totally at a loss as to what had upset Abby so much. If it wasn't the business, was it her parents? He knew she was close to them. Had one of them had bad news about their health? She'd said something about her mother being diagnosed with coeliac disease. Had that been masking something more sinister?

He was really worried by the time he got back to the car.

She'd stopped crying, but her face was pale and she was still looking worried sick.

'I don't have tissues,' he said, 'but I have this.' He handed her the bottle of water. 'I'm going to drive us somewhere quiet, then you're going to talk to me. I know something's wrong. If I can do anything to help you fix it, I will, but even if I can't then talking about it will help you feel a bit better.'

She looked at him. 'That has to be the most hypo-critical thing you've ever said.'

He stared at her. 'What?' He couldn't believe she was picking a fight with him, when he was trying his best to be supportive.

'"Talking about it will help."' She actually used her fingers to make fake quotation marks round the words, and that stung. 'It didn't, five years ago.'

That stung even more, because he knew it was true—and because now she knew why. 'You mean, because I didn't talk,' he said. 'I've kind of learned that one the hard way.' He couldn't stop a note of acid creeping into his voice when he added, 'And, believe it or not, I might have grown up a bit since then.'

But Abigail wasn't one to pick a fight. She was straight-talking, but she didn't deliberately start arguments. 'You're trying to deflect me,' he said. 'Don't. Just tell me whatever it is.'

She lifted her chin. 'You're not going to like this.'

'Let me be the judge of that.'

She took a deep breath. 'OK. You wanted it straight, so I'll give it to you straight. I'm pregnant.'

As the words sank in, his head spun.

Abigail was going to have a baby.

His baby.

'But… How?'

'Oh, come on, Dr Powell,' she scoffed. 'You did biology A level and a doctorate in biochemistry—at Cambridge, no less. You *know* how babies are made.'

'Of course I know how babies are made,' he said. 'But how—?' No, that was the wrong question. 'When?'

She swallowed hard. 'It has to be the night of Ruby's wedding.' Her breath hitched. 'I can't remember if we used a condom. My head's blank. But it has to be then.'

He knew she was right. They hadn't made love again until two nights ago, and it would be way too soon for her to know that she was pregnant from then.

Had they used a condom, that first night?

He thought about it, and his head drew a blank, too.

And he didn't know what to say.

He opened his mouth, and nothing came out.

Panic flooded through him.

A father.

Would he even make a good father? Everyone had thought he was close to his own father, and in some ways he had been; but half the time he'd worked so hard, driven himself, just to prove himself to Jim. It had felt almost like being in a competition. And not in a good way.

He hadn't been great as a son, as a brother, as a husband. So how could he possibly be a good dad?

Abby knew that look.

She'd seen it in Brad's eyes before, after Jim's death. The look that told her he was bottling up his feelings and he was going to withdraw from everyone.

So much for thinking that they'd gone a long way to sort out the issues between them. So much for thinking that Brad would change. He might *want* to change, but maybe at the end of the day that was simply asking too much of him and he couldn't.

It looked as if she was going to be bringing up the baby alone.

No. No, no, no. Brad fought against the panic. This was where it had gone wrong last time, because he hadn't talked. This was way too important for him to mess up. Even if the wrong words came out, he could fix that. He might have to grovel for weeks, but at least they'd be talking. Silence was what would drive her away.

'Right now,' he said, 'I don't know what to say. I need to think about this. But what I do know is that

I'm here for you. Now and always. That's not going to change. Ever.'

She didn't look as if she believed him. Then again, he'd let her down before. How did he convince her that it would be different, now? He took her hand. 'When did you first realise?'

'Today. When you dropped me off at the café, I walked in and the smell of cooking bacon made me feel really queasy. And then I didn't want my coffee.' She dragged in a breath. 'I thought I was being ridiculous and making two plus two make twenty, until I counted back and realised my period's a week overdue.'

'So Ruby's wedding was right in the middle of your cycle.' He knew he was analysing this instead of making the right emotional noises, but for pity's sake he was a *scientist*. Analysing things was the way he managed his life. It was the way he'd work out what to do next. 'And you did a test?'

Another tear slid down her cheek. 'I even went two towns away to buy one, to a supermarket where I knew nobody would have a clue who I was.'

So nobody would gossip. That was the thing about living in a small town: everyone knew everyone else, and also knew all their business. If anyone had seen Abby buying a pregnancy test today, the whole of Great Crowmell would have known by now.

'Good idea,' he said. 'And it was positive.' It was a statement, not a question. Even though she was probably panicking every second that she waited for the results, Abby wouldn't have misread it.

She nodded. 'I bought one of the digital ones, the ones that actually use words instead of coloured lines, so there could be no mistake. No squinting at it and trying to work out if there's really a line or if you just think it's there. Plain text.'

'Also a good idea,' he said.

She was pregnant.

With his baby.

If this had happened when they'd still been married, he would've been thrilled. He would still have been a student, so money would've been tight, but they would've managed.

Now, financially he was in a much better position. He'd inherited money from his father and invested it well; plus he'd been promoted rapidly at work. If Abigail wanted to stay at home with the baby, he could afford to support her.

Emotionally, they could still be poles apart. These last few days, he'd thought they'd grown closer. He'd known that he was still in love with the woman who'd stolen his heart when they'd been teenagers. He'd woken up with her in his arms this morning, and he'd felt happier than he had in years. Tonight was supposed to be about their future. About whether they were going to give each other a second chance and get back together.

Technically, she'd be the one giving him a second chance. He was the one who'd messed up.

But now the situation was different. She was expecting their baby. So there was only one thing they could do, and everything else would just have to fall into place from that. 'OK. It's obvious what we have to do. We'll get married again,' he said.

CHAPTER ELEVEN

THAT WAS BRAD'S answer to their situation? A blithe 'we'll get married again'? No discussion, no finding out how she felt, no telling her how he felt? Abigail could barely believe what she was hearing. And this couldn't have been further from the first time he'd asked her to marry him, when he'd promised to love her for the rest of time.

'No,' she said.

He frowned. 'What do you mean, no?'

'We haven't discussed *anything*, Brad. Not how we feel about each other, not whether we actually want to keep seeing each other in the future, not the logistics with me living here and you living three hours away in London...' She shook her head. 'We can't get married.'

'It's not as simple as just whether we want to see each other or not,' he said. 'The situation's changed. We have a baby to consider now.'

'And that's why I can't marry you,' she said. 'Last time we were married, your dad died and you didn't cope with it. You pushed me away—and I let you do it, so it's not all your fault and I'm not dumping the blame on you. But you froze me out, Brad. Next time we have to face something awful in our lives—and the chances are we will—what happens then? Will you freeze me *and* the baby out?'

He looked hurt. 'I'm older, now. Wiser. I hope.'

'You *hope*.' She knew she was being unfair, maybe even cruel, but this was too important to be swept under the carpet. 'But you can't be sure.'

'I talked to you after the lighthouse. And I told you things yesterday I'd never really talked about to anyone else.'

Which was a big thing for him, but it still wasn't enough to allay her fears. And the only way she could think of now was to tell him straight. 'What happens if it's something really awful—God forbid, if something happens to your mum or to Ruby? Or you get made redundant, or...' She blew out a breath. 'There are all sorts of things that could get in the way. How do you know you're not going to freeze me out again, next time things get tough?'

'Because I'll try harder, this time. I know where I messed up. I won't repeat my mistakes.'

He might not intend to, but she could see the panic in his eyes. He might not be able to help himself. 'If it was just me to consider, I might take the risk. But, as you said, we have a baby to think of now.' She raked a hand through her hair. 'I say "baby". At this stage it's just a handful of cells.'

He went white. 'Are you suggesting...?'

'A termination? No.' She shook her head. 'That's not the answer for me. I'm keeping the baby. I know Mum and Dad will be there for me—your mum and Ruby will be there, too. I'll have support as a single mum.'

His eyes were very, very dark. 'Is that what you

want? To bring the baby up on your own and have nothing to do with me?'

'No,' she said tiredly. 'Of course I don't want that. We'd make arrangements for access. I'd never keep the baby from you. Your family will be very much part of this baby's life.'

'My family, but not me.'

'You're three hours away, Brad. In London. It's not a workable situation for a relationship, living that far apart.' She blew out a breath. 'And that's something else we haven't discussed.' Where they'd live, if they tried to make a second go of their marriage. There was so very much to think about, and she wasn't sure she could do this. 'I don't expect you to leave London and come back here.'

'My career's in London.' He paused. 'But I could retrain. I could teach chemistry in secondary school. The education authority is crying out for science teachers.'

'You'd hate every second of it. You love the lab— you always have, and you always will. I could see you working with undergraduates, maybe, but only in a job where you got to do a big chunk of research as well. I won't ask you to give that up.'

His expression was very serious. 'And you love your job here. Not just the job, the place. And your family's here. I can't ask you to give that up.'

She shook her head in sheer frustration. 'I can't see any way to compromise, Brad. If we're to be together, one of us has to move and uproot everything.'

'So what's your solution?' he asked.

Not moving to London. Not being isolated with a small baby, hours away from her family and with Brad working ridiculous hours at the lab so she and their child would barely see him.

'I don't know.' She swallowed miserably. 'I thought tonight we were going to talk about things. About what we want.'

'Then let's do that. What do you want, Abby?'

Him. And the baby. And her business. *Everything*.

Which was greedy.

She couldn't have it all.

And if she told him what she really wanted... He'd already offered to retrain as a school teacher and move back here, two things she knew he'd hate. How could she ask him to do that? It would only make him miserable, and in the end he'd grow to resent her and the baby. Their marriage would crumble again, only this time there'd be someone else hurt by the fallout.

She couldn't see any way out of it.

She was about to tell him so when his phone shrilled.

To her surprise, he ignored it.

'Brad, that might be important.'

'Then whoever it is will either leave a message or ring back,' he said.

His phone went again, and this time he glanced at the screen before rejecting the call.

'Who was it?' she asked.

'Sunetra.'

His number two at the lab. She frowned. 'Brad, it's eight o'clock at night. That's not a normal time to ring someone about work. So it must be important.'

'You're more important than work.'

That made her feel slightly better, but if she'd had a call about work at this time of the evening she'd know there was a problem and she'd want to act on it. 'Call her back,' she said.

He sighed, but did so; though Abigail couldn't tell from his side of the conversation if there was a problem or what Sunetra wanted from him.

When he ended the conversation, he looked at her. 'The reason it's late is because Sunetra was staying on to wait for some results in the lab. It seems we might have had a bit of a breakthrough and she wanted to let me know.'

'That's good, isn't it?'

'Yes.' But he didn't look as excited about it as she'd expected. 'I'm going to ring my boss and tell him I need to stay here for a bit longer.'

She shook her head. 'Brad, it sounds as if your team needs you there. You can't let them down. You have a responsibility to them—just as I have a responsibility to my team.'

'I know, but I don't want to let *you* down, Abby.'

He was clearly torn between his duty to work and his duty to her. But he hadn't mentioned a word about his feelings towards her, just about his responsibilities. So she'd make this easy for him.

'We're at stalemate. And maybe we need some time apart to think.'

Time apart to think.

Brad had been here before. Five years ago. And that was where it had all unravelled. Time apart had turned into a divorce.

'No.'

She frowned. 'What do you mean, no?'

'No, we don't need time apart to think. We need time

together to think.' He raked a hand through his hair. 'You're right—I do need to be in London. But I want to be here with you.'

'You can't be in two places at once. And you have responsibilities at work.'

'Last time you said we needed time apart to think, I let you go—and it was the worst decision I ever made,' he said. 'I'm not making that mistake again.'

'I'm not the one who's going, this time.'

'Fair point. And this isn't an open-ended thing. Because I'll be back tomorrow night. Whatever promises I have to make, whatever I have to do to make things work in the lab, I'll be back for you tomorrow. We'll both have had time to think about the baby and what we want. And we're going to talk, Abby. I'm going back to London now, but this isn't over. Not by a long way.'

He drove her back to her cottage. As he parked outside, he really wanted to kiss Abby and tell her he loved her and make a family with her, but he didn't want to put any pressure on her. He wanted her to be with him because she wanted to be with him, not because she thought she had a duty to the baby.

'I'll see you tomorrow,' he said.

She looked as if she didn't quite believe him, and that hurt. Yes, he'd let her down in the past—but they were both older and wiser. Faced with that same situation, he knew they'd both do things differently now.

'Have a safe journey,' she said. 'Text me when you get back.'

'It'll be late.'

'That's OK. Just text me.'

'OK.'

For a moment, he thought she was going to reach

over and kiss him. And then he'd tell her that he loved her and never wanted to let her go again.

But she didn't.

She just looked bone-deep tired and miserable.

Which was pretty much how he felt, too, and he hated having to leave. Though he knew she was right. He had responsibilities and there were conversations he really needed to have at work. Because, even if Abby didn't want to be with him any more, she was having his baby. And he wanted to be there for her and their child. He didn't want to be the dad who turned up on the odd weekend and took the child to the playground and a fast-food place. He wanted to be part of their lives. Be there for every scan and antenatal class, the first day at nursery and the first day at school, all the nativity plays and sports days.

He waited until Abby was safely back inside the cottage before he drove back to London. And he thought about their situation all the way back.

She was right in that he didn't want to teach in a secondary school. He'd miss his work in the lab so much. But if it was a choice between doing a job he didn't love and being with the woman he loved, or doing the job he loved and being without Abby, then it would be an easy decision. He wanted to be with her and the job came second. He wanted a second chance with her and he wanted to see their child grow up. Most of all he wanted to make a proper family with Abby.

The way she saw it, either she had to give up her entire life and move to London to be with him, or he had to give everything up and move back to Norfolk.

But surely there had to be a middle way, where they could both get what they wanted?

He thought about it some more.

The previous summer, a headhunter had called him and offered him a job up in Manchester. He'd considered it seriously and had almost accepted, but in the end he'd talked to his boss and negotiated more responsibility in his job.

Maybe he could talk to the headhunter to see if anything was available nearer to Great Crowmell than London. Maybe Cambridge; it would still be two hours away from Great Crowmell, but that was better than three hours. More doable.

The next morning, he was in the lab early, but before he left the house he'd already bought flowers online to be delivered to Abby at breakfast time, along with the message *See you tonight. B.* Again, he'd been close to writing *I love you*, but he didn't want to pressure her. Just let her know that he wasn't going to let her down.

He'd also left a message with the headhunter he'd spoken to, outlining his availability and saying that he'd call at lunchtime to discuss the options.

He sorted out his team's questions, agreed the next steps for the project, and then went to speak to his boss.

'Good to have you back, Brad,' Dominic said.

This was where Brad knew he was supposed to say that it was good to be back. Which it was; and at the same time it wasn't.

'Can I be frank with you, Dominic?' he asked.

'Sure.'

'There isn't an easy way to say this, because I love my job here and I love working with my team—but I need to move out of London. I'm sorry, but I'm going to have to resign without seeing the project through to the end.'

'Move out of London?' Dominic frowned. 'Why? Is there a problem at home? Is there anything we can help with?'

Brad shook his head. 'It's all a bit up in the air at the moment, to be honest—it's for personal reasons.'

'OK.'

Dominic had been a great support. The least Brad could do was tell him the truth. 'I know you won't tell anyone before I'm ready to break the news.' Brad looked his boss straight in the eye. 'I just found out that I'm going to be a dad. And that's something I can't do from three hours away. It's not commutable, and I don't want to be a part-time dad.'

'No, of course not.' Dominic blinked. 'Well, this is a bit out of left field. I didn't even realise you were seeing someone, let alone that it was serious enough to start a family. I don't know what to say—um, congratulations?'

'I'm seeing my ex,' Brad said, 'and the baby wasn't planned. But I'm hoping we're going to be able to make things work, second time round.'

'As you're resigning, does that mean you have another job lined up?'

'Not yet,' Brad admitted. 'I might end up retraining. I was thinking of maybe teaching chemistry.'

'And you'd be happy doing that?'

'If it meant I could be with Abby and the baby, yes. But that's plan B,' Brad admitted. 'I'm keeping my options open.'

'If you want my opinion,' Dominic said, 'I think you'd hate teaching in a school because you'd miss the research side too much. And I also think you'd be a huge loss to the industry if you switched to teaching. I wish there was some way to keep you here, because I

don't want to lose you.' He frowned. 'Would your partner consider moving to London?'

'That would mean moving a three-hour drive away
from both our families. So if she moved here, that would
mean she'll be pregnant and know nobody in the area—
or, if she waited until the baby was born before she
moved, she'd have a small baby and know nobody in
the area. It's not fair to do that to her.'

'She'd make friends at antenatal classes, and at the
baby groups.'

Abby would make friends easily, Brad knew. But
that wasn't the issue. 'I don't want to make her uproot
everything. And, to be honest, I know how much she
loves it back in Norfolk. It's not just her home and her
family, it's her family business as well.' Last time, Abby
had put him first, uprooted herself and gone with him
to Cambridge—and he'd let her down. This time, it was
his turn to make the move. To put her first. 'So I need
to go back to Norfolk.'

'Don't hand your notice in just yet,' Dominic said.
'Give me a few days. I know people in other labs. People
I trained with. They're always looking for good people.
One of them might have an opening.'

'I was going to sign on with an agency, too,' Brad
said. 'Talk to the people who headhunted me last year.'

'Much as I'm going to hate losing you from the team,
it looks as if you've got it all sorted out.' Dominic rolled
his eyes. 'Not that I'd expect anything less from you.
Your organisational skills put everyone else's to shame.'

'Obviously I'll work out my notice,' Brad said, 'but
I have a lot of time in lieu owing.'

'I'm sure the HR team can work something out,'
Dominic said. 'Thank you for being honest with me.'

He sighed. 'I really wish you weren't going. But I understand. You must really, really love her.'

'I do,' Brad said. 'I was the one who messed it up, last time. And I'm going to be the one to fix it, this time.'

Who would be ringing her doorbell at this time of the morning? Abigail wondered.

Thankfully she'd always been a lark rather than an owl, so she was already up and dressed.

She answered the door to see a delivery man half hidden behind a huge bouquet of flowers.

'Ms Scott?'

'Yes.'

'These are for you. Could you sign for them, please?' The delivery man gave her the handset so she could sign on the screen, then handed her the flowers.

'Thank you,' she said, and took the flowers into the kitchen.

They were gorgeous, bright and summery, all yellows and blues.

But who would be sending her flowers—especially at this time of the morning, when it was well before normal delivery times? Someone had definitely pulled some strings or paid a massive premium to get them to her before she went to work.

Brad?

Her heart gave a little leap of excitement.

And then she thought about it. Were the flowers his way of saying sorry, he wasn't going to make it tonight?

Her hands shook slightly as she opened the envelope.

And the message left her none the wiser.

See you tonight. B.

Not even a kiss. Nothing emotional at all. She still didn't have a clue how he felt.

On the other hand, he'd got the flowers to her at a crazy time. And this didn't look like any old bouquet. He'd asked them to include little yellow pompom chrysanthemums with dark centres that looked like tiny sunflowers, flowers she'd admired in the stately home gardens with him earlier in the week. It was a detail she knew hadn't slipped past him. He'd chosen them deliberately because he knew she liked them.

And maybe he'd just sent them to let her know he wasn't going to let her down. This time. A statement that he'd be there tonight and then they'd talk properly.

A tear leaked down her cheek.

She so wanted this to work out. But, for that to happen, one of them was going to have to make a huge sacrifice—and the whole thing scared her stupid.

She rested one hand across her abdomen. 'Whatever happens, baby, you're going to be loved. I can guarantee that,' she said. But whether she and Brad would be living together and bringing their child up together—and where—she really didn't know.

She picked up her phone and texted him.

Thank you for the flowers. They're beautiful. Loved the pompoms. See you tonight.

And please, please let it work out.

The Friday night traffic was worse than usual, Brad thought.

He'd left London at six, hoping the worst of the rush hour would be over and he could get to Abby by nine—

but there seemed to be roadworks and temporary traffic lights everywhere, holding him up at every stage.

He called her at seven, but her mobile phone went through to voice mail; clearly she was either busy or she hadn't heard the phone ring. 'I'm on my way,' he said, 'but the traffic's terrible. I'll be with you as soon as I can.'

She didn't call him back, so either she hadn't picked up the message or she didn't want to talk to him. He really hoped it was the former. Sure, he could go and stay with his mother, or find a room in a hotel somewhere, and then sit on her doorstep the next morning until she emerged for her usual run, but he just wanted to be with Abby.

He was thoroughly fed up with sitting in a queue of traffic, but at least all the delays gave him a chance to practise what he wanted to say to Abby. He just hoped that she'd actually listen to him.

A phone call with news from Dominic, half an hour later, cheered him up slightly.

Though it was half-past nine before he reached Great Crowmell, and it took him another ten minutes to find a parking space because the car park was much busier than he'd expected. But finally he knocked on Abigail's door.

She looked as if she hadn't slept properly the previous night, and there were dark smudges under her eyes.

'Sorry—I'm really late. Maybe it would be better to do this tomorrow,' he said.

'No, come in,' she said. 'Have you eaten?'

'Yes,' he lied. He didn't want food—he wanted Abby. And he didn't want to give her an excuse for distraction.

'At least let me make you a cup of coffee.'

'Not if the smell makes you feel queasy.'

'It's fine.' She bustled around the kitchen. 'Your flowers were lovely.'

'I got your message.' He smiled. 'I'm glad you noticed I picked the flowers deliberately.' The day they'd talked about going to Monet's garden together in the spring.

'How did you get someone to deliver so early?' she asked.

'The Internet can be a wonderful thing,' he said.

And then he couldn't stand it any more. 'Abby.'

'What?'

He took the tin of coffee from her and put it on the worktop, then drew her into his arms. 'I missed you.'

'You were only gone a day.'

That bright, breezy tone meant she was trying to hide her feelings. And it gave him hope. 'I still missed you.' He dragged in a breath. 'Forget the coffee. I need to tell you something.'

She went very still. 'Oh?'

Did she really think he was going to let her down again? He pulled back slightly, keeping his arms loosely round her but making sure she could see his eyes. Making sure she had no cause to doubt his sincerity. 'Last night, I tried not to put any pressure on you. But I'm done with trying to be noble. I need you to know the truth. Abigail Scott, you're the love of my life—you always have been, you always will be, and I want to be with you.'

She looked as if she was about to say something, and he gave the tiniest shake of his head. 'Hear me out, because I've been practising this all the way from London and I want to get it right. Five years ago, I was very, very stupid. I thought I was doing the right thing in let-

ting you go in order to find the happiness you deserve
with someone else. But it's the worst thing I ever did
and I've regretted it every single day since. I bury myself in work so I don't have time to realise how empty
my life is without you.

'But I want you back, Abby. I want you and I want
our baby. I want the life we should've had together if I
hadn't gone into meltdown when Dad died. And I don't
want to be a part-time. Actually, I'm scared as hell I'll
make as much of a mess of being a dad as I have of
being a son, a brother and a husband, but I'm going to
do whatever it takes to make this work. I want to be a
full-time family, with you. I know you don't want to
live in London because it's too far away from our family, so I'm moving back to Norfolk.'

She looked utterly shocked. 'But—' she began.

'Hear me out, Abby,' he said again. 'Yes, I love my
job, but I love you more. If it's a choice between you,
then you'll always win. I'm coming home to you.'

'But I don't want to give you an ultimatum, Brad. I
don't want you to give up the job you love.'

'I don't have to,' he said. 'I didn't tell you, but last
year I was headhunted to work for a company in Manchester. I turned it down because my boss gave me more
responsibilities and I wanted to see my current project
through, but I got in touch with the headhunters today
to see if they had anything else available.'

'Did they?' She looked hopeful.

'No,' he said, 'but my boss trained with someone who
runs a lab in Norwich, and he's put in a good word for
me. It's not absolutely definite, and there are no guaran-
tees I'll get the job, but they're ringing me on Monday
to arrange an interview. It'll be a mix of lab work and

teaching postgraduate students, which suits me fine. Plus my hours will be reasonable and it'll be only a forty-minute commute from here—that's less time than it takes me to get to my lab now. Even if they don't offer me the job, then I can find something. The main thing is I'll be here with you.' He took a deep breath. 'The first time I asked you this question, I pretty much knew the answer before I asked.' The second time, she'd said no. Would this be third time lucky? 'This time, I don't. It scares the hell out of me that you'll say the words I don't want to hear, but even if you do I'll be here for you and the baby. That's not going to change.' He swallowed hard, then dropped to one knee in front of her. 'I love you, Abby. I always will. Will you marry me and make a family with me and our baby?'

He loved her.

Loved her enough to put her before the job she thought was his life.

And he was telling her that she could have it all. She didn't have to wrench herself away from their family, she didn't have to give up her job to follow him—this time, he was making the changes. He'd found a compromise that would work for both of them. And he wanted to marry her again.

All she had to do was say yes.

'You shouldn't have to do all the compromising,' she said.

'You did all the compromising last time,' he said. 'So I think it's my turn.'

'Not necessarily,' she said. 'Maybe I could open a branch of Scott's in Norwich and run all the admin from there. Then you wouldn't have such a long commute.'

He coughed. 'Abby, that was a yes or no question. And you're killing me, making me wait for the answer. I'm not promising you perfection, because I'm only human. But I'll try my hardest not to let you down again. To be a much better husband than I was before and a good dad. I love you. Nobody else has ever come close to making me feel the way I feel about you.' He looked up at her, his eyes dark and beseeching. 'Will you marry me again? Make a family with me and our baby?'

She took his hand and drew him to his feet. 'I love you, too. Always have and always will. Yes, I'll marry you.'

He wrapped his arms round her and kissed her lingeringly. 'I was so scared you'd say no.'

'I never have been able to resist you, Brad. But it took me a long while to pick myself up again when you filed for divorce.'

'It was the worst mistake of my life,' he said. 'No more hair shirts and no more white chargers.'

'Agreed.' She paused. 'Though, this time round, I think we owe our family the party we deprived them of last time.'

'Absolutely.'

'And your sister gets to be my bridesmaid.' She smiled. 'And we pour a glass of champagne on your dad's grave so Jim gets to share it, too.'

'I'd like that.' He kissed her. 'All that time we wasted… We've got some making up to do.'

She grinned as he scooped her up into his arms and carried her out of the kitchen. 'I thought you'd never ask…'

EPILOGUE

A year later

'OK. YOU'RE DONE,' Gina, the hairdresser, said with a smile.

Abby looked at her reflection. 'I can barely believe this is me.'

'Wait until you've got the dress and shoes on,' Ruby said.

'Mummy looks amazing, doesn't she, Jessie?' Annie said, cuddling her granddaughter.

The baby gurgled, as if to agree, and everyone smiled.

Ruby helped Abby into her dress, straightened her veil and then stood back. 'Wow. You look amazing.'

Abby's dress was cream, with a full-length tulle skirt, and a bodice of raw silk with a spray of roses across it.

'So do you,' Abby said. Ruby's dress was similar to Abby's, but in duck-egg blue.

Ruby hugged her. 'I'm so thrilled to be getting my sister back. Not that I ever didn't see you as my sister. And I still can't believe you got back together with Brad at my wedding.'

'Contagious things, weddings,' Abby said with a grin, and hugged her back.

There was a knock on the door. 'Am I allowed in?' Stuart asked.

'Sure. It's just the bridegroom who's not allowed,' Ruby said.

Stuart came in with a large box. 'Flowers.'

Both Abby and Ruby had simple bouquets of cream roses and there was also a single red rose from Brad.

I love you and I can't wait to marry you.

Abby blinked away the tears. She couldn't wait to marry him, too.

'You look beautiful, love,' Stuart said. 'Let's go downstairs and have a glass of champagne while we're waiting for the cars. And I need a cuddle from this young lady here.' He scooped Jessica from his wife's arms and blew a raspberry at the baby, who chuckled and waved her hands in glee.

Once the cars had arrived and Annie, Jessica and Ruby had left, Stuart looked at his daughter. 'You and Brad seem settled,' he said quietly, 'but I need to know you're sure about this.'

'Absolutely sure,' Abby said. 'This is the wedding we should have had, the first time round—and this time it's for keeps.'

The first part of their wedding was a very small register office do, with just their immediate family attending; and then Brad kissed Abby. 'I love you,' he said. 'And this time our marriage is for keeps.'

'For keeps,' she agreed.

And then they headed to the church for the blessing, where the rest of their family and friends were waiting.

Brad waited at the top of the aisle. He turned round as the organist began to play the traditional 'Wedding March', to see Abby walking towards him. She was even more beautiful now than she'd been ten years ago when they had first married; and as she walked towards him he felt as if his whole body was bubbling with sheer happiness.

Although the blessing didn't involve an exchange of rings or giving away of the bride, they'd discussed the service with the vicar to make it feel as much like a wedding as possible, with Stuart and Rosie reading Shakespeare and Elizabeth Barrett Browning respectively, hymns, flowers and the church bell pealing as they walked back down the aisle after the service.

Everyone threw the bird-friendly confetti at them, and then while the photographer was organising some of the group shots they went to James's grave and poured a glass of champagne next to his headstone.

'I know you're here with us today in spirit, Jim,' Abby said. 'And I promise you I'll love your son for ever.'

'Sorry we eloped, the first time round,' Brad said. 'We're doing it right, this time. Sharing with our family and friends, the way we should've done last time.'

After the photographs had finished, they headed for the hotel—the one where they'd gone to the prom together and kissed for the very first time, because they'd both agreed that was the right place to hold their wedding breakfast.

And Brad felt happier than he'd ever thought possible

as he sat at the table with his four-month-old daughter asleep on his lap, the love of his life next to him, and their family and friends surrounding them.

This time, they were doing it right.

Stuart kicked off the speeches after the meal, as the father of the bride. 'Welcome, everyone,' he said. 'I'm pleased to say that this time Abigail and Bradley didn't run off to Gretna Green—but I guess that's harder to do when you have a baby.' Everyone laughed. 'I'm going to keep this short, and say I'm delighted to welcome Brad back into the family, where he's always belonged,' Stuart said. 'Please raise your glasses to the bride and groom, Abby and Brad.'

'Abby and Brad,' everyone chorused.

Brad couldn't quite bear to wake Jessica by transferring her to his wife's arms, so he stood up and gave his speech with his daughter in his arms. 'I'd like to thank everyone for coming, and as Stuart said this time we didn't run off to Gretna Green. Actually, it wasn't so much because of Jessica, because she's happy to go anywhere, but we didn't think you'd forgive us for depriving you of a party for the second time.'

There were claps and hoots and cheers.

'Ten years on, we're both older and wiser—at least, I think we are,' Brad continued. 'I would like to thank Stuart, Annie, Mum and George for all their help over the wedding arrangements and for being wonderful grandparents; and I'd like to thank my twin Ruby for being the best bridesmaid ever. And I'd like you all to raise a glass to my gorgeous bride, Mrs Abby Powell— I'm so proud of her. For most people, moving house or having a baby or opening a new branch of the family business in a different town would be quite enough to do in a year. Not for my new wife, because she's done all three—and she was named local businesswoman of the year, last week. She's brilliant. And I'm very lucky she agreed to marry me again.' He lifted his glass. 'To Abby.'

'To Abby,' everyone echoed.

Colin stood up next. 'I'm absolutely thrilled that my brother-in-law chose me as best man. I knew he actually wanted his sister as his best woman, but his bride called first dibs on her, so he was pretty much stuck with me. So I'm going to keep it short and sweet—please raise your glasses to the bride and groom, Abby and Brad.'

And then Abby stood up. 'I'd like to thank you all for coming today. This is the wedding we probably should have given you last time, and I think it's fitting that we're celebrating here because this is the place where Brad and I first danced together at the school prom—he kissed me for the very first time in the rose garden here. I'd like to thank my parents for being brilliantly supportive about me moving some of the family business to Norwich, my parents again and Rosie and George for being wonderful grandparents and excellent babysitters, and Ruby—well, she never actually stopped being my sister as far as I was concerned, but it's nice for it to be official again. To Jessica, for being the sweetest-tempered baby in the world; to Jim, who I'm very sure is here with us in spirit; and most of all to Brad, the love of my life, for finding a compromise so we both won.' She smiled. 'Now we're done with all the talking bits—let's get this party started!'

Jessica was scooped up by Rosie. 'Go and have the first dance,' she said, shooing Brad and Abby onto the dance floor.

They walked into the centre, and the band started to play the song that Brad had danced to with Abby for the very first time, at the school prom: 'Make You Feel My Love.'

'We did it right, this time,' he said softly as they began to dance. 'Celebrating with all our family and friends—including our little girl.'

'Three magpies,' she said.

He smiled. 'The old superstition turned out to be right. And I'm the luckiest man on earth. Thank you for giving me a second chance.'

'This time,' she said, 'it's for keeps. You and me. Always.'

'Always,' he said, and kissed her.

* * * * *

DETECTIVE
BARELLI'S
LEGENDARY
TRIPLETS

MELISSA SENATE

Dedicated to my darling Max.

Chapter One

The first thing Norah Ingalls noticed when she woke up Sunday morning was the gold wedding band on her left hand.

Norah was not married. Had never been married. She was as single as single got. With seven-month-old triplets.

The second thing was the foggy headache pressing at her temples.

The third thing was the very good-looking stranger lying next to her.

A memory poked at her before panic could even bother setting in. Norah lay very still, her heart just beginning to pound, and looked over at him. He had short, thick, dark hair and a hint of five-o'clock shadow along his jawline. A scar above his left eyebrow. He

was on his back, her blue-and-white quilt half covering him down by his belly button. An innie. He had an
impressive six-pack. Very little chest hair. His biceps
and triceps were something to behold. The man clearly
worked out. Or was a rancher.

Norah bolted upright. Oh God. Oh God. Oh God. He
wasn't a rancher. He was a secret service agent! She remembered now. Yes. They'd met at the Wedlock Creek
Founder's Day carnival last night and—

And had said no real names, no real stories, no real
anything. A fantasy for the night. That had been her
idea. She'd insisted, actually.

The man in her bed was not a secret service agent.
She had no idea who or what he was.

She swallowed against the lump in her parched
throat.

She squeezed her eyes shut. What happened? *Think,
Norah!*

There'd been lots of orange punch. And giggling,
when Norah was not a giggler. The man had said something about how the punch must be spiked.

Norah bit her lower lip hard and looked for the man's
left hand. It was under the quilt. Her grandmother's
hand-me-down quilt.

She sucked in a breath and peeled back the quilt
enough to reveal his hand. The same gold band glinted
on his ring finger.

As flashes of memories from the night before started
shoving into her aching head, Norah eased back down,
lay very still and hoped the man wouldn't wake before
she remembered how she'd ended up married to a total

stranger. The fireworks display had started behind the Wedlock Creek chapel and everything between her and the man had exploded, too. Norah closed her eyes and let it all come flooding back.

A silent tester burst of the fireworks display, red and white just visible through the treetops, started when she and Fabio were on their tenth cup of punch at the carnival. The big silver punch bowl had been on an un-manned table near the food booths. Next to the stack of plastic cups was a lockbox with a slot and a sign atop it: Two Dollars A Cup/Honor System. Fabio had put a hundred-dollar bill in the box and taken the bowl and their cups under a maple tree, where they'd been sitting for the past half hour, enjoying their punch and talk-ing utter nonsense.

Not an hour earlier Norah's mother and aunt Chey-enne had insisted she go enjoy the carnival and that they'd babysit the triplets. She'd had a corn dog, won a little stuffed dolphin in a balloon-dart game, which she'd promptly lost somewhere, and then had met the very handsome newcomer to town at the punch table.

"Punch?" he'd said, handing her a cup and putting a five-dollar bill in the box. He'd then ladled himself a cup.

She drank it down. Delicious. She put five dollars in herself and ladled them both two more cups.

"Never seen you before," she said, daring a glance up and down his six-foot-plus frame. Muscular and lanky at the same time. Navy Henley and worn jeans and cowboy boots. Silky, dark hair and dark eyes. She could look, but she'd never touch. No sirree.

He extended his hand. "I'm—"

She held up her own, palm facing him. "Nope. No real names. No real stories." She was on her own tonight, rarely had a moment to herself, and if she was going to talk to a man, a handsome, sexy, no-ring-on-his-finger man—something she'd avoided since becoming a mother—a little fantasy was in order. Norah didn't date and had zero interest in romance. Her mother, aunt and sister always shook their heads at that and tried to remind her that her faith in love, and maybe herself, had been shaken, that was all, and she'd come around. That was all? Ha. She was done with men with a capital *D*.

He smiled, his dark brown eyes crinkling at the corners. Early thirties, she thought. And handsome as sin. "In that case, I'm…Fabio. A…secret service agent. That's right. Fabio the secret service agent. Protecting the fresh air here in Wedlock Creek."

She giggled for way too long at that one. Jeez, was there something in the punch? Had to be. When was the last time she'd giggled? "Kind of casually dressed for a Fed," she pointed out, admiring his scuffed brown boots.

"Gotta blend," he said, waving his arm at the throngs of people out enjoying the carnival.

"Ah, that makes sense. Well, I'm Angelina, international flight attendant." Where had *that* come from? Angelina had a sexy ring to it, she thought. She picked up a limp fry from the plate he'd gotten from the burger booth across the field. She dabbed it in the ketchup on the side and dangled it in her mouth.

"You manage to make that sexy," he said with a grin.

Norah Ingalls, single mother of drooling, teething triplets, sexy? LOL. Ha. That was a scream. She giggled again and he tipped up her face and looked into her eyes.

Kiss me, you fool, she thought. *You Fabio. You secret service agent.* But his gaze was soft on her, not full of lascivious intent. Darn.

That was when he suggested they sit, gestured at the maple tree, then put the hundred in the lockbox and took the bowl over to their spot. She carried their cups.

"Have more punch," she said, ladling him a cup. And another. And another. He told her stories from his childhood, mostly about an old falling-down ranch on a hundred acres, but she wasn't sure what was true and what wasn't. She told him about her dad, who'd been her biggest champion. She told him the secret recipe for her mother's chicken pot pie, which was so renowned in Wedlock Creek and surrounding towns that the *Gazette* had done an article on her family's pie diner. She told him everything but the most vital truth about herself.

Tonight, Norah was a woman out having fun at the annual carnival, allowing herself for just pumpkin-hours to bask in the attention of a good-looking, sexy man who was sweet and smart and funny as hell. At midnight—well, 11:00 p.m. when the carnival closed— she'd turn back into herself. A woman who didn't talk to hot, single men.

"What do you think the punch is spiked with?" she

asked as he fed her a cold french fry and poured her another cup.

He ran two fingers gently down the side of her cheek. "I don't know, but it sure is nice to forget myself, just for a night when I'm not on duty."

Duty? *Oh, right*, she thought. He was a secret service agent. She giggled, then sobered for a second, a poke of real life jabbing at her from somewhere.

Now the first booms of the fireworks were coming fast and there were cheers and claps in the distance, but they couldn't see the show from their spot.

"Let's go see!" she said, taking his hand to pull him up.

But Fabio's expression had changed. He seemed lost in thought, far away.

"Fabio?" she asked, trying to think through the haze. "You okay?"

He downed another cup of punch. "Those were fireworks," he said, color coming back into his face. "Not gunfire."

She laughed. "Gunfire? In Wedlock Creek? There's no hunting within town limits because of the tourism and there hasn't been a murder in over seventy years. Plus, if you crane your neck, you can see a bit of the fireworks past the trees."

He craned that beautiful neck, his shoulder leaning against hers. "Okay. Let's go see."

They walked hand in hand to the chapel, but by the time they got there—a few missed turns on the path due to their tipsiness—the fireworks display was over.

The small group setting them off had already left the dock, folks clearing away back to the festival.

The Wedlock Creek chapel was all lit up, the river behind it illuminated by the glow of the almost full moon.

"I always dreamed of getting married here," she said, gazing up at the beautiful white-clapboard building, which looked a bit like a wedding cake. It had a vintage Victorian look with scallops on the upper tiers and a bell at the top that almost looked like a heart. According to town legend, those who married here would—whether through marriage, adoption, luck, science or happenstance—be blessed with multiples: twins or triplets or even quadruplets. So far, no quintuplets. The town and county was packed with multiples of those who'd gotten married at the chapel, proof the legend was true.

For some people, like Norah, you could have triplets and not have stepped foot in the chapel. Back when she'd first found out she was pregnant, before she'd told the baby's father, she'd fantasized about getting married at the chapel, that maybe they'd get lucky and have multiples even if it was "after the fact." One baby would be blessing enough. Two, three, even four—Norah loved babies and had always wanted a houseful. But the guy who'd gotten her pregnant, in town on the rodeo circuit, had said, "Sorry, I didn't sign up for that," and left town before his next event. She'd never seen him again.

She stared at the chapel, so pretty in the moonlight, real life jabbing her in the heart again. *Where is that punch bowl?* she wondered.

"You always wanted to marry here? Then let's get married," Fabio said, scooping her up and carrying her into the chapel.

Her laughter floated on the summer evening breeze. "But we're three sheets to the wind, as my daddy used to say."

"That's the only way I'd get hitched," he said, slurring the words.

"Lead the way, cowboy." She let her head drop back.

Annie Potterowski, the elderly chapel caretaker, local lore lecturer and wedding officiant, poked her head out of the back room. She stared at Norah for a moment, then her gaze moved up to Fabio's handsome face. "Ah, Detective Barelli! Nice to see you again."

"You know Fabio?" Norah asked, confused. Or was his first name really Detective?

"I ran into the chief when he was showing Detective Barelli around town," Annie said. "The chief's my second cousin on my mother's side."

Say that five times fast, Norah thought, her head beginning to spin.

And Annie knew her fantasy man. Her fantasy groom! *Isn't that something*, Norah thought, her mind going in ten directions. Suddenly the faces of her triplets pushed into the forefront of her brain and she frowned. Her babies! She should be getting home. Except she felt so good in his arms, being carried like she was someone's love, someone's bride-to-be.

Annie's husband, Abe, came out, his blue bow tie a bit crooked. He straightened it. "We've married sixteen couples tonight. One pair came as far as Texas to get hitched here."

"We're here to be the seventeenth," Fabio said, his arm heavy around Norah's.

"Aren't you a saint!" Annie said, beaming at him. "Oh, Norah, I'm so happy for you."

Saint Fabio, Norah thought and burst into laughter. "Want to know a secret?" Norah whispered into her impending husband's ear as he set her on the red velvet carpet that created an aisle to the altar.

"Yes," he said.

"My name isn't really Angelina. It's Norah. With an *h*."

He smiled. "Mine's not Fabio. It's Reed. Two *e*'s." He staggered a bit.

The man was as tipsy as she was.

"I never thought I'd marry a secret service agent," she said as they headed down the aisle to the "Wedding March."

"And we could use all your frequent flyer miles for our honeymoon," Reed added, and they burst into laughter.

"Sign here, folks," Annie said as they stood at the altar. The woman pointed to the marriage license. Norah signed, then Reed, and Annie folded it up and put it in an addressed, stamped envelope.

I'm getting married! Norah thought, gazing into Reed's dark eyes as he stood across from her, holding her hands. She glanced down at herself, confused by her shorts and blue-and-white T-shirt. Where was her strapless, lace, princess gown with the beading and sweetheart neckline she'd fantasized about from watching *Say Yes to the Dress*? And should she be getting married in her beat-up slip-on sneakers? They were hardly white anymore.

But there was no time to change. Nope. Annie was already asking Reed to repeat his vows and she wanted to pay attention.

"Do you, Reed Barelli, take this woman, Norah Ingalls, to be your lawfully wedded wife, for richer and for poorer, in sickness and in health, till death do you part?"

"I most certainly do," he said, then hooted in laughter.

Norah cracked up, too. Reed had the most marvelous laugh.

Annie turned to Norah. She repeated her vows. Yes, God, yes, she took this man to be her lawfully wedded husband.

"By the power vested in me by the State of Wyoming, I now pronounce you husband and wife! You may kiss your bride."

Reed stared at Norah for a moment, then put his hands on either side of her face and kissed her, so tenderly, yet passionately, that for a second, Norah's mind cleared completely and all she felt was his love. Her new husband of five seconds, whom she'd known for about two hours, truly loved her!

Warmth flooded her, and when rice, which she realized Abe was throwing, rained down on them, she giggled, drunk as a skunk.

Reed Barelli registered his headache before he opened his eyes, the morning sun shining through the

sheer white curtains at the window. Were those em-
broidered flowers? he wondered as he rubbed his aching temples. Reed had bought a bunch of stuff for his
new house yesterday afternoon—everything from down
pillows to coffee mugs to a coffee maker itself, but he
couldn't remember those frilly curtains. They weren't
something he'd buy for his place.

He fully opened his eyes, his gaze landing on a stack
of books on the bedside table. A mystery. A travel guide
to Wyoming. And *Your Baby's First Year.*

Your Baby's First Year? Huh?

Wait a minute. He bolted up. Where the hell was he?
This wasn't the house he'd rented.

He heard a soft sigh come from beside him and
turned to the left, eyes widening.

Holy hell. There was a woman sleeping in his bed.

More like he was in *her* bed, from the looks of the
place. He moved her long reddish-brown hair out of her
face and closed his eyes. Oh Lord. Oh no. It was her—
Angelina slash Norah. Last night he'd given in to her
game of fantasy, glad for a night to eradicate his years
as a Cheyenne cop.

He blinked twice to clear his head. He wasn't a Cheyenne cop anymore. His last case had done him in and,
after a three-week leave, he'd made up his mind and
gotten himself a job as a detective in Wedlock Creek,
the idyllic town where he'd spent several summers as
a kid with his maternal grandmother. A town where it
seemed nothing could go wrong. A town that hadn't
seen a murder in over seventy years. Hadn't Norah mentioned that last night?

Norah. Last night.

He lifted his hand to scrub over his face and that was when he saw it—the gold ring on his left hand. Ring finger. A ring that hadn't been there before he'd gone to the carnival.

What the…?

Slowly, bits and pieces of the evening came back to him. The festival. A punch bowl he'd commandeered into the clearing under a big tree so he and Norah could have the rest of it all to themselves. A clearly heavily *spiked* punch bowl. A hundred-dollar bill in the till, not to mention at least sixty in cash. Norah, taking his hand and leading him to the chapel.

She'd always dreamed of getting married, she'd said.

And he'd said, "Then let's get married."

He'd said that! Reed Barelli had uttered those words!

He held his breath and gently peeled the blue-and-white quilt from her shoulder to look at her left hand—which she used to yank the quilt back up, wrinkling her cute nose and turning over.

There was a gold band on her finger, too.

Holy moly. They'd really done it. They'd gotten married?

No. Couldn't be. The officiant of the chapel had called him by name. Yes, the elderly woman had known him, said she'd seen the chief showing him around town yesterday when he'd arrived. And she'd seemed familiar with Norah, too. She knew both of them. She wouldn't let them drunk-marry! That was the height of irresponsible. And as a man of the law, he would demand she explain herself and simply undo whatever it was they'd signed. Dimly, he recalled the marriage license, scrawling his name with a blue pen.

Norah stirred. She was still asleep. For a second he couldn't help but stare at her pretty face. She had a pale complexion, delicate features and hazel eyes, if he remembered correctly.

If they'd made love, *that* he couldn't remember. And he would remember, drunk to high heaven or not. What had been in that punch?

Maybe they'd come back to her place and passed out in bed?

He closed his eyes again and slowly opened them. *Deep breaths, Barelli.* He looked around the bedroom to orient himself, ground himself.

And that was when he saw the framed photograph on the end table on Norah's side. Norah in a hospital bed, in one of those thin blue gowns, holding three newborns against her chest.

Ooh boy.

Chapter Two

"I'm sure we're not really married!" Norah said on a high-pitched squeak, the top sheet wrapped around her as she stood—completely freaked out—against the wall of her bedroom, staring at the strange man in her bed.

A man who, according to the wedding ring on her left hand—and the one on his—*was* her husband.

She'd pretended to be asleep when he'd first started stirring. He'd bolted upright and she could feel him staring at her. She couldn't just lie there and pretend to be asleep any longer, even if she was afraid to open her eyes and face the music.

But a thought burst into her brain and she'd sat up, too: she'd forgotten to pick up the triplets. As her aunt's words had come back to her, that Cheyenne didn't expect her to pick up the babies last night, that she'd take them to the diner this morning, Norah had calmed down. And slowly had opened her eyes. The sight of the stranger awake and staring at her had her leaping out of bed, taking the sheet with her. She was in a camisole and underwear.

Oh God, had they...?

She stared at Reed. In her bed. "Did we?" she croaked out.

He half shrugged. "I don't know. Sorry. I don't think so, though."

"The punch was spiked?"

"Someone's idea of a joke, maybe."

"And now we're married," she said. "Ha ha."

His gaze went to the band of gold on his finger, then back at her. "I'm sure we can undo that. The couple who married us—they seemed to know both of us. Why would they have let us get married when we were so drunk?"

Now it was her turn to shrug. She'd known Annie since she was born. The woman had waitressed on and off at her family's pie diner for years to make extra cash. How could she have let Norah do such a thing? Why hadn't Annie called her mother or aunt or sister and said, *Come get Norah, she's drunk off her butt and trying to marry a total stranger*? It made no sense that Annie hadn't done just that!

"She seemed to know you, too," Norah said, wishing she had a cup of coffee. And two Tylenol.

"I spent summers in Wedlock Creek with my grandmother when I was a kid," he said. "Annie may have known my grandmother. Do the Potterowskis live near the chapel? Maybe we can head over now and get this straightened out. I'm sure Annie hasn't sent in the marriage license yet."

"Right!" Norah said, brightening, tightening the sheet around her. "We can undo this! Let's go!"

He glanced at his pile of clothes on the floor beside the bed. "I'll go into the bathroom and get dressed." He stood, wearing nothing but incredibly sexy black boxer briefs. He picked up the pile and booked into the bathroom, shutting the door.

She heard the water run, then shut off. A few minutes later the door opened and there he was, dressed like Fabio from last night.

She rushed over to her dresser, grabbed jeans and a T-shirt and fresh underwear, then sped past him into the bathroom, her heart beating like a bullet train. She quickly washed her face and brushed her teeth, got dressed and stepped back outside.

Reed was sitting in the chair in the corner, his elbows on his knees, his head in his hands. How could he look so handsome when he was so rumpled, his hair all mussed? He was slowly shaking his head as if trying to make sense of this.

"So you always wanted to be a secret service agent?" she asked to break the awkward silence.

He sat up and offered something of a smile. "I have no idea why I said that. I've always wanted to be a cop. I start at the Wedlock Creek PD on Monday. Guess you're not a flight attendant," he added.

"I've never been out of Wyoming," she said. "I bake for my family's pie diner." That was all she'd ever wanted to do. Work for the family business and perfect her savory pies, her specialty.

The diner had her thinking of real life again, Bella's, Bea's and Brody's beautiful little faces coming to mind. She missed them and needed to see them, needed to hold them. And she had to get to the diner and let her family know she was all right. She hadn't called once to check in on the triplets last night. Her mom and aunt had probably mentioned that every hour on the hour. *No call from Norah? Huh. Must be having a good time.* Then looking at each other and saying *Not* in unison, bursting into laughter and sobering up fast, wondering what could have happened to her to prevent her from calling every other minute to make sure all was well with the babies.

Her phone hadn't rung last night, so maybe they'd just thought she'd met up with old friends and was having fun. She glanced at her alarm clock on the bedside table. It was barely six o'clock. She wouldn't be expected at the diner until seven.

Reed was looking at the photo next to the clock. The one of her and her triplets taken moments after they were born. He didn't say a word, but she knew what he was thinking. Anyone would. *Help me. Get me out of this. What the hell have I done? Triplets? Ahhhhh!* She was surprised he didn't have his hands on his screaming face like the kid from the movie *Home Alone.*

Well, one thing Norah Ingalls was good at? Taking care of business. "Let's go see Annie and Abe," she said. "They wake up at the crack of dawn, so I'm sure they'll be up."

His gaze snapped back to hers. "Good idea. We can catch them before they send the marriage license into the state bureau for processing."

"Right. It's not like we're really married. I mean, it's not *legal*."

He nodded. "We could undo this before 7:00 a.m. and get back to our lives," he said.

This was definitely not her life.

Norah poked her head out the front door of her house, which, thank heavens, was blocked on both sides by big leafy trees. The last thing she needed was for all of Wedlock Creek to know a man had been spotted leaving her house at six in the morning. Norah lived around the corner from Main Street and just a few minutes' walk to the diner, but the chapel was a good half mile in the other direction.

"Let's take the parallel road so no one sees us," she said. "I'm sure you don't want to be the center of gossip before you even start your first day at the police station."

"I definitely don't," he said.

They ducked down a side street with backyards to the left and the woods and river to the right. At this early hour, no one was out yet. The Potterowskis lived in the caretaker's cottage to the right of the chapel. Norah dashed up the steps to the side door and could see eighty-one-year-old Annie in a long, pink chenille bathrobe, sitting down with tea and toast. She rang the bell.

Annie came to the door and beamed at the newlyweds. "Norah! Didn't expect to see you out and about so early. Shouldn't you be on your honeymoon?" Annie peered behind Norah and spied Reed. "Ah, there you are, handsome devil. Come on in, you two. I just made a pot of coffee."

How could the woman be so calm? Or act like their getting married was no big deal?

Norah and Reed came in but didn't sit. "Annie," Norah said, "the two of us were the victims of spiked punch at the festival last night! We were drunk out of our minds. You had to know that!"

Annie tilted her head, her short, wiry, silver curls bouncing. "Drunk? Why, I don't recall seeing you two acting all nutty and, trust me, we get our share of drunk couples and turn them away."

Norah narrowed her eyes. There was no way Annie hadn't known she was drunk out of her mind! "Annie, why would I up and marry a total stranger out of the blue? Didn't that seem weird?"

"But Reed isn't a stranger," Annie said, sipping her coffee. "I heard he was back in town to work at the PD." She turned to him. "I remember you when you were a boy. I knew your grandmother Lydia Barelli. We were dear friends from way back. Oh, how I remember her hoping you'd come live in Wedlock Creek. I suppose now you'll move to the ranch like she always dreamed."

Reed raised an eyebrow. "I've rented a house right in town. I loved my grandmother dearly, but she was trying to bribe me into getting married and starting a family. I had her number, all right." He smiled at Annie, but his chin was lifted. The detective was clearly assessing the situation.

Annie waved her hand dismissively. "Well, bribe or not, you're married. Your dear grandmother's last will and testament leaves you the ranch when you marry. So now you can take your rightful inheritance."

Norah glanced from Annie to Reed. What was all this about a ranch and an inheritance? If Reed had intended to find some drunk fool to marry to satisfy the terms and get his ranch, why would he have rented a house his first day in town?

The detective crossed his arms over his chest. "I have no intention of moving to the ranch, Annie."

"Oh, hogwash!" Annie said, waving her piece of toast. "You're married and that's it. You should move to the ranch like your grandmamma intended, and poor Norah here will have a father for the triplets."

Good golly. Watch out for little old ladies with secret agendas. Annie Potterowski had hoodwinked them both!

Norah watched Reed swallow. And felt her cheeks burn.

"Annie," Norah said, hands on hips. "You did know we were drunk! You let us marry anyway!"

"For your own good," Annie said. "Both of you. But I didn't lure you two here. I didn't spike the punch. You came in here of your own free will. I just didn't stop you."

"Can't you arrest her for this?" Norah said to Reed, narrowing her eyes at Annie again.

Annie's eyes widened. "I hope you get a chance to leave town and go somewhere exotic for your honeymoon," she said, clearly trying to change the subject from her subterfuge. "New York City maybe. Or how about Paris? It's so romantic."

Norah threw up her hands. "She actually thinks this is reasonable!"

"Annie, come on," Reed said. "We're not *really* married. A little too much spiked punch, a wedding chapel right in our path, no waiting period required—a recipe for disaster and we walked right into it. We're here to get back the marriage license. Surely you haven't sent it in."

"We'll just rip it up and be on our way," Norah said, glancing at her watch.

"Oh dear. I'm sorry, but that's impossible," Annie said. "I sent Abe to the county courthouse in Brewer about twenty minutes ago. I'm afraid your marriage license—and the sixteen others from yesterday—are well on their way to being deposited. There's a mail slot right in front of the building. Of course, it's Sunday and they're closed, so I reckon you won't be able to drive over to try to get it back."

Reed was staring at Annie with total confusion on his face. "Well, we'll have to do something at some point."

"Yeah," Norah agreed, her head spinning. Between all the spiked punch and the surprise this morning of the wedding rings, and now what appeared to be this crazy scheme of Annie's to not undo what she'd allowed to happen…

"I need coffee," Reed said, shaking his head. "A vat of coffee."

Norah nodded. "Me, too."

"Help yourself," Annie said, gesturing at the coffee-pot on the counter as she took a bite of her toast.

Reed sighed and turned to Norah. "Let's go back to your house and talk this through. We need to make a plan for how to undo this."

Norah nodded. "See you, Annie," she said as she headed to the door, despite how completely furious she was with the woman. She'd known Annie all her life and the woman had been nothing but kind to her. Annie had even brought each triplet an adorable stuffed bas-set hound, her favorite dog, when they'd been born, and had showered them with little gifts ever since.

"Oh, Norah? Reed?" Annie called as they opened the door and stepped onto the porch.

Norah turned back around.

"Congratulations," the elderly officiant said with a sheepish smile and absolute mirth glowing in her eyes.

Reed had been so fired up when he'd left Norah's house for the chapel that he hadn't realized how chilly it was this morning, barely fifty-five degrees. He glanced over at Norah; all she wore was a T-shirt and her hands were jammed in her pockets as she hunched over a bit. She was cold. He took off his jacket and slipped it around Norah's shoulders.

She started and stared down at the jacket. "Thank you," she said, slipping her arms into it and zipping it up. "I was so out of my mind before, I forgot to grab a sweater." She turned to stare at him. "Of course, now you'll be cold."

"My aching head will keep me warm," he said. "And I deserve the headache—the literal and figurative one."

"We both do," she said gently.

The breeze moved a swath of her hair in her face, the sun illuminating the red and gold highlights, and he had the urge to sweep it back, but she quickly tucked it behind her ear. "I'm a cop. It's my job to serve and protect. I had no business getting drunk, particularly at a town event."

"Well, the punch was spiked with something very strong. And you weren't on duty," she pointed out. "You're not even on the force till tomorrow."

"Still, a cop is always a cop. Unfortunately, by the time I realized the punch had to be spiked, I was too affected by it to care." He wouldn't put himself in a position like that again. Leaving Cheyenne, saying yes to Wedlock Creek—even though it meant he couldn't live in his grandmother's ranch—trying to switch off the city cop he'd been… He'd let down his guard and he'd paid for it with this crazy nonsense. So had Norah.

Damn. Back in Cheyenne, his guard had been so up he'd practically gotten himself killed during a botched stakeout. Where the hell was the happy medium? Maybe he'd never get a handle on *just right*.

"And you said you were glad to forget? Or something like that?" she asked, darting a glance at him.

He looked out over a stand of heavy trees along the side of the road. *Let it go*, he reminded himself. No re-hashing, no what-ifs. "I'm here for a fresh start. Now I need a fresh start to my fresh start." He stopped and shook his head. What a mess. "Sixteen couples besides us?" he said, resuming walking. "It's a little too easy to get married in the state of Wyoming."

"Someone should change the law," Norah said. "There should be a waiting period. Blood tests required. Something, anything, so you can't get insta-married."

That was for sure. "It's like a mini Las Vegas. I wonder how many of those couples meant to get married."

"Oh, I'm sure all of them. The Wedlock Creek Wedding Chapel is famous. People come here because of the legend."

He glanced at her. "What legend?"

"Just about everyone who marries at the chapel becomes the parent of multiples in some way, shape or form. According to legend, the chapel has a special blessing on it. A barren witch cast the spell the year the chapel was built in 1895."

Reed raised an eyebrow. "A barren witch? Was she trying to be nice or up to no good?"

"No one's sure," she said with a smile. "But as the mother of triplets, I'm glad I have them."

Reed stopped walking.

She'd said it. It was absolutely true. She was the mother of *triplets*. No wonder Annie Potterowski had called him a saint last night. The elderly woman had thought he was knowingly marrying a single mother of three babies! "So you got married at the chapel?" He supposed she was divorced, though that must have been one quick marriage.

She glanced down. "No. I never did get married. The babies' father ran for the hills about an hour after I told him the news. We'd been dating for only about three months at that point. I thought we had something special, but I sure was wrong."

Her voice hitched on the word *wrong* and he took her hand. "I'm sorry." The jerk had abandoned her? She was raising baby triplets on her own? One baby seemed like a handful. Norah had three. He couldn't even imagine how hard that had to be.

She bit her lip and forced a half smile, slipping her hand away and into her pocket. "Oh, that's all right. I have my children, who I love to pieces. I have a great family, work I love. My life is good. No complaints."

"Still, your life can't be easy."

She raised an eyebrow. "Whose is? Yours?"

He laughed. "Touché. And I don't even have a pet. Or a plant for that matter."

She smiled and he was glad to see the shadow leave her eyes. "So, what's our plan for getting back our marriage license? I guess we can just drive out to Brewer first thing in the morning and ask for it back. If we get to the courthouse early and spring on them the minute they open, I'm sure we'll get the license back before it's processed."

"Sounds good," he said.

"And if we can't get it back for whatever reason, we'll just have the marriage annulled."

"Like it never happened," he said.

"Exactly," she said with a nod and smile.

Except it had happened and Reed had a feeling he wouldn't shake it off so easily, even with an annulment and the passage of time. The pair of them had gotten themselves into a real pickle as his grandmother used to say.

"So I guess this means you really didn't secretly marry me to get your hands on your grandmother's ranch," Norah said. "Between renting a house the minute you moved here yesterday and talking about annulments, that's crystal clear."

He thought about telling her why he didn't believe in marriage but just nodded instead. Last night, as he'd picked her up and carried her into that chapel, he'd been a man—Fabio the secret service agent—who *did* believe in marriage, who wanted a wife and a house full of kids. He'd liked being that guy. Of course, with the light of day and the headache and stone-cold reality, he was back to Reed Barelli, who'd seen close up that marriage wasn't for him.

Reed envisioned living alone forever, a couple of dogs to keep him company, short-term relationships with women who understood from the get-go that he wasn't looking for commitment. He'd thought the last woman he'd dated—a funny, pretty woman named Valerie was on the same page, but a few weeks into their relationship, she'd wanted more and he hadn't, and it was a mess. Crying, accusations and him saying over and over *But I told you on the first date how I felt.* That was six months ago and he hadn't dated since. He missed sex like crazy, but he wasn't interested in hurting anyone.

They walked in silence, Norah gesturing that they should cross Main Street. As they headed down Norah's street, Sycamore, he realized they'd made their plan and there was really no need for that coffee, after all. He'd walk her home and then—

"Norah! You're alive!"

Reed glanced in the direction of the voice. A young blond woman stood in front of Norah's small, white Cape Cod house, one hand waving at them and one on a stroller with three little faces peering out.

Three. Little. Faces.

Had a two-by-four come out of nowhere and whammed him upside the head?

Just about everyone who marries at the chapel becomes the parent of multiples in some way, shape or form.

Because he'd just realized that the legend of the Wedlock Creek chapel had come true for him.

Chapter Three

Norah was so relieved to see the babies that she rushed over to the porch—forgetting to shove her hand into her pocket and hide the ring that hadn't been on her finger yesterday.

And her sister, Shelby, wasn't one to miss a thing. Shelby's gaze shifted from the ring on Norah's hand to Reed and his own adorned left hand, then back to Norah. "I dropped by the diner this morning with a Greek quiche I developed last night, and Aunt Cheyenne and Mom said they hadn't heard from you. So I figured I'd walk the triplets over and make sure you were all right." She'd said it all so casually, but her gaze darted hard from the ring on Norah's hand to Norah, then back again. And again. Her sister was dying for info. That was clear.

"I'm all right," Norah said. "Everything is a little topsy-turvy, but I'm fine." She bent over and faced the stroller. "I missed you little darlings." She hadn't spent a night away from her children since they were born.

Shelby gave her throat a little faux clear. "I notice you and this gentleman are wearing matching gold wedding bands and taking walks at 6:30 a.m." Shelby slid her gaze over to Reed and then stared at Norah with her "tell me everything this instant" expression.

Norah straightened and sucked in a deep breath. Thank God her sister was here, actually. Shelby was practical and smart and would have words of wisdom.

"Reed Barelli," Norah said, "this is my sister, Shelby Mercer. Shelby, be the first to meet my accidental husband, Detective Reed Barelli of the Wedlock Creek PD...well, starting tomorrow."

Shelby's green eyes went even wider. She mouthed *What?* to Norah and then said, "Detective, would you mind keeping an eye on the triplets while my sister and I have a little chat?"

Reed eyed the stroller. "Not at all," he said, approaching warily.

Norah opened the door and Shelby pulled her inside. The moment the door closed, Shelby screeched, *"What?"*

Norah covered her face with her hands for a second, shook her head, then launched into the story. "I went to the carnival on Mom and Aunt Cheyenne's orders. The last thing I remember clearly is having a corn dog and winning a stuffed dolphin, which I lost. Then it's just flashes of the night. Reed and I drinking spiked punch—the entire bowl—and going to the chapel and getting married."

"Oh, phew," Shelby said, relief crossing her face. "I thought maybe you flew to Las Vegas or something crazy. There's no way Annie or Abe would have let you get drunk-married to some stranger. I'm sure you just *think* you got married."

"Yeah, we'd figured that, too," Norah said. "We just got back from Annie's house. Turns out she knows Reed from when he spent summers here as a kid. Apparently she was friends with his late grandmother. She called him a saint last night. Annie married us with her blessing! And our marriage license—along with sixteen others—is already at the county courthouse."

"Waaah! Waah!" came a little voice from outside.

"That sounds like Bea," Norah said. "I'd better go help—"

Shelby stuck her arm out in front of the door. "Oh no, you don't, Norah Ingalls. The man is a police officer. The babies are safe with him for a few minutes." She bit her lip. "What are you two going to do?"

Norah shrugged. "I guess if we can't get back the license before it's processed, we'll have to get an annulment."

"The whole thing is nuts," Shelby said. "Jeez, I thought my life was crazy."

Norah wouldn't have thought anything could top what Shelby had been through right before Norah had gotten pregnant. Her sister had discovered her baby and a total stranger's baby had been switched at birth six months after bringing their boys home from the Wedlock Creek Clinic. Shelby and Liam Mercer had gotten married so that they could each have both boys—and along the way they'd fallen madly in love. Now the four of them were a very happy family.

"You know what else is crazy?" Norah said, her voice going shaky. "How special it was. The ceremony, I mean. Me—even in my T-shirt and shorts and grubby slip-on sneakers—saying my vows. Hearing them said back to me. In that moment, Shel, I felt so…safe. For the first time in a year and a half, I felt safe." Tears pricked her eyes and she blinked hard.

She was the woman who didn't want love and romance. Who didn't believe in happily-ever-after anymore. So why had getting married—even to a total stranger—felt so wonderful? And yes, so safe?

"Oh, Norah," her sister said and pulled her into a hug. "I know what you mean."

Norah blew out a breath to get ahold of herself. "I know it wasn't real. But in that moment, when Annie pronounced us husband and wife, the way Reed looked at me and kissed me, being in that famed chapel…it was an old dream come true. Back to reality, though. That's just how life is."

Shelby squeezed her hand. "So, last night, did the new Mr. and Mrs. Barelli…?"

Norah felt her cheeks burn. "I don't know. But if we did, it must have been amazing. You saw the man."

Shelby smiled. "Maybe you can keep him."

Norah shook her head. Twice. "I'm done with men, remember? *Done*."

Shelby let loose her evil smile. "Yes, for all other men, sure. Since you're married now."

Norah swallowed. But then she remembered this wasn't real and would be rectified. Brody let out a wail and once again she snapped back to reality. She was no one's bride, no one's wife. There was a big difference between old dreams and the way things really were. "I'd better go save the detective from the three little screechers."

Norah opened the door and almost gasped at the sight on the doorstep. Brody was in Reed's strong arms, the sleeves of his navy shirt rolled up. He lifted the baby high in the air, then turned to Bea and Bella in the stroller and made a funny face at them before lifting Brody again. "Upsie downsie," Reed said. "Downsie upsie," he added as he lifted Brody again.

Baby laughter exploded on the porch.

Norah stared at Reed and then glanced over at Shelby, who was looking at Reed Barelli in amazement.

"My first partner back in Cheyenne had a baby, and whenever he started fussing, I'd do that and he'd giggle," Reed explained, lifting Brody one more time for a chorus of more triplet giggles.

Bea lifted her arms. Reed put Brody back and did two upsie-downsies with Bea, then her sister.

"I'll let Mom and Aunt Cheyenne know you might not be in today," Shelby said very slowly. She glanced at Reed, positively beaming, much like Annie had done earlier. "I'll be perfectly honest and report you have a headache from the sweet punch."

"Thanks," Norah said. "I'm not quite ready to explain everything just yet."

As her sister said goodbye and walked off in the direction of the diner, Norah appreciated that Shelby hadn't added a "Welcome to the family." She turned back to Reed. He was twisting his wedding ring on his finger.

"So you were supposed to work today?" he asked.

"Yes—and Sundays are one of the busiest at the Pie Diner—but I don't think I'll be able to concentrate. My mom and aunt will be all over me with questions. And now that I think about it, with the festival and carnival continuing today, business should be slow. I'll just make my pot pies here and take them over later, once we're settled on what to say if word gets out."

"Word will get out?" he said. "Oh no—don't tell me Annie and Abe are gossips."

"They're *strategic*," Norah said. "Which is exactly how we ended up married and not sent away last night."

"Meaning they'll tell just enough people, or the right people, to make it hard for us to undo the marriage so easily."

"She probably has a third cousin at the courthouse!" Norah said, throwing up her hands. But town gossip was the least of her problems right now, and boy did she have problems, particularly the one standing across from her looking so damned hot.

She turned from the glorious sight of him and racked her brain, trying to think who she could ask to babysit this morning for a couple hours on such short notice so she could get her pies done and her equilibrium back.

Her family was out of the question, of course. Her sister was busy enough with her own two kids and her secondhand shop to run, plus she often helped out at the diner. There was Geraldina next door, who might be able to take the triplets for a couple of hours, but her neighbor was another huge gossip and maybe she'd seen the two of them return home last night in God knew what state. For all Norah knew, Reed Barelli had carried her down the street like in *An Officer and a Gentleman* and swept her over the threshold of her house.

Huh. Had he?

"You okay?" he asked, peering at her.

Her shoulders slumped. "Just trying to figure out a sitter for the triplets while I make six pot pies. The usual suspects aren't going to work out this morning."

"Consider me at your service, then," he said.

"What?" she said, shaking her head. "I couldn't ask that."

"Least I can do, Norah. I got you into this mess. If I remember correctly, last night you said you'd always wanted to get married at that chapel and I picked you up and said 'Then let's get married.'" He let out a breath. "I still can't quite get over that I did that."

"I like being able to blame it all on you. Thanks." She smiled, grateful that he was so…nice.

"Besides, and obviously, I like babies," he said, "and all I had on my agenda today was re-familiarizing myself with Wedlock Creek."

"Okay, but don't say I didn't try to let you off the hook. Triplet seven-month-olds who are just starting to crawl are pretty wily creatures."

"I've dealt with plenty of wily creatures in my eight-year career as a cop. I've got this."

She raised an eyebrow and opened the door, surprised when Reed took hold of the enormous stroller and wheeled in the babies. She wasn't much used to someone else...being there. "Didn't I hear you tell Annie that you had no intention of ever getting married? I would think that meant you had no intention of having children, either."

"Right on both counts. But I like other people's kids. And babies are irresistible. Besides, yours already adore me."

Brody was sticking up his skinny little arms, smiling at Reed, three little teeth coming up in his gummy mouth.

"See?" he said.

Norah smiled. "Point proven. I'd appreciate the help. So thank you."

Norah closed the door behind Reed. It was the strangest feeling, walking into her home with her three babies—and her brand-new husband.

She glanced at her wedding ring. Then at his.

Talk about crazy. For a man who didn't intend to marry or have kids, he now had one huge family, even if that family would dissolve tomorrow at the courthouse.

As they'd first approached Norah's house on the way back from Annie and Abe's, Reed had been all set to suggest they get in his SUV, babies and all, and find someone, anyone, to open the courthouse. They could root through the mail that had been dumped through the slot, find their license application and just tear it up. Kaput! No more marriage!

But he'd been standing right in front of Norah's door, cute little Brody in his arms, the small, baby-shampoo-smelling weight of him, when he'd heard what Norah had said. Heard it loud and clear. And something inside him had shifted.

You know what else is crazy, how special it was. The ceremony, I mean. Me—even in my T-shirt and shorts and grubby slip-on sneakers—saying my vows. Hearing them said back to me. In that moment, Shel, I felt so... safe. For the first time in a year and a half, I felt safe.

He'd looked at the baby in his arms. The two little girls in the stroller. Then he'd heard Norah say something about a dream come true and back to reality.

His heart had constricted in his chest when she'd said she'd felt safe for the first time since the triplets were born. He'd once overheard his mother say that the only time she felt safe was when Reed was away in Wedlock Creek with his paternal grandmother, knowing her boy was being fed well and looked after.

Reed's frail mother had been alone otherwise, abandoned by Reed's dad during the pregnancy, no child support, no nothing. She'd married again, more for security than love, but that had been short-lived. Not even a year. Turned out the louse couldn't stand kids. His mother had worked two jobs to make ends meet, but times had been tough and Reed had often been alone and on his own.

He hated the thought of Norah feeling that way— unsteady, unsure, alone. This beautiful woman with so much on her shoulders. Three little ones her sole responsibility. And for a moment in the chapel, wed to him, she'd felt safe.

He wanted to help her somehow. Ease her burden. Do what he could. And if that was babysitting for a couple hours while she worked, he'd be more than happy to.

She picked up two babies from the stroller, a pro at balancing them in each arm. "Will you take Bea?" she asked.

He scooped up the baby girl, who immediately grabbed his cheek and stared at him with her huge gray-blue eyes, and followed Norah into the kitchen. A playpen was wedged in a nook. She put the two babies inside and Reed put Bea beside them. They all immediately reached for the little toys.

Norah took an apron from a hook by the refrigerator. "If I were at the diner, I'd be making twelve pot pies—five chicken and three turkey, two beef, and two veggie—but I only have enough ingredients at home to do six—three chicken and three beef. I'll just make them all here and drop them off for baking. The oven in this house can't even cook a frozen pizza reliably."

Reed glanced around the run-down kitchen. It was clean and clearly had been baby-proofed, given the covered electrical outlets. But the refrigerator was strangely loud, the floor sloped and the house just seemed...old. And, he hated to say it, kind of depressing. "Have you lived here long?"

"I moved in a few months after finding out I was pregnant. I'd lived with my mom before then and she wanted me to continue living there, but I needed to grow up. I was going to be a mother—of three—and it was time to make a home. Not turn my mother into a live-in babysitter or take advantage of her generosity. This place was all I could afford. It's small and dated but clean and functional."

"So a kitchen, living room and bathroom down-stairs," he said, glancing into the small living room with the gold-colored couch. Baby stuff was every-where, from colorful foam mats to building blocks and rattling toys. There wasn't a dining room, as far as he could see. A square table was wedged in front of a win-dow with one chair and three high chairs. "How many bedrooms upstairs?"

"Only two. But that works for now. One for me and one for the triplets." She bit her lip. "It's not a palace. It's hardly my dream home. But you do what you have to. I'm their mother and it's up to me to support us."

Everything looked rumpled, secondhand, and it prob-ably was. The place reminded him of his apartment as a kid. His mother hadn't even had her own room. She'd slept on a pull-out couch in the living room and folded it up every morning. She'd wanted so much more for the two of them, but her paycheck had stretched only so far. When he was eighteen, he'd enrolled in the po-lice academy and started college at night, planning to give his mother a better standard of living. But she'd passed away before he could make any of her dreams come true.

A squeal came from the playpen and he glanced over at the triplets. The little guy was chewing on a cloth book, one of the girls was pressing little "piano" keys and the other was babbling and shaking keys.

"Bea's the rabble-rouser," Norah said as she began to sauté chicken breasts in one pan, chunks of beef in another, and then set a bunch of carrots and onions on the counter. "Bella loves anything musical, and Brody is the quietest. He loves to be read to, whereas Bea will start clawing at the pages."

"Really can't be easy raising three babies. Especially on your own," he said.

"It's not. But I'll tell you, I now know what love is. I mean, I love my family. I thought I loved their father. But the way I feel about those three? Nothing I've ever experienced. I'd sacrifice anything for them."

"You're a mother," he said, admiring her more than she could know.

She nodded. "First and foremost. My family keeps trying to set me up on dates. Like any guy would say yes to a woman with seven-month-old triplets." She glanced at Reed, then began cutting up the carrots. "I sure trapped you."

He smiled. "Angelina, international flight attendant, wasn't a mother of three, remember? She was just a woman out having a good time at a small-town carnival."

She set down the knife and looked at him. "You're not angry that I didn't say anything? That I actually let you marry me without you knowing what you were walking into?"

He moved to the counter and stood across from her. "We were both bombed out of our minds."

She smiled and resumed chopping. "Well, when we

get this little matter of our marriage license ripped up before it can be processed, I'll go back to telling my family to stop trying to fix me up and you'll be solving crime all over Wedlock Creek."

"You're not looking for a father for the triplets?" he asked.

"Maybe I should be," she said. "To be fair to them. But right now? No. I have zero interest in romance and love and honestly no longer believe in happily-ever-after. I've got my hands full, anyway."

Huh. She felt the same way he did. Well, to a point. Marriage made her feel safe, but love didn't. Interesting, he thought, trying not to stare at her.

As she pulled open a cabinet, the hinge broke and it almost hit her on the head. Reed rushed over and caught it before it could.

"This place is falling down," he said, shaking his head. "You could have been really hurt. And you could have been holding one of the triplets."

She frowned. "I've fixed that three times. I'll call my landlord. She'll have it taken care of."

"Or I could take care of it right now," he said, surveying the hinge. "Still usable. Have a power drill?"

"In that drawer," she said, pointing. "I keep all the tools in there."

He found the drill and fixed the hinge, making sure it was on tight. "That should do it," he said. "Anything else need fixing?"

"Wow, he babysits *and* is handy?" She smiled at him. "I don't think there's anything else needing work," she said, adding the vegetables into a pot bubbling on the stove. "And thank you."

When the triplets started fussing, he announced it was babysitting time. He scooped up two babies and put them in Exersaucers in the living room, then raced back for the third and set Brody in one, too. The three of them happily played with the brightly colored attachments, babbling and squealing. He pulled Bea out—he knew she was Bea by her yellow shirt, whereas Bella's was orange—and did two upsie-downsies, much to the joy of the other two, who laughed and held up their arms.

"Your turn!" he said to Bella, lifting her high to the squeals of her siblings. "Now you, Brody," he added, putting Bella back and giving her brother his turn.

They sure were beautiful. All three had the same big cheeks and big, blue-gray eyes, wisps of light brown hair. They were happy, gurgling, babbling, laughing seven-month-olds.

Something squeezed in his chest again, this time a strange sensation of longing. With the way he'd always felt about marriage, he'd never have this—babies, a wife making pot pies, a family. And even in this tired old little house, playing at family felt…nicer than he expected.

Brody rubbed his eyes, which Reed recalled meant he was getting tired. Maybe it was nap time? It was barely seven-thirty in the morning, but they'd probably woken before the crack of dawn.

"How about a story?" he asked, sitting on the braided rug and grabbing a book from the coffee table. *"Lulu Goes to the Fair."* A white chicken wearing a baseball cap was on the cover. "Your mother and I went to the fair last night," he told them. "So this book will be perfect." He read them the story of Lulu wanting to ride the Ferris wheel but not being able to reach the step until two other chickens from her school helped her. Then they rode the Ferris wheel together. The end. Bella and Brody weren't much interested in Lulu and her day at the fair, but Bea was rapt. Then they all started rubbing their eyes and fussing.

It was now eight o'clock. Maybe he'd put the babies back in the playpen to see if he could help Norah. Not that he could cook, but he could fetch.

He picked up the two girls and headed back into the kitchen, smiled at Norah, deposited the babies in the playpen and then went to get Brody.

"Thank you for watching them," she said. "And reading to them."

"Anytime," he said. Which felt strange. Did he mean that?

"You're sure you didn't win Uncle of the Year or something? How'd you get so good with babies?"

"Told you. I like babies. Who doesn't? I picked up a few lessons on the job, I guess."

Why had he said "anytime" though? That was kind of loaded.

With the babies set for the moment, he shook the thought from his scrambled head and watched Norah cook, impressed with her multitasking. She had six tins covered in pie crust. The aromas of the onions and chicken and beef bubbling in two big pots filled the kitchen. His stomach growled. Had they eaten breakfast? He suddenly realized they hadn't.

"I made coffee and toasted a couple of bagels," she said as if she could read his mind. She was so multi-talented, he wouldn't be surprised if she could. "I have cream cheese and butter."

"You're doing enough," he said. "I'll get it. What do you want on yours?"

"Cream cheese. And thanks."

He poured the coffee into mugs and took care of the bagels, once again so aware of her closeness, the physicality of her. He couldn't help but notice how incredibly sexy she was, standing there in her jeans and maroon T-shirt, the way both hugged her body. There wasn't anywhere to sit in the kitchen, so he stood by the counter, drinking the coffee he so desperately needed.

"The chief mentioned the Pie Diner is the place for lunch in Wedlock Creek. I'm sure I'll be eating one of those pies tomorrow."

She smiled. "Oh, good. I'll have to thank him for that. We need to attract the newcomers to town before the burger place gets 'em." She took a long sip of her coffee. "Ah, I needed that." She took another sip, then a bite of her bagel. She glanced at him as if she wanted to ask something, then resumed adding the pot pie mixtures into the tins. "You moved here for a fresh start, you said?"

He'd avoided that question earlier. He supposed he could answer without going into every detail of his life.

He sipped his coffee and nodded. "I came up for my grandmother's funeral a few months ago. She was the last of my father's family. When she passed, I suddenly wanted to be here, in Wedlock Creek, where I'd spent those good summers. After a bad stakeout a few weeks ago that almost got me killed and did get my partner injured, I'd had it. I quit the force and applied for a job in Wedlock Creek. It turns out a detective had retired just a few weeks prior."

"Sorry about your grandmother. Sounds like she was very special to you."

"She was. My father had taken off completely when I was just a month old, but my grandmother refused to lose contact with me. She sent cards and gifts and called every week and drove out to pick me up every summer for three weeks. It's a three-hour drive each way." He'd never forget being seven, ten, eleven and staring out the window of his apartment, waiting to see that old green car slowly turn up the street. And when it did, emotion would flood him to the point that it would take him a minute to rush out with his bag.

"I'm so glad you had her in your life. You never saw your dad again?"

"He sent the occasional postcard from all over the west. Last one I ever got was from somewhere in Alaska. Word came that he died and had left instructions for a sea burial. I last saw him when I was ten, when he came back for his dad's funeral—my grandfather."

"And your mom?"

"It was hard on her raising a kid alone without much money or prospects. And it was just me. She remarried, but that didn't work out well, either, for either of us." He took a long slug of the coffee. He needed to change the subject. "How do you manage three babies with two hands?"

She smiled and lay pie crust over the tins, making some kind of decoration in the center. "Same way you did bringing the triplets from the kitchen to the living room. You just have to move fast and be constantly on guard. I do what I have to. That's just the way it is."

An angry wail came from the playpen. Then another. The three Ingalls triplets began rubbing their eyes again, this time with very upset little faces.

"Perfect timing," she said. "The pies are assembled." She hurried to the sink to wash her hands, then hurried over to the playpen. "Nap time for you cuties."

"I'll help," Reed said, putting down his mug.

Brody was holding up his arms and staring at Reed. Reed smiled and picked him up, the little weight sweet in his arms. Brody reached up and grabbed Reed's cheek, like his sister had, not that there was much to grab. Norah scooped up Bea and Bella. They headed upstairs, the unlined wood steps creaky and definitely not baby-friendly when they would start to crawl, which would probably be soon.

The nursery was spare but had the basics. Three cribs, a dresser and changing table. The room was painted a pale yellow with white stars and moons stenciled all over.

"Ever changed a diaper?" she asked as she put both babies in a crib, taking off their onesies.

"Cops have done just about everything," he said. "I've changed my share of diapers." He laid the baby on the changing table. "Phew. Just wet." He made quick work of the task, sprinkling on some cornstarch powder and fastening a fresh diaper.

"His jammies are in the top drawer. Any footsie ones."

Reed picked up the baby and carried him over to the dresser, using one hand to open the drawer. The little baby clothes were very neatly folded. He pulled out the top footed onesie, blue cotton with dinosaurs. He set Brody down, then gently put his little arms and legs into the right holes, and there Brody was, all ready for bed. He held the baby against his chest, Brody's impossibly little eyes drooping, his mouth quirking.

He tried to imagine his own father holding him like this, his own flesh and blood, and just walking away. No look back. No nothing. How was it possible? Reed couldn't fathom it.

"His crib is on the right," Norah said, pointing as she took one baby girl out of the crib and changed her, then laid her down in the empty crib. She scooped up the other baby, changed her and laid her back in the crib.

He set Brody down and gave his little cheek a caress. Brody grabbed his thumb and held on.

"He sure does like you," Norah whispered.

Reed swallowed against the gushy feeling in the region of his chest. As Brody's eyes drifted closed, the tiny fist released and Reed stepped back.

Norah shut off the light and turned on a very low lullaby player. After half a second of fussing, all three babies closed their eyes, quirking their tiny mouths and stretching their arms over their heads.

"Have a good nap, my loves," Norah said, tiptoeing toward the door.

Reed followed her, his gold band glinting in the dim light of the room. He stared at the ring, then at his surroundings. He was in a nursery. With the woman he'd accidentally married. And with her triplets, whom he'd just babysat, read to and helped get to nap time.

What the hell had happened to his life? A day ago he'd been about to embark on a new beginning here in Wedlock Creek, where life had once seemed so idyllic out in the country where his grandmother had lived alone after she'd been widowed. Instead of focusing on reading the WCPD manuals and getting up to speed on open cases, he was getting his heart squeezed by three eighteen-pound tiny humans.

And their beautiful mother.

As he stepped into the hallway, the light cleared his brain. "Well, I guess I'd better get going. Pick you up at eight thirty tomorrow for the trip to Brewer? The courthouse opens at nine. Luckily, I don't report for duty until noon."

"Sounds good," she said, leading the way downstairs. "Thanks for helping. You put Brody down for his nap like a champ."

But instead of heading toward the door, he found himself just standing there. He didn't want to leave the four Ingalls alone. On their own. In this falling-down house.

He felt...responsible for them, he realized.

But he also needed to take a giant step backward and catch his breath.

So why was it so hard to walk out the door?

Chapter Four

At exactly eight thirty on Monday morning, Norah saw Reed pull up in front of her house. He must be as ready to get this marriage business taken care of as she was. Yesterday, after he'd left, she'd taken a long, hot bubble bath upstairs, ears peeled for the triplets, but they'd napped for a good hour and a half. In that time, a zillion thoughts had raced through her head, from the bits and pieces she remembered of her evening with Fabio to the wedding to waking up to find Detective Reed Barelli in her bed to how he played upsie-downsie with the triplets and read them a story. And fixed her bagel. And the cabinet.

She couldn't stop thinking about him, how kind he'd been, how good-natured about the whole mess. It had been the man's first day in town. And he'd found himself married to a mother of three. She also couldn't stop thinking about how he'd looked in those black boxer briefs, how tall and muscular he was. The way his dark eyes crinkled at the corners.

After the triplets had woken up, she'd gotten them into the stroller and moseyed on down to the Pie Diner with her six contributions. She'd been unable to keep her secret and had told her mother and aunt everything, trying to not be overheard by their part-time cook and the two waitresses coming in and out. She'd explained it all and she could see on her sister's face how relieved Shelby was at not having to keep her super-juicy family secret anymore.

"That Annie!" Aunt Cheyenne had said with a wink. "Always looking out for us."

Arlena Ingalls had had the same evil smile. "Handsome?"

"Mom!" Norah had said. "He's a stranger!"

"He's hardly that now," her mother had pointed out, glancing at an order ticket and placing two big slices of quiche Lorraine on a waitress's tray.

Aunt Cheyenne had laughed. "I have to hand it to you. We send you to the carnival for your first night out in seven months and you come home married. And to the town's new detective. I, for one, am very impressed."

After talk had turned to who had possibly spiked the punch, Norah, exasperated, had left. Her mother had offered to watch the triplets this morning so that Norah could get her life straightened out and back together. "If you absolutely have to," her mother had added.

Humph, Norah thought now, watching Reed get out

of his dark blue SUV. As if marriage was the be-all and end-all. As if a good man was a savior. They didn't even know if Reed was a good man.

But she did, dammit. That had been obvious from the get-go, from the moment he'd stuffed that hundred in the till box to pay what he'd thought was fair for swiping all the punch to picking her up and taking her into the chapel to fulfill her dream of getting married there. He was a good man when bombed out of his ever-loving mind. He was a good man stone-cold sober, who played upsie-downsie with babies, making sure each got their turn. He'd fixed her broken cabinet.

And damn, he really was something to look at. His thick, dark hair shone in the morning sun. He wore charcoal-colored pants, a gray button-down shirt and black shoes. He looked like a city detective.

In the bathtub, as she'd lain there soaking, and all last night in bed, in between trips to the nursery to see why one triplet or another was crying or shrieking, she'd thought about Reed Barelli and how he'd looked in those boxer briefs. She was pretty sure they hadn't had sex. She would remember, wouldn't she? Tidbits of the experience, at least. There was no way that man, so good-looking and sexy, had run his hands and mouth all over her and she hadn't remembered a whit of it.

Anyway, their union would be no more in about a half hour. It was fun to fantasize about what they might have done Saturday night, but only because it was just that—fantasy. And Reed would be out of her life very soon, just someone she'd say hi to in the coffee shop or grocery store. Maybe they'd even chuckle at the crazy time they'd up and gotten married by accident.

She waited for the doorbell to ring, but it didn't. Reed wouldn't be one to wait in the car and honk, so she peered out the window. He stood on the doorstep, typing something into his phone. Girlfriend, maybe. The man had to be involved with someone. He'd probably been explaining himself from the moment he'd left Norah's house this morning. Poor guy.

Her mom had already come to pick up the babies, so she was ready to go. She wore a casual cotton skirt and top for the occasion of getting back their marriage license, but in the back of her mind she was well aware she'd dolled up a little for the handsome cop. A little mascara, a slick of lip gloss, a tiny dab of subtle perfume behind her ears.

Which was all ridiculous, considering she was spending her morning undoing her ties to the man!

A text buzzed on her phone.

Not sure if the cutes are sleeping, so didn't want to ring the doorbell.

Huh. He hadn't been texting a girlfriend; he'd been texting *her*. Maybe there was no girlfriend.

She glanced at the text again. The warmth that spread across her heart, her midsection, made her smile. The cutes. An un-rung doorbell so as not to disturb the triplets. If she needed more proof that Reed Barelli was top-notch, she'd gotten it.

She took a breath and opened the door. Why did he

have to be so good-looking? She could barely peel her eyes off him. "Morning," she said. "My mom has the triplets, so we're good to go."

"I got us coffee and muffins," he said, holding up a bag from Java Joe's. "Light, no sugar, right? That's how you took your coffee yesterday."

She smiled. "You don't miss much, I've been noticing."

"Plight of the detective. Once we see it, it's imprinted."

"What kind of muffins?" she asked, trying not to stare at his face.

"I took you for a cranberry-and-orange type," he said, opening the passenger door for her.

She smiled. "Sounds good." She slid inside his SUV. Clean as could be. Two coffees sat in the center console, one marked *R*, along with a smattering of change and some pens in one of the compartments.

"And I also got four other kinds of muffins in case you hate cranberry and orange," he said, handing her the cup that wasn't marked regular.

Of course he had, she thought, her heart pinging. She kept her eyes straight ahead as he rounded the hood and got inside. When he closed his door, she was ridiculously aware of how close he was.

"Thanks," she said, touched by his thoughtfulness.

"So, it's a half hour to the courthouse, we'll get back our license and that's that." He started the SUV and glanced at her.

She held his gaze for a moment before sipping her coffee to have something to do that didn't involve looking at him.

Would be nice to keep the fantasy going a little longer, she thought. *That we're married, a family, my mom is babysitting while we go off to the county seat to... admire the architecture, have brunch in a fancy place.* Once upon a time, this was all she'd wanted. To find her life's partner, to build a life with a great guy, have children, have a family. But everything had gotten turned on its head. Now she barely trusted herself, let alone anyone she wasn't related to.

Ha, maybe that was why she seemed to trust Reed. He was related to her. For the next half hour, anyway.

By the time they arrived at the courthouse, a beautiful white historic building, she'd finished her coffee and had half a cranberry-and-orange muffin and a few bites of the cinnamon chip. Reed was around to open her door for her before she could even reach for the handle. "Well, this is it—literally and figuratively."

"This is it," she repeated, glancing at him. He held her gaze for a moment and she knew he had to be thinking, *Thank God. We're finally here. Let's get this marriage license ripped up!*

They headed inside. The bronze mail slot on the side of the door loomed large. She could just imagine sneaky, old Abe Potterowski racing over and shoving all the licenses in. As they entered through the revolving door, Norah glanced at the area under the mail slot. Just an empty mail bucket was there.

Empty. Of course it was. Every step of this crazy process was going to be difficult.

After getting directions to the office that handled marriage licenses, they took the elevator to the third floor.

Maura Hotchner, County Clerk was imprinted on a plaque to the left of the doorway to Office 310. They went in and Norah smiled at the woman behind the desk.

"Ms. Hotchner, my name is Norah—"

"Good morning!" the woman said with a warm smile. "Ms. Hotchner began her maternity leave today. I'm Ellen Wheeler, temporary county clerk and Ms. Hotchner's assistant. How may I help you?"

Norah explained that she was looking for her marriage license and wanted it back before it could be processed.

"Oh dear," Ellen Wheeler said. "Being my first day and all taking over this job, I got here extra early and processed all the marriage licenses deposited into the mail slot over the weekend. Do you believe there were seventeen from Wedlock Creek alone? I've already put the official decrees for all those in the mail."

Norah's heart started racing. "Do you mean to tell me that my marriage to this man is legally binding?"

The county clerk looked from Norah to Reed, gave him a "my, you're a handsome one" smile, then looked back at Norah. "Yes, ma'am. It's on the books now. You're legally wed."

Oh God. Oh God. Oh God. This can't be happening.

She glanced at Reed, whose face had paled. "Can't you just erase everything and find our decree and rip it up? Can you just undo it all? I mean, you just processed it—what?—fifteen minutes ago, right? That's what the delete key is for!"

The woman seemed horrified by the suggestion. "Ma'am, I'm sorry, but I most certainly cannot just 'erase' what is legally binding. The paperwork has been processed. You're officially married."

Facepalm. "Is this the correct office to get annulment forms?" Norah asked. At least she wouldn't walk out of there empty-handed. She would get the ball rolling to undo this…crazy mistake.

Ellen's face went blank as she stared from Norah to Reed to their wedding rings and then back at Norah. "I have them right here."

Norah clutched the papers and hurried away. She could barely get to the bench by the elevators without collapsing.

Reed put his hand on her shoulder. "Are you all right? Can I get you some water?"

"I'm fine," she said. "No, I'll be fine. I just can't believe this. We're married!"

"So we are," he said, sitting beside her. "We'll fill out the annulment paperwork and I'm sure it won't take long to resolve this."

She glanced at the instruction form attached to the form. "Grounds for annulment include insanity. That's us, all right."

He laughed and held her gaze for a moment, then shoved his hands into his pockets and looked away.

"I guess I'll fill this out and then give it to you to sign?" she said, flipping through the few pages. She hated important forms with their tiny boxes. She let out a sigh.

He nodded and reached out his hand. "Come on. Let's go home."

For a split second she was back in her fantasy of him

being her husband and having an actual home to go to that wasn't falling down around her with sloping floors and a haunted refrigerator. She took his hand and never wanted to let go.

She really was insane. She had to be. What the hell was going on with her? It's like she had a wild crush on this man.

Her husband!

As Reed turned onto the road for Wedlock Creek, he could just make out the old black weather vane on top of his grandmother's barn in the distance. The house wasn't in view; it was a few miles out from here, but that weather vane, with its arrows and mother and baby buffalo, had always been a landmark when that old green car would get to this point for his stay at his grandmother's.

"See that weather vane?" he said, pointing.

Norah bent over a bit. "Oh yes, I do see it now."

"That's my grandmother's barn. When I was a kid heading up here from our house, I'd see that weather vane and all would be right in the world."

"I'd love to see the property," she said. "Can we stop?"

He'd driven over twice Saturday morning, right after he'd arrived in Wedlock Creek, but he'd stayed in the car. He loved the old ranch house and the land, and he'd keep it up, but it was never going to be his, so he hadn't wanted to rub the place in his own face. Though, technically, until his marriage was annulled, it *was* his. His grandmother must be mighty happy right now at his situation. He could see her thinking he'd finally settle down just to be able to have the ranch, then magically fall madly in love with his wife and be happy forever. Right.

He pulled onto the gravel road leading to the ranch and, as always, as the two-story, white farmhouse came into view, his heart lurched. Home.

God, he loved this place. For some of his childhood, when his grandfather had been alive, he'd stayed only a week, which was as long as the grouchy old coot could bear to have him around. But when he'd passed, his grandmother had him stay eight weeks, almost the whole summer. A bunch of times his grandmother had told his mother she and Reed could move in, but his mother had been proud and living with her former mother-in-law had never felt right.

Norah gasped. "What a beautiful house. I love these farmhouses. So much character. And that gorgeous red door and the black shutters…"

He watched her take in the red barn just to the left of the house, which was more like a garage than a place for horses or livestock. Then her gaze moved to the acreage, fields of pasture with shade trees and open land. A person could think out here, dream out here, *be* out here.

"I'd love to see inside," she said.

He supposed it was all right. He did have a key, after all. Always had. And he was married, so the property was out of its three-month limbo, since he'd fulfilled the terms of the will.

He led the way three steps up to the wide porch that wrapped around the side of the house. How many chocolate milks had he drunk, how many stories had his grandmother told him on this porch, on those two rocking chairs with the faded blue cushions?

The moment he stepped inside, a certain peace came over him. Home. Where he belonged. Where he wanted to be.

The opposite of how he'd felt about the small house he'd rented near the police department. Sterile. Meh. Then again, he'd had the place only two days and hadn't even slept there Saturday night. His furniture from his condo in Cheyenne fit awkwardly, nothing quite looking right no matter where he moved the sofa or the big-screen TV.

"Oh, Reed, this place is fantastic," Norah said, looking all around. She headed into the big living room with its huge stone fireplace, the wall of windows facing the fields and huge trees and woods beyond.

His grandmother had had classic taste, so even the furniture felt right to him. Brown leather sofas, club chairs, big Persian rugs. She'd liked to paint and her work was hung around the house, including ones of him as a boy and a teenager.

"You sure were a cute kid," Norah said, looking at the one of him as a nine-year-old. "And I'm surprised I never ran into you during your summers here. I would have had the biggest crush on that guy," she added, pointing at the watercolor of him at sixteen.

He smiled. "My grandmother didn't love town or people all that much. When I visited, she'd make a ton of food and we'd explore the woods and go fishing in the river just off her land."

The big, country kitchen with its white cabinets and

bay window with the breakfast nook was visible, so she walked inside and he followed. He could tell she loved the house and he couldn't contain his pride as he showed her the family room with the sliders out to a deck facing a big backyard, then the four bedrooms upstairs. The master suite was a bit feminine for his taste with its flowered rose quilt, but the bathroom was something—spa tub with jets, huge shower, the works. Over the years he'd updated the house as presents for his grandmother, happy to see her so delighted.

"I can see how much this place means to you," Norah said as they headed back downstairs into the living room. "Did it bother you that your grandmother wrote her will the way she did? That you had to marry to inherit it?"

"I didn't like it, but I understood what she was trying to do. On her deathbed, she told me she knew me better than I knew myself, that I did need a wife and children and this lone-wolf-cop nonsense wouldn't make me happy."

Maybe your heart will get broken again, but loss is part of life, Lydia Barelli had added. *You don't risk, you don't get.*

Broken again. Why had he ever told his grandmother that he'd tried and where had it gotten him? Those final days of his grandmother's life, he hadn't been in the mood to talk any more about the one woman he'd actually tried to be serious about. He'd been thinking about proposing, trying to force himself out of his old, negative feelings, when the woman he'd been seeing for almost a year told him she'd fallen for a rich lawyer—sorry. He hadn't let himself fall for anyone since, and that was over five years ago. Between that and what he'd witnessed about marriage growing up? Count him out.

Reed hadn't wanted to disappoint his beloved grandmother and had told her, "Who knows what the future holds?" He couldn't outright lie and say he was sure he'd change his mind about marriage. But he wouldn't let his grandmother go on thinking no one on this earth would ever love him. She wouldn't have been able to abide that.

"*Have* you been happy?" Norah asked, glancing at him, then away as if to give him some privacy.

He shrugged. "Happy enough. My work was my life and it sustained me a long time. But when I lost the only family I had, someone very special to me, I'll tell you, I *felt* it."

"It?" she repeated.

"Loss of…connection, I guess."

She nodded. "I felt that way when my dad died, and I had my mother, aunt and sister crying with me. I can't imagine how alone you must have felt."

He turned away, looking out the window. "Well, we should get going. I have to report to the department for my orientation at noon. Then it's full-time tomorrow."

"Thanks for showing me the house. I almost don't want to leave. It's so…welcoming."

He glanced around and breathed in the place. They had to leave. *He* had to leave. Because this house was never going to be his. And being there hurt like hell.

Chapter Five

Reed sat in his office in the Wedlock Creek Police Department, appreciating the fact that he had an office, even if it was small, with a window facing Main Street, so he could see the hustle and bustle of downtown. The two-mile-long street was full of shops and restaurants and businesses. The Pie Diner was just visible across the street if he craned his neck, which he found himself doing every now and again for a possible sighting of Norah.

His wife for the time being.

He hadn't seen her around today since dropping her off. But looking out the window had given him ideas for leads and follow-ups on a few of the open cases he'd inherited from his retired predecessor. Wedlock Creek might not have had a murder in over seventy years—

knock on wood—but there was the usual crime, ranging from the petty to the more serious. The most pressing involved a missing person's case that would be his focus. A thirty-year-old man, an ambulance-chasing attorney named David Dirk who was supposed to get married this coming Saturday, had gone missing three days ago. No one had heard from him and none of his credit cards had been used, yet there was no sign of foul play.

David Dirk. Thirty. Had to be the same guy. When Reed was a kid, a David Dirk was his nearest neighbor and they'd explore their land for hours during the summers Reed had spent at his grandmother's. David had been a smart, inquisitive kid who'd also had a father who'd taken off. He and Reed would talk about what jerks their dads were, then laud them as maybe away on secret government business, unable to tell their wives or children that they were really saving the world. That was how much both had needed to believe, as kids, that their fathers were good, that their fathers did love them, after all. David's family had moved and they'd lost touch as teenagers and then time had dissolved the old ties.

Reed glanced at the accompanying photo stapled to the left side of the physical file. He could see his old friend in the adult's face. The same intense blue eyes behind black-framed eyeglasses, the straight, light brown hair. Reed spent the next hour reading through the case file and notes about David's disappearance.

The man's fiancée, Eden Pearlman, an extensions specialist at Hair Palace on Main Street, was adamant that something terrible had happened to her "Davy Darling" or otherwise he would have contacted her. According to Eden, Davy must be lying gravely injured in a ditch somewhere or a disgruntled associate had hurt him, because marrying her was the highlight of his life. Reed sure hoped neither was the case. He would interview Ms. Pearlman tomorrow and get going on the investigation.

In the meantime, though, he called every clinic and hospital within two hours to check if there were any John Does brought in unconscious. Each one said no. Then Reed read through the notes about David's last case, which he'd won big for his client a few days prior to his disappearance. A real-estate deal that had turned ugly. Reed researched the disgruntled plaintiff, who'd apparently spent the entire day that David was last seen at a family reunion an hour away. Per the notes, the plaintiff was appealing and had stated he couldn't wait to see his opponent and his rat of a lawyer in court again, where he'd prevail this time. Getting rid of David in some nefarious way certainly wouldn't get rid of the case; Reed had his doubts the man had had anything to do with David's disappearance.

So where are you, David? What the heck happened to you?

Frustrated by the notes and his subsequent follow-up calls getting him nowhere, Reed packed up his files at six. Tomorrow would be his first full day on the force and he planned to find David Dirk by that day's end. Something wasn't sitting right in his gut about the case, but he couldn't put his finger on it. He'd need to talk to the fiancée and a few other people.

As he left the station, he noticed Norah coming out of a brick office building, wheeling the huge triple stroller.

He eyed the plaque on the door: Dr. Laurel McCray, Pediatrician. Brody in the front was screaming his head off. Bella was letting out shrieks. Or was that Bea? All he knew for sure was that one of the girls, seated in the middle, was quiet, picking up Cheerios from the narrow little tray in front of her and eating them.

He crossed the street and hurried up to her. "Norah? Everything okay?"

She looked as miserable as the two little ones. "I just came from their pediatrician's office. Brody was tugging at his ear all afternoon and crying. Full-out ear infection. He's had his first dose of antibiotics, but they haven't kicked in yet."

"Poor guy," Reed said, kneeling and running a finger along Brody's hot, tearstained cheek. Brody stopped crying for a moment, so Reed did it again. When he stood, Brody let out the wail of all wails.

"He really does like you," Norah said, looking a bit mystified for a moment before a mix of mom weariness came over her. "Even Bella has stopped crying, so double thank you."

As if on cue, Bella started shrieking again and, from the smell of things, Reed had a feeling she wasn't suffering from the same issue as her brother. People walking up and down the street stared, of course, giving concerned smiles but being nosey parkers.

Norah's shoulders slumped. "I'd better get them home."

"Need some help?" he asked. "Actually, I meant that rhetorically, so don't answer. You do need help and I'm going home with you."

"Reed, I can't keep taking advantage of how good you are with babies."

"Yes, you can. I mean, what are husbands for if not for helping around the house?"

She laughed. "I can't believe you actually made me laugh when I feel like crying."

"Husbands are good for that, too," he said before he could catch himself. He was kidding, trying to lighten her load, but he actually *was* her husband. And there was nothing funny about it.

"Well, you'll be off the hook in a few days," she said. "I filled out the annulment form and all you have to do is sign it and I'll send it in. It's on my coffee table."

She hadn't wasted any time. Or Norah Ingalls was just very efficient, despite having triplet babies to care for on her own. He nodded. "Well, then, I'm headed to the right place."

Within fifteen minutes they were in Norah's cramped, sloping little house. He held poor Brody while Norah changed Bella, who'd stopped shrieking, but all three babies were hungry and it was a bit past dinnertime.

Reed was in charge of Brody, who was unusually responsive to him, especially when his little ears were hurting, so he sat in front of Brody's high chair, feeding him his favorite baby food, cereal with pears. Norah was on a chair next to him, feeding both girls. Bella was in a much better mood now that her Cheerios had been replenished and she was having pureed sweet potatoes. Bea was dining on a jar of pureed green beans.

Reed got up to fill Brody's sippy cup with water when he stopped in his tracks.

On the refrigerator, half underneath a Mickey Mouse magnet, was a wedding invitation.

Reed stared at it, barely able to believe what he was seeing.

Join Us For
The Special Occasion of Our Wedding
Eden Pearlman and David Dirk...

Norah was invited to the wedding? He pulled the invitation off the fridge. "Bride or groom?" he asked, holding up the invitation.

Norah glanced up, spoon full of green bean mush midway to Bea's open mouth. "Groom, actually. I'm surprised he invited me. I dated David Dirk for two weeks a couple years ago. He ditched me for the woman he said was the love of his life. She must be, because I got that invitation about six weeks ago."

"You only dated for two weeks?" Reed asked.

She nodded. "We met at the Pie Diner. He kept coming in and ordering the pot pie of the day. I thought it was about the heavenly pot pies, but apparently it was me he liked. He asked me out. We had absolutely nothing in common and nothing much to talk about over coffee and dinner. But I'll tell ya, when my sister, Shelby, needed an attorney concerning something to do with her son Shane, I recommended David based on his reputation. He represented her in a complicated case and she told me he did a great job."

He tucked that information away. "No one has seen or heard from him in three days. According to the case notes, his fiancée thinks there was foul play, but my predecessor found no hint of that."

"Hmm. David was a real ambulance chaser. He had a few enemies. Twice someone said to me, 'How could you date that scum?'"

His eyebrow shot up. "Really? Recall who?"

"I'll write down their names for you. Gosh, I hope David's okay. I mean, he was a shark, but, like I said, when Shelby *needed* a shark, he did well by her. I didn't get to know him all that well, but he was always a gentleman, always a nice guy. We just had nothing much to say to each other. Zero chemistry."

He was about to put the invitation back on the fridge. "Mind if I keep this?" he asked.

She shook her head. "Go right ahead." She turned back to her jars of baby food and feeding the girls. "Brody seems calmer. The medicine must have kicked in." She leaned over and gave his cheek a gentle stroke. "Little better now, sweet pea?"

Brody banged on his tray and smiled.

"Does that mean you want some Cheerios?" Reed asked, sitting back down. He handed one to Brody, who took it and examined it, then popped it in his mouth, giving Reed a great gummy smile, three little jagged teeth making their way up.

Bea grabbed her spoon just as Norah was inching it toward her mouth and it ended up half in Bea's hair, half in Norah's.

"Oh, thanks," Norah said with a grin. "Just what I wanted in my hair." She tickled Bea's belly. "And now the three of you need a bath." She laughed and shook her head.

By eight o'clock, Norah had rinsed the baby food from her hair, all three babies had been fed, bathed, read to and it was time for bed. Reed stood by the door as Norah sang a lullaby in her lovely whispered voice. He almost nodded off himself.

"Well, they're asleep," she said, walking out of the nursery and keeping the door ajar. "I can't thank you enough for your help tonight, Reed."

"It was no trouble."

For a moment, as he looked into her hazel eyes, the scent of pears clinging to her shirt, he wanted to kiss her so badly that he almost leaned forward. He caught himself at the last second. What the hell? He couldn't kiss Norah. They weren't a couple. They weren't even dating.

Good Lord, they were married.

And he wanted to kiss her, passionately, kiss her over to that lumpy-looking gold couch and explore every inch of her pear-smelling body. But he couldn't, not with everything so weird between them. And things were definitely weird.

He was supposed to sign annulment papers. But those papers on the coffee table had been in his line of vision for the past two hours and he'd ignored them. Even after Norah had mentioned them when they'd first arrived tonight. "There are the papers," she'd said, gesturing with her chin. Quite casually.

But he'd bypassed the forms and fed Brody instead. Rocked the little guy in his arms while Norah gave his sisters a bath. Changed Brody into pajamas and sang his own little off-key lullaby about where the buffalos roamed.

And all he could think was *How can I walk away from this woman, these babies? How can I just leave them?*

He couldn't. Signing those annulment papers would mean the marriage never happened. They'd both walk away.

He didn't want to. Or he couldn't. One or the other. He might not want love or a real marriage, but that didn't mean he couldn't step up for Norah.

And then the thought he'd squelched all day came right up in Technicolor.

And if you stay married to Norah, if you step up for her, you can have your grandmother's ranch. You can live there. You can go home. You can all go home, far away from this crummy little falling-down house.

Huh. Maybe he and his new bride could make a deal.

They could *stay* married. She'd feel safe every day.

And he could have the Barelli ranch fair and square.

She'd said she was done with romance, done with love. So was he.

He wondered what she'd think of the proposition. She might be offended and smack him. Or simply tell him the idea was ludicrous. Or she might say, "You know what, you've got yourself a deal" and shake on it. Instead of kiss. Because it would be an arrangement, not anything to do with romance or feelings.

He'd take these thoughts, this idea, back to the sterile rental and let it percolate. A man didn't propose a romance-less marriage without giving it intense consideration from all angles.

But only one thought pushed to the forefront of his head: that he wasn't walking away from Norah and the triplets. No way, no how. Like father, *not* like son.

* * *

Norah was working on a new recipe for a barbecue pot pie when the doorbell rang. Which meant it wasn't Reed. He'd just left ten minutes ago and wouldn't ring the bell knowing the triplets were asleep. Neither would her sister, mother or aunt.

Please don't be someone selling something, she thought as she headed to the front door.

Amy Ackerman, who lived at the far end of the street, stood at the door, holding a stack of files and looking exasperated. "Oh, thank God, you're here, Norah. I have to ask the biggest favor."

Norah tried to think of the last time someone had asked a favor of her. Early in her pregnancy, maybe. Before she started showing for sure. People weren't about to ask favors from a single mother of triplets.

"Louisa can't teach the zero-to-six-month multiples class and it starts Wednesday!" Amy shrieked, balancing her files in her hands. "Sixteen people have signed up for the class, including eight pregnant mothers expecting multiples. I can't let them down."

Amy was the director of the Wedlock Creek Community Services Center, which offered all kinds of classes and programming for children and adults. The multiples classes were very popular—the center offered classes in preparing for and raising multiples of all ages. How to feed three-week-old twins at once. How to change triplets' diapers when they were all soaked. How to survive the terrible twos with two the same age. Or three. Or four, in several cases.

During her pregnancy, Norah had taken the prep class and then the zero-to-six-month class twice herself.

At the time, she'd been so stressed out about what to expect that she'd barely retained anything she'd learned, but she remembered being comforted by just being there. She'd been the only one without a significant other or husband, too. She'd gotten quite a few looks of pity throughout and, during any partner activities, she'd had to pair up with the instructor, Louisa.

"Given that you just graduated from the real-life course now that the babes are seven months," Amy said, "will you teach it? You'll get the regular fee plus an emergency bonus. The class meets once a week for the next six weeks."

Norah stared at Amy, completely confused. "Me? Teach a class?"

"Yes, you. Who better? Not only do you have triplets, but you're a single mom. You're on your own. And every time I see you with those three little dumplings, I think, 'There goes a champ.'"

Huh. Norah, champ. She kind of liked it.

She also knew she was being buttered up big-time. But still, there was sincerity in Amy's eyes and the woman had always been kind to her. In fact, the first time Norah had signed up for the zero-to-six-month class, Amy had waived the course fee for her, and it wasn't cheap.

But how could she teach a class in anything? She was hardly a pro at being the mother of triplets. Last week Norah had made the rookie mistake of guiding her shopping cart in the grocery store a little too close to the shelves. Bella had managed to knock over an entire display of instant ramen noodles and either Bea or Brody had sent a glass jar of pickles crashing to the floor, blocking the path of a snooty woman who'd given Norah a "control your spawn" dirty look.

Then there was the time Norah had been waiting for a phone call from the pediatrician with test results, couldn't find her phone in her huge tote bag with its gobs of baby paraphernalia and had let go of the stroller for a second to dig in with both hands. The stroller had rolled away, Norah chasing after it. She'd caught someone shaking his head at her. Then there were all the times Norah had been told her babies should be wearing hats, shouldn't have pacifiers and "Excuse me, but are you really feeding your child nonorganic baby food? Do you know what's in that?"

Not to mention all the secret shame. How Brody had almost fallen off the changing table when she'd raced to stop Bea from picking up the plastic eye from a stuffed animal that had somehow come off in her crib. Norah could go on and on and on. She was no Super Mom of Multiples, ages zero to six months.

Thinking of all that deflated her, despite the fact that a minute ago, just being asked to teach the course had made her feel almost special, as though she had something to share with people who could use her help.

"Amy, I'm sorry, but I don't think—" Norah began.

Amy held up a hand. "If anyone is qualified to teach this class, it's you, Norah. And I promise you, I'm not just saying that because I'm desperate. Though I am desperate to find the right instructor. And that's you."

Norah frowned. "I make so many mistakes. All the time."

"Oh. You mean you're human? It's *not* easy taking care of baby triplets? Really?"

Norah found herself smiling. "Well, when you put it like that."

"There's no other way to put it."

"You know what, Amy? Sign me up. I will teach the class." Yeah, she would. Why not? She most certainly *had* been taking care of triplet babies—on her own— for seven months.

But she would have to hire a sitter or ask her mom or aunt to watch the triplets while she taught.

The fee for teaching was pretty good; paying a sitter every week would still leave a nice little chunk left over, and now she'd be able to afford to buy a wall-unit air conditioner for the downstairs. Norah had a feeling her mom and aunt would insist on watching the babies, though; both women had taken the class when Norah was in her ninth month. And even Shelby had signed up when she'd found herself the mother of not one but two six-month-old babies and needed to learn how to multitask on the quick.

The relief that washed over Amy's face made Norah smile. "You've saved me! Here's Louisa's syllabus and notes. You don't have to use her curriculum, though. You may have different ideas. It's your class now, so you make it your own."

That sounded good. "I'm looking forward to it," she said. "And thanks for asking me."

As Amy left, Norah carried the folder into the kitchen and set it down beside the bowl containing her special barbecue sauce, which wasn't quite there yet. Norah's regular barbecue sauce was pretty darn good, but she liked creating specials for the pot pies and wanted something with more of a Louisiana bite. She'd try a new batch, this time with a drop more cayenne pepper and a smidge less molasses. She'd just have to keep trying bits and dashes until she got it just right, which, now that she thought about it, was sometimes how parenting went. Yeah, there were basics to learn, but sometimes you had to be there, doing it, to know what to do.

As she headed to the coffeepot for a caffeine boost, she noticed the manila envelope on the counter. The annulment papers were inside. A yellow Post-it with Reed's name on the outside. Tomorrow she'd drop it off at the station and he'd sign them and she'd send them in or he would. And that would be the end of that.

No more Reed to the rescue, which had been very nice today.

No more fantasy husband and fantasy father.

No more sexy man in her kitchen and living room.

More than all that, she liked the way Reed made her feel. Despite his offers to help, he never looked at her as though she was falling apart or unable to handle all she had on her plate. He made her feel like she could simply use another hand…a partner.

Could the annulment papers accidentally fall behind the counter and disappear? She smiled. She liked this new and improved Norah. Kicking butt and teaching a class. Suddenly wanting her accidental husband to stick around.

Maybe because she knew he wouldn't?

Anyway, one out of two wasn't bad, though. At least she had the class.

Tomorrow she'd be out a husband.

Chapter Six

Norah had filled her tenth pulled pork pot pie of the morning when she noticed Reed Barelli pacing the sidewalk that faced the back windows of the Pie Diner's kitchen. He seemed to be deep in thought. She was dying to know about what. His missing person's case? Or maybe even…her? The annulment papers he'd forgotten to sign last night on his way out?

It's not like I reminded him, she thought. The way he'd come to her rescue last night like some Super Husband had brought back all those old fantasies and dreams. Of someone having her back. Someone to lean on, literally and figuratively. And, oh, how she would love to lean on that very long, sexy form of his, feel those muscular arms wrapped around her.

Focus on your work, she admonished herself. She

topped the pot pie with crust and made a design in the center, then set the pie on the tray awaiting the oven for the first of the lunch rush.

"Norah?" a waitress named Evie called out. "There's someone here to see you."

Had to be Reed. He was no longer out back. She quickly washed her hands and took off her apron, then left the kitchen. Reed sat at the far end of the counter. Since it was eleven, late for breakfast and early for lunch, the Pie Diner had very few customers. He was alone at the counter except for their regular, Old Sam, who sat at the first spot just about all day, paying for one slice of pie and coffee and getting endless refills and free pot pie for lunch, which had been the case for over a decade. Norah's mom had a soft spot for the elderly widower who reminded her of her late dad, apparently.

Reed looked…serious. Her heart sank. He must be there to sign the papers.

"I have the papers in my bag," she said. "Guess we both forgot last night. Follow me to the back office and you can sign them there if you want."

He glanced around, then stood and trailed her into the kitchen. The large office doubled as a kiddie nook and the triplets were napping in their baby swings.

She grabbed her tote bag from where it hung on the back of the desk chair and pulled out the annulment papers from the manila envelope.

But Reed wasn't taking the papers. He was looking at the babies.

"I'm glad they're here," he said. "Because I came to

say something kind of crazy and seeing the triplets reinforces that it's actually not crazy. That *I'm* not crazy."

She stared at him, no idea what he could be talking about.

He took the papers from her and set them down on the desk. "Instead of signing those, I have a proposition for you."

Norah tilted her head and caught her mother and aunt and sister all staring at them. She could close the door and give them some privacy, but then she'd only have to repeat what he'd said to her family, so they might as well get the earful straight from him. Besides, they'd never forgive her if she shut them out of this juicy part.

"A proposition?" she repeated.

Out of the corner of her eye, she could see her mother, sister and aunt all shuffle a step closer to the office.

He nodded. "If I sign those papers and you return them to the county clerk, poof, in a week, we're not married anymore. Never happened. Drunken mistake. Whoops. Except it *did* happen. And the intensive couple of days I've been a part of your life makes me unable to just walk away from you and Bella, Bea and Brody. I can't. A man doesn't do that, Norah."

Did she hear a gasp or two or three coming from the kitchen?

She stared at him. "Reed. We got married by accident. By drunken mistake, as you perfectly put it."

"Maybe so. But we also got married. We both stood up there and said our vows. Drunk off our tushes or not, Norah, we got married."

She gaped at him. "So you feel you have to stand by

vows you made under total insanity and drunken duress? Why do you think both of those are grounds for annulment?"

"I stand by you and the triplets. And if we're married, if we stay married, I also get to have the Barelli ranch fair and square. I was never planning on getting married. You said you weren't, either. We're both done with love and all that nonsense about happily-ever-after. So why not partner up, since we're already legally bound, and get what we both need?"

"What do I need exactly?" she asked, narrowing her eyes on him.

"You need a safe home, for one. A place big enough for three children growing every single day. You need financial stability and security. You need someone there for you 24/7, having your back, helping, sharing the enormous responsibility of raising triplets. That's what you need."

No kidding. She did need that. She *wanted* that more than she could bear to admit to herself. She also wanted to take responsibility for her own life, her own children, and do it on her own. And it was harder than she even imagined it would be, than her mother had warned her it would be when she'd been so set on moving out and going it alone.

She couldn't be stubborn at the triplets' expense. She would focus on that instead of on how crazy Reed's proposal was. Because when it came right down to it, he was absolutely right about what she needed.

And what *he* needed was his grandmother's ranch. She'd witnessed just how great that need was when they'd been together at the house. The ranch meant so much to him. It was home. It was connection to his family. It was his future. And his being able to call the ranch home came down to her saying yes to his proposition.

Hmm. That proposition was a business deal of sorts. She thought, at least. "I get stability and security and you get the Barelli ranch."

He eyed her and she could tell he was trying to read her. She made sure she had on her most neutral expression. She had no idea what she thought of his proposal. Stay legally married to a man she'd known for days? For mutual benefit?

"Right," he said. "I need it more than I ever realized. It's home. The only place that's ever felt like home. You could move out of that falling-down, depressing little place and move to the ranch with room and wide-open spaces for everyone."

Her house *was* falling down and depressing. She hated those steep, slippery wooden stairs. And the lease was month to month. It would be a snap to get out of.

But the man was talking about serious legal stuff. Binding. He was talking about keeping their marriage on the books.

She looked up at him. "So we just rip up the papers and, voilà, we're married?"

"We are truly married, Norah. Yeah, we can go through with the annulment. Or we can strike a bargain that serves us both. Neither of us is interested in a real marriage about love and all that jazz. We've both been burned and we're on the same page. Our marriage would be a true partnership based on what we need. I think we'll be quite happy."

Quite happy? She wasn't so sure she'd be even close to happy. Comfortable, maybe. Not afraid, like she was almost all the time.

And what would it be like to feel the way she had during the ceremony? Safe. Secure. Cherished. Sure, the man "promising" those things had been drunk off his behind, but here he was, sober as a hurricane, promising those things all over again.

Maybe not to cherish her. But to stand at her side. God, she wanted that. Someone trustworthy at her side, having her back, being there.

But what did Reed Barelli, bachelor, know about living 24/7 with babies? What if she let herself say yes to this crazy idea, moved to that beautiful homestead and breathed for the first time in over seven months, and he couldn't handle life with triplets after a week? He had no idea what he was in for.

She raised an eyebrow. "What makes you think you want to live with three seven-month-old, teething babies? Are you nuts?"

He smiled. "Insane, remember?"

He had to be. She had to be. But what did she have to lose? If the partnership didn't work out, he would sign the papers and that would be that.

She could give this a whirl. After all, they were already married. She didn't have to do anything except move into a beautiful ranch house with floors that didn't creak or slope and with an oven that worked all the time.

Of course, she would be living with Reed Barelli. Man. Gorgeous man. What would *that* be like?

"Let's try," he whispered.

She looked up at him again, trying to read him. If she said, "Yes, let's try this wild idea of yours," he'd get his ranch. If she said no, he'd never have the only place that had ever felt like home. Reed wouldn't marry just to get the ranch; she truly believed that. But because of a big bowl of spiked punch, he had his one chance. He'd been so kind to her, so good to the triplets.

Brody let out a sigh and Norah glanced over at her son. His little bow-shaped mouth was quirking and a hand moved up along his cheek. The partnership would benefit the triplets and that was all she needed to know.

"I was about to say 'Where do I sign?' but I guess I'm not signing, after all." She picked up the papers and put them back in her tote bag.

The relief that crossed Reed's face didn't go unnoticed. Keeping that ranch meant everything to him. Even if it meant being awakened at 2:00 a.m. by one, two or three crying babies. And again at 3:00 a.m.

Out of the corner of her eye, Norah caught her mother hurrying back over to her station, pretending to be very busy whisking eggs. She poked her head out of the office. "Did y'all hear this crazy plan of his?"

"What? No, we weren't eavesdropping," her mother said. "Okay, we were. And I for one think his crazy plan isn't all that crazy."

"Me, too," Cheyenne said from in front of the oven. "You each get what you need."

Even if it's not what we really want, Norah thought.

Reed didn't want to be married. Just as she didn't. Sure, it felt good and safe. But even a good man like Reed couldn't be trusted with her stomped-on heart. No one could. It wasn't up for grabs, hadn't been since the day after she'd found out she was pregnant and had been kicked to the curb.

Shelby sidled over and took Norah's hand. "You don't mind if I borrow your wife, do you?" she asked Reed.

What also didn't go unnoticed? How Reed swallowed, uncomfortably, at the word *wife*.

Wife. Norah was someone's wife. Not just someone's—this man's. This handsome, kind, stand-up man.

"Of course," he said. "I'll keep an eye on the triplets."

Shelby gave him a quick smile, then led Norah by the hand to the opposite end of the kitchen. "Don't forget to figure out the rules."

"The rules?" Norah repeated.

"Just what kind of marriage will this be?" her sister asked. "He used the word *partnership*, but you're also husband and wife. So are you sharing a bedroom?"

Norah felt her face burn. She was hardly a prude, but the thought of having sex with Reed Barelli seemed… sinful in a very good way. They'd hardly worked up to the level of sex. Even if they were married. They weren't even at the first-kiss stage yet.

Norah pictured Reed in his black boxer briefs. "I guess we'll need to have a conversation about that."

"Yeah, you will," Shelby said. "Been there, done that with my own husband back when we first got together. Remember, Liam and I only got married so we could each have both our babies—the ones we'd raised for six months and the ones who were biologically ours."

Norah would never forget that time in Shelby's life. And the fact that all had turned out very well for her sister was a bonus. It wasn't as if Norah and Reed Barelli were going to fall in love. She had zero interest in romance. Yes, Reed was as hot as a man got, but nice to look at was different than feeling her heart flutter when she was around him. That wasn't going to happen. Not to a woman who'd been burned. Not to a busy mother of baby triplets. And it certainly wouldn't happen to Reed. He was even more closed to the concept of love and romance than she was. And as if he'd fall for a woman who'd lost all sex appeal. She smelled like strained apricots and spit-up and baby powder when she wasn't smelling like chicken pot pie. She wasn't exactly hot stuff these days.

"No matter what you're thinking, Norah, don't forget one thing," Shelby said.

Norah tilted her head. "What's that?"

Shelby leaned in and whispered, "He's a man."

"Meaning?"

"What's the statistic about how many times per second men think about sex?" Shelby asked.

Norah let out a snort-laugh and waved a hand down the length of herself. "Oh yeah, I am irresistible." She was half covered in flour. Her hair was up in a messy bun. She wore faded overalls and yellow Crocs.

"Trust me," Shelby said. "The issue will arise." She let out a snort herself. "Get it? *Arise*." She covered her mouth with her hand, a cackle still escaping.

"You're cracking jokes at a time like this?" Norah said, unable to help the smile.

"I'm just saying. You need to be prepared, Norah. Your life is about to change. And I'm not just talking about a change in address."

That was for sure. She'd be living with a man. Living with Reed Barelli. "Your words of wisdom?" she asked her sister.

"Let what happens happen. Don't fight it."

Norah narrowed her eyes. "What's gonna happen?"

"Let's see. Newlyweds move in together…"

Norah shook her head. "You can stop right there, sistah. We may be newlyweds, but like Reed said, this is a partnership. No hanky-panky. This isn't about romance or love. Nothing is *arising*."

"We'll see. But just know this, Norah. It's nice to be happy. Trust me on that."

Norah loved that her sister was happy. But the pursuit of happiness wasn't why Norah was saying yes to Reed's proposition.

"I'm finally at a good place, Shel," Norah said. "It took me a long time to bounce back from being abandoned the way I was. Lied to. Made a fool of. I might not be skipping all over town, but I'm not *un*happy. And I'm not throwing away my equilibrium when my first and foremost job is to be a good mother. I will not, under any circumstances, fall for a guy who's made it crystal clear he feels the same way I do—that love is for other people."

Shelby squeezed her hand. "Well, just know that anytime you need a sitter for an evening out with your husband, I'm available."

"I no longer need sitters because I'll have a live-in sitter."

"Answer for everything, don't you?" Shelby said with a nudge in Norah's midsection. She threw her arms around her and squeezed. "Everything's going to be fine. You'll see."

Norah went back into the office and stared hard at her sleeping babies, then at Reed, who leaned against the desk looking a bit...amused, was it?

"Your sister is right," he said. "Everything *is* going to be fine."

Norah wasn't so sure of that.

And had he heard *everything* they'd said?

Chapter Seven

Thanks to the Wedlock Creek PD going digital, copies of all the case files were now a click away and on Reed's smartphone. He was almost glad to have a confounding case to focus on for the next couple of hours while Norah packed for herself and the triplets.

For a while there he'd thought she might say no. The idea *was* crazy. To stay married? As a business partnership? Nuts. Who did that?

People like him whose wily grandmother had him over a barrel.

People like her who could use a solid place to land.

When he'd left the Pie Diner, the annulment papers back in the envelope, unsigned, the ranch rightfully his after a visit to his grandmother's attorney, an unfamiliar shot of joy burst inside him to the point he could have been drunk on spiked punch. The ranch was home for real. He'd wake up there every day. Walk the land he'd explored as a child and teenager. Finally adopt a dog or two or three and a couple of black cats that he'd always been partial to. He was going home.

But right now he was going to find David Dirk, who hadn't been seen or heard from in days. Reed sat in his SUV and read through the notes on his phone. Dirk's fiancée, Eden Pearlman, twenty-five, hair stylist, never before married, no skeletons in the closet, per his predecessor's notes, had agreed to meet with him at her condo at the far end of Main Street.

He stood in front of the building and took it in: five-story, brick, with a red canopy to the curb and a part-time doorman who had seen David Dirk leave for his office four days ago at 8:45 a.m., as usual, briefcase in one hand, travel mug of coffee in the other. He'd been wearing a charcoal-gray suit, red-striped tie. According to his predecessor's notes, David had had a full day's appointments, meetings with two clients, one prospective client, but had mostly taken care of paperwork and briefs. His part-time administrative assistant had worked until three that day and noted that David had seemed his usual revved-up self. Except then he vanished into thin air instead of returning home to the condo he shared with his fiancée of eight months.

Looking worried, sad and hopeful, Eden closed the door behind Reed and sat on a chair.

Reed sat across from her. "Can you tell me about the morning you last saw Mr. Dirk?"

Eden pushed her light blond hair behind her shoulders and took a breath. "It was just a regular morning. We woke up, had breakfast—I made him a bacon-and-cheese omelet and toast—and then David left for his office. He texted me a Thinking about you, beautiful at around eleven. That's the last time I heard from him. Which makes me think whatever went wrong happened soon after because he would have normally texted a cute little something a couple hours later and he didn't. He always texted a few times a day while at work. I just know something terrible happened! But I don't want that to be true!" She started crying, brown streaks under her eyes.

Reed reached for the box of tissues on the end table and handed it to her. She took it and dabbed at her eyes. "I know this isn't easy, Ms. Pearlman. I appreciate that you're talking to me. I'm going to do everything I can to find your fiancé. I knew David when I was a kid. We used to explore the woods together when I'd come up summers to stay with my grandmother. I have great memories of our friendship."

She sniffled and looked up at him. "So it's personal for you. That's good. You'll work hard to find my Davy Doo."

He wondered if any old girlfriend of his had ever referred to him as Reedy Roo or whatever. He hoped not. "What did you talk about over breakfast?" he asked.

"The wedding mostly. He was even trying to convince me to elope to Las Vegas—he said he wanted me to be his wife already and that we could even fly out that night. He's so romantic."

Hmm, making a case for eloping? Had Dirk wanted to get out of town fast? Was there a reason he'd wanted to go to Las Vegas in particular? Or was there a reason he'd wanted to marry Eden even faster than the week-end? "Did you want to elope?"

She shook her head. "My mother would have my head! Plus, all the invitations were out. The wedding is this Saturday!"

"Where?" he asked, trying to recall the venue on the invitation.

"The Wedlock Creek chapel—this Saturday night," she said, sniffling again. "What if he's not back by then?"

"I'm going to go out there and do my job," he said. "I'll be in touch as soon as I have news."

She stood and shook his hand. "Thanks, Detective. I feel better knowing an old friend of David's is on the case."

Back in his SUV, Reed checked David Dirk's financials again. None of his credit cards had been used in the past twenty-four hours. Reed's predecessor had talked to five potential enemies of David's from opposing cases, but none of the five had struck the retired detective as holding a grudge. Reed flipped a few more pages in the man's notes. Ah, there it was. "According to friends and family, however, David wouldn't have just walked out on Eden. He loved her very much."

So what did happen to you, David Dirk? Reed wondered.

Reed had sent a small moving truck with two brawny guys to bring anything Norah wanted from the house to the ranch, but since the little rental had come furnished, she didn't have much to move. Her sister had given her way too many housewarming gifts from her secondhand shop, Treasures, so Norah had packed up those items and her kitchen stuff and everything fit into a small corner of the moving truck. It was easier to focus on wrapping up her picture frames than on actually setting them on surfaces in Reed's home.

She was moving in with him? She was. She'd made a deal.

Norah had never lived with a man. She'd lived on her own very briefly in this little dump, just under a year, and while she liked having her own place and making her way, she'd missed hearing her mom in the kitchen or singing in the shower. Did Reed sing in the shower? Probably not. Or maybe he did. She knew so little about him.

She gave the living room a final sweep. This morning she'd done a thorough cleaning, even the baseboards because she'd been so wired, a bundle of nervous energy about what today and tomorrow and the future would be like. She was taking a big leap into the unknown.

"We're all set, miss," the big mover in the baseball cap said, and Norah snapped out of her thoughts.

She was about to transfer the triplets from their playpen to their car seats, then remembered her mom had them for the day to allow Norah a chance to settle in at Reed's. She stood in the doorway of her house, gave it a last once-over and then got in her car. She pulled out, the truck following her.

In fifteen minutes they were at the farmhouse. Reed told the movers to place all the items from the truck in the family room and that Norah would sort it all later.

Once the movers were gone and it was just Norah and Reed in the house, which suddenly seemed so big and quiet, it hit her all at once that this was now her home. She *lived* here.

"I want you to feel comfortable," he said. "So change anything you want."

"Did we talk about sleeping arrangements?" she asked, turning away and trying to focus on an oil painting of two pineapples. They hadn't, she knew that full well.

"I'll leave that to you," he said.

"As if there's more than one option?"

He smiled. "Why don't you take the master bedroom? It's so feminine, anyway." He started for the stairs. "Come, I'll give you more of a tour."

She followed him to the second level. The first door on the left was open to the big room with its cool white walls and huge Oriental rug and double wood dresser and big round mirror. A collection of old perfume dispensers was on a tray. A queen-size four-poster was near the windows overlooking the red barn, the cabbage-rose quilt and pillows looking very inviting. Norah could see herself falling asleep a bit easier in this cozy room. But still. "I feel like you should have the master suite. It's your house, Reed."

"I'd really rather have the room I had as a kid. It's big and has a great view of the weeping willow I used to read under. My grandmother kept it the same for when I'd come visit through the years. I'm nostalgic about it. So you take the master."

"Well, if you insist that I take the biggest room with

the en suite bath, who am I to say no?" She grinned and he grinned back. She walked inside the room and sat on the bed, giving it a test. "Baby-bear perfect. I'll take it." She flopped back and spread out her arms, giving in to this being home.

"Good, it's settled."

A vision of Reed Barelli in his black boxer briefs and nothing else floated into her mind again, the way he'd looked lying next to her, all hard planes and five-o'clock shadow, long, dark eyelashes against his cheeks. She had a crazy thought of the two of them in bed.

And crazy it was, because their marriage was platonic. Sexless.

Focus, Norah. Stop fantasizing, which is bad for your health, anyway. Men can't be trusted with any part of your anatomy. That little reminder got her sitting up. "My sister says we need to talk about how this is going to work."

"Your sister is right. I made a pot of coffee before you came. Let's go talk."

She followed him downstairs and into the kitchen. On the refrigerator was a magnet holding a list of emergency numbers, everything from 9-1-1 to poison control to the clinic and closest hospital. His work and cell numbers were also posted, which meant he'd put up this sheet for her.

He poured coffee and fixed hers the way she liked, set them both on the round table in front of the window and sat down. "I have a feeling we'll just have to deal with things as they come up."

She sat across from him, her attention caught by the

way the light shone on the side of his face, illuminating his dark hair. He was too handsome, his body too muscular and strong, his presence too…overwhelming.

"But I suppose the most important thing is that you feel comfortable here. This is now your home. Yours and the triplets. You and they have the run of the place. The crawl of the place."

She smiled. "I guess that'll take some getting used to." She glanced out the window at the fields she could imagine Bella, Bea and Brody running like the wind in just several months from now.

"No rush, right?" he said.

I could do this forever, she finished for him and realized that really was probably the case for him. He seemed to be at ease with the situation, suddenly living with a woman he'd accidentally slash drunk-married, appointing himself responsible for her and her three children. Because he wasn't attracted to her physically, most likely. Or emotionally. Men who weren't interested in marriage generally went for good-time girls who were equally not interested in commitment. Norah Ingalls was anything but a good-time girl. Unless you counted their wedding night. And you couldn't because neither of them could remember it.

Detective Reed Barelli's job was to serve and protect and that was what he was doing with his accidental wife. That was really what she had to remember here—and not let her daydreams get a hold on her. The woman he'd thought he was getting was Angelina, international flight attendant. Not Norah.

There was no need to bring up her sister Shelby's

bedroom questions again or exactly what kind of marriage this was. That was clear. They were platonic. Roommates. Sharing a home but not a bed. Helping each other out. Now that she had that square in her mind, she felt more comfortable. There were boundaries, which was always good. She could ogle her housemate, stare at his hotness, but she'd never touch, never kiss and never get her heart and trust broken again.

"Anything else we should cover?" he asked.

She bit her lip. "I think you're right. We'll deal with whatever comes up. Right now we don't know what those things might be."

"For instance, you might snore really loud and keep me awake all night and I'll have to remember to shut my door every night to block out the freight train sounds."

She smiled. "I don't snore."

"Not an issue, then," he said, and she realized that, again, he was trying to break the ice, make her feel more comfortable.

She picked up her mug. "You know who might keep you awake, though? The three teething seven-month-olds you invited to live here with you."

"They're supposed to do that, so it's all good."

"Does anything rattle you?" she asked, wondering if anything did.

"Yes, actually. A few things. The first being the fact that we're married. Legally married."

Before she could even think how to respond to that, he changed the subject.

"So what's on your agenda for today?" he asked.

"I figure I'll spend the next couple of hours unpacking, then I'll be working this afternoon. It's Grandma's Pot Pie Day, so I'll be making about fifty classics—chicken, beef, vegetable—from my grandmother's recipes. Oh—and I'll be writing up a class syllabus, too."

He took a sip of his coffee and tilted his head. "A class syllabus?"

She explained about the director of the community services center asking her to teach the multiples class for parents and caregivers of zero-to-six-month-olds. "I tried to get out of it—I mean, I'm hardly an expert—but she begged."

"You *are* an expert. You're a month out of the age group. Been there, done that and lived to tell the tale. And to teach the newbies what to do."

She laughed. "I guess so!"

Norah always thought of herself as barely hanging on, a triplet's lovie falling out of the stroller, a trail of Cheerios behind them on the sidewalk, a runny nose, a wet diaper. Well-meaning folks often said, "I don't know how you do it," when they stopped Norah on the street to look at the triplets. Most of the time she didn't even feel like she *was* doing it. But all three babies were alive and well and healthy and happy, so she must be. She could do this and she would. She *did* have something to offer the newbie multiples moms of Wedlock Creek.

She sat a little straighter. She had graduated from the zero-to-six-month age range, hadn't she? And come through just fine. She was a veteran of those first scary six months. And yeah, you bet your bippy she'd done it alone. With help from her wonderful family, yes. But alone. She could teach that class blindfolded.

He covered her hand with his own for a moment and she felt the two-second casual touch down to her toes.

"Well, I'd better start unpacking," she said, feeling like a sixteen-year-old overwhelmed by her own feelings.

"If you need help, just say the word."

He was too good. Too kind. Too helpful. And too damned hot.

She slurped some more coffee, then stood and carried the mug into the family room, where the movers had put her boxes. But she wanted to be back in the kitchen, sitting with…her husband and just talking.

Her husband. She had a husband. For real. Well, sort of for real.

She didn't expect it to feel so good. She'd just had an "I'm doing all right on my own" moment. But it was nice to share the load. Really, really nice.

After walking Norah to the Pie Diner and taking a slice of Grandma's Classic Beef Pot Pie to go, Reed was glad the diner was so busy, because he kept seeing Norah's mom and aunt casting him glances, trying to sneak over to him for news and information about how Norah's move-in had gone. Luckily, they'd kept getting waylaid by customers wanting more iced tea and "could they have sausage instead of bacon in their quiche Lorraine?" and "were the gluten-free options really gluten free?"

Move-in had gone just fine. He was comfortable around Norah for some reason he couldn't figure out.

He'd never lived with a woman, despite a girlfriend or two dumping him over his refusal for even that, let alone an engagement ring.

As far as tonight went, he'd simply look at his new living arrangement the way he would with any roommate. They were sharing a home. Plain and simple. The snippets he'd overheard from Norah's conversation with her sister wouldn't apply. There would be no sex. No kissing. No romance. As long as he kept his mind off how pretty and sexy she was and remembered why they were staying married, he'd be fine.

That settled in his head, he hightailed it out of the Pie Diner with his to-go bag and took a seat at a picnic table edging the town green, waving at passersby, chatting with Helen Minnerman, who had a question about whether it was against the law for her neighbor's Chihuahua to bark for more than a minute when outside—no, it was not—and helping a kid around ten or eleven up from under his bike when he slid from taking a turn too fast.

Life in Wedlock Creek was like this. Reed could get used to this slower pace. A man could think out here in all this open space and fresh air, which was exactly what he was doing, he realized. Too much thinking. About his new wife and what it would be like to wake up every morning knowing she was in bed down the hall. In the shower, naked under a spray of steamy water and soap. Making waffles in his kitchen. Their kitchen. Caring for babies who had him wrapped around their tiny fingers after just a few days of knowing them.

But all his thinking hadn't gotten him closer to finding David Dirk. In fifteen minutes he was meeting Dirk's closest friend, a former law associate, so hopefully the man would be able to shed some light.

Reed finished the last bite of the amazing beef pot pie, then headed for Kyle Kirby's office in a small, brick office building next to the library.

Kirby, a tall, lanky man with black eyeglasses, stood when Reed entered, then gestured for him to sit. "Any luck finding David?"

Reed sat. "Not yet. And to be honest, not much is making sense. I've looked into all the possibilities and I'm at a loss."

Kirby was chewing the inside of his lip—as if he knew more than he wanted to say. He was looking everywhere but at Reed.

Reed stared at him. "Mr. Kirby, if you know where David is or if he's okay or not, tell me now."

Was that sweat forming on the guy's forehead despite the icy air-conditioning?

"I wish I could help. I really do." He stood. "Now, if those are all your questions, I need to get back to work."

Reed eyed him and stood. This was strange. Reed had done his homework on Kyle Kirby's relationship with David and the two were very close friends, had been since David had moved back to Wedlock Creek to settle down after graduating from law school. Kirby had no skeletons in his closet and there was no bad blood between him and David. So what was the guy hiding?

Frustrated, Reed put in a couple more hours at the station, working on another case—a break-in at the drugstore. A promising lead led to a suspect, and another hour later, Reed had the man in custody. The solid police work did nothing to help his mood over his inability to figure out what had happened to David. It was as if he had just vanished into thin air.

One staff meeting and the receptionist's birthday cake celebration later, Reed headed home. He almost drove to the house he'd rented and would need to find a new tenant for. It still hadn't sunk in that the Barelli ranch was his, was home, and that when he arrived, he wouldn't walk into an empty house. Norah would be there. Bella, Bea and Brody would be there. And tonight he was grateful for the company. Company that wouldn't be leaving. *That* would definitely take some getting used to.

He pulled up at the ranch, glad to see Norah's car. Inside he found her in the kitchen, the triplets in their big playpen near the window. Bella was chewing on a cloth book, Brody was banging on a soft toy piano and Bea was shaking a rattling puppy teether. The three looked quite happy and occupied.

"Something sure smells good," he said, coming up behind Norah and peeking into the big pot on the stove. "Pot pies for the diner?"

"Meatballs and spaghetti for us," she said. "I remember you mentioned you loved meatballs and spaghetti the night we met, so I figured it would be a good first dinner for us as—"

He smiled. "Official husband and wife."

"Official husband and wife," she repeated. She turned back to the pot, using a ladle to scoop out the meatballs and fragrant sauce into a big bowl. Was it Reed's imagination or did she look a little sad?

"You okay?" he asked.

She didn't answer. She picked up the pot of spaghetti and drained it into a colander over the sink, then added it to the bowl of meatballs and stirred it. Before he could say another word, the oven timer dinged and she took out heavenly smelling garlic bread.

"Well, can I at least help with anything?" he asked.

"Nope. The babies have eaten. Dinner is ready. The table is set. So let's eat."

She'd poured wine. There was ice water. A cloth napkin. He hadn't been treated to this kind of dinner at home in a long, long time, maybe not since he'd last visited his grandmother just weeks before she'd died.

"This is nice. I could get used to this," he said. "Thank you."

"You will get used to it because I love to cook and, given everything you're doing for me and the triplets, making dinner is the least I can do."

But as they chatted about their days and the triplets and she filled him in on some upcoming events in town, Norah seemed to get sadder. And sadder. Something was wrong.

"Norah. This marriage is meant to be a true partnership. So if something is bothering you, and something clearly is, tell me. Let's talk about it."

She poked at her piece of garlic bread. "It's silly."

"I'm sure it's not."

"It's just that, there I was, cooking at the stove in this beautiful country kitchen, my dream kitchen, the triplets happily occupied in the playpen, and my husband comes home, except he's not really my husband in the way I always thought it would go. I'm not complaining, Reed. I'm just saying this is weird. I always wanted something very different. Love, forever, growing old together on the porch. The works."

"It's not quite what I expected for myself, either," he said, swirling a bite of spaghetti. "It'll take some getting used to. But we'll get to know each other and soon enough we'll seem like any other old married couple."

"Kind of backward to have to get to know your spouse." She gave him a wistful smile and took a sip of wine.

"The triplets' father—you wanted to marry him?"

Norah put down her fork as though the mention of him cost her her appetite. "I just don't understand how someone could seem one way and truly be another way. I got him so wrong. I thought he was crazy about me. He was always talking about us and the future. But then the future presented itself in the form of my pregnancy and everything changed. I'll never forget the look on his face when I told him I was pregnant. A combo of freaked out and horrified."

"Sorry."

"And now everything I wanted—the loving husband, the babies, a home for us—is right here and it's all..."

He touched her hand. "Not like the old dreams."

She lifted her chin and dug her fork into a meatball with gusto. "I'm being ridiculous. I'm sitting here moping over what isn't and what wasn't. My life is my life. Our deal is a good one. For both of us. And for those three over there," she added, gesturing at the playpen. She focused on them for a moment and then turned back to him. "Okay, full speed ahead on the marriage partnership. My head is back in the game."

The meatball fell off her fork and plopped back onto her plate, sending a splatter of sauce onto both of them—her cheek and his arm. They both laughed and then he reached out and dabbed away the sauce from her cheek as she did the same to his arm.

"Anytime you need to talk this through, just tell me," he said. "And we'll work it out."

"You, too, you know."

He nodded. "Me, too."

As she pushed around spaghetti and twirled it but never quite ate any more, he realized she had the same funny pit in the middle of her stomach that he had in his, just maybe caused by a different emotion. She'd wanted something so much more—big passion, real romance, everlasting love—and had to settle for plain ole practical for a good reason. He'd planned on going it alone, never committing, but he had committed in a huge way, even if his heart wasn't involved. He was responsible for this family of four. Family of five now, including him.

He wouldn't let Norah down. Ever. But he knew he'd never be able to give her what she wanted in the deepest recesses of her heart.

Chapter Eight

There was no way Reed was getting any sleep tonight. Not with Norah down the hall, sleeping in who knew what. Maybe she slept naked, though he doubted she'd choose her birthday suit for her first night in her new home with her new partnership-husband. Twice he'd heard her get out of bed—the floor creaked a bit in that room—and go into the nursery. One of the babies had been fussing a bit and she sang a lullaby that almost had him drifting off. Almost. Norah had a beautiful voice.

He glanced at the clock: 2:12 a.m. He heard a faint cry. Then it grew louder. If he wasn't mistaken, that was Brody. He waited a heartbeat for the telltale creak of the master bedroom floor, but it didn't come. Only another cry did.

Reed got out of bed, making sure he was in more

than his underwear. Check. A T-shirt and sweats. He headed to the nursery and gently pushed the door open wider. One frustrated, red-faced little one was sitting up in his crib, one fist around the bar.

"Hey there, little guy," Reed said in his lowest voice to make sure he wouldn't wake Brody's sisters. "What's going on? What's with the racket?"

Brody scrunched up his face in fury that Reed wasn't picking him up fast enough. His mouth opened to let loose a wail, but Reed snatched him up and, as always, the sturdy little weight of him felt like pure joy in his arms. Brody wore light cotton footie pajamas and one sniff told Reed he was in the all clear for a middle-of-the-night, heavy-duty diaper change. He brought the baby over to the changing table and took off the wet diaper, gave Brody a sprinkle of cornstarch, then put on a new diaper like a pro. All the while, Brody looked at him with those huge slate-blue eyes.

Reed picked him up and held him against his chest, walking around the nursery while slightly rocking the little guy. Brody's eyes would flutter closed, then slowly open as if making sure Reed hadn't slipped him inside his crib and left. This went on four more times, so Reed sat in the rocker and Brody let out the sigh of all sighs and closed his eyes, his lips quirking and then settling.

"Guess that means you're comfortable, then," Reed whispered. He waited a few seconds, then stood, but the baby opened his eyes. Reed almost laughed. "Busted. You caught me." Reed sat back down, figuring he might be there awhile. Maybe all night. "Want to hear a story?"

Brody didn't make a peep in response, but Reed took that for a yes anyway.

"Once upon a time, there was a little boy named Beed Rabelli. That's not me, by the way."

Did Brody believe him? Probably not. But it made the story easier to tell.

"Well, this little kid, Beed, did everything to try to win his father's approval. His father's interest. But no matter what Beed did, pretending to be interested in things he really didn't even like, his father barely paid attention to him. He only came around every now and then as it was. But one day, Beed's dad never came around again and Beed started getting postcards from far-off places."

Brody moved his arm up higher by his ear and Reed smiled at how impossibly adorable the baby was. And what a good listener.

"So one day, Beed and his friend David Dirk were riding bikes and exploring the woods and they got to talking about how even though they pretty much had the same type of not-there dad, it didn't mean their dads didn't love them or care about them. Their dads were just…free spirits who had to follow the road in their souls. Or something like that. Anyway, Brody, I just want you to know that your father is like that and that's why he's not here. I don't want you to spend one minute wondering why he doesn't care about you, because I'm sure he does. He's just following that road that took him far away from here and—"

Reed stopped talking. Where the hell was this coming from? Why was he saying anything of this to Brody?

Because he cared about this little dude, that was why. And it was important to know because at some level it was very likely true.

He heard a sniffle and glanced toward Bea's and Bella's cribs. They were both fast asleep. He heard the sound again and realized it was coming from outside. Reed put Brody gently back inside his crib, and *booyah*—the baby did not open those eyes again. Either Reed had bored him to sleep or a story worked like it always had since time began.

He tiptoed out to investigate the sound of the sniffle. Was Norah so upset about her lost dreams that she was crying in the middle of the night?

He froze at the sight of her standing to the left of the nursery door, tears in her eyes.

"Norah? What's wrong?"

She grabbed him, her hands on the sides of his face, and pulled him close, laying one hell of a kiss on him. Damn, she smelled so good and her skin was so soft. Everything inside him was on fire. He backed her up against the wall and pressed against her, deepening the kiss, his hands roaming her neck, into her hair, down along her waist. He wanted to touch her everywhere.

"So you're not upset," he whispered against her ear, then trailed kisses along her beautiful neck.

"I was touched enough that you'd gotten up at a baby crying," she said. "And then as I was about to walk in, I heard you talking to Brody and couldn't help eavesdropping. I can't tell you how anxious I've been about the questions that would be coming my way someday, maybe at age three or four. 'Where's my father? Why doesn't Daddy live with us? Why doesn't Daddy ever see us? Doesn't he care about us?'"

Norah wiped under her eyes and leaned the front of her luscious body against Reed's. "I had no idea what I would say, how I could possibly make it okay for them. And one 2:00 a.m. diaper change later, you've settled it."

"Eh, I didn't say anything I hadn't worked out over the past twenty-nine years."

She smiled and touched his face, and he leaned his cheek against it. Then he moved in for another kiss, hoping reality and the night-light in the hallway wouldn't ruin the moment and make her run for her room.

She didn't. She kissed him back, her hands on his chest, around his neck, in his hair. He angled them down the hall toward his room and they fell backward onto his bed, the feel of her underneath him, every part of her against him, almost too much to bear.

He slid his hands under her T-shirt and pulled it over her head, then tugged off his own shirt and flung it behind him. He lay on top of her, kissing her neck, her shoulder, between her luscious breasts.

And then he felt her shift. Just slightly. The equivalent of a bitten lower lip. A hesitation.

He pulled back and looked at her. "Too fast?"

"Way too fast," she said. "Not that I'm not enjoying it. Not that I didn't start it."

He laughed. "That was hot. Trust me."

Her smile faded. "You've made it very clear what this marriage is, Reed. 'Friends with benefits' when we're married is too weird. Even for us. I think we need to keep some very clear boundaries."

She turned away from him and quickly put her T-shirt back on. He did the same.

"An emotional moment, the middle of the night, then there's me, still probably highly hormonal. Of course I jumped your bones."

She's trying to save face. Let her. "Believe me, if you hadn't kissed me, I would have kissed you first."

"Oh," she said, a bit of a smile back on her pretty face. "I guess we know where we stand, then. We're foolishly attracted to each other on a purely physical level, and we went with the moment, then wised up. We'll just keep our hands to ourselves from now on. So that this partnership has a fighting chance."

She was right. If they screwed this up with great sex, that could lead to who knew what, like other expectations, and suddenly she would be throwing annulment papers at him, all his plans to stand by her and the triplets would fall to pot. And so would this ranch—home.

He nodded. Twice to convince himself of just how right she was. "We both know where romance leads. Trouble. Heartache. Ruin."

"Well, at least the mystery is gone. You've seen my boobs."

He had to laugh. But he sobered up real fast when he realized the mystery was hardly gone. He had yet to truly touch her.

"So if I let what happens happen and then we realize it's a bad idea, what does that mean?" Norah asked Shelby the next morning as they sat at a corner table for two in Coffee Talk, their favorite place to catch up in Wedlock Creek. Their huge strollers against the wall behind them, triplets asleep and Shelby's toddler sons drifting off after a morning running around the playground, the sisters shared a huge slice of delicious crumbly coffee cake. Of course they'd never have pie anywhere but at their own family restaurant.

"Ooh, so something happened?" Shelby asked, sipping her iced mocha.

"In the middle of the night last night, I thought I heard one of the babies crying, but when I went to the nursery, Reed was sitting in the rocker with Brody in his arms, telling him a story about himself and relating it to Brody. I stood there in tears, Shel. This is going to sound crazy, but in that moment, my heart cracked open."

Shelby's mouth dropped open. "You're falling in love!"

"Oh God, I think I am. I was so touched and so hormonal that I threw myself at him. But then I realized what an idiot I was being and put the kibosh on that."

"What? Why?"

"Shelby, he's made it crystal clear he married me for his ranch. And because he feels some kind of chivalrous duty toward me, as if annulling our marriage means he's walking away from his responsibilities. He's not responsible for us!"

"He feels he is," Shelby said. "The man's a police officer. Serve and protect. It's what he does."

Maybe that was a good reminder that Reed was operating on a different level—the cop level, the responsibility level. His father had walked away from him and his mother, the triplets' father had walked away from them and Norah, and Reed couldn't abide that, couldn't stand it. So he was stepping in. Attracted to her physically or not, Reed's feelings where she was concerned weren't of the romantic variety. He was trying to right wrongs.

"Um, excuse me?" a woman asked as she approached the table.

"Hi," Norah said. "Can we help you?"

"I noticed your triplets," she said, looking at Bella, Bea and Brody, who were all conked out in their stroller wedged up against the wall. "So it's true? If you get married at the Wedlock Creek chapel, you'll have multiples?"

"I didn't get married at the chapel and still had triplets," Norah said.

"And I did get married at the chapel and had one baby," Shelby said, "but ended up with twins, sort of." At the woman's puzzled expression, she added, "It's a long story."

Norah took a sip of her iced coffee. "Well, the legend does say if you marry at the chapel you'll have multiples in some way, shape or form. Are you hoping for a houseful of babies all at the same time?" she asked the woman.

"My fiancé is a twin and so we have a good chance of having twins ourselves, but he wants to increase our luck. I just figure the legend is just that—a silly rumor."

"No way," Shelby said. "Last year alone, there were five multiple births—two sets of triplets and three twins. The year before, four sets of twins and one set of triplets. The year before that, one set of quadruplets and two sets of twins. And that's just in Wedlock Creek."

The woman paled. She truly seemed to lose color. "Oh. So the legend is actually true?"

"Well, as true as a legend can be," Shelby said. "But

this town is full of multiples. We can both personally attest to that."

"Um, is that a bad thing?" Norah asked gently.

"Well, twins just seem like a lot," the woman said. "One seems like a lot. I want to be a mother, but two at once? I don't know. I don't think I want to help our chances, you know?"

Norah smiled. "Then you definitely don't want to marry at the Wedlock Creek chapel." She upped her chin out the window. "See that woman? Pregnant with triplets. All boys!"

The woman swallowed. "I think we'll marry at the Brewer Hotel. Thanks!" she said and practically ran out.

Shelby laughed. "One baby *is* a lot of work. She's not wrong."

"But the more the merrier," Norah said, lifting her iced coffee for a toast.

"Got that right," Shelby said and tapped her cup. "Of course, you know what this means."

"What what means?"

"You and Reed got married at the chapel. You're going to have more multiples. Omigod, Norah, you're going to have, like, ten children."

She imagined three babies that looked like Reed Barelli. The thought made her smile.

"Jeez, you are far gone," Shelby said.

"Heaven help me. But I am."

She was falling in love with her business partner of a husband. She had to put the brakes on her feelings. But how did you do that when the floodgates just opened again?

Chapter Nine

That night, Norah arrived at the Wedlock Creek Community Services Center with her stack of handouts, her laptop, for her slideshow on her favorite baby products, and a case of the jitters. As she stood at the front of the room, greeting students as they entered, she took a fortifying gulp of the coffee she'd brought in a thermos. As she'd left the ranch, she was surprised by how much she wished Reed had been there to see her off and give her a "you've got this" fist bump or something. She was beginning to need him a little too much for comfort. But he was working late, following up on a promising lead about David Dirk, who was still missing.

A woman's belly entered the room before she did. "If my water breaks while I'm sitting down, here's my husband's cell number," she said to Norah with a smile. "I'm not due for another month, but you never know."

You never know. No truer words ever spoken.

Norah smiled and took the card with the woman's husband's information. "I'm glad you're here. And if your water does break, I've got my cell phone at the ready and a list of emergency medical numbers."

"Pray I don't give birth until after the last class!" the woman said on a laugh. "I need to learn everything!" she added and slowly made her way over to the padded, backed benches that had been brought in specifically for women in her condition.

There were several pregnant women with their husbands, mothers, mothers-in-law and various other relatives all wanting to learn the basics of caring for newborn multiples. Several women had infant multiples already. Norah glanced around the room, seeing excitement and nerves on the faces. That was exactly how she'd felt when she'd shown up for the first class.

She was about to welcome her students when the door opened and Reed walked in. "Sorry I'm a minute late," he said, handing her a printout of his online registration form. He took an empty seat next to one of the husbands, giving the man a friendly nod.

Reed was taking her class?

Of course he was.

Norah smiled at him and the smile he gave her back almost undid her. *Don't think about what happened in the hallway last night*, she ordered herself. *Stop thinking about his hands on your bare skin. You're standing in front of a room full of people!*

She sucked in a breath, turned her attention away

from Reed and welcomed her students. "Eight months ago, I was all of you," she said. "I was nine months' pregnant with BGG triplets—that's boy, girl, girl—and I was a nervous wreck. Not only was I about to give birth to three helpless infants who would depend on me for everything, but I was a single mother. I will tell you right now that the most important thing I have learned about being the mother of triplets, particularly in my position, is to ask for help."

Norah looked around the room. All eyes were on her, interested, hanging on her every word, and some were actually taking notes.

So far, so good, she thought. "Ladies, don't expect your husbands to read your minds—if you want him to change Ethan while you change Emelia, ask him! No passive-aggressive stewing at the changing table while he's watching a baseball game. Speak up. Ask for what you need!"

"She's talking to you, Abby," the man next to Reed said and got a playful sock in the arm from his wife.

The students laughed. This was actually going well! She was standing there giving advice. People were responding! "And men, while you have infant twins or triplets or quadruplets, you're not going to be watching the game unless you have a baby or two propped in your arms, one hand on a bottle, the other burping another's little back."

A guy got up and headed for the door. "Just kidding," he said with a grin. More laughter.

Norah smiled. "And you grandmothers-to-be…what I learned from my mother? You're the rock. You're going to be everything to the mother and father of newborn multiples. Not only do you have experience, even if it's not with multiples yourselves, but you've been there, done that in the parenting department. You love those little multiples and you're there to help. Sometimes your brand-new mother of a daughter or daughter-in-law may screech at you that she's doing it her way. Let her. Maybe it'll work, maybe it won't. But what matters is that you're supporting one another. You're there."

She thought of her mother and her aunt Cheyenne and her sister. Her rocks. She couldn't have done it without them—their love and support and good cheer.

"So that's my number one most valuable piece of information I can offer you. Ask for help when you need it. When you think you'll need it. Because you will need it. If some of you don't have a built-in support system, perhaps you can create one when you go home tonight. Friends. Caring neighbors. Folks from your house of worship. Think about the people you can turn to."

From there, Norah started up her slideshow of products she'd found indispensable. She talked about cribs and bassinets. Feeding schedules and sleep schedules. How laundry would take over entire evenings.

"You did all that on your own?" a woman asked.

"I lived on my own, but I have a fabulous mother, fabulous aunt and fabulous sister who were constantly over, taking shifts to helping me out, particularly that first crazy month. So when I tell you help is everything, I mean it. Just don't forget that thank-yous, hugs and homemade pies go a long way in showing appreciation for their support."

Fifty-five minutes later the class was winding down. Norah let them know that in two weeks she'd be bringing in her triplets for show-and-tell with her mom as a volunteer assistant, demonstrating how to perform necessary tasks with three babies. After a question-and-answer session, Norah dismissed the students.

Huh. She'd really done it. She'd taught a class! And she was pretty darn good at it.

One of the last to pack her notebook and get up was a woman who'd come to the class alone. Early thirties with strawberry blond hair, she looked tired and defeated and hadn't spoken much during the period. She walked up to Norah with tears in her eyes.

Oh no. This woman had the look of multiple-itis.

"I have twin six-week-olds," the woman said. "My mother is with them now, thank God. They're colicky and I'm going to lose my mind. My husband and I argue all the time. And I only have twins—the bare minimum to even have multiples—and I'm a falling-apart wreck!"

Norah put her hand on the woman's arm. "I totally hear you." She offered the woman a commiserating smile. "What's your name?"

"Sara Dirk."

Norah noticed Reed's eyebrows shoot up at the name Dirk.

"Welcome, Sara. I'm really glad you're here. I haven't personally dealt with colic, but I've known colicky babies, and let me tell you, you might as well have sextuplets."

Sara finally smiled. "They don't stop crying. Except to breathe. I don't know how my mother does it—the screeching doesn't even seem to bother her. She just walks up and down with one baby while she watches the other in the vibrating baby swing, then switches them. I hear those cries that go on forever and I just want to run away."

Reed walked over and sat in the chair at the side of the desk, collecting Norah's handouts. She knew he was intently listening.

"That's wonderful that your mom is so supportive, Sara. I tell you what. Stop by the Pie Diner tomorrow and let anyone there know that Norah said they're to give you two of your and your mom's favorite kinds of pies on the house."

"I love the Pie Diner's chocolate peanut butter pie. It always cheers me up for a good ten minutes."

Norah smiled. "Me, too. And I'll research some tips for dealing with colic," she said. "I'm sure you have already, but I'll talk to the mothers I know who've dealt with it and survived. I'll email you the links."

"Thanks," she said. "I really appreciate it."

Reed stood with Norah's folders and laptop. He extended his hand to Sara. "Did I hear you say your last name is Dirk?"

Sara nodded.

"Are you related to David Dirk?" he asked.

Sara nodded. "My husband's first cousin."

"I'm Reed Barelli, a detective with the Wedlock Creek Police Department. I also knew David when I was a kid. I'm trying to find him."

"I sure hope he's okay," Sara said. "We just can't figure out what could have happened. The night before he went missing, he stopped by for a few minutes to drop off a drill he'd borrowed from my husband and he seemed so happy."

"Any particular reason why—besides the upcoming wedding, I mean?" Reed asked.

"He said something had been bothering him but that he'd figured out a solution. And then the twins started screaming their heads off, as usual, and there went the conversation. He left and that was the last time I saw him."

"Do you know what was bothering him?" Reed asked.

"No idea. I know he's madly in love with Eden. Things are going well at work, as far as I know."

"When did you see him before that last time?" Reed asked.

"Hmm, maybe a couple nights before. We—my husband and I—needed a sitter for an hour and my mother couldn't do it, so we begged David. He and Eden watched the twins. Do you believe that after babysitting our little screechers, that woman is hoping for triplets or even quadruplets? Craziest thing. She loves the idea."

"More power to her," Norah said.

"Well, I'd better get back and give my mother a break. See you next week, Norah. Oh, and, Detective Barelli, I do hope you find David. Eden must be out of her mind with worry."

Norah watched Reed wait until Sara had left, then hurried to the door and closed it.

"Are you thinking what I'm thinking?" he asked.

"I have so many thoughts running through my head that it could be any number of them."

"About David Dirk. And why he suddenly went missing."

Norah tilted her head and stared at Reed. "What do you mean?"

"Well, let's recount the facts and evidence. David

Dirk has a cousin with colicky twins. David Dirk and his fiancée babysit said colicky twins. Despite the screeching in their ears for over an hour, Eden is hoping for multiples."

Norah wasn't sure where he was going with this. "Okay," she said. "What does that have to do with his disappearance?"

"Well," he continued, "she and David are to be married at the Wedlock Creek chapel, where legend says those who marry will be blessed with multiples. The night before he went missing, David told Sara something was bothering him but he'd figured out a solution. Cut to David's fiancée telling me that on the morning he disappeared, he'd asked her to elope. But she reminded him how badly she wanted to marry at the chapel."

Ah. Now she was getting it. "Oh boy."

"Exactly. Because why would David want to elope instead of marrying at the Wedlock Creek chapel?

"The only reason folks in this town don't get married there is because they don't want multiples." But was David really so freaked out by his cousin's colicky babies and his fiancée wanting sextuplets that he ran away? No way. Who would do that? She herself had dated him, and he'd seemed like a stand-up guy, even if they'd had zero to talk about other than the weather and which restaurants they liked in town.

She remembered the woman who'd approached her and Shelby in the coffee shop yesterday. She'd wanted to avoid that legend like the ole plague. So maybe it was true. David had run!

"I'm thinking so," Reed said. "It's the only thing that makes sense. Yesterday I spoke with a friend of his who seemed nervous, like he was hiding something. Maybe he knew the truth—that David took off on his own—and had been sworn to secrecy."

"What a baby David is," Norah said.

"Pun intended?"

Norah laughed. "Nope. He's just really a baby. Why not tell Eden how he felt? He has family and friends scared that something terrible happened to him. He had a friend lie to a police officer."

"Based on everything I've heard, I'm ninety-nine percent sure he took off on his own. I just have to find him. Maybe the friend can shed some light. I doubt he'll tell me anything, though."

"So how will you find David, then?"

"The right questions," Reed said. "And maybe my own memories of where David would go when his world felt like it was crashing down. I might know where he is without even realizing it. I need to do some thinking."

She nodded. "So let's go home, then."

"Home to the ranch. I like the sound of that."

Norah smiled and took his hand before she realized they weren't a couple. Why did being a couple feel so natural, then?

"Tell me more about the legend of the Wedlock Creek chapel," Reed said to Norah as they sat in the living room with two craft beers and two slices of the Pie Diner's special fruit pie of the day—Berry Bonanza.

"Well, as far as I know, back in the late 1800s, a woman named Elizabeth Eckard, known for being a bit peculiar, married her true love at the chapel."

"Peculiar how?"

"Some say she was a witch and could cast spells," Norah explained. "It was just rumor, but most shunned her just in case they got on her bad side."

Reed raised an eyebrow. "Apparently her true love wasn't worried."

Norah smiled. "Legend says he was so in love with Elizabeth, he married her against his parents' wishes, who refused to have anything to do with them."

"Jeez. Harsh."

"Yup. But he loved her and so he married her at the beautiful chapel that she had commissioned to be built. Elizabeth had inherited a bit of money and wanted the new town of Wedlock Creek to have a stately chapel for services of all kinds."

Reed took a bite of the pie. "That must have buttered up the townspeople. Did his family come around?"

"Nope. And the townspeople still shunned her. Some even avoided services at the chapel. But some started noticing that those who attended church seemed luckier than those who didn't. And so everyone started going."

Reed shook his head. "Of course."

"Well, the luck didn't extend to Elizabeth. All she wanted was children—six. Three boys and three girls. But she never did get pregnant. After five years of trying, her husband told her there was no point being married to her if she couldn't give him a family, and he left her."

"That's a terrible story," Reed said, sipping his beer.

Norah nodded. "But Elizabeth loved children and ended up turning her small house into a home for orphans. She had the children she'd always wanted so much, after all. But when her only sister found herself in the same position, not getting pregnant, her sister's husband went to the officiants of the chapel and demanded an annulment. That night, Elizabeth crept out to the chapel at midnight and cast a spell that those who married at the chapel would not only be blessed with children, but multiples."

"Come on," Reed said.

Norah shrugged. "Nine months later, Elizabeth's sister had twin girls. And all the couples who married at the church that year also had multiples. Whispers began that Elizabeth had blessed the church with a baby spell."

"Did she ever marry again? Have her own multiples?"

Norah shook her head. "No, but she took in orphans till her dying day, then hired people to keep the home going. It was going strong until the 1960s, when foster care became more prominent."

"It's crazy that I actually think that David Dirk, reasonable, intelligent, suspicious of everything, believes in this legend to the point that he fled town to avoid marrying at the chapel. It's just an old legend. There's no blessing or spell."

"Then what accounts for all the multiples?" Norah asked.

"A little help from science?" he asked.

"Maybe sometimes," she said. "But I know at least ten women who married at the chapel and had multiples without the help of a fertility doctor."

"Don't forget me," he said.

"You?"

"I married at the chapel and now I have triplets."

She smiled, but the beautiful smile faded. "Are you their father, Reed? I mean, we didn't actually ever talk about that. You said you felt responsible for them and me. You said you would help raise them and help support them and be there for them. But are you saying you want to be their father?"

He flinched and realized she caught it. "I—" He grabbed his beer and took a swig, unsure how to answer. *Did* he want to be the triplets' father? He was their mother's husband—definitely. He was doing all the things Norah said when it came to caring for Bella, Bea and Brody. He was there for them. But was he their *father*?

That word was loaded.

"This is a partnership," she said, her voice formal as she sat straighter. "Of course you're not their *father.*" She waved a hand in the air and made a strange snorting noise, then cut a forkful of berry pie. "It was silly of me to even use the term." A forced smile was plastered on her face. "So where do you think David Dirk is?"

Should he let her change the subject? If he were half the person she thought he was, he wouldn't. They'd talk this out. But he had no idea how he felt about this. Their *father*? Was he anyone's father? Could he be? Did he *want* to be?

"Norah, all I know for sure is that I want to take care of the four of you. I'm responsible for you all."

Her lips were tightly pressed. "Because you drunk-married me."

"I'm legally wed to you. It might have been because of spiked punch, but being married serves us both."

"You got your ranch," she said, staring at him. "And I got some security. I just have to keep reminding myself of that. Why we're here. Why we did this. Crazy as it really is."

Was it all that crazy? No. They both got what they needed.

He wasn't anyone's father. Reed Barelli? A father? With his craptastic model of paternity?

"It's good to know, to remember, what we are," she said, her voice higher pitched.

Higher pitched because she was upset? Or because she was stating a fact? They'd almost had sex, but she'd called a halt and wisely so. She knew messing around with their partnership could have terrible consequences. Anything that could put conflict between them could ruin a good thing. And this marriage was a good thing. For both of them.

He was no one's father. He was Norah's husband and caretaker of her children. Guardian of them all.

None of this sounded right. Or felt right. His shoulders slumped and he slugged down the rest of the beer.

"Maybe I should go pick up the babies," she said. "My mom wants to keep them overnight, but I'm sure she'd rather have a solid night's sleep."

She wanted—needed—a buffer, he realized. And so did he.

"I'll go with you," he said. "Tell you the truth, I miss their little faces."

She bit her lip and lifted her chin, and he also realized he'd better stop saying things like that, despite the fact that it was the truth. His affection for the triplets was also a good thing—the fact that they had his heart meant he'd be a good provider, a good protector.

And that was what he'd vowed to be.

Chapter Ten

The next morning, Norah woke very early and made twelve pot pies to deliver to the Pie Diner, the need to keep her eyes and mind on the various pots and timers a help in keeping her mind off Reed. But as she slid the last three pies from the oven, the smell of vegetable pot pie so comforting and tantalizing that she took out a frozen one to heat up for her breakfast, she couldn't stop hearing him say he wasn't the triplets' father.

She knew that. And of course, he didn't say it outright because he was Reed Barelli. But she'd been under the impression that fatherhood was part of the deal. Until she'd heard what had come stumbling out of her own mouth last night. He'd said again that being married, spiked punch or not, served them both. And she'd said something like, "Right, you got your ranch, I got some security."

Security. That was very different than "a father for my children."

Her shoulders slumped. Maybe she hadn't thought this through quite far enough. A father for her kids should have been first on her list, no?

Except you weren't looking for a father for your kids, dummy, she reminded herself. *You weren't looking for anyone. You got yourself in a situation and you didn't undo it so that you and your babies could have that security: a safe house, another caring adult, the financial burden lifted a bit, one more pair of hands. All that in a kind, supportive—and yes, sexy as all get-out—husband.*

No one, certainly not Reed Barelli, had used the word *father*.

Okay. She just had to let it sink in and accept it. Her marriage was platonic. Her husband was not her children's father. She had a good setup. It was good for the both of them.

"Do people eat pot pie for breakfast?" Reed asked as he walked into the kitchen in a T-shirt and navy sweats. Even his bare feet were sexy. His hair was adorably rumpled and as the sunlight illuminated half his face, he looked so beautiful she just stood there and stared at him until he tilted his head.

"Pot pie is appropriate for all meals," she said. "Seven a.m. Three p.m. Six p.m."

"Good, because this kitchen smells so good I'm now craving it."

"You're in luck because I have six frozen in the freezer. Just pop one in the oven for a half hour. It'll be ready when you're out of the shower." She glanced at her watch. "I'm going to drop these off at the Pie Diner and pick up the babies, bring them home and then go to Sara Dirk's with some frozen pot pies. I think she could use a freezer full of easily reheatable meals."

"That's thoughtful of you. Tell you what. Why don't you go to Sara's and I'll deliver the pies and pick up the rug rats and bring them home. I'm not on duty till noon."

"I can pick up the triplets," she said, her stomach twisting. "They're my children and I—"

"Norah," he said, stepping closer. He took both her hands and held them. "That's why I'm here. That's why you're here. I'm now equally responsible for them. So go."

He sure did use the word *responsible* a lot. She had to keep that in mind. *Responsible* was how he'd gotten himself married to her in the first place. He'd heard the plaintive, wistful note in her voice—*I've always dreamed of getting married here*—and instead of running for the hills, he'd felt responsible for her lost dreams and picked her up in his arms and carried her inside the chapel and vowed to love, honor and cherish her for the rest of his days.

She glanced down at their entwined hands. Why did it have to feel so good? Why did she have to yearn for more than the deal they'd struck? "Thank you, then," she managed to say, moving to the freezer to pull out six pot pies for Sara. The icy blast felt good on her hot, Reed-held hands and brought her back to herself a bit. "I'll pop one in the oven for you. Thirty minutes, okay?"

"Got it. See you back at home in a bit."

Back at home. Back at home. As she carried her bag

to the door, she looked around and realized this ranch didn't feel like home, that she wasn't quite letting herself feel that it was hers, too. It wasn't. Not really. Just like Reed wasn't the triplets' father.

Because he was holding back just as she was. For self-preservation.

Stop thinking, she ordered herself as she got into her car and turned on the radio, switching the station until she found a catchy song she couldn't resist singing along to. A love song that ended up reminding her of the hot guy taking a shower right now. Grr, why did everything always come back to Reed Barelli?

"So how's married life?" Norah's mother, Arlena, asked as she set a slice of apple pie in front of Reed at the counter of the Pie Diner.

"Things are working out great," Reed said quite honestly.

"It's nice having someone to come home to, isn't it?" Cheyenne said, sidling up with a coffeepot in each hand. She refilled two tables behind them, then poured Reed a fresh cup.

"You two," Shelby chided. "Leave the poor detective alone. We all know theirs isn't a real marriage."

Reed stiffened, glancing at Shelby. Norah's sister was sharp and cautious, a successful business owner, and had held her own against one of the wealthiest and most powerful businessmen in Wedlock Creek, Liam Mercer, whom she'd eventually married. He felt like Shelby was trying to tell him something. Or trying to get across a message. But what?

Their marriage *was* real. They might not be loving and cherishing, but they were honoring each other's deepest wishes and needs.

But still, he couldn't shake what she'd said. *Not a real marriage. Not a real marriage. Not a real marriage.*

If their union wasn't real, then why would he feel such responsibility for her children? And he did. He had from day one when he'd woken up with the wedding ring and seen that photo of Norah and her triplets on the day they were born.

"Well, everyone's happy, including my beloved little grandbabies, so that's what matters," Arlena said, taking away Reed's empty plate.

Cheyenne nodded.

Shelby nodded extra sagely.

Arlena returned with the stroller, parking it beside Reed. "Look who's here to take you home," she cooed to the triplets. She frowned, then looked at him. "What do they call you?"

"Call me?" he repeated.

"Call you," Norah's mother repeated. "Da-da? Papa? Reed? Mama's husband?"

He felt his cheeks sting. Had Norah talked to her mom about their conversation? He doubted there'd been time. "They don't talk yet, so, of course, they don't call me anything."

"They'll be taking any day," she said, clearly uninterested in letting this line of questioning go. He should suggest detective work on the side for Arlena Ingalls.

He swallowed and got up from the bar stool, refusing to take the twenty Cheyenne tried to foist back at him. He put the bill under his empty coffee mug and got out of there fast with the giant stroller. Or as fast as anyone could make their way around tables in a diner while pushing a three-seat stroller with a yellow-and-silver polka-dotted baby bag hanging off the handle.

Anyway, what he'd said in regard to "how married life was" was true: things *were* great. He and Norah had to get used to each other—that was all. Yes, he'd made a mistake in not being clear about the father title, but the subject hadn't come up even though it was really the root and heart of staying married in the first place.

What the hell was wrong with him? How could he be so damned dense sometimes?

And what *were* the triplets going to call him?

He didn't like the idea of them calling him Reed.

Humph.

Frowning again, he settled the babies in their car seats, got the stroller in the trunk of his SUV and drove to the ranch, grateful, as always, that he was making this drive, that he was going home to the ranch. The summer sun lit the pastures through the trees and, as expected, the sight of the homestead relaxed Reed in a way nothing could. He remembered running out to the crazy weeping willow, which always looked haunted, with David Dirk when they were nine, David talking about his uncle who'd just won a quarter million dollars in Vegas and "was so lucky" that their lives were changing. He remembered David saying that if only his mother could win that kind of money, they'd have everything and wouldn't need anything else. As if money alone—

Wait a minute. Reed pulled the car over and stared hard at that weeping willow.

Could David have gone to Las Vegas? To try to win a pot of money to make having multiples more palatable? Or just easier? Or maybe he'd gone there to hide out for a few days before the wedding, to think through what he wanted?

He pulled out his phone and called David's bank. In seconds he was switched over to the manager and reintroduced himself as the detective working on the Dirk disappearance. Reed's predecessor had noted that David hadn't taken out a large sum of cash before he'd gone missing. But David had never been a gambler. He wouldn't risk more than five hundred bucks on slots and tables, even for the chance of a big payday. "Can you tell me if David withdrew around five hundred dollars the week of the tenth?"

"He withdrew two hundred and fifty dollars on the eleventh. Then another hundred on the twelfth."

Well, hardly enough cash for even a cheap flight, a cheap motel and quarters for a few slot machines. But he might have had cash socked away, too.

It was just a hunch. But Reed would bet his ranch that David Dirk was in Vegas, sitting at a slot machine and freaking out about what he was doing—and had done.

Before Norah even got out of her car, she could hear the loud, piercing wails from inside Sara Dirk's house. Screeching babies.

Norah rang the bell and it was a good minute before Sara opened the door, a screaming baby against her chest and frazzled stress etched on her tired face. Behind Sara, Norah could see the other twin crying in the baby swing.

"I thought you could use some easy meals to heat up," Norah said, holding up the bag of pies. "I brought you every kind of pot pie we make at the Pie Diner."

Sara looked on the verge of tears. "That's really nice of you," she managed to say before the baby in her arms let out an ear-splitting wail.

"Could you use a break?" Norah asked, reaching out her arms.

"Oh God, yes," Sara said, handing over the baby girl. "This is Charlotte. And that's Gabrielle," she added, rushing over to the crying one in the swing. She scooped her out and rocked her, and the baby quieted.

Norah held Charlotte against her chest, rubbing the baby's back and murmuring to her.

"A few minutes' reprieve," Sara said. "They like the change, but then they'll start up again."

"Is your husband at work?" Norah asked, giving Charlotte's back little taps to burp her.

Sara nodded. "He works at the county hospital and starts at 5:00 a.m. But the poor guy was up for a couple hours before then. He's such a great dad. He calls and texts as often as he can to check to see if I'm okay, if they're okay."

Norah smiled. "Support is everything."

Sara nodded. "It really is. David's fiancée said she'd come over this morning to help out. I feel so bad for her. Is there still no word on David?"

"Not that I know of."

The doorbell rang and there was Eden, her blond hair in a ponytail. Norah knew Eden from the Pie Diner, like just about everyone in town, so no introductions were necessary. And since David had done his share of dating among the single women in town, Norah's two weeks as David's girlfriend hardly merited a second thought. There wouldn't be any awkwardness in that department with Eden, thank heavens.

Eden burst into tears. "You know what I think?" she asked, taking Gabrielle from Sara and rocking the baby in her arms while sniffling. "I think David up and left. I think he changed his mind about me and didn't want to break my heart. But—" She let out a wail. "He broke it anyway." She cried, holding the baby close against her, her head gentle against Gabrielle's head.

"That man loves you to death," Sara said. "Everyone knows that."

"Well, he's either dead in a ditch somewhere or he left on his own because he doesn't want to marry me," Eden said, sniffling.

Norah handed her a tissue. It wasn't her place to mention Reed's theory. But maybe she could work in the subject of the chapel to see if Eden brought up whether or not David wanted multiples the way she did.

Before Norah could even think about how to pose a question about marrying at the chapel, Eden's phone rang. Sara took Gabrielle as Eden lunged for her phone in her bag, clearly hoping it was her fiancé.

"It's him!" Eden shrieked. "It's David!"

Norah stared at Eden as she screamed, "Hello, Davy

Doo?" into her phone and then realized she should at least pretend to give the woman some privacy.

Eden was listening, her blue eyes narrowing with every passing second, her expression turning murderous. "*What?* I was kidding when I got to your cousin's house today and said I was sure you left on your own because of me! I just said that so everyone would say 'Of course that's not true.' But it is!" she screamed so loudly that both babies startled and stopped fussing entirely.

Whoa boy. So Reed's theory was right.

"Yes, I hear the twins crying again, David. I'm in the same house with them. It's what babies do!" Silence. Eyes narrowing some more. Death expression. And then she said through gritted teeth, "I don't want just *one* baby. I want triplets! Or even quadruplets! Twins at the least!" More listening. More eyes narrowing. "Well, fine! Then I guess we're through!" She stabbed at the End Call button with her finger, threw the phone in her bag, then stormed out. A second later she was back. "I'm sorry you had to hear that. Apparently I was engaged to a weenie twerp! No offense to your husband or his family, Sara," she added, then stormed out again.

Norah stared at Sara, who looked as amazed as Norah felt.

"Omigod," Sara said. "What was that?"

Norah shifted little Charlotte in her arms. "A little miscommunication in expectations before the wedding."

"A little?" Sara shook her head. "And I don't know if I'd classify that as miscommunication. Eden has been talking about getting married at the chapel and having triplets from the first family dinner she was invited to.

David knew what she wanted. He probably didn't think too much about it until his cousin had twins—colicky twins—and he realized what he'd be in for. David has witnessed some whopper arguments between me and my husband. He probably just ran scared with the wedding coming so close."

"Well, I'm glad he's okay—that he wasn't hurt or anything like that," Norah said, realizing something had changed. She gasped—Charlotte had fallen asleep in her arms. She glanced at Sara, who was beaming. Sara pointed to the nursery and Norah tiptoed into the room and laid the baby in her crib. The little creature didn't even stir.

"I owe you," Sara said. "Thank you!"

They glanced at Gabrielle, who was rubbing her eyes and yawning. Easily transferred to the vibrating swing, she, too, was asleep a few seconds later.

"I get to have coffee!" Sara said. "Thank you so much for staying to help."

"Anytime," Norah said. "See you at the next class. Oh, and if your husband hears from David, will you let Reed know?"

"Will do," Sara said.

As Norah headed home, eager to see her own baby multiples, she wondered if she was the one with the problem. She'd picked three men who didn't want to be fathers. She'd dated David, albeit for two weeks. Then her babies' father. Now Reed.

She was chewing that over when she opened the front door to find Reed sitting in the family room with all three babies in their swings, cooing and batting at their little mobiles. He was reading them a story from a brightly colored book with a giraffe on the cover.

Not a father, huh? Sure. The man was father material whether he liked it or not. Knew it or not.

"Have I got news for you," she said and then told him the whole story about Eden and the phone call from David.

Reed shook his head. "At least he's not dead—yet, anyway. Once Eden gets her hands on him…"

"I didn't get the sense he told her where he was or when or if he was coming home."

"I'm ninety-nine percent sure I know where he is—Las Vegas. But it's a big place, and since he's not using his credit cards, he could be at any super-cheap hole-in-the-wall motel. Though now that he's let the cat out of the bag that he's alive and well and afraid of triplets, he might start using his cards and check in somewhere cushy while he lets Eden digest the news."

Not a minute later a call came in from the station. An officer reporting that David Dirk had finally used his MasterCard to check into the fancy Concordia Hotel on the Strip.

"I have to say, Detective. You're good."

"Does that mean you're coming to Vegas with me?" he asked.

Chapter Eleven

Just like that, Norah found herself on a plane to Las Vegas, a city she'd never been to, with Reed beside her, studying the floor plans of the Concordia Hotel and the streets of Vegas on his iPad.

As she stared out at the clouds below, she knew the answer she should have given was "No. Of course not. I'm not going." But what had come out of her mouth, with barely any hesitation was "Yes." This trip wasn't a honeymoon. Or a vacation. But it wasn't strictly business, either. Or Wedlock Creek police business. David Dirk had every right to disappear; once Reed knew for sure that the man had willingly left town, the case had been closed. But Reed wanted to find David and talk to him old friend to old friend. Bring him home. And Norah wanted some time away from real life with her…husband.

Why, she wasn't quite sure. What would be different in a new environment? They were the same people with the same gulf between them.

Still, the trip was a chance. To experience Reed off duty, away from home, where neither of them had any of their usual responsibilities. To see who they were together in a completely different environment. Maybe there would be nothing between them and Norah could just start to accept that their relationship was exactly what she'd agreed to. A platonic marriage slash business partnership for mutual benefit.

The only problem with that was the fact that just sitting this close to Reed, their sides practically touching, she'd never been so aware of a man and her physical attraction to him in her entire life.

"Of course, I booked us separate rooms," Reed said, turning to glance at her. "Right across the hall from each other."

Too bad the Concordia wasn't completely booked except for one small room with a king-size bed, she thought, mesmerized by the dark hair on his forearms and how the sunlight glinted on his gold wedding band, the one that symbolized their union.

Before she knew it, the plane had landed and they were checking in at the front desk, then being shown to their rooms. Reed had 401. Norah was in 402.

"Meet you in the hallway in twenty minutes?" he asked. "I don't have much of a plan to find David other than to sit in the lobby for a while to see if he passes through. We might get lucky. I tried calling David's friend Kyle Kirby, the one who seemed to be withholding, but he didn't answer his phone or my knock at his door. We're gonna have to do this the boring way."

"It's my chance to see you doing surveillance work," she said. "Not boring at all. See you in twenty," she added and hurried inside her room with her weekend bag.

The room was a bit fancier than she'd expected. King-size bed, wall of windows and a fuzzy white robe hanging on the bathroom door. She called her mom to check on the triplets, who were fine and having their snack, then she freshened up and changed into a casual skirt, silky tank top and strappy sandals.

Twenty minutes later, when she went into the hallway, Reed was standing there and she caught his gaze moving up and down the length of her. He liked strappy, clearly. Good.

He was amazingly handsome, as always. He wore dark pants and a dark buttoned shirt, no tie. He looked like a detective.

They sat in the well-appointed lobby for forty minutes, pretending to be poring over maps of the Strip and brochures and dinner menus. No sign of David. Many people came through the lobby, all shapes and sizes and nationalities. Norah noticed a coffee bar across the lobby and had a hankering for an iced mocha. She definitely needed caffeine.

"Want something?" she asked Reed, who was glancing over the lobby, his gaze shooting to the chrome revolving doors every time they spun.

"Iced coffee, cream and sugar. And thanks."

"Coming right up," she said and sauntered off, wondering if he took his eyes off his surveillance to watch her walk away. She turned back to actually check and almost gasped. He *was* watching her. But then he darted his eyes back to the revolving door. Busted!

This meant that no matter what he had to say about ignoring their attraction to each other, he ignored it only when he had to. There was hope to change things between her and the detective. And she was going for it. What happened in Vegas didn't have to stay in Vegas all the time, right?

Her mood uplifted with her secret plan, Norah stood behind a group of women who had very high-maintenance drink orders—double no whip this and no moo that—and studied the board to see if she wanted to try something besides her usual iced mocha when someone said, "Norah?"

She whirled around.

And almost gasped again.

David Dirk himself was staring at her, his mouth agape. "Holy crap, it *is* you," he said, walking over to her. Tall and lanky with light brown hair and round, black glasses, he held an iced coffee in one hand and a small white plate with a crumb cake in the other. "I never took you for a Vegas type."

What did *that* mean? That she couldn't let loose and have fun? Let down the ole hair and have a cocktail or three? Throw away a couple hundred bucks? Okay, maybe fifty at most.

I'm actually here with the detective who's been searching for you for days, she wanted to say. But who knew what David's frame of mind was? He might bolt.

"I'm here with my husband," she said, holding up her left hand and giving it a little wave. She turned and looked toward where Reed was sitting, staring at him hard for a second until she caught his attention. When he looked up and clearly saw David, his eyes practically bugged out of his head.

She turned back to David, who was staring at her ring.

"Oh, wow, congrats!" David said, a genuine smile on his face. "I didn't know you got married. Good for you. And good for your triplets." He bit his lip, looked at the ring again and then promptly burst into tears. He put the drink and the crumb cake down on the counter beside them and slashed each hand under his eyes. "I'm supposed to be getting married tomorrow night. At the chapel," he added, looking stricken.

He sniffled and Norah reached into her bag for her little packet of tissues. He took the whole packet and noisily blew his nose.

"But…?" she prompted, despite knowing exactly what the *but* was.

Tears slipped down his cheeks. Had he always been such a crier? They'd gone to two movies during the two weeks they'd dated, action flicks with very little pathos, so she hadn't had a chance to see him show much emotion.

"I…" He dabbed at his eyes with a wadded-up tissue.

"Whoa, David? David Dirk?" Reed asked with great feigned surprise as he walked up to them.

David stared at Reed, clearly trying to place him. His mouth dropped open, then curved into a grin. "No way. No flipping way! Reed Barelli? Who I last saw when I was thirteen?"

"It's me, man," Reed said, extending his hand.

Instead of taking his hand, David pulled Reed into a hug and sobbed. "You're probably wondering how my life is after all these years. I'll tell you. It sucks. I've ruined everything. Destroyed the best thing that ever happened to me." He pulled a few tissues from the packet and dabbed at his eyes again.

"Why don't we go get a beer?" Reed said, his arm slung around David's shoulders. "We'll catch up." He turned to Norah. "You'll be all right on your own for a couple of hours, honey?"

Honey. It was for show, but it warmed her heart nonetheless.

"Sure," she said. "I'll hit the shops. Maybe get a massage."

"Wait," David said. "*You two* are married? How'd you even meet?" he asked, looking from Reed to Norah.

"Long story," Reed said. "I'll tell you all about it over a cold one. And you can fill me in on what's going on with you."

David nodded, his shoulders slumped. "I let the best thing that ever happened to me get away."

"There's always a second chance if you don't screw it up," Reed said as they headed toward the bar.

Here's hoping so, Norah thought. *For everyone.*

The waiter placed two craft beers and a plate of nachos with the works on the square table in front of Reed and David. David took a chug of his beer, then said, "Okay, you first. How'd you meet Norah?"

He told David the entire story. The truth and nothing but the truth. He and Norah had talked about being generally tight-lipped about their story of origin, but he had a feeling David could use the information and apply it to himself.

Now it was David's eyes that were bugging out of his head.

"Oh man," David said, chugging more beer. "So you'll get it. You got married at the chapel. And now you're the father of triplets."

There was that word again. *Father*.

"What I can't believe is that you actually proposed *staying* married," David said. "The woman handed you annulment papers, man! You were home free."

"I couldn't just walk away from Norah and the babies. How could I?" He knew he didn't need to add, "You of all people should know that." He was sure David had heard it loud and clear. And from his old friend's expression, Reed was certain.

"I don't want to walk away from Eden," David said. "I love her. I know I screwed up by running away. But I had to think. I had to get my head on straight. Spending time with my cousin and those screaming colicky twins of his made me realize I'm not ready for that. I don't want that."

"You don't want *what*, exactly?" Reed asked. "A colicky baby? Twins? Or kids at all?"

David pulled a nacho onto his plate but just stared at it. "I don't know."

How could such a smart guy know so little? "Why not just tell Eden the truth?"

David frowned. "I did when I called her yesterday. She was so angry at me she hung up." Tears glistened in the guy's eyes and he ate the loaded nacho chip in one gulp.

"I think you should call Eden. FaceTime her, actually. And tell her exactly how you feel. Which sounds to me like you love her very much and want to marry her, but you're not ready for children and certainly not ready for multiples."

"That's it, exactly. I want kids someday. Just not now. And not all at once."

"Tell her. You need to have faith in your relationship with her, David. And remember, that showing her you didn't have faith in her, in your relationship, by running, is probably what is stinging her the most."

David seemed to think about that. He nodded, then took a sip of his beer. "So is it as awful as I think?"

Reed took a swig of his beer. "Is what?"

"Living with three screaming babies."

"Actually, I love those little buggers." The minute he said it, he felt his smile fade. He'd do anything for them. Of course he loved them. He had since the day he'd first upsie-downsied Bea on the rickety porch of Norah's old rental house.

"Really?" David asked, eyes wide behind the black-framed glasses.

"Yeah. Huh. I guess being a father can be more in-stinctive than I thought. There's really nothing to it other than caring and showing up and doing what needs to be done."

David nodded. "Right. I guess I don't want to do any of that—yet."

Reed laughed. "Then you shouldn't. And don't have to. Not everyone is ready for parenthood at the same time." He thought about Norah, who'd had to be ready. And him, too, in a way. But something told Reed he'd been ready for a long time. Waiting to give his heart to little humans in the way his own father hadn't been willing.

So. He *was* their father. Father. Daddy. He laughed, which made David look at him funny.

"Just thinking about something," Reed said.

David got up and polished off his beer, putting a twenty on the table. "I'm gonna go FaceTime Eden. Wish me luck. I'm gonna need it."

"Go get her," Reed said.

But as he sat there, finishing his beer and helping himself to the pretty good nachos, he realized something that twisted his gut.

Maybe he'd been focusing on the father thing as an excuse not to focus on the marriage thing. Maybe it was only *husband* he had the issue with. *Husband* that he didn't want to be.

Deep down he knew it was true. Of course it was true; it was the whole reason he'd proposed what he'd proposed. A sham of a marriage. So he'd get what he really wanted. His ranch. And a chance to still be the father he'd never had. A chance to do right.

But he also knew deep down that it wasn't what Norah wanted. At all. And she was so independent-minded and used to being on her own that he was pretty sure she wouldn't give up her dreams so soon. She'd tell him the plan wasn't working, that she needed more and she'd hold out for a man who could be a father and a husband.

She deserved that.

Reed sat there long after his beer was gone, his appetite for the nachos ruined. What the hell was going to happen to him and Norah?

* * *

If Norah wasn't mistaken, Reed was being…distant.

While Reed had been with David at the bar, she'd gone into the hotel's clothing boutique and bought herself a little black dress she'd have no use for at home. It wasn't cheap and she'd likely wear it every few years, since it was kind of a classic Audrey Hepburn sleeveless with just the right amount of low neckline to make Norah feel a bit more daring than her usual mom-of-three self.

She and Reed had agreed to meet at six thirty for dinner at an Italian restaurant in their hotel that was supposed to have incredible food. But when she came out of her room at six thirty on the nose, all dolled up, including a light dab of perfume in the cleavage, Reed seemed surprised. And kept his eyes on her face. Not even a peek at her in the hotsy-totsy dress.

Instead, he filled her in on what had happened with David, how he'd texted his old buddy an hour ago to ask if he'd spoken to Eden and how things had gone. David hadn't gotten back to him.

Love, marriage, parenthood, life. Why was it so complicated? Why did wanting one thing mean you had to give up another thing? Compromise was everything in life and relationships.

Can I give up wanting what I used to dream about? she asked herself as they walked into Marcello's, so romantic and dimly lit and full of candles and oil paintings of nudes and lovers that Norah figured Reed hadn't known what they were in for. *Can I stay married to a man I'm falling in love with when it's platonic and he wants to keep it that way forever?*

Maybe not forever. Maybe just till the triplets were grown and off starting their lives and he could finally take a breath from the sense of responsibility he felt. Oh, only eighteen years. No biggie.

Face-palm. Could she live this way for eighteen years?

Norah had just noticed a sign on an easel by the long zinc bar that said Closed For Private Event when a woman rushed up to them. The restaurant was closed? Or the bar?

"Oooh," the woman said, ushering them inside the restaurant "You two had better hurry. There's only one table left. Otherwise you'll have to eat standing at the counter along the back."

Huh? She glanced at Reed, who shrugged, and they followed the hostess to a small round table for two. A man and a woman sat a table on a platform in the center of the dining room, a candle between them, wineglasses and a plate of bruschetta.

Hmm, bruschetta, Norah thought. She definitely wanted some of that. "Maybe it's their anniversary," she told Reed. "And they're high rollers or something, so they get a platform."

"You never know in Vegas," he said, his dark eyes flashing in the dimly lit room. He looked so damned hot, this time all in black, again tieless but wearing a jacket and black shoes.

They were seated and Norah couldn't help but notice the fortyish couple at the table beside theirs. The woman sat with her arms crossed over her chest, looking spitting mad. The man was gobbling up Italian bread and slathering it with butter.

"How can you even eat when I'm this upset!" the woman hiss-whispered.

The man didn't quite roll his eyes, but he didn't stop buttering the bread or popping it in his mouth.

"Welcome!" said the woman at the platform table.

Norah turned her attention to her. She and the man beside her stood. They had microphones. Gulp. This was clearly the "special event." Had she and Reed crashed a wedding or something?

Should they get up now and slink out? While all eyes were focused on the couple and it was dead quiet otherwise?

"We'll slip out when she stops talking, when it's less noticeable," Reed whispered.

Norah nodded. *Awk*ward.

"I know it's not easy for you to be here," the woman continued, turning slowly around the room to speak to all tables. "And because you are here, you've taken the first step in your relationship recovery."

Okay, what? Relationship recovery?

Reed raised an eyebrow and looked at Norah; now it was her turn to shrug.

"My name is Allison Lerner," the woman on the platform said. "My husband, Bill, here, and I have been married for thirty-six years. Yes, we got married at eighteen—*badump!* No, seriously, ladies and gents, we have been married for thirty-six years. Some of those years were so bumpy we threatened each other with divorce every other day. Some months were good. Some days were amazing. Do you want to know *why* we didn't divorce despite the arguments, problems, issues, this, that and the other?"

"Yes!" a woman called out.

Allison smiled. "We didn't divorce because—and this is the big secret—we *didn't want* to. Not really. Even when we hated each other. We didn't want to not be married to each other. Not really."

"What the hell kind of special event is this?" Reed whispered. "They're the entertainment?"

"God, I hope not," Norah whispered back.

"All of you taking tonight's Relationship Recovery seminar are here because you don't want to divorce or separate or go your separate ways, either. So enjoy a glass of wine, folks, order your appetizers and entrées, and once the waiters are off in the kitchen, we'll start the hard work of saving our relationships. Because we want to!"

Norah glanced around. The woman with the arms crossed over her chest had tears in her eyes. Her husband was rubbing her arm—half-heartedly, but hey, at least he was doing something. The entire restaurant must be booked for the seminar.

"I sure got this one restaurant choice wrong," Reed said. "Shall we?" he asked, throwing down his napkin.

"Sir, you can do this," Allison Lerner said from behind them as she put a hand on Reed's arm. She and her husband must have been on the lookout for runners. "You deserve this. You both do. Give yourselves—and your marriage," she added, glancing at their wedding rings, "a chance."

"No, I—" Reed started to say.

"Allison is right," Norah said to Reed. "We need to learn how to fight for our marriage instead of against it."

As Reed gaped at her, she realized how true that

was. Reed was fighting against it without even knowing it because he didn't want a real marriage. Norah was fighting against it because she wanted more when she'd agreed to less. Did that even make sense? No wonder she was so confused about her feelings.

"We need to figure out how to make this work, right?" Norah said. "Let's stay."

Reed stared at her, then glanced at Allison's patiently kind face. He sat back down.

"I'm thinking of pasta," Norah said, opening her menu.

He raised his eyebrow at her. Scowled a bit. Then she saw the acquiescence in his eyes and the set of his shoulders. "Okay, okay. I'm in." He opened his menu.

They ordered a delicious-sounding seafood risotto as an appetizer. Norah chose the four-cheese-and-mushroom ravioli for an entrée; Reed went with the stuffed filetto mignon. Norah sure hoped he'd offer her a bite.

"Everyone, take a sip of your beverage—wine, soda, water, what have you," Bill Lerner said from the platform.

Norah and Reed picked up their glasses, clinked and took a sip. The woman next to them frowned. There was no clinking at their table.

"Okay, now put down your drinks," Bill said. "Turn to your partner. Look at your partner and say the first nice thing that comes to you in reference to your partner. Ladies, you begin."

Norah turned to Reed. This was an easy one. "I love how you are with the triplets. I love how you read to them and blow raspberries on Brody's and Bea's arms but not Bella's because you know she doesn't like it. I love that you know which of them likes sweet potatoes and which hates carrots. I feel like I can relax as a parent in my own home…well, *your* home, for the first time since they were born because you're there. Really, really there. It's a good feeling. Better than I even hoped it would be."

Norah felt tears spring to her eyes. She hadn't meant to say all that. But every word was true. Oh hell. That was the entire reason she'd agreed not to rip up the annulment papers—so that exactly what had happened would happen. And she wanted things to change? She wanted more? She was being selfish. Demanding more of Reed than he wanted to give. Putting the triplets' good new fortune in jeopardy. Mommy's love life had to come second. Period.

Reed took her hand and held it. "Thank you. That means a lot to me. Those babies mean a lot to me."

She almost burst into tears but held back the swell of emotion by taking a sip of wine.

"Okay, gentlemen," Allison said from the platform. "Your turn. Say the first true and nice thing you feel about your partner."

Reed took a sip of his wine and then looked at Norah. "I admire you. You've got your act together. You're lovely. You're kind. You're funny. I like seeing you around the house."

Norah laughed. She liked what he'd said. Maybe it wasn't quite as personal as what she'd said, but it came down to him liking her, really liking her, as a person. And liking having her around.

"Okay, gentlemen," Bill said into the mic. "Now look

at your partner and tell her how you felt about what she said."

Reed put down his glass of wine, which from his expression, he clearly wanted to gulp. "Maybe I am the triplets' father, after all."

Norah did feel tears sting her eyes this time and she didn't wipe them away. She was also speechless.

"I realized it before you said what you said. I realized it from talking to David Dirk. I love those babies, Norah. They have my heart. I am their father. If they'll have me."

Norah bit her lip. "They'll have you." *I'll have you.*

"Okay, ladies, now tell your partner how the nice thing he said about you made you feel."

Norah took Reed's hand and squeezed it. "You'll never say anything that I'll treasure more than what you just did. The triplets come first. That's just how it is with me."

He tilted his head as if considering something. But he didn't say anything. He just nodded.

"Whew!" Allison said from the platform. "That is quite a bit of work we did all before the entrées were served! Feel free to talk about what we just did or change the subject and enjoy dinner. Once you've had a chance to eat, we'll resume with the next exercise. Of course, after dinner, we'll get into the heavy lifting."

"Luckily we've got plans," Reed whispered. "So we'll have to skip the heavy lifting."

Norah smiled. "Oh?"

"There's something I want to show you. Something more fun than heavy lifting."

"I feel like my head was put back on straight," she

said. "So I'd say this Relationship Recovery seminar was a huge success. In just one exercise."

He squeezed her hand but again didn't say anything and cut into his delicious-looking filetto mignon. He cut a bite and instead of lifting the fork to his mouth, reached it out to hers. "Ladies first."

She smiled, feeling her moment-ago resolve to focus on the partnership and not her heart start to waver. How was she supposed to avoid her feelings for Reed Barelli when he was so wonderful?

She took the bite and closed her eyes at how tender and delicious the steak was. "Amazing," she said. "Thank you."

She scooped a ravioli onto his plate. "For you."

And then they ate, drank and didn't talk more about the exercise, which the poor woman at the next table was trying to get her husband to do.

"So you really like my hair this way?" she'd said three times.

The husband shoveled his pasta into his mouth and barely looked up. "Honestly, Kayla, with your hair blonder like that, you look just like you did the day I got the nerve to talk to you after earth science class junior year of high school. Took me a month to get the courage."

The woman gasped and looked like she might faint. Pure joy crossed her face and she reached out her hand and squeezed her husband's. "Oh, Skip."

Sometimes people knew how to say the right things at the right time.

Reed glanced over at the Lerners on the platform. They had their arms linked and were feeding each other fettuccine. Norah's and Reed's plates were practically empty, both of them having just declared they couldn't eat another bite. "I say we slip out now."

Norah smiled. "Let's go."

Reed put a hundred-dollar bill and a fifty on the table, then took her hand and made a point of asking a waiter where the restrooms were, pointing and gesturing for show. They dashed over to the entrance and then quickly ran up the hall. They were free.

"That was unexpected," Norah said on a giggle as they stopped around the corner of the lobby. Her first giggle since her wedding night.

"But worthy," Reed said. "Our marriage feels stronger. We actually did some good work in there."

Norah smiled. "We did. So what did you want to show me?"

"Follow me." He pressed the elevator button. Once they were inside, he pressed the button marked Roof. They rode up forty-two floors and exited into a hallway without any doors except one with a sign that said Roof. Reed pushed open the door and she followed.

It was a roof deck, with couches and chairs and flowers and a bar staffed with a waiter in a tuxedo. Reed took her hand and led her over to the other side of the deck, away from the small groups gathered. She gasped at the view of the Strip, sparkling lights everywhere, all underneath a canopy of stars.

"Something else, huh?" he asked, looking up and then around at the lights.

"Yeah," she said. "Something else. You sure don't see a view like this in Wedlock Creek."

Would she appreciate it even more if Reed were

standing a drop closer? With his arm around her? Or behind her, pressed against her, both of his strong arms wrapped around her? Yes, she would. But hadn't she said she wasn't going to be greedy and selfish? She knew what was important. She had to remember that and not want more.

Reed's phone buzzed in his pocket. He pulled it out and read the screen. "It's David Dirk," he whispered. He turned toward the view. "Hey, David." He listened, then smiled. "Great news. And yes, we'd love to. See you in two hours."

Norah's eyebrows shot up. "We'd love to what?"

"Seems we're invited to be David and Eden's witnesses at their wedding at the Luv U Wedding Chapel."

Norah was surprised. "Wait. Eden flew here? She's giving up the Wedlock Creek chapel and her dream of triplets?"

"I guess she did some soul-searching and decided what she wanted most."

Norah nodded. "That's the key. What you want most. You have to follow that even if it involves some compromise."

And what she wanted most was a good life for her children, the security and safety Reed would provide, the love and kindness, the role model he'd be. She wanted that for her triplets more than she wanted anything. Even if her own heart had to break to get it.

He'd be there, right? Even if he was a million miles away at the same time.

"Wow," Norah said. "She must really love him."

"Well, she's still getting some assurance. Turns out

there's a legend associated with the Luv U Wedding Chapel."

"And what would that be?"

"Eden's parents eloped there the summer after high school, scandalizing both sets of parents. Twenty-five years later the Pearlmans are happy as can be. According to Pearlman family legend, if you marry at the Luv U Wedding Chapel in Las Vegas, you're pretty much guaranteed happily-ever-after."

Norah laughed. "That's a really good legend."

Reed nodded. "This has turned out to be a pretty busy day for us. First a marriage counseling seminar over dinner and now we're witnesses at a legend-inspired wedding that almost didn't happen."

"Like ours," she said. "It's pretty crazy that it happened at all."

He looked into her eyes and squeezed her hand. "I'm glad it did happen, Norah. Our insane wedding changed my life. For the much, much better."

She squeezed his hand back. "Mine, too."

Because I'm in love with my husband. A good thing *and* exactly what wasn't supposed to happen.

I love you, Reed Barelli, she shouted in her head. *I love you!*

She wondered what he was shouting in his head.

Chapter Twelve

"Well, it's not the Wedlock Creek Wedding Chapel," Eden said, reaching for her "something borrowed," her grandmother's seed-pearl necklace. "But if getting married here blessed my parents with twenty-five so-far happy years and four children, I'll take it."

Norah clasped the pretty necklace for Eden and looked at her reflection in the standing mirror in the bridal room of the Luv U Wedding Chapel. The bride looked absolutely lovely in her princess gown with more lace and beading than Norah had ever seen on one dress. "I love it. Your own family legend."

Eden bit her lip and looked at Norah in the mirror. "Do you really believe in the Wedlock Creek legend? I mean, you had triplets without getting married there."

"Well, actually, I did get married there, just after the

fact. So maybe the fates of the universe knew that down the road I'd be getting married at the chapel and so I got my triplets. Just early." She rolled her eyes. "Oh, who the hell knows? I think Reed will tell you the legend is true, though. He got married at the chapel and voilà— father of triplets."

Eden laughed. "Poor guy." Her smile faded as she stared at herself. "Do you think I'm an idiot for forgiving David and marrying him on his terms after what he pulled?"

"I think you know David best and you know what's right and what feels right. No one else can tell you otherwise."

Eden adjusted her long, flowy veil. "I know he loves me. But he did a real bonehead thing just running away. I mean, I *really* thought something happened to him." She frowned. "Maybe he's too immature to get married. I know I'm not about to win Person of the Year or anything, but still."

"Well, he got scared and he didn't know how to deal with it, so he fled. He didn't want to lose you by telling you how he really felt. In the end, though, he did call you and tell you the truth. You two worked it out, because here you are."

Eden's smile lit up her pretty face. "It'll make one hell of a family story, huh? I'll be telling my grandkids about the time Grandpa ran for the hills to avoid having quadruplets."

Norah laughed. "You just might have quadruplets anyway. You never know."

"Mwahaha," Eden said, doing her best evil-laugh impersonation. She turned around to face Norah. "So is this your honeymoon? Is that why you and Reed are here?"

Honeymoons were for real newlyweds. She sighed inwardly. There she went again, wanting more.

Was it wrong to want more when it came to love? If your heart was bursting?

Eden was eyeing her, so she'd better say something reasonable. She had no idea what Reed had told David about the two of them and how they'd ended up married. Probably the truth. She knew Reed Barelli well enough to know that he didn't lie.

"I suppose it's like a mini honeymoon. Reed just started at the police department, so he can't take off any real time." She kind of liked saying that. It was true— in a way. This was like their honeymoon. And since they *were* newlyweds, they should have this time away.

"He must really love you," Eden said, turning back to the mirror to freshen her pink-red lipstick. "He married a single mother of seven-month-old triplets."

Norah felt her heart squeeze. How she wished that were true. Of course, they couldn't go backward and fall in love and then get married. They'd already done the backward thing by getting married first, then actually getting to know each other. She smiled, her heartache easing just a bit. There was hope there, no? If you started out backward, you could only go forward. And forward was love and forever.

Unless your husband was Reed "No Romance" Barelli.

Did a man who didn't believe in romance bring his dry-eyed deal of a wife to see a breathtaking view forty-two flights above the city? Did he do any of the sweet and wonderful things Reed had done? Including offering her the first bite of his incredible filetto mignon?

"He's a great guy," Norah said. He sure was.

Eden smiled and checked that her pearl drop earrings were fastened. "You're so lucky. You have your triplets and your hot new detective husband who's madly in love with you. You have everything."

Oh, if only.

After tearing up a time or two at the wedding and doing her official job as Witness One, Norah watched as David Dirk, looking spiffy in a tuxedo, lifted his bride and carried her out of the Luv U chapel. Reed threw rice and then it was time for the next couple to say their I Do's, so Norah and Reed headed out into the balmy July Las Vegas air.

"Case closed with a happy ending," Reed said. "The best kind of case."

"I think they're going to be just fine," she agreed. "But he'll probably keep doing dumb things."

Reed laughed. "No doubt." He looked over at her. "So should we head back to the hotel? Have a nightcap on the terrace?"

"Sounds good," she said. And too romantic. But there was nothing she'd rather do than continue this night of love and matrimony with her own husband.

They passed a lot of couples holding hands. Brides and grooms with their heads popped out of limo sunroofs, screaming, "I did!" The happy, drunken energy reminded her of her wedding night.

In ten minutes they were back at the Concordia, taking the elevator to the fourth floor. Reed's room was just like hers. The king-size bed in the center of the room had her attention. Suddenly all she could think about was waking up the morning after her wedding, the shock of seeing Fabio-Reed in her bed, half-naked except for the hot, black boxer briefs, the hard planes of his chest and rippling muscles as he shifted an arm, the way his long eyelashes rested on his cheeks.

"Do you think that on our wedding night we...?" She trailed off, staring at the bed.

"We what?"

"Had sex," she said, turning to face him.

He placed his key card on the dresser, took off his jacket and folded it over the desk chair, then went over to the minibar. "No. In fact, I'm ninety-nine percent sure."

"How?"

He poured two glasses of wine from the little bottles. "Because if I made love to you, Norah, I never would have forgotten it." He held her gaze and she felt her cheeks burn a bit, the warmth spreading down into her chest, to her stomach, to her toes.

She took the wineglass he held out and took a sip, then moved over to the windows, unable to stand so close to him or to look directly at him without spontaneously combusting. Being in his room, the bed, images of him, the very thought of his gorgeous face and incredibly hot body... She wanted him with a fierceness she couldn't remember ever experiencing. She wanted to feel his hands and mouth all over her. She wanted him to be her husband—for real.

Maybe she could show him how it could be, how good it could be between them. That if she of all people could let go of mistrust and walls and actually let herself risk feeling something, then he could, too, dammit. There was no way she could be married to this man, share a home and life with him, and not have him in every sense of the word. And the fact that he was clearly attracted to her gave her the cojones to take a long sip of her wine, put down the glass and sit on the edge of the bed.

He was watching her, but he stayed where he was. On the other side of the bed, practically leaning against the wall.

So now what? Should she throw herself at him? No way was she doing that.

Ugh, this was stupid. Forget it. She wasn't going to beg this man—any man—to want her; all of her, heart, mind, soul, body. Hadn't her smart sister told her to let what would happen just happen? She shouldn't be forcing it.

She sighed a wistful sigh and stood. "Well, I guess I'll head to my room, maybe watch a movie. Something funny." She needed funny. A good laugh.

"Sounds good," he said. "I could go for funny." He grabbed the remote control off the desk and suddenly the guide was on the screen. "Hmm, *Police Academy 3*, *Out of Africa*, *Jerry Maguire* or *Full Metal Jacket*?"

Uh-oh. She hadn't meant they watch together. They

were going to lie down on the bed, inches apart, and watch a movie? Really?

"Unless you were hinting that you're sick of me and don't want company," he said with a smile. "I could never get tired of you, so I forget not everyone is dazzled by me 24/7."

She burst out laughing. Hot *and* funny. Who needed the movie? She'd just take him.

"I've seen *Jerry Maguire* at least five times, but you really can't see that enough," she said.

"Really? I've never seen it."

You. Complete. Me, she wanted to scream at him and then grab him down onto the bed and kiss him everywhere on his amazing body.

"Wait, we can't watch a movie without popcorn," he said, picking up the phone. Was the man really ordering from room service? Yes, he was. He asked for a big bowl of popcorn, freshly popped, two sodas, a bottle of a good white wine and two slices of anything chocolate.

Amazing. "You really know how to watch a movie," she said.

He grinned. "The way I see it, you might as well do everything right."

Yup. That was why he hadn't rushed the annulment papers to the county clerk's too-efficient replacement. Because he did things right. Like stay married to a mother of teething seven-month-old triplets who'd lived in a falling-down dump and made her living by the pot pie.

Twenty minutes later, their little movie feast delivered, they settled on the bed, on top of the blanket, the big bowl of popcorn between them, to watch *Jerry Maguire*.

"Oh, it's the *Mission Impossible* dude," he said, throwing some popcorn into his mouth. They were both barefoot and Norah couldn't stop looking at Reed's sexy feet.

"Don't see many movies, huh?" she asked.

"Never really had much time. Hopefully now in Wedlock Creek, I will. Slower pace of life and all that."

She nodded and they settled down to watch. Reed laughed a lot, particularly at the scenes with Cuba Gooding Jr. By the time Renée Zellweger said Tom Cruise had her at hello, Norah was mush and teary-eyed.

"Softy," Reed said, slinging his arm over so that she could prop up against him. She did.

Great. Now they were cuddling. Sort of. His full attention was on the movie. Norah found it pretty difficult to keep her mind on the TV with her head against Reed's shoulder and him stretched out so close beside her. She ate popcorn and dug into the chocolate cake to take her mind off Reed and sex.

But as the credits rolled, Reed turned onto his side to face her. "Do you believe in that 'you complete me' stuff?"

She turned onto her side, too. "Believe in it? Of course I do."

"So someone else can complete you?" he asked. "You're not finished without a romantic partner?"

"What it *means* is that your romantic partner brings out the best in you, makes you realize and understand the depth of your feelings, makes you feel whole in a way you never did before, that suddenly nothing is missing from your life."

He smiled. "I don't know, Norah. I think it was just a good line."

She shook her head. "Nope. She completes him and he knows it."

He reached out to move a strand of hair that had fallen across her face, but instead of pulling his hand back, he caressed her cheek. "You're a true romantic."

"You are, too. You just don't know it," she said. It was so true. Everything he did was the mark of a romantic. His chivalry. His code of honor. His willingness to watch *Jerry Maguire*. The man had ordered popcorn and chocolate cake from room service, for God's sake. He was a romantic.

The thought made her smile. But now he was staring at her mouth.

His finger touched her lip. "Popcorn crumb," he said.

"Does popcorn have crumbs?"

"Yes," he whispered, his face just inches away. He propped up on his elbow and moved another strand of hair away from her face. There was a combination of tenderness and desire in his eyes, in his expression.

He was *thinking*, she realized, fighting the urge to move his head down and kiss her. *Win out, urge*, she telepathically sent to his brain. *Do it. Kiss her. Kiss. Her.*

And then he did. Softly at first. Passionately a second later.

He moved on top of her, his hands in her hair, his mouth moving from her lips to her neck. She sucked in a breath, her hands roaming his back, his neck, his hair. Thick, silky hair. "Tell me to stop, Norah. This is nuts."

"I don't want you to stop. I want you to make love to me."

He groaned and tore off his shirt, then unzipped her dress. She sat up and flung the dress off before he could change his mind. His eyes were on her lacy bra. Her one sexy, black undergarment with panties to match, chosen for this possibility.

And it was happening. Mmm. Yes, it was happening! She lay back, his eyes still on her cleavage. That was good. He was not thinking. He was only feeling. And the moment her hands touched the bare skin of his chest, he was hers. He groaned again and his mouth was on hers, one hand undoing his pants and shrugging out of them while the other unsnapped her bra like a pro.

Suddenly they were both naked. He lay on top of her and propped up on his forearms. "I can't resist you, Norah. I don't have *that* much self-control."

She smiled. "Good."

By the time he reached for the foil-wrapped little packet in his wallet, she was barely able to think for the sensations rocketing every inch, every cell, of her body. But she was vaguely aware that he'd brought a condom. Probably a whole box. Which meant he'd anticipated that something could happen between them.

Her husband *wasn't* lost to her behind that brick wall he'd erected between him and love, him and *feeling*. There was hope for them. That was all she needed to know. In that moment her heart cracked wide-open and let him in fully, risks be damned.

And then he lay on top of her and suddenly they were one, all thought poofing from her head.

Reed's phone was on silent-vibrate, but as a cop he'd long trained himself to catch its hum. He must have drifted off to sleep after two rounds of amazing sex with Norah. His wife. Sex that they weren't supposed to have. Not part of the deal.

He glanced over at her. She lay next to him, turned away on her side, asleep, he figured from her breathing. Her long reddish-brown hair flowed down her sexy bare shoulders. Just looking at her had him stirring once more, wanting her like crazy, but then his phone vibrated again on the bedside table. Then again. And again. What the hell could this be at almost one thirty in the morning?

David Dirk was what it was. A series of texts.

I owe u, man. Good talk we had earlier.

I'm lying here next to my gorgeous wife, feeling so lucky.

I might as well have won a mil downstairs, bruh.

I'm realizing the depth of my love for this woman means she comes 1st.

The selfish crap is stopping. I love Eden 2 death and
I'm putting her needs above my own.

Double-date back in the Creek, dude?

Well, good for David Dirk. And Eden. The guy had
flipped out, fled town in a spectacularly immature fashion, but had worked it out with himself and laid his heart
bare to the woman he loved. And they'd both ended up
getting what they'd wanted: each other—still with a
hearty dose of legend on their side.

So why was Reed feeling so…unsettled? He put the
phone back on the table and lay very still, staring up
at the ceiling.

Because he wasn't putting Norah's needs above his
own? She wanted the whole shebang—love, romance,
snuggles while watching *Jerry Maguire*, a shared, true
partnership. And what was he giving her? Just the partnership. Fine, he threw in some snuggles while watching the biggest date-night movie of all time.

And then made mad, passionate love to his wife of
"convenience." His life-plan partner.

He shook his head at himself.

He got to feel like a better man than his father was
when he was too much of a coward to marry and plan
a family of his own. He got to have his ranch when his
grandmother would be sorely disappointed at the "marriage" he'd engineered to have the Barelli homestead.

Meanwhile he was keeping Norah from finding what
she really wanted. She'd agreed to the marriage deal;
she herself had said she wanted nothing to do with love

or romance or men. But something had changed for her. Because her heart had opened up. Somehow. Married to a brick wall like him.

Whereas he was still unbreakable and unblastable.

He turned his head and looked at Norah, reaching for a silky strand of her hair. Sex with her was everything he'd thought it would be; they fit perfectly together, they were in rhythm. But afterward, part of him had wanted to hit the streets and just breathe it out. He'd stayed put for her, like he was doing her some kind of big favor. Which had made him feel worse about what he could and couldn't give her.

There was only one thing to do, he realized as he lay there staring back up at the ceiling.

One way out of the mess he'd created by thinking this kind of marriage could work, could be a thing.

Yes. The more he thought about what he needed to do, the more he knew it was the right thing. He'd have to take an hour off work in the morning, but he'd make up the time and then some.

Decision made, he turned over and faced the beige-and-white-striped wallpaper until he realized Norah was a much better sight to fall asleep to. He wanted to reach out and touch her, to wrap his arms around her and tell her how much he cared about her, for her, but he couldn't.

Nothing about Reed Barelli escaped Norah's notice. So she'd caught on to his distance immediately. It had started in the hotel room when she'd woken up five minutes ago. All the warmth from the night before was gone, replaced by this…slight chill. He was polite. Respectful. Offering to run out for bagels or to call room service.

She sat up in bed, pulling the top sheet and blankets up to her chest. *Keep it light, Norah*, she warned herself. "All that hot sex does have me starving," she said with a smile, hoping to crack him.

Instead of sliding back into bed for another round, he practically raced to the phone. "I'll call room service. Omelet? Side of hash browns?"

Deep endless sigh. If she couldn't have him, she may as well eat. She hadn't been kidding. She *was* starving. "Western omelet. And yes to hash browns. And a vat of coffee."

He ordered two of that.

She could still feel the imprint of his lips on hers, all over her, actually. The scent of him was on her. He was all over her, inside her, with her. She felt like Cathy in *Wuthering Heights*—"*I am Heathcliff!*"

Maybe not the most hopeful reference for the Barellis of Wedlock Creek.

"Here you go," he said, handing her the fluffy terry robe, compliments of the Concordia. "Use mine."

Either he didn't want to see her naked anymore or he was just being kind and polite and respectful. She knew it was all the latter. Last night, everything he did had shown how much he'd wanted to see her naked, how much he'd wanted *her*. And now it was all over. Light of day and all that other back-to-Cinderella, back-to-a-pumpkin reality.

They ate on the terrace, making small talk. He asked

how the triplets were, since of course she'd already called to check in on them. They were all fine. The Pie Diner was fine. The police station was fine. Eden and David were fine. Everything was fine but them. What had changed so drastically overnight?

He pushed his hash browns around on his plate. "Norah, we need to talk. Really talk."

Oh hell. She put down her coffee mug. "Okay."

He cleared his throat, then took a long sip of his coffee. Then looked out at the view. Then, finally, he looked at her. "I will stand by you, beside you, and be a father to Bella, Bea and Brody. I want to be their father."

"But…?" she prompted, every nerve ending on red alert.

"But I sense—no, I *know*—that you want more. You want a real marriage. And I'm holding you back from that. If you want to find a man who will be both husband and father, I don't want to hold you back, Norah. You deserve everything."

"I deserve everything, but you won't give me everything," she said, pushing at her hash browns. Anything to avoid directly looking into his eyes.

"I wish I could, Norah. I don't have it in me. I guess it's been too long, too many years of shutting down and out. My job made it easy. I swore off all that stuff, said 'no more,' and I guess I really meant it."

Crud. She wished there was something lying around on the floor of the terrace that she could kick. A soda can. Anything. "So I'm supposed to decide whether I want half a marriage or to let you go so I can find everything in one man."

He glanced out toward the Strip, at the overcast sky. "Yes."

Half of him or the possibility of everything with another? She'd take a quarter of Reed Barelli.

Oh, really, Norah? That's all you deserve? A man who can't or won't give more of himself?

He wanted to serve and protect the community and his family. Same thing to him. She shook her head, trying to make sense of this, trying to make it work for her somehow. But she wasn't a town. She wasn't a bunch of houses or people. She was his *wife*.

"And if I hand you the annulment papers to sign, you're prepared to give up the Barelli ranch? Your heart and soul?"

His expression changed then, but she couldn't quite read it. There was pain, she was pretty sure.

"Yes, I'm fully prepared to give it up."

God. She sucked in a breath and turned away, trying to keep control of herself. "Well, then. If you're willing to give up the ranch that means so much to you, I think we both know we need to get those annulment papers over to the courthouse."

She slid off her wedding ring, her heart tearing in two. "Here," she managed to croak out, handing it to him. "I don't want it."

He bit his lip but pocketed it. Then she pushed out of her chair, ran back into the room, grabbed her clothes off the floor and rushed across the hall into her room.

She sat on the edge of her bed and sobbed.

Chapter Thirteen

"What? You're just gonna let him go?" Aunt Cheyenne said with a frown.

Norah stirred the big pot of potatoes on the stove in the kitchen of the Pie Diner. She'd asked herself that very question on the flight back home and all night in her bedroom at the ranch. Reed had packed a bag and had gone to the one hotel in town to give her "some privacy with your thoughts."

She'd wanted to throw something at him then. But she'd been too upset. When the door had closed behind him, she was just grateful the triplets were with her mother so that she could give in to her tears and take the night to get it out of her system. Come morning, she'd known she'd have to turn into a pot pie baker and a mother and she wouldn't have the time or the luxury of a broken heart.

"Not like I have much choice," she said.

"Uh, Norah, a little more gently with that spoon," her mother said from her station across the kitchen. "The potatoes aren't Reed."

Norah took a deep breath and let up on the stirring. She offered her mom a commiserating smile. "I'll be okay. The potatoes will be okay. The only one who won't be okay is that stubborn brick wall I married by accident."

"Fight for him!" Cheyenne said. "The man is so used to being a lone wolf that he doesn't feel comfortable having a real-life partner. He's just not used to it. But he likes being married or he wouldn't have suggested staying married—no matter what."

Norah had thought of that. Her mind had latched on to so many hopeful possibilities last night. But then she'd come back to all he'd said on the terrace in Las Vegas. "He's giving up the ranch to undo it," Norah reminded her aunt.

"Because he thinks you're losing out," her mother said, filling six pie crusts with the fragrant beef stew she and Cheyenne had been working on this morning. "He wants you to have everything you deserve. The man loves you, Norah."

She shook her head. "If he loved me, he'd love me. And we wouldn't have had that conversation in Vegas." Tears poked her eyes and she blinked them back. The triplets were in the office slash nursery having their nap and she needed to think about them. In Reed, they'd have a loving father but would grow up with a warped view of love and marriage because their parents' lack of love—kisses, romance, the way a committed couple acted—would be absent. They would be roommates, and her children would grow up thinking that was how married people behaved. No sirree.

The super annoying part? She couldn't even go back to the old Norah's ways of having given up on love and romance. Because she'd fallen hard for Reed and she knew she was capable of that much feeling. She did want it. She wanted love. She wanted a father for her babies. She wanted that man to be the same.

She wanted that man to be Reed.

He didn't want to be that man. Or couldn't be. Whatever!

Being Fabio was his fantasy, though, she suddenly realized. A man who *did* want to marry. Fabio had suggested it, after all. Fabio had carried her into that chapel.

Could there be hope?

A waitress popped her head into the kitchen "Norah? There's someone here to see you. Henry Peterfell." The young woman filled her tray with her order of three chicken pot pies and one beef and carried it back out.

"Henry Peterfell is here to see me?" She glanced at her mother and aunt. Henry Peterfell was a pricey attorney and very involved in local government. What could he want with Norah?

She wiped her hands on her apron and went through the swinging-out door into the dining room. Fifty-something-year-old Henry, in his tan suit, sat at the counter, a Pie Diner yellow to-go bag in front of him. "Ah, Ms. Ingalls. I stopped in to pick up lunch and realized I had some papers for you to sign in my brief-case, so if you'd like, you can just John Hancock them here. Or you can make an appointment to come into the office. Whatever is more convenient."

Panic rushed into her stomach. "Papers? Am I being sued?"

Oh God. Was Reed divorcing her? Perhaps he figured they couldn't annul the marriage because they'd made love. *You're the one who gave him back your ring*, she reminded herself, tears threatening again. *Of course he's divorcing you.*

"Sued? No, no, nothing like that." He set his leather briefcase on the counter and pulled out a folder. "There are three sets. You can sign where you see the neon arrow. There, there and there," he said, pointing at the little sticky tabs.

Norah picked up the papers. And almost fell off the chair.

"This is a deed," she said slowly. "To the Barelli ranch."

"Yes," the lawyer said. "Everything is in order. Lovely property."

"Reed turned the ranch over to me? The ranch is now mine?"

"That's right. It's yours. Once you sign, of course. There, there and there," he said, gesturing.

Norah stared at the long, legal-size papers, the black type swimming before her eyes. *What?* Why would Reed do this?

"Mr. Peterfell, would it be all right if I held on to these to read first?"

"Absolutely," he said. "Just send them to my office or drop them off at your convenience."

With that, he and his briefcase of unexpected documents were gone.

Reed had deeded the ranch to her. His beloved ranch. The only place that had ever felt like home to him.

Because he didn't feel he deserved it now that they were going to split up? That had to be the reason. He wasn't even keeping it in limbo in case he met someone down the road, though. He was that far gone? That sure he was never going to share his heart with anyone?

A shot of cold swept through her at the thought. How lonely that would be.

She wasn't letting him get away that easily. Her aunt and mother were right. She was going to fight for him. She was going to fight for Fabio. Because there was a chance that Reed did love her but couldn't allow himself to. And if the feeling was there, she was going to pull it out of him till he was so happy he made people sick.

The thought actually made her smile.

Reed stood in the living room of his awkward rental house—the same old one, which of course was still available because it was so blah—trying to figure out why the arrangement of furniture looked so wrong. Maybe if he put the couch in front of the windows instead of against the wall?

This place would never look right. Or feel right. Or be home.

But giving Norah the ranch had been the right thing to do. Now she'd have a safe place to raise the triplets with enough room for all of them, fields to roam in, and she'd own it free and clear. She'd never have to worry about paying rent again, let alone a mortgage or property taxes—he'd taken care of that in perpetuity.

And he had a feeling his grandmother was looking down at him, saying, *Well, you tried. Not hard enough, but you tried and in the end you did the right thing. She should have the ranch, you dope.*

He *was* a dope. And Norah should have the ranch.

The doorbell rang. He had a feeling it was Norah, coming to tell him she couldn't possibly accept the ranch. Well, tough, because he'd already deeded it to her and it was hers. He'd even talked over the legalities with his lawyer; he'd married, per his grandmother's will, and the ranch was his fair and square. His to hand over.

He opened the door and it was like a gut punch. Two days ago they'd still had their deal. Two nights ago they'd been naked in bed together. And then yesterday morning, he'd turned back into the Reed he needed to be to survive this thing called life. Keeping to himself. No emotional entanglements.

And yet his first day in town he'd managed to get married and become a father to three babies. He was really failing at no emotional entanglements.

"I can't accept this, Reed," she said, holding up a legal-size folder.

"You have no choice. It's yours now. The deed is in your name."

She scowled. "It's your home."

"I'd rather you and the triplets have it. My grandmother would rather that, too. I have no doubt."

"So you get married, get your ranch and then give up the ranch, but the wife who's not really your wife gets to *keep* the ranch. That makes no sense."

"Does anything about our brief history, Norah?" An image floated into the back of his mind, Fabio and Angelina hand in hand, him scooping her up and carrying her into the chapel with its legend and sneaky, elderly caretakers slash officiants.

She stared at him hard. "I'll accept the ranch on one condition."

He raised an eyebrow. "And that would be?"

"I need your help for my multiples class. I'd like you to be a guest speaker. Give the dad's perspective."

No, no, no. What could *he* contribute? "I've only been a dad for a little while," he said. "Do I really have anything to truly bring to the class? And now with things so…up in the air between us."

Up in the air is good, she thought. Because it meant things could go her way. Their way. The way of happiness.

"You have so much to contribute," she said. "Honestly, it would be great if you could speak at all the remaining classes," she said. "Lena Higgins—she's the one expecting all boy triplets—told me her husband wasn't sure he felt comfortable at the class last week and might not be joining her for the rest because the class seemed so mom-focused. Poor Lena looked so sad. A male guest speaker will keep some of the more reluctant dads and caregivers comfortable. Especially when it's Reed Barelli, detective."

He didn't quite frown, so that was something. "I don't know, Norah. I—"

"Did you see how scared some of those dads looked?" she asked. "For dads who are shaking over the responsibility awaiting them—you could set their minds at ease. I think all the students will appreciate the male perspective."

Some of the guys in the class, which had included fathers, fathers-to-be and grandfathers, had looked like the ole deer in the headlights. One diaper was tough on some men who thought they were helpless. Two, three, even four diapers at the same time? Helpless men would poof into puddles on the floor. He supposed he could be a big help in the community by showing these guys they weren't helpless, that they had the same instincts—and fears—as the women and moms among them.

Step up, boys, he thought. That would be his mission.

Ha. He was going to tell a bunch of sissies afraid of diaper wipes and onesies and double strollers to step up when he couldn't step up for the woman he'd do anything for?

Anything but love, Reed?

He shook the thought out of his weary brain. His head ran circles around the subject of his feelings for Norah. He just couldn't quite get a handle on them. Because he didn't want to? Or because he really was shut off from all that? Done with love. Long done.

She was tilting her head at him. Waiting for an answer.

"And if I do this, you'll accept the ranch as yours?" he said.

She nodded.

He extended a hand. "Deal."

She shook his hand, the soft feel of it making him want to wrap her in his arms and never let her go.

"We make a lot of deals," she said. "I guess it's our thing."

He smiled. "The last one failed miserably." He failed miserably. Or had Norah just changed the rules on him by wanting more? They'd entered their agreement on a handshake, too. He wasn't really wrong here. He just wasn't…right.

"This one has less riding on it," she said. "You just have to talk about how you bonded with the triplets. How you handle changing time. Feeding time. Bedtime. What's it like to come home from work and have three grumpy, teething little ones to deal with. How you make it work. How it's wonderful, despite everything hard about it. How sometimes it's not even hard."

He nodded and smiled. "I'll be there," he said. He frowned, his mind going to the triplets. "Norah, how are things going to work now? I mean, until you find the right man, I want to be there for you and the babies. I want to be their father."

"Until I find a father who can be that and a real husband?"

"Okay, it's weird, but yes."

She frowned. "So you're going to get all enmeshed in their lives, give a hundred percent to them, and then I meet someone who fits the bill and you'll just back off? Walk away? Bye, triplets?"

Hey, wait a minute.

"Look, Norah, I'm not walking away from anything. I want to be their father. I told you that. But I want you to have what you need, too. If I can't be both and some-one else can…"

Someone else. Suddenly the thought of another man touching her, kissing her, doing upsie-downsie with his babies…

His babies. Hell. Maybe he should back off now. Or he'd really be done for. Maybe they both needed a break from each other so they could go back to having what they wanted. Which was all messed up now.

She lifted her chin. "Let's forget this for now. Any-time you want to see Bella, Bea and Brody, you're wel-come over. You're welcome at the ranch anytime."

He nodded, unable to speak at the moment.

She peered behind him, looking around the living room. "The couch should go in front of the windows. And that side table would be better on that wall," she said, pointing. "The mirror above the console table is too low. Should be slightly above eye level."

"That should help. Thank you. I can't seem to get this place right."

"I'm not sure I want it to feel right," she said. "Wait, did I say that aloud?" She frowned again. "Everything is all wrong. I don't like that you left your home, Reed. That place is your dream."

"That place is meant for a family. I want you to have it."

She looked at him for a long moment. He could see her shaking her head without moving a muscle. "See you in class."

He watched her walk to her car. The moment she got in, he felt her absence and the weight of one hell of a heavy heart.

Chapter Fourteen

Word had spread that Detective Reed Barelli, who'd become de facto father to the Ingalls triplets by virtue of marrying their mother at the Wedlock Creek chapel with its Legend of the Multiples, would be a guest speaker at tonight's zero-to-six-month multiples class. There were more men than women this time, several first-timers to the class who practically threw checks at Norah. At this rate, she'd be raking it in as a teacher.

She hadn't even meant to invite him to speak—especially not as a condition of her keeping the ranch. The sole condition, no less. But it had been the best she could come up with, just standing there, not knowing what to say, how to keep him, how to get him to open up the way she had and accept the beautiful thing he was being offered: love. She did want him to be a speaker in her class, and it would get them working together, so that was good. She couldn't try to get through to him if they were constantly apart now that he'd moved out.

They hadn't spent much time together in three days.

He'd come to the ranch to see the triplets every day since their return from Las Vegas. He'd help feed them, then read to them, play with them. Blow raspberries and do upsie-downsies. And then he'd leave, taking Norah's heart with him.

Now here he was, sitting in the chair beside her desk with his stack of handouts, looking so good she could scream.

"Welcome, everyone! As you may have heard through the grapevine, tonight we have a guest speaker. Detective Reed Barelli. When Reed and I got married, he became the instant father of three seven-month-old teething babies. Was he scared of them? Nope. Did he actually want to help take care of them? Yes. Reed had never spent much time around babies and yet he was a natural with my triplets. Why?"

She looked at Reed and almost didn't want to say why. Because it proved he could pick and choose. The triplets. But not her.

She bit back the strangled sob that rose up from deep within and lifted her chin. She turned back toward the class. "Because he wanted to be. That is the key. He *wanted* to be there for them. And so he was. And dads, caregivers, dads-to-be, grandfathers, that's all you have to know. That you want to be there for them. So, without further ado, here is Detective Reed Barelli."

He stood, turned to her and smiled, then addressed

the class. "That was some introduction. Thank you, Norah."

She managed a smile and then sat on the other side of the desk.

"Norah is absolutely right. I did want to be there for the triplets. And so I was. But don't think I had a clue of how to take care of one baby, let alone three. I know how to change a diaper—I think anyone can figure that out. But the basics, including diapers and burping and sleep schedules and naps? All that, you'll learn here. What you won't learn here, or hell, maybe you will because I'm talking about it, is that taking care of babies will tell you who you are. Someone who steps up or someone who sits out. Be the guy who steps up."

A bunch of women stood and applauded, as did a few guys.

"Is it as easy as you make it sound?" Tom McFill asked. "My wife is expecting twins. I've never even held a baby before."

"The first time you do," Reed said, "everything will change. That worry you feel, that maybe you won't know what you're doing? It'll dissipate under the weight of another feeling—a surge of protection so strong that you won't know what hit you. All you'll know is that you're doing what needs to be done, operating by instinct and common sense, Googling what you don't know, asking a grandmother. So it's as hard and as easy as I'm making it sound."

A half hour later Norah took over, giving tutorials on feeding multiples, bathing multiples and how to handle sleep time. Then there was the ole gem: what if both babies, or three or four, all woke up in the middle of the night, crying and wet and hungry. She covered that, watching her students taking copious notes.

Finally the class was over. Everyone crowded around Reed, asking him questions. By the time the last student left and they were packing up to go, it was a half hour past the end of the class.

"You were a big hit," she said. "I knew I called this one right."

"I'm happy to help out. I knew more than I thought on the subject. I'd stayed up late last night doing research, but I didn't need to use a quarter of it."

"You had hands-on training."

"I miss living with them," he said, and she could tell he hadn't meant to say that.

She smiled and let it go. "Most people would think you're crazy."

"I guess I am."

Want more, she shouted telepathically. *Insist on more! You did it with the babies, now do it with me. Hot sex every night, fool!* But of course she couldn't say any of that. "Well, I'd better get over to the diner to pick up the triplets."

"They're open for another half hour, right? I could sure go for some beef pot pie."

She stared at him. Why was he prolonging the two of them being together? Because he wanted to be with her? Because he really did love the triplets and wanted to see them?

Because he missed her the way she missed him?

"I have to warn you," she said as they headed out.

"My family might interrogate you about the state of our marriage. Demand to know when we're patching things up. *If* we will, I should say."

"Well, we can't say what we don't know. That goes for suspects and us."

Humph. All he had to do was say he'd be the one. The father and the husband. It was that easy!

On the way to their cars, she called her mom to let her know she and Reed would be stopping in for beef pot pies so they'd be ready when they arrived. Then she got in her car and Reed got in his. The whole time he trailed her in his SUV to the Pie Diner, she was so aware of him behind her.

The diner was still pretty busy at eight thirty-five. Norah's mom waved them over to the counter.

"Norah, look who's here!"

Norah stared at the man sitting at the counter, a vegetable pot pie and lemonade in front of him. She gasped as recognition hit. "Harrison? Omigod, Harrison Atwood?" He stood and smiled and she threw her arms around him. Her high school sweetheart who'd joined the army and ended up on the east coast and they'd lost contact.

"Harrison is divorced," Norah's mom said. "Turns out his wife didn't want children and he's hoping for a house full. He told me all about it."

Norah turned beet red. "Mom, I'm sure Harrison doesn't want the entire restaurant knowing his business."

Harrison smiled. "I don't mind at all. The more people know I'm in the market for a wife and children, the better. You have to say what you want if you hope to get it, right?"

Norah's mother smiled at Norah and Reed, then looked back at Harrison. "I was just telling Harrison how things didn't work out between the two of you and that you're available again. The two of you could catch up. High school sweethearts always have such memories to talk over."

Can my face get any redder? Norah wondered, shooting daggers at her busybody mother. What was she trying to do?

Get her settled down, that was what. First Reed and now a man she hadn't seen in ten years.

Norah glanced at Reed, who seemed very stiff. He was stealing glances at Harrison every now and then.

Harrison had been a cute seventeen-year-old, tall and gangly, but now he was taller and more muscular, attractive, with sandy-brown hair and blue eyes and a dimple in his left cheek. She'd liked him then, but she'd recognized even then that she hadn't been in love. To the point that she'd kept putting him off about losing their virginity. She'd wanted her first time to be with a man she was madly in love with. Of course, she'd thought she was madly in love with a rodeo champ, but he'd taken her virginity and had not given her anything in return. She'd thought she was done with bull riders and then, wham, she'd fallen for the triplets' father. Maybe she'd never learn.

"Harrison is a chef. He studied in Paris," Aunt Cheyenne said. "He's going to give us a lesson in French cooking. Isn't that wonderful? You two must have so much in common," she added, wagging a finger between Norah and Harrison.

"Well, I'd better get going," Reed said, stepping back. "I have cases to go over. Nice to see you all."

"But, Reed, your pot pie just came out of the oven," Norah's mother said. "I'll just go grab it."

Norah watched him give Harrison the side-eye before he said, "I'll come with you. I want to say goodnight to the triplets."

"They are so beautiful," Harrison said with so much reverence in his voice that Norah couldn't help the little burst of pride in her chest. Harrison sure was being kind.

Reed narrowed his gaze on the man, scowled and disappeared into the kitchen behind her mother.

And then Aunt Cheyenne winked at Norah and smiled. Oh no. Absolutely not. She knew what was going on here. Her mother and aunt realized they had Norah's old boyfriend captive at the counter and had been waiting for Norah and Reed to come in so they could make Reed jealous! Or, at least, that was how it looked.

Sneaky devils.

But they knew Reed wasn't in love with her and didn't want a future with her. So what was the point? Reed would probably push her with Harrison, tell her to see if there was anything to rekindle.

But as cute and nice as Harrison was, he wasn't Reed Barelli. No one else could be.

Every forkful of the pot pie felt as if it weighed ten pounds in his hand. Reed sat on his couch, his lonely dinner tray on the coffee table, a rerun of the baseball game on the TV as a distraction from his thoughts.

Which were centered on where Norah was right now. *Probably on a walking date with Harrison,* he said in his mind in a singsong voice. High school sweethearts would have a lot to catch up on. A lot to say. Memories. Good ones. There were probably a lot of firsts between them.

Reed wanted to throw up. Or punch something.

Just like that, this high school sweetheart, this French chef, would waltz in and take Reed's almost life. His wife, his triplets. His former ranch, which was now Norah's. A woman who wanted love and romance and a father for her babies might be drawn to the known—and the high school sweetheart fit that bill. Plus, they had that cooking thing in common. They might even be at the ranch now, Harrison standing behind Norah at the stove, his arms around her as he showed her how to Frenchify a pot pie. You couldn't and shouldn't! Pot pies were perfect as they were, dammit.

Grr. He took a swig of his soda and clunked it down on the coffee table. What the hell was going on here? He was jealous? Was this what this was?

Yes. He was jealous. He didn't want Norah kissing this guy. Sleeping with this guy. Frenchifying pot pies with this guy.

He flung down his fork and headed out, huffing into his SUV. He drove out to the ranch, just to check. And there was an unfamiliar car! With New York plates!

Hadn't Norah's mother said Harrison had lived on the east coast?

He was losing her right now. And he had let it happen.

This is what you want, dolt. You want her to find everything in one man. A father for her triplets. A husband for herself. Love. Romance. Happiness. Forever. You don't want that. So let her go. Let her have what she always dreamed of.

His heart now weighing a thousand pounds, he turned the SUV around and headed back to his rental house, where nothing awaited him but a cold pot pie and a big, empty bed.

"Upsie-what?" Harrison said, wrinkling his nose in the living room of the Barelli ranch. Correction. The Ingalls ranch. The Norah Ingalls ranch.

Norah frowned. "Upsie-downsie," she repeated. "You lift her up, say 'Upsie' in your best baby-talk voice, then lower her with a 'downsie'!"

They were sitting on the rug, the triplets in their Exersaucers, Bella raising her hands for a round of upsie-downsie. But Harrison just stared at Bella, shot her a fake smile and then turned away. Guess not everyone liked to play upsie-downsie.

Bella's face started to scrunch up. And turn red. Which meant any second she was about to let loose with a wail. "Waaaah!" she cried, lifting her arms up again.

"Now, Bea, be a good girl for Uncle Harrison," he said. "Get it, *Bea* should *be* a good girl. LOL," he added to no one in particular.

First of all, that was Bella. And did he just LOL at his own unfunny "joke"? Norah sighed. No wonder she hadn't fallen in love with Harrison Atwood in high school. Back then, cute had a lot to do with why she'd liked him. But as a grown-up, cute meant absolutely nothing. Even if a man looked like Reed Barelli.

"I'd love to take you out to a French place I know over in Brewer," he said. "It's not exactly Michelin-starred, but come on, in Wyoming, what is? I'm surprised you stuck around this little town. I always thought you'd move to LA, open a restaurant."

"What would give you that idea?" she asked.

"You used to talk a lot about your big dreams. Wanting to open Pie Diners all across the country. You wanted your family to have your own cooking show on the Food Network. Pot pie cookbooks on the *New York Times* bestseller list."

Huh. She'd forgotten all that. She did used to talk about opening Pie Diners across Wyoming, maybe even in bordering states. But life had always been busy enough. And full enough. Especially when she'd gotten pregnant and then when the triplets came.

"Guess your life didn't pan out the way you wanted," Harrison said. "Sorry about that."

Would it be wrong to pick up one of the big foam alphabet blocks and conk him over the head with it?

"My life turned out pretty great," she said. *I might not have the man I love, but I have the whole world in my children, my family, my job and my little town.*

"No need to get defensive," he said. "Jeez."

God, she didn't like this man.

Luckily, just then, Brody let loose with a diaper explosion, and Harrison pinched his nostrils closed. "Oh boy. Something stinks. I guess this is my cue to leave. LOL, right?"

"It was good to see you again, Harrison. Have a great rest of your life."

He frowned and nodded. "Bye." He made the mistake of removing his hand from his nose, got a whiff of the air de Brody and immediately pinched his nostrils closed again.

She couldn't help laughing. "Buh-bye," she said as he got into his car.

She closed the door, her smile fading fast. She had a diaper to change. And a detective to fantasize about.

Chapter Fifteen

Reed kept the door of his office closed the next morning at the police station. He was in no mood for chitchat and Sergeant Howerton always dropped in on his way from the tiny kitchen to talk about his golf game and Officer Debowski always wanted to replay any collars from the day before. Reed didn't want to hear any of it.

He chugged his dark-brew coffee, needing the caffeine boost to help him concentrate on the case he was reading through. A set of burglaries in the condo development. Weird thing was, the thief, or thieves, was taking unusual items besides the usual money, jewelry and small electronics. Blankets and pillows, including throw pillows, had been taken from all the hit-up units.

Instead of making a list of what kind of thief would go for down comforters, he kept seeing Norah and the high school sweetheart with their hands all over each other. Were they in bed right now? He had to keep blinking and squeezing his eyes shut.

He wondered how long the guy had stayed last night. Reed should have made some excuse to barge in and interrupt them a bunch of times. Checking on the boiler or something. Instead, he'd reminded himself that the reason the French chef was there was because of Reed's own stupidity and stubbornness and inability to play well with others. Except babies.

He slammed a palm over his face. Were they having breakfast right now? Was Norah in his button-down shirt and nothing else? Having pancakes on the Barelli family table?

Idiot! he yelled at himself. *This is all your fault.* He'd stepped away. He'd said he couldn't. He'd said he wouldn't. And now he'd lost Norah to the high school sweetheart who wanted a wife and kids. They were probably talking about the glory days right now. And kissing.

Dammit to hell! He got up and paced his office, trying to force his mind off Norah and onto a down-feather-appreciating burglar. A Robin Hood on their hands? Or maybe someone who ran a flea market?

He's going to give us lessons in French cooking, Norah's mother had said. Suddenly, Reed was chopped liver to the Ingalls women, having been replaced by the beef bourguignon pot pie.

So what are you going to do about this? he asked himself. *Just let her go? Let the triplets go? You're their father!*

And he was Norah's husband. Husband, husband,

husband. He tried to make the word have meaning, but the more it echoed in his head, the less meaning it had. Husband meant suffering in his memories. His mother had had two louses and his grandfather had been a real doozy. He thought of his grandmother trying to answer Reed's questions about why she'd chosen such a grouch who didn't like anyone or anything. She'd said that sometimes people changed, but even so, she knew who he was and, despite his ways, he'd seemed to truly love her and that had made her feel special. She'd always said she should have known if you're the only one, the exception, there might be a problem.

So what now? Could he force himself to give this a real try? Romance a woman he had so much feeling for that it shook him to the core? Because he was shaken. That much he knew.

His head spinning, he was grateful when his desk phone rang.

"Detective Barelli speaking."

"Reed! I'm so glad I caught you. It's Annie. Annie Potterowski from the chapel. Oh dear, I'm afraid there's a bit of a kerfuffle concerning your marriage license. Could you come to the chapel at ten? I've already called Norah and she's coming."

"What kind of kerfuffle?" he asked. What could be more of a kerfuffle than their entire wedding?

"I'll explain everything when you get here. 'Bye now," she said and hung up.

If there was one good thing to come from this kerfuffle, it was that he knew Norah would be apart from the high school sweetheart, even for just a little while.

* * *

"Annie, what on earth is going on?" Norah asked the elderly woman as she walked into the chapel, pushing the enormous stroller.

"Look at those li'l dumplings!" Abe said, hurrying over to say hello to the triplets. He made peekaboo faces and Bea started to cry. "Don't like peekaboo, huh?" Abe said. "Okay, then, how about silly faces?" He scrunched up his face and stuck out his tongue, tilting his head to the left. Bea seemed to like that. She stopped crying.

"I'm just waiting for Detective Barelli to arrive," Annie said without looking at Norah.

Uh-oh. What was this about?

"Ah, there he is," Annie said as Reed came down the aisle to the front of the chapel.

Reed crossed his arms over his chest. "About this kerfuffle—"

"Kerfuffle?" Norah said. "Anne used the words *major problem* when she called me."

Annie bit her lip. "Well, it's both really. A whole bunch of nothing, but a lot of something."

Reed raised an eyebrow.

"I'll just say it plain," Abe said, straightening the blue bow-tie that he wore almost every day. "You two aren't married. You spelled your names wrong on the marriage license."

"What?" Norah said, her head spinning.

"The county clerk's temporary replacement checked her first week's work, just in case she made rookie errors, and discovered only one. On your marriage license. She sent back the license to you and Reed and to the chapel, since we officiated the ceremony. You didn't receive your mail yet?"

Had Norah even checked the mail yesterday? Maybe not.

"I was on a case all day yesterday and barely had time to eat," Reed said. "But what's this about spelling our names wrong?"

Anne held up the marriage license. "Norah, you left off the *h*. And, Reed, you spelled your name *R-e-a-d*. I know there are lots of ways to spell your name, but that ain't one of them."

"Well, it's not like you didn't know we were drunk out of our minds, Annie and Abe!" Norah said, wagging a finger at them.

"I didn't think to proofread your names, for heaven's sake!" Annie said, snorting. "Now we're supposed to be proofreaders, too?" she said to Abe. "Each wedding would take hours. I'd have to switch to my reading glasses, and I can never find them and—"

"Annie, what does this mean?" Reed asked. "You said we're not married. Is that true? We're not married because our names were spelled wrong?"

"Your legal names are not on that document or on the official documents at the clerk's office," Abe said.

"So we're not married?" Norah repeated, looking at Reed. "We were never actually married?"

"Well, double accidentally, you were," Annie said. "The spiked punch and the misspelling. You were married until the error was noted by the most efficient county clerk replacement in Brewer's history."

I'm not married. Reed is not my husband.

It's over.

Her stomach hurt. Her heart hurt. Everything hurt.

Reed walked over to Norah and seemed about to say something. But instead he knelt down in front of the stroller. "Hey, little guys. I miss you three."

Brody gave Reed his killer gummy smile, three tiny teeth poking up.

She glanced at his hand. He still wore his wedding ring even though she'd taken hers off. Guess he'd take it off now.

"We'll leave you to talk," Annie said, ushering Abe into the back room.

Norah sat in a pew, a hand on the stroller for support. She wasn't married to Reed. How could she feel so bereft when she never really had a marriage to begin with?

"We can go back to our lives now," she said, her voice catching. She cleared her throat, trying to hide what an emotional mess she was inside. "I'll move out of the ranch. Since we were never legally married, I'm sure that affects possession of the ranch. You can't deed me something you didn't rightfully inherit."

She was babbling, talking so she wouldn't burst into tears.

He stood, giving Bea's hair a caress. "I guess Harrison will be glad to hear the news."

"Harrison?"

"Your high school sweetheart," he said. "The one you spent the night with."

She narrowed her eyes at him. "What makes you think we spent the night together?"

"I drove by the house to see if his car was there."

"Why? Why would you even care? You don't have feelings for me, Reed."

He looked away for a moment, then back at her. "I have a lot of feelings for you."

"Right. You feel responsible for me. You care about me. You're righting wrongs when you're with me."

He shook his head but didn't say anything.

"I should get back to work," she said.

"Me, too," he said.

She sucked in a breath. "I guess when we walk out of here, it's almost like none of it ever happened. We were never really married."

"I felt married," he said. Quite unexpectedly.

"And you clearly didn't like the feeling." She waited a beat, hoping he'd say she was wrong.

She waited another beat. Nothing.

"There's nothing between me and Harrison," she said without really having to. What did it matter to Reed anyway? His urge to drive by the ranch had probably been about him checking up on her, making sure she'd gotten back okay, the detective in him at work. "He did come over for a bit and was so insufferable I couldn't wait for him to leave."

He looked surprised. "But what about all the firsts you two shared?"

"Firsts? I had my first kiss with someone else. I lost my virginity to someone else. I did try sushi for the first time with Harrison. I guess that counts."

"So you two are *not* getting back together," he said, nodding.

"We are definitely not."

"So my position as father of the triplets still stands."

"That's correct," she said even though she wanted to tell him no, it most certainly did not. This was nuts. He was going to be their father in between semi-dates and short-term relationships until the real thing came along for her?

"I'd like to spend some time with them after work, if that's all right," he said. "I have presents for them for their eight-month birthday."

Her heart pinged. "It's sweet that you even know that."

"You only turn eight months once," he said with a weak smile.

And you find a man like Reed Barelli once in a lifetime, she thought. *I had you, then lost you, then didn't ever really have you, and now there's nothing.* Except his need to do right by the triplets, be for them what he'd never had.

"Time to go, kiddos," she said, trying to inject some cheer in her voice. "See you later, then," she said, wondering how she'd handle seeing him under such weird circumstances. Were they friends now?

"I'll get the door," he said, heading up the aisle to open it for her. He couldn't get rid of her fast enough.

Her heart breaking in pieces, she gripped the stroller and headed toward the Pie Diner, knowing she'd never get over Reed Barelli.

"Your grandmother would have loved Norah."

Reed glanced up at the voice. Annie Potterowski was walking up the chapel aisle toward where he sat in a pew in the last row. He'd been sitting there since Norah had left, twenty minutes or so. He'd married her in this place. And been unmarried to her here. He couldn't seem to drag himself out.

"Yeah, I think she would have," Reed said.

Annie sat beside him, tying a knot in the filmy pink scarf around her neck. "Now, Reed, I barely know you. I met you a few times over the years when you came to visit Lydia. So I don't claim to be an expert on you or anything, but anyone who's been around as long as I have and marries people for a living knows a thing or two about the human heart. Do you want to know what I think?"

He did, actually. "Let me have it."

She smiled. "I think you love Norah very much. I think you're madly in love with her. But this and that happened in your life and so you made her that dumb deal about a partnership marriage."

He narrowed his eyes at her. "How'd you know about that?"

"I listen, that's how. I pick up things. So you think you can avoid love and feeling anything because you were dealt a crappy hand? Pshaw," she said, adding a snort for good measure. "We've all had our share of bad experiences."

"Annie, I appreciate—"

"I'm not finished. You don't want to know the upbringing I had. It would keep you up at night feeling sorry for me. But when Abe Potterowski came calling, I looked into that young man's eyes and heart and soul, and I saw everything I'd missed out on. And so I said yes instead of no when I was scared to death of my feelings for him. And it was the best decision I ever made."

He took Annie's hand in his and gave it a gentle squeeze.

"I was used to shutting people out," she continued. "But you have to know when to say yes, Reed. And your grandmother, God bless her sweet soul, only ever wanted you to say yes to the right woman. Don't let her get away." Annie stood and patted his shoulder. "Your grandmother liked to come in here and do her thinking. She sat in the back row, too, other end, though."

With that, Annie headed down the aisle and disappeared into the back room.

Leaving Reed to do some serious soul-searching.

Chapter Sixteen

"Not married?" Shelby repeated, her face incredulous as she cut up potatoes for the lunch-rush pot pies.

Norah shook her head, recounting what Annie and Abe had said.

"Oh hell," her mother said. "I really thought you two would work it out."

"You pushed Harrison on me last night!" Norah complained even though she knew why.

"Yeah, but I only did that because he was here when you called and said you and Reed were stopping in for pot pies. I wanted Reed to know he had competition for your heart."

"Well, he doesn't. Harrison was awful. He freaked the minute one of the triplets did number two in his presence."

"Norah, you and Reed belong together," Aunt Cheyenne said as she filled six pie tins with beef stew. "We can all see that."

"I thought we did," Norah said, tears threatening her eyes. "But he never wanted a real relationship. He wanted to save me. And he wanted the ranch."

"The ranch he gave up for you?" her mother asked. "You do something crazy like that when you love someone so much they come first."

"There's that responsibility thing again," Norah said, frowning. "Putting me first. Everything for me, right? He wants me to have 'everything I deserve.' Except for him."

"Coming through," called a male voice.

Norah glanced up at her handsome brother-in-law, Liam Mercer, walking into the kitchen, an adorable toddler holding each of his hands. Despite being in the terrible twos, Norah's nephews, Shane and Alexander, were a lot of fun to be around.

Liam greeted everyone, then wrapped his wife in a hug and dipped her for a kiss, paying no mind to the flour covering her apron. Norah's heart squeezed in her chest as it always did when she witnessed how in love the Mercers were.

You should hold out for that, she told herself. *For a man who loves you like Liam loves Shelby. Like Dad loved Mom.*

Like I love Reed, she thought with a wistful sigh.

In just a few hours he'd be at the ranch, which they'd both have to give up, and the wonderful way he was with the triplets would tear her heart in two. She could have everything she'd ever wanted if Reed would just

let go of all those old memories keeping him from opening his heart.

Hmm, she thought. Since being around the triplets
did have Reed Barelli all mushy-gushy and as close to
his feelings as he could get, maybe she could do a little
investigative detective work of her own to see if those
"feelings" he spoke of having for her did reach into the
recesses of his heart. She knew he wanted her—their
night in Las Vegas had proved that, and she knew he
cared for her. That was obvious and he'd said it straight-
out. But could he enter into a romantic relationship with
her and hold nothing back?

The man was so good at everything. Maybe she
could get him to see that he could be great at love, too.

"Something smells amazing," Reed said when Norah
opened the door. For a moment he was captivated by the
woman herself. She wore jeans and a pale yellow tank
top, her long, reddish-brown hair in a low ponytail, and
couldn't possibly be sexier. His nose lifted at the mouth-
watering aroma coming from somewhere nearby. "Steak?"

"On the grill with baked potatoes and asparagus at
the ready."

"Can't wait. I'm starving." He set a large, brown
paper bag down by the closet. "Where are the brand-
new eight-month-olds?"

She smiled. "In their high chairs. They just ate."

"Perfect. It's party time." He trailed her into the
kitchen carrying the bag. He set it on the kitchen table
and pulled out three baby birthday hats, securing one
on each baby's head.

"Omigod, the cutest," Norah said, reaching for her phone to take pictures. She got a bunch of great shots. Including Reed in several.

"For the eight-month-olds," Reed said, putting a chew rattle on Bea's tray. And one on Bella's and one on Brody's. "Oh, I set up a college fund for them today. And got them these new board books," he added, pulling out a bunch of brightly colored little hardcovers. At first he'd gone a little overboard in the store, putting three huge stuffed animals in his cart, clothing and all kinds of toys. Then he'd remembered it wasn't even their first birthday and put most of the stuff back.

"Thank you, Reed," she said. "From the bottom of my heart, thank you. I can't tell you how much it means to me that they're so special to you."

"They're very special to me. And so are you, Norah." With the babies occupied in their chairs with their new rattles, he moved closer to their mother and tilted up her chin. "I'm an idiot."

"Oh?" she asked. "Why is that?"

"Because I almost lost you to that French chef. Or any other guy. I almost lost you, Norah."

"What are you talking about? I'm alive." She waved a hand in front of herself.

"I mean I almost lost out on being with you. Really being with you."

"But I thought—"

"I couldn't get the triplets gifts and not get you something, too," he said. "This is for you." He handed her a little velvet box.

"What's this?" she asked.

"Open it."

She did—and gasped. The round diamond sparkled in the room. "It's a diamond ring. A very beautiful diamond ring."

He got down on one knee before her. "Norah, will you marry me? For real, this time? And sober?"

"But I thought—"

"That I didn't love you? I do. I love you very much. But I was an idiot and too afraid to let myself feel anything. Except these little guys here changed all that. They cracked my heart wide-open and I had to feel everything. Namely how very deeply in love with you I am."

She covered her mouth with her hands. "Yes. Yes. Yes. Yes."

He grinned and stood and slid the ring on her finger. "She said yes!" he shouted to the triplets, then picked her up and spun her around.

"I couldn't be happier," she said.

"Me, either. I get you. I get the triplets. And, hey, I get to live in the ranch because the owner is going to be my wife."

She smiled and kissed him and he felt every bit of her love for him.

"So the Luv U Wedding Chapel?" she asked. "That would be funny."

He shook his head. "I was thinking the Wedlock Creek Wedding Chapel."

Her mouth dropped open. "Wait. Are you forgetting the legend? You *want* more multiples?"

"Sure I do. I think five or six kids is just about perfect."

She laughed. "We really must be insane. But you'll

be in high demand to teach the multiples classes. You'll never have a minute to yourself."

"I'll be too busy with my multiples. And my wife."

"I love you, Reed."

"I love you, too."

After calling her mother, aunt and sister with the news—and Reed could hear the shrieks and cheers from a good distance away, Reed called Annie Potterowski at the chapel.

"So, Annie… Norah and I would like to book the chapel for an upcoming Saturday night for our wedding ceremony. We're thinking a month from now if there are any openings."

Now it was Annie's turn to shriek. "You're making your grandmother proud, Reed. How's the second Saturday in August? Six p.m.?"

"Perfect," he said. Norah had told him a month would be all she'd need to find a wedding dress and a baby tux for Brody and two bridesmaids' dresses for Bella and Bea. Her family was already all over the internet.

"And we'll spell our names right this time," he added.

A few hours later the triplets were in their cribs, the dishes were done and Reed was sitting with his fiancée on the sofa, stealing kisses and just staring at her, two glasses of celebratory champagne in front of them.

"To the legend of the Wedlock Creek chapel," he said, holding up his glass. "It brought me my family and changed my life forever."

Norah clinked his glass and grinned "To the chapel— and the very big family we're going to have."

He sealed that one with a very passionate kiss.

Epilogue

One year later

Reed stood in the nursery—the twins' nursery—marveling at tiny Dylan and Daniel. Five days ago Norah had given birth to the seven-pounders, Dylan four ounces bigger and three minutes older. Both had his dark hair and Norah's perfect nose, slate-blue eyes that could go Norah's hazel or his dark brown, and ten precious fingers and ten precious toes.

Norah was next door in the triplets' nursery, reading them their favorite bedtime story. Soon they'd be shifting to "big kid" beds, but at barely two years old they were still smack in the middle of toddlerhood. He smiled at the looks they'd gotten as they'd walked up and down Main

Street yesterday, Norah pushing the twins' stroller and him pushing the triplets'.

"How do you do it?" someone had asked.

"Love makes it easy," Reed had said. "But we have *a lot* of help."

They did. Norah's family and the Potterowskis had set up practically around-the-clock shifts of feeding them, doing laundry and entertaining the triplets the first couple of days the twins were home. Many of their students from the past year had also popped by with gifts and offers to babysit the triplets, couples eager to get some first-hand experience at handling multiples.

Even the Dirks had come by. David and a very pregnant Eden—expecting twins without having ever said "I do" at the Wedlock Creek chapel.

"I've got this," David had said, putting a gentle hand on his wife's belly. "I thought I'd be scared spitless, but watching you two and taking your class—easy peasy."

Reed had raised an eyebrow. David might be in for the rude awakening he'd been trying to avoid, but Reed wasn't about to burst his bubble. They'd have help just like the Barellis did. That was what family and friends and community were all about.

Norah came in then and stood next to him, putting her arm around him. "The triplets are asleep. Looks like these guys are close."

"Which means we have about an hour and a half to ourselves. Movie?"

She nodded. "*Jerry Maguire* is on tonight. Remember when we watched that?"

He would never forget. He put his arms around her

and rested his forehead against hers. "Did I ever tell you that you complete me?"

She shook her head. "You said it was nonsense."

"Didn't I tell you I was an idiot? You. Complete. Me. And so do they," he added, gesturing at the cribs. "And the ones in the room next door."

She reached up a hand to his cheek, her happy smile melting his heart. Then she kissed him and they tiptoed out of the nursery.

But Dylan was up twenty minutes later, then Daniel, and then the triplets were crying, and suddenly the movie would have to wait. Real life was a hell of a lot better, anyway.

* * * * *